Praise for Maritta Wolff and *Whistle Stop*

"An extraordinary novel. . . . [At twenty-two] little Miss Wolff is as thoroughly informed about the seamy side of life in a Midwestern factory town as if she had spent fifty years in police courts, reformatory schools, honkey tonks, and slums. She was (in print, at least) as tough and unrelentingly realistic as James Farrell and a dozen times more entertaining. Her dialogue was wonderfully effective in its reflection of the way the English language is manhandled by average Americans. Her story itself was exciting and melodramatic and unnecessarily sensational. But beneath its brassy glitter was a warm affection for ordinary people that was most appealing."
—Orville Prescott, *The New York Times* (1947)

"[Wolff] is a realistic photographer and . . . narrator of tense, violent action. . . . I think you'd better read *Whistle Stop* and keep an eye on Miss Wolff. If she can write this way at twenty-two, she should be good for a banning in Boston before she's twenty-five."
—Clifton Fadiman, *The New Yorker* (1941)

"Beneath all the humor there is a bitter and genuine emotion."
—Edith Walton, *The New York Times Book Review* (1941)

"An astonishing first novel. . . . It has an unusual and strictly ungirlish talent back of it. . . . I read *Whistle Stop* with almost unbroken interest."
—Ralph Thompson, *The New York Times* (1941)

"Maritta Wolff is a careful, patient craftsman. She achieves, piece by piece, a mosaic of breadth, impact, and artistry."
—Thomas Sugrue, *The New York Times* (1947)

Whistle Stop

A NOVEL

Maritta Wolff

Scribner

NEW YORK   LONDON   TORONTO   SYDNEY

SCRIBNER

1230 Avenue of the Americas
New York, NY 10020

First Scribner trade paperback edition 2005

SCRIBNER and design are trademarks of Macmillan Library Reference USA, Inc. used under license by Simon & Schuster, the publisher of this work.

For information regarding special discounts for bulk purchases, please contact Simon & Schuster Special Sales at 1-800-456-6798 or business@simonandschuster.com

Designed by Kyoko Watanabe

Manufactured in the United States of America

10   9   8   7   6   5   4   3   2   1

Library of Congress Cataloging-in-Publication Data
Wolff, Maritta, 1918–
Whistle stop: a novel/Maritta Wolff.—1st Scribner trade pbk. ed.
p. cm.
1. City and town life—Fiction. 2. Middle West—Fiction. 3. Depressions—Fiction. 4. Criminals—Fiction. 5. Suspense fiction. gsafd 6. Love stories. gsafd I. Title.

PS3545.O346W48   2005
813'.52—dc22   2004059012

ISBN 0-7432-5486-4

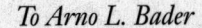

To Arno L. Bader

Book One

1

A^{S SOON AS THE SUN ROSE FROM THE HORIZON THE} heat began, cutting short the cool freshness and the summer morning songs of birds. Kenny Veech, walking in on the highway north of the village, took off his coat and slung it over his shoulder. One of his shoe soles had come loose at the toe, and when he walked it made a scuffling, slapping noise against the concrete. He walked with his shoulders hunched and his head down, half asleep from the warmth of the sun and the rhythmic sound of his flapping shoe sole.

The village lay down the road in front of him. Above the green crowns of trees rose two pointed church steeples and a great stand-pipe water tank. But Kenny Veech did not lift his head to look. He took scant notice of the occasional automobiles that he met, most of them carrying factory workers into the city for the morning shift, waving his arm abstractedly sometimes in response to the shrill blare of their auto horns.

Kenny Veech passed the village limits sign and crossed over onto the strip of sidewalk that began abruptly just beyond it. He walked perceptibly faster now as the houses grew thicker. The street was quiet and empty, but in the sun it bore a fresh alert look like a shiny scrubbed morning face. At the last house before the store buildings, a sagging faded frame structure set close to the pavement in the front and on the far side jammed up against the used-car lot of the town garage, Kenny Veech turned in.

He cut through the small unkempt yard to the back of the house. The little wooden back porch sagged and teetered under his weight. The door was open, covered by the rusty screen. The house was still, but living, somnambulistic with sleeping people. Kenny threw his coat on the warped porch boards and sat down on the top step. He stretched his big, well-muscled frame, yawning, with his arms out wide and his eyes shut, and then he pressed his hands down through his tousled light hair over his eyes and face. He lifted his foot and studied the condition of the loose shoe sole carefully; then he yawned again. He went through his coat pockets for cigarettes, but found none. He collected all the coins from various pockets in one hand, and after he put the coat down again, he counted them, poking at them with one finger as they lay in his brown palm. A nickel, three pennies, one Canadian penny and a slot-machine slug. He counted twice to make sure; then he put them in the breast pocket of his soiled white shirt. His face relaxed suddenly, and the assurance and mockery went out of the eyes. He looked puzzled and hurt and bewildered, like a child, and finally desperate. He dropped his head between his knees and sat still, his hands clasped across the back of his neck.

The sun shone down hotter over the weeds in the back yard and the untidy bit of garden, and onto the porch boards. Flies crawled lazily on the screen door and over his arms; the bees among the weeds kept up a continual humming. A train went through, and the vibrations shook the whole house; the porch jiggled and swayed under him.

In the stillness again, there came a sound of heavy feet in the kitchen. Kenny, on the steps, did not stir or lift his head. Molly Veech moving around the kitchen in her old bedroom slippers carefully avoided the back door. Each one was perfectly aware of the other. In a minute or two Molly came to the door and unhooked the screen. Kenny waited for her voice without moving, and she stood for a second looking at him. Her body, corsetless, sagged comfortably under her faded cotton dress, and her straight gray hair hung carelessly behind her ears.

"Well, I'll be darned," she said at last in her full pleasant voice, but not surprised at all.

Kenny sat up immediately and twisted around on the step toward her. His face was good-humored and careless again. He yawned and stretched elaborately. "Hi yah, Mom!"

She smiled with him involuntarily, and then, as her face softened, she struggled to keep it severe. "Now lookit here," she said. "I been telling you you gotta cut this kind of business out and I ain't just been talking to hear myself neither. . . ."

"The coffee hot yet, Mom?" he asked her fondly.

"No, not yet. I ain't got the water pumped. Lord, what do you think folks are gonna say, you hanging around Ashbury all night, and then not walking in here till after daylight in the morning. I tell yuh . . ."

"What you got?" he said.

"Huh? Oh, I got a dress of Josie's to iron out for her to wear to school this morning." She held it over one arm, the bottom of it rubbing carelessly against the rusty screen.

"Well, ain't that something," he said, indignantly, sitting up straight. "What's the matter of Josie getting up an' ironing her own dress instead of putting all that work on you, Ma?"

She moved back from the door, mollified by his concern for her. "Oh, it ain't no work, I hate to get her up till she has to."

He got up briskly and took the water pail from the kitchen to the pump at the back door. He pumped fast and noisily, whistling over the squeaking and groaning of the old pump.

When he carried the pail of water in, his mother had the ironing board set up and was straightening out the dress over it. "Here you are, Mom," he said. He came up behind her and put his arms around her. She pulled him up against her and kissed him. "You're a bum," she said contentedly. "You're nothing but a good-for-nothing, lazy, old bum."

He sat in the chair by the table while she pressed the flimsy white dress. "Say, Mom, gimme a dime, will you? I wanta go uptown and get some cigarettes before breakfast. I'm all outa cigarettes."

"Ain't you got no money?" she said.

"Not a cent," he said, turning out pockets one after another.

"Good," she said, "I'm glad of it. You smoke too many cigarettes, anyway. It'll be good for you if you don't have none today."

"Ah hell, Mom!"

She hung the fresh dress over the back of a chair, and put the ironing board away. Jud Higgins came out of the bedroom off the kitchen, pulling at his suspenders. He grinned at them, wrinkling up his face under the stubby white whiskers, and went out the back door and down the path among the weeds to the little wooden outhouse.

"What's old pickle puss grinnin' about this morning?" Kenny said.

"I tell you, Kenny, you can't keep on fooling around like this," she said. "You're going to ruin your health. Lord, drinking and smoking and staying up all night. How'd you get home?"

"I got a ride out of Ashbury with a guy I know that drives a truck, and then I walked in from the main road."

While she stirred the kettle of oatmeal on the stove, Sam Veech came into the kitchen silently and went to the sink. He was a heavy, mild, slow-motioned man. He washed methodically, wiped his face on the rough towel and combed his hair neatly. He did not speak to either his wife or son, and their voices died out when he appeared. When he was through he went into the living room and picked up the tattered library book from the center table and went out onto the front porch. In a minute they heard the squeak of the porch swing. At the sound, Molly gave an exaggerated sigh and looked at Kenny, lifting her eyebrows and shaping her mouth.

He answered her with ready sympathy. "I thought you was gonna get the old man on the W.P.A."

"Well, I'm still aiming to," she said. "Only it ain't so easy to get on as it used to be."

She put the dishes of steaming oatmeal around the stained oil-cloth-covered table, and Kenny turned his chair around. While she filled the cups from the heavy coffee pot, she yelled, "Come on, breakfast's ready." Her voice echoed through the house, and there was a sound over their heads of bed springs squeaking. Sam Veech came in obediently and smoothed his hair once before the crooked kitchen mirror above the sink.

Molly said, "Say, Kenny, how much was they selling raspberries for up to Ashbury? I been figuring on putting up some red raspberries this year. They make nice eating sauce. I oughta get 'em while they're nice berries yet. This dry weather they ain't gonna be nice for long."

"I dunno, I didn't notice no raspberries."

Sam pulled his chair out and said mildly, "I should think you could get raspberries right here in town. I see some of Dettler's berries in Clark's store yesterday, and they was real nice. He's got a big patch of red and black ones both, and he lets pickers in to pick on shares."

Kenny sugared his oatmeal quietly. Molly put the coffee pot back on the stove and went to the screen door. "Mr. Higgins!" she called. "Come on in here; we're eating!"

Dorothy crowded into the kitchen door before Carl, and slid her thin little body in between the chair and table without pulling the chair out. Her face under her frizzy blonde hair was surprisingly secret and artificial. She spoke to nobody in particular in a childish treble. "Carl stole my money," she said, twisting her bare feet around the chairrungs and looking at Kenny beside her out of the corners of her eyes.

"Oh, hell," Carl said.

Molly put the milk bottle in the middle of the table and sat down heavily in her chair. She split the situation apart and dealt with it deftly. "Dor'thy, if you don't quit that lyin' all the time, I'm goin' to tell your mother on you, and she'll take care of you proper. Carl, you better cut out that swearin' and cussin'. I ain't gonna have you hangin' around this house a-talking like that."

Kenny poked his finger into the little girl's thin ribs, and grinned at Carl over the table top. "What you so sour about, kid? Whatsa matter, you got some kinks in your love life? Did you hear the kid's got a girl? Oh, boy, what a girl! You just oughta see him hanging around downtown waiting for Franny Cope to walk by. He ain't even got the nerve to ask her for a date, but he gets his money's worth every time he sees her, man, oh, man!

"Oh, how I love to see you, Franny—
Wigglin' your little fanny . . ."

Dorothy laughed shrilly, not a laugh at all, but a sort of hysterical cry, above Kenny's laughter.

The red color spread over Carl's thin face to the edge of his untidy black hair. "Shut your God-damn mouth, will you?"

Jud Higgins banged the screen door. "Where'm I gonna eat? Ain't got no place set for me. Pretty pass when I ain't welcome to eat with nobody no more. But I been expectin' it. I seed it a-coming."

"Oh, Lord!" Molly said, getting up. "There ain't no use a-dishing up your breakfast, Mr. Higgins, when nobody knows how long you're gonna set out there in that toilet. Here, here's your oatmeal, and you set right down there and eat it now."

She filled up Kenny's coffee cup and sat down again. She stirred her own coffee placidly. "Lord, I wish I had some of them red raspberries of Dettler's to put up. Carl, why don't you go right over to Dettler's when you get your breakfast et, and see if you can't pick today?"

Jud spoke with his mouth full while little trickles of milk rolled down his chin out of the corners of his mouth, catching in the short whiskers. "If you picked berries over there to Dettler's, the old son of a bitch would cheat you out of all your pickin'. Worst God-damn crook a-livin'!" He choked on the oatmeal, lumps of it flying out of his mouth.

"Carl, you hurry up and eat and go on over there," Molly said.

Carl turned white and put his cup down; his voice was jerky with anger. "My God, you make me sick. You know I got a job delivering for the meat market. You think I'm gonna quit my job and go over there and pick berries! My God, you oughta know! What's the matter with you?" His voice sputtered out and his lips trembled and his dark eyes were blazing.

"That's no way to talk to your mother. If you can't talk decent and civil you better keep still." Molly became more indignant with every word she spoke. "When it comes to eating, I notice you're willing and able, right here every meal a-scoopin' it away; but when it comes to helpin' get ahold of something to eat, why, that's different."

"Where's my money going that I get at the meat market? Where's that going? I don't do a God-damn thing but eat here, I don't. Where's two-thirds of every pay check I get to the meat market going?"

"If you think I'm gonna have you running after that Cope girl, you're crazy," Molly replied, disregarding Carl's question. "She's tough, that's what she is." Molly's breath was running out. "She's always been tough, and I won't have . . ."

Carl suddenly became coherent, and yelled at the top of his lungs. "My God, you make me sick, the whole bunch of you. I'm workin', ain't I, and turning in my money here; but what about him?" He leveled his finger at Kenny across the table. "What about him?

What's the matter with him going over to Dettler's and picking some berries? Nobody says a thing about him picking a berry or doing one single God-damn lick of work anywhere. No, he can lay around here and eat what the rest of us get out and earn. He can go to Ashbury every damn night and spend the money you give him to do it with, drinking and chasing women, and not get home till morning, and then sleep all day long so he'll be in good shape to go back to Ashbury tonight. That's perfectly all right, ain't it? What's the matter with . . ."

Kenny said, "You mind your own business for a change, you little . . ."

"I'm telling you," Molly said, "you better cut out that cussin' and swearin', mister."

It was as if the sudden bright anger was a contagious thing that swept around the table.

Sam Veech raised his soft voice and inserted it into the commotion. "No son of mine is gonna do that kind of business, tearing around all night long and then coming dragging in here in the morning. I always been a decent lawabiding man. We ain't that kind of folks . . ."

Molly interrupted him. "What you expect Kenny to do, sit around here waitin' for a job to come to him? If he don't go to Ashbury once in awhile to see if they ain't takin' on men in the shops again, how you think he's ever . . . ?"

Dorothy closed her eyes and twitched all over with nervous excitement. "Damn liar, damn liar," she yelled over and over.

"Oh, sure," Carl said. "The best time of day to start looking for a job is eight o'clock at night, sure, and if you do a good job of looking you can't get home till morning. And the best place for looking is every God-damn beer joint and whore house and poolroom on Water Street, and . . ."

Sam's voice was tremulous. "There's other jobs besides the shops, ain't there? He could pick berries couldn't he, or anything he can get? When I was his age there wasn't no shops to work in, and I didn't sit around home eating off . . ."

"Oh, go to hell," Kenny said coolly.

Molly leaned across the table and pounded on it with her fist until the dishes rattled. "You better shut your mouth, Sam Veech! What have you got to say, I'd like to know? What you doin' day after day but settin' out there in that porch swing on your behind a-readin' those cussed lib'ry books and a-swinging back and forth, back and forth, while your fambly has to get out and hustle for the victuals you swill down three times a day regular as clockwork? I'd like to know and . . ."

"Damn liar, damn liar," Dorothy crooned, swaying in ecstasy, her eyes still shut.

Sam Veech stumbled up out of his chair. Old Jud laughed, his eyes darting from face to face, and reached over for his half-eaten dish of oatmeal.

Josette came in then, sweeping her father aside out of the doorway. She was a tall full-bodied girl, with firm breasts under her cotton slip, and rounded brown arms and shoulders. Her motions were all hurried, and there were little worry wrinkles across her forehead and around her eyes. "Ma, did you get my dress pressed? It's terribly late. Is there any hot water left for me to wash in?" She took the tea kettle off the stove as she spoke and poured water into the washbasin in the sink.

"Oh, Lord," Molly said, "I clean forgot to call you. You hurry up there and get washed and I'll set your breakfast on. You got time to eat your breakfast."

Josette scrubbed herself with the soapy faded washcloth. "You needn't worry about my oversleeping. Nobody could get any sleep with the racket you were making down here. All of you yelling as loud as you could, and the language you were using . . . I don't see what you think the neighbors think of us, the way you all were . . ."

"Oh, God," Kenny said. "Ain't we somebody, now Ernie is sending us to business college? We're getting too good for our own family now, ain't we? All we want to do is run around with Midge Clark, on account of her daddy runs a store, whenever Midge Clark will look at yuh, and that ain't too often."

"Well, maybe I am too good," she said, without turning around.

"I'm surprised you ever bother to come home at all," Carl said vindictively, shoving his chair back.

"You don't think I want to, do you?" she said, her voice muffled by the dress as she pulled it down over her head. "What do you think I'm doing, if it isn't trying to get out of here just as quick as I can? All that's the matter with you, Carl Veech, is that you're jealous, that's all. Well, maybe Ernie would help you go to school if you attended to your business better in high school and got better marks and was nice to Ernie and . . ."

"Yeah, you said it that time," Carl called back to her from the living room. "You better get down off your high horse. You aren't any smarter than anybody else. You just sugared around Ernie and got him to send you up there and . . ." The rush of a train put an end to his words. Carl went out banging the door behind him. The air was close and hot and there was a lazy buzz of activity around the store buildings. Carl walked toward the meat market, his eyes and ears blind to everything, fitting his stride to the old refrain of his mind, "My God, I've got to get out of this. I've got to get away from here."

Back in the kitchen, Josette put lipstick on her mouth.

Molly said, "You come on and eat here. They'll be stopping for you in a minute, and you'll have to go. You can't keep skipping meals like this; it ain't good for you. First thing you know, you'll be getting sick. I'll put up your lunch right away."

"No," Josette said, with hair pins in her mouth. "I haven't got time for you to fix it. I'll have to buy my lunch in Ashbury again, or else go without. It seems funny you can't get around in the morning and . . ."

"Well, maybe you better buy something then. You got some money?"

Josette rearranged the brown curls above her forehead. "Well, I've got some, but I've got to buy typing paper today and I think I've got to have another book and . . ."

"I better give you some." Molly disappeared into the living room.

"If you'd cut out some of that primping, you could put up your own dinner for a change instead of taking Ma's money day after day . . ."

"Oh, for heaven's sake, you should talk about saving Ma's money . . ." Josette drank her coffee standing by the table, with her eyes staring out of the window to the street. Kenny sat alone at the table, slouched back at ease in his chair.

Molly came back with her purse in her hand and gave Josette some change. "Ain't Jen getting up?" she said.

"I don't know," Josette said. "She went back to sleep after I got up. I think you ought to talk to her, Ma. The way she's running around now, it's a disgrace . . ."

Josette closed her purse on the money with a snap under Kenny's eyes.

An automobile horn made an insistent raucous sound outside. Josette caught up her books and purse and rushed out, calling good-bye absently over her shoulder, and setting a cool pretty smile on her mouth, ready to face what she thought of as the real beginning of her day—the moment when the front screen slammed behind her, and drowned out the porch swing squeaking under her father's weight.

"Lord," Molly said, "I ain't good for nothing once breakfast is over, everybody rushing around so. You want some more coffee, Kenny? Wait a minute and I'll throw out those grounds in your cup and you can have all fresh."

She stirred her coffee leisurely, and the flies buzzed and crawled over the dirty table and dishes. "You know," she said, "if Ernie comes in tonight, I believe I'll have him see about buying me some red raspberries somewhere. I wanted to put up a few of the red ones this year. They make real nice sauce, and I want to get them now while they're nice yet. They won't stay nice long, in this hot dry weather."

Kenny felt again for the cigarettes. "Say, Ma, guess who I seen in Ashbury last night. She offered to give me a ride home, only I wasn't ready to come yet. Rita!"

"Rita Sibley? Why, that was nice of her. But then she's always been nice to me. All the while she and Ernie was having trouble, and after she divorced him and even since she got married again, she's always been real nice. Is she staying here in town since her school was out?"

"Yeah, she was just up to Ashbury seeing a movie or something. Joe is working nights now, I guess."

"How was she looking?" Molly asked.

"Swell. She's damn good-looking woman, and she knows how to dress too. I guess she was too good for old Ernie, at that."

"Well," Molly said, "I wouldn't say that exactly. I never want to take sides, or anything like that, but I guess Ernie and Rita couldn't make a go of it for lots of reasons."

"She sure is a swell-looking woman," Kenny said again, his voice trailing out after his thoughts.

"I oughta do some hoeing in that garden," his mother said. "I guess I better get out there before this sun gets any hotter. Mary'll want her breakfast in a minute. You tell her everything's hot there on the stove."

"Yeah," Kenny said absently, his mind busy with the image of Rita and her hair pale blonde against her brown skin . . .

Molly poured milk in the cat's dish. She lingered in the door for a moment and finally ambled out among the weeds to the little garden plot.

Kenny shoved dishes aside before him on the table and pillowed his head on his elbows. He drowsed a little, his thoughts unrolling like a slow smoke spiral. Rita Sibley's thin scented body; a funny little squirt named Bill who used to hang around Ashbury till he went out to Milwaukee and hired out as a shooter for some mob there, and made good money, they said, except he got killed the other day; his mother out in the garden with her hoe striking sharp steel against stones, an awful good old girl at that, they didn't come any better; a factory whistle cutting the air open. So the little squirt named Bill was dead. What was it like to be dead? Something black to be afraid of, especially if it hurt, and you couldn't tell him that it didn't hurt to die. Then, underneath, a little insistent tick: you're wasting your time; you ain't getting any younger; you ought to have a job and get some place. What you oughta do is get out of this dump and go away some place and amount to something. . . .

His mind came back to the kitchen table with a snap at the touch of Mary's hand along his forehead.

"G'morning, Ken."

He sat up straight, blinking his eyes in the sunlight, and his whole manner changed in her presence. He became more contained, more sophisticated, his voice lowered and slowed as if it was drawn down by her own low husky voice. "G'morning, Mary. How are you? Mom left your breakfast on the stove. Wait a minute, I'll set these dirty dishes off the table for you." He got up immediately and began to stack the dishes together.

Mary said, "Thanks." She took the discolored ragged fly swatter from a hook by the stove and began to kill the flies on the table. The old swatter became a delicate precise instrument in her hands. She struck leisurely and accurately, littering the floor with the little crumpled bodies. She was small, with fine clear features, her head not quite to Kenny's shoulder, her body slight and well formed. Her hair was smooth and short, lying in big golden-brown waves on her head. It was her mouth perhaps, absurdly small and rosy, that gave her a peculiarly childlike quality.

Kenny stacked the dirty dishes carelessly on the stove. "Say, Mary, you got a cigarette?"

She took a long flat silver case out of her pocket and opened it for him. He struck a match down his trouser leg and held it for her before he lit his own. "God, that tastes good. You sure do treat yourself to the best, don't you?"

She squinted her eyes from the smoke while she filled her coffee cup, and then she sat down beside him at the table, and sipped the hot black coffee.

Kenny watched her admiringly. "Ain't you gonna eat something?"

She shook her head. "No, I'll pick up something after I get down to the hotel."

She smoked silently, and Kenny leaned forward on his arms, watching her.

At last she said, "How's everything?"

"Oh, so-so," he said guardedly. "Same old crowd, same old thing. You know, sometimes I get so God-damn sick of it I could . . ."

"Yeah, I know." She looked him full in the face. Her eyes were startlingly blue, set in deep brown shadows, infinitely old, and infinitely weary.

He put his hand out suddenly and covered hers on the table. "How's things with you, kid?"

"So-so; same old thing," she said indifferently. She twisted her fingers up around his thumb. They sat quietly looking deep into each other's eyes.

"Lew was in Chicago last week, huh?" he said.

"Yeah, I kept things running at the hotel. He got back last night."

She looked away again, out of the window, but he kept his eyes upon her face.

"I was talking to Rita Sibley in Ashbury last night," he said suddenly.

"Yeah?"

"Yeah, that's the way I got it figured."

She laughed shortly, tipping her head back. It was as if some detailed communication had passed between them that made any further discussion of the subject unnecessary. They were silent again for a long time.

"Where's Ma?" she said finally.

"Out there in the garden. You want to see her before you go downtown?"

They were silent again as if they were both loath to put an end to the quiet moments sliding by there in the kitchen while the sun rose higher and higher.

Mary got up and shoved her chair back. "Go on up and get some sleep, Ken." She fumbled in the pocket of her modish black linen dress. She took out a crumpled five-dollar bill and wadded it up small in her hand, and slid it into his, closing his fingers tight over it. They smiled then, both of them, for the first time.

She went to the door and called, "Hey, Mom!"

Molly Veech stood up straight in the garden back of the weeds, and wiped the sweat off her face. "You ready to go downtown, Mary? I'll be right in."

She threw her hoe down carelessly across a tangle of tomato plants and came to the house, hoisting her heavy body clumsily up the steps.

"Where's Kenny?" she said.

"He's gone upstairs to bed."

Molly sat down hard on a chair, wiping the sweat off her face. "My, you look nice and cool this morning."

"Is Dorothy behaving all right? She doesn't give you any trouble, does she?"

"Lord, no," Molly said. "She ain't a bit of trouble. She's an awful funny little kid in a lot of ways, but she ain't no trouble having around." Molly went on comfortably, fanning herself with a piece of newspaper. "I figure I'll have Ernie get me some red raspberries somewhere to put up; they make real nice sauce."

"I'll get some and have them sent up when I get downtown."

"No, you ain't gonna do no such thing. Lord knows you do enough around here. Let Ernie get the berries."

"Josette doing all right in school? I haven't seen the kid in a week," Mary said.

"Just fine, I guess. Say, Mary," Molly lowered her voice, "I wanted to talk to you about Jen. Josie claims we ought to talk to her or something. She's doing an awful lot of running around lately. She's mixed up with a kind of tough crowd, you know. That Frances Cope and her are thicker than spatter. She's gone every night. They do an awful lot of drinking and stuff, and I just don't know . . . Honest, for twins, Jen and Josie ain't no more alike than black and white. I just don't know what we oughta . . ."

Mary snapped open the silver cigarette case. "Jen's a good kid. She don't use her head, but she's a good kid."

"Well," Molly said reflectively. "But I tell you what, Mary, I wish you'd talk to her. You're a lot older and you know Jen thinks you're just about it, if you'd just kind of talk to her . . ."

Mary did not answer. Molly settled back, savoring this confidential moment with her oldest daughter. "Well, I'll tell you, I don't know. There's a lot to having a family of kids besides just feeding them and getting the clothes to put on their backs, a whole lot more. And it's always been me that had to do it. You know your father ain't never been no help to me in raising up you kids. It's always been me, and sometimes I just don't know. Now, you take Kenny. What you think we oughta do about Kenny? I always figured as he got older he'd straighten out. He's an awful good-hearted kid, good as gold, but I don't know . . ."

"Kenny'll be all right," Mary said briefly.

"Well, I just don't know," Molly said insistently. "And then there's Carl. I just can't make head nor tail to that boy. Now he's getting older he's changing. Just this last year in high school I noticed it. He's changing. He's always acting like he's mad and spiteful about something. Maybe we ain't been able to do so much for him, but I done the best I could. I give him a place to stay and three meals a day, and next year he'll be graduating from high school, but I just can't make him out, the way he acts. He ain't like no kid I ever saw before. Sometimes I just don't know . . ."

Mary threw her cigarette down and said, "It's getting late, Mom, I gotta be going."

"Lord," Molly said, getting up. "It seems like I never see you to talk to, just a little piece in the morning like this sometimes, before you go to the hotel. You don't get home till so late every night."

"I'm sorry, Mom. You got plenty of money?"

"Sure, I ain't even busted that ten-dollar bill you give me Saturday night yet."

"Okay, g'bye, Mom."

"G'bye, Mary." Molly followed her out to the porch, and watched her down the street. She walked swiftly with her small head held high and a rhythm of motion all through her body.

"Move over," Molly Veech said to Sam in the porch swing. He slid over on the wooden slats obediently and she sat down, tipping the porch swing low on her end of it.

"Mary's an awful pretty woman, ain't she?" she said. "I tell you, I don't know what this fambly woulda done without her. There's folks in this town that ain't got enough to do tending to their own business that likes to talk about Mary, but I'll tell you I ain't never felt a single bit ashamed . . ."

She rocked the porch swing back and forth, with the chains groaning in protest at her weight.

"Mary ain't like most folks," her mother said. "She never was, even when she was just a little girl, and you can't expect her to live and act just like ordinary folks. She's an awful queer one, but I never been a bit ashamed . . ."

Sam Veech closed the book, with his finger stuck in among the pages to keep his place. He swung silently beside Molly, with his eyes turned away toward town, watching Mary's bright head shining in the sun as far as he could see it.

"I kinda figured maybe she'd marry Lew Lentz and settle down," Sam said. "But I guess she ain't a-going to."

"Don't it beat all," Molly said. "I've heard the story plenty times that he's just crazy to marry her too."

Sam nodded. "That's where folks get the idea she's just out after his money."

"Lord," Molly said indignantly, "they oughta know better. Mary's took up with plenty men before this that didn't have a cent to their names. They oughta know better'n to go saying things like that behind Mary's back."

"Well, I don't know," Sam said, opening his book once more.

Molly kept the swing in motion contentedly. "Mary ain't like other folks," she said. "She ain't never been like other folks. Nobody knows what's goin' on in that head a hers. Seems like she ain't got feelings even like most folks have—not that she ain't the nicest, best-hearted girl in the world. Lord, all she's done for this fambly, and all. You just can't tell what's going on in her head, that's all." Molly sighed suddenly and gave up the puzzle.

"Anyway," she said, "I'd just give anything to know why she keeps hanging on to Lew Lentz when she won't marry him and Lord knows it ain't his money she's after. I'd just give anything to know."

Sam did not answer her. He was already lost in the pages of the library book.

2

MARY VEECH'S DAUGHTER LAY ON HER STOMACH in the grass that grew tall where the old street-car tracks had been taken up, now that bus service was assured the village. She peeped up out of the tangle of grass and weeds, well hidden, at the panorama of backyards, garden plots, and billowing clothes lines. The sun shone down hot on her body through her thin cotton dress. The air was full of muted lethargic sound; insects, and children's voices, automobiles on Main Street, radios. But Dorothy's skinny little body was tense and alert on the ground. Black ants crawled over her bare legs, but she never noticed them. She crawled forward in the grass silently like a little animal. The grass swayed over her as she lay motionless again, and one long green stem of it, straddled by a shiny golden-colored shelled bug, bobbed against her cheek.

Suddenly she got up and darted through an opening in the fence into a neat, well-kept garden plot beyond. Along its edge, the tame asparagus grew in an irregular line. She broke off the thick tender stalks with her wiry fingers, keeping her eyes turned toward the house beyond. She picked until her hands were full, and then she bundled the asparagus into the skirt of her dress and went on picking.

A door slammed somewhere, and as quickly as she had come, she darted back again and sank down into the tall weeds on the other side.

A few moments later Dorothy rapped on the back door of a house down the street and turned a sweet, ingratiating smile on the woman in the apron who came to answer. She held out a scant handful of the asparagus and said in a piping childish voice, "You want to buy some asparagus? It's only five cents."

The woman smiled back at her through the screen door. "Why, hello there, Dorothy. My, that's nice asparagus. It's real fresh, isn't it? And only a nickel a bunch! I tell you what, I'll take two bunches. How's that?"

"That will be fine." Dorothy smiled all across her face, so that the woman laughed.

"You wait just a minute and I'll get the money for you."

Dorothy sorted out something slightly under two handfuls of the asparagus from her stock and handed it in the door to the woman when she returned.

Her customer dropped the coins into her hand. "There. Here is a dime and two pennies for you."

Dorothy's face turned rosy with appealing delight. "Oh, thank you very much!"

The woman laughed again as the child gathered up her asparagus from the porch. She watched Dorothy out of sight and sighed as she put away the asparagus that she had no use for, thinking sentimentally of what a lovely child that little Veech girl was (but then love children so often were), and how sad it was that the poor little thing would never have a chance to grow up right; no telling if the

Veech family was good to her or not. Then, of course, the kind of a mother she had . . .

As soon as Dorothy turned away from the porch the smile disappeared from her face, leaving it blank and closed and artificial again. She walked carefully with her armful of asparagus, looking from time to time to see that the coins did not spill out of her pocket.

She went on to the next house with her wares, and to the next, methodically, until she had sold it all. Finally putting her hand into her pocket over the money, she ran for home.

Once there, she sneaked by her grandfather into the house and straight up the stairs. In the bare hallway, lined with open bedroom doors framing glimpses of untidy, unmade beds, stood an old pasteboard box full of remnants of broken toys, cast-offs of the whole Veech family that Dorothy too had long ago outgrown. She crouched down beside it, reaching in among the dusty broken clutter. She pulled out a tin box, opened it and dropped her little handful of money on top of the rest that she had hidden there. She looked long at her savings, with her face expressionless, and then she hid the box again, down in among the toys.

She stood up and teetered uncertainly on her bare feet, and then slipped in to the small bedroom where her mother slept alone. Dorothy herself since babyhood had slept in the cot at the foot of her grandmother and grandfather's bed. This room in which Mary Veech lived the few hours of the day that she spent at home was somehow subtly full of her presence. It was a small, sparsely furnished room, with a clothes closet at one end and a window at the other. There was a large wooden bed in the room, and a low dresser, neat and bare, with a mirror hanging over it. The floor lacked rugs and was unpainted. The one touch of luxury was the large padded cretonne-covered easy chair and foot-rest that stood before the window with a little bare table beside it, to hold an ash tray.

Dorothy hung onto the edge of the dresser, peering at herself in the mirror. She tipped her head this way and that, posing it and studying her own reflection. She stepped back a little, her lips moving as if she was holding a noiseless conversation with someone invisible to the common eye. Her posing became more elaborate and grotesque as half-formed expressions passed across her face. She was now the leading character in some vague but profound and melodramatic tragedy.

At that moment Jen entered, barefooted and quiet, clad only in brassiere and scant silk step-ins. She stopped short to watch Dorothy in front of the looking glass. She was quite like Josette, her twin, an inch or so shorter perhaps, with a slightly different cast of features. Her hair was rolled up in more elaborate curls, and her mouth was looser, fuller-lipped. She lacked the quality of energy and vigor of her sister. She bore the romantic name of Jennine, although no one ever called her that. The twins were the only ones of the Veech children for whom Sam Veech had had the responsibility of choosing names, because their birth was the only one that ever seriously incapacitated Molly. There had never been a discussion of names for twins, so Sam was completely free to choose, and he had picked Jennine and Josette, his choice being somewhat shaped by a war novel he had been reading at that time, in which two French girls bearing those names had figured prominently. Molly had considered such names highly inappropriate and quite in keeping with the general inefficiency of her husband when it came to meeting the problems of living, so she molded them into Jen and Josie, to the end of preserving the congruity of the family nomenclature.

"What you doing here?" Jen said suddenly, and Dorothy skipped at the sound of her voice. "Go on, get out of here, you ain't got any business fooling around in your mother's room."

Dorothy stared at her silently, motionless.

"Go on!" Jen said again. "Can't you hear me? Maybe nobody else around here makes you mind, but when I say something to you, you're gonna do it."

She advanced on the little girl and tried to push her out of the room. Dorothy stood her ground, struggling and clawing without a sound. They scuffled together. "Why, you little brat, you!" Jen said. Together they bumped against the footboard of the big wooden bed. Kenny's head appeared abruptly as he sat up in the middle of the neat white bedspread. Neither one of them had noticed him lying there, and they stopped short at the sight of him.

"What the hell's going on here? You ain't got any business in here. Go on, get out, both of you."

Dorothy looked at Jen uncertainly. "Huh," Jen said. "I got just as much right in here as you have. I just come in to get some nail polish outa the drawer, that's all."

Kenny's face was sullen and sleepy and threatening. "You keep outa Mary's stuff. She don't want you rummaging around in her things, stealin' everything you can get away with. Go on! get out!" he said shortly. "What you waiting for?"

Jen pushed Dorothy out ahead of her and slammed the door shut behind them with all of her strength. She stalked back to her room at the other end of the hall. Dorothy padded down to the kitchen where Molly was washing dishes, and said with her sweetest smile, "Grandma, can I have a nickel to buy an ice cream cone? It's awful hot. I want an ice cream cone."

"Why, sure you can." Molly wiped her wet hands on the sides of her dress and went to her purse on top of the cupboard. "Ice cream is the best thing there is for little girls this kind of weather. Here's a nickel. You skip with it, but don't you stay out in that sun too much nor walk too fast."

"Okay," Dorothy said.

"What you been doing this morning, Dor'thy?"

Dorothy swung on a chair-back and searched her mind. "Ooooooh, playin' with the kids."

"Well, you be careful and stay outa the sun. Today is sure a scorcher. I guess we're in for a pretty hot summer. I'm about bushed when it gets hot like this. I ain't gonna cook no meals today till it gets cooler. Anybody that wants any dinner is gonna have to get it themselves. I'm gonna lay down awhile and see if I can't get cooled off."

Dorothy edged away, out of the sound of her grandmother's voice. On the front porch her grandfather slept, and the book fell from his hand. Dorothy sidled off down the street, stepping carefully on the hot cement and squeezing the nickel tight in her sweaty little hand.

3

THE SUN HAD DROPPED AWAY, LEAVING A ROSY stain behind in the clear white sky, and all of the insects of the night had taken up their noisy incessant business of living when Pat Thompson climbed the front steps at the Veeches, to call for Josette. He lingered a moment on the porch to talk to Sam and then went on through the house to the kitchen, where Molly was doing the supper dishes.

As a matter of fact, Josette was not at home. She had left a half-hour before with Midge Clark in complete disregard of the date she had made with Pat. Molly tried valiantly to smooth the matter over, as she leisurely wiped the last of the dishes, plodding back and forth across the cooling kitchen, in the glare of the one electric light bulb hanging from the cord in the middle of the ceiling. But Pat was glum and hurt. This was no ordinary date for him. He had come tonight to bring Josette the news of a promotion he had received to a better job in the factory in Ashbury where he worked.

Jud Higgins came out into the kitchen and fumbled with the dipper and pail, getting a drink of water, and Pat made his reluctant departure over Molly's protests that he remain and spend the evening with them.

Jud stared after him. "What's he doing a-hanging around here?" he said to Molly.

"Lord, Mr. Higgins," Molly said shortly as she crammed the dishes into the cupboard, "Pat's been a-looking after Josie for three years now. You oughta know by now what he's a-doing a-hanging around here."

"Josie'll never take up with him," Jud said, grinning as he wiped the water off his chin with the back of his hand. "He ain't good enough to suit Josie. Ain't nobody good enough to suit her, around here."

"You ain't got no business going around talking things like that," Molly said. "Say, you didn't see Ernie hanging around up to the poolroom did you? I kinda wanted to see Ernie about getting me some red raspberries to put up, they make awful nice eating sauce and I . . ."

"No, I didn't," said Jud.

"You don't need to be so short about it," Molly said. "I just thought you mighta seen him, that's all. You ain't going to bed now, are you? Lord, I don't see how you can sleep till it cools off a little."

"Yes, I be," Jud said. He disappeared into the little dark bedroom off the kitchen. Molly reached for the chain on the light. "I better put this light off. The light calls the bugs something awful, and they can come in anywhere they're a-mind to through these screens."

A sudden yowl mixed with muttered cursing came from the bedroom, and the old striped cat ran out into the kitchen on his stiff skinny legs, his eyes wild and his stub of tail erect.

"You oughta be ashamed, Mr. Higgins, kicking that poor old cat around the way you do. When you're as old as that cat is how'd you like it if everybody kicked you around all the time?"

"Ain't gonna sleep with no damn cat in my bed," Jud wailed.

"Nobody's asking you to," Molly said as she let the cat out of the door. "He just likes to lay in there on the bed, that's all. All you gotta do is put him off gentle. That ain't the thing of it though. You go outa your way all the time to kick that poor old cat around. It's a shame," she said, watching the fragile old body slink away into the weeds.

Carl Veech wandered home, watching the stars come out in a sky clear and liquid as the water of the stagnant weed-choked lake at the edge of the village. Twilight and early evening more than any other time of the day drove Carl into a frenzy of discontent. Every automobile that passed through the village, every passenger train, every bus, every airplane flying high in the evening sky brought Carl resentment. He had a feeling of people everywhere doing amusing things together after nightfall while he was forgotten in this remote corner of nowhere.

Half a block from home he met Pat Thompson, and he stopped a minute and spoke to him curtly, reluctant to leave off his orgy of self-pity and dissatisfaction.

Pat was as tall as Carl but much broader across his well-proportioned shoulders. Carl was always aware of this, and he resented it. They stood silently, for they disliked each other and had

no common interest to share. They spoke at last of the heat, shuffling their feet over the sidewalk in the dark and swinging at mosquitoes. They lingered a moment more and parted, each thankful to
be rid of the other.

As Carl moved off again down the quiet street, Kenny called
from behind him and he stood and waited.

"What you doin' up in this end of town?" Kenny said, as he
joined him.

Carl became instantly defensive and wary of this friendly over-
ture from his elder brother. "Nothing. I just been walking around
awhile trying to get cooled off before I went home. What you doing
up here?"

"Oh, hell," Kenny said cheerfully. "After the ball game I went
uptown with Smitty and Bob and had a beer and then Smitty got to
thinking he'd left his catcher's glove laying over there by the ball
diamond somewhere so I walked back with him to get it."

"Did you find it?"

"Naw, it wasn't around there nowhere. Somebody musta picked
it up. Smitty went on over to Simpsons' to see if they had it."

The brothers walked along slowly over the broken sidewalk by
the vacant lot, with the weed stalks that leaned out over the sidewalk
catching at their legs.

"Who was that you was talking to—Thompson?"

"Yeah," Carl said briefly.

"He's a hell of a guy!"

"He sure is."

"I tell yuh there's something about that guy," Kenny said. "I hate
his guts."

"Me too," Carl said. "I suppose he was just coming home from
our house."

"I bet he was at that. Ain't that a hell of a thing."

"Him and Josie? It sure is."

The brothers were in unwonted agreement, and it surprised both
of them.

Kenny looked at Carl cautiously. "I don't know but what he's
about as good as Josie, at that. God, it's getting so it makes me sick
to my stomach to be around Josie."

"Yeah, me too. They're about two of a kind."

They felt good and fond and approving of each other. Out of that feeling Kenny said, "Say, you got a cigarette on you, kid?" And Carl said, "Sure, just a minute. Let me give you a light." They walked on together with their red cigarette ends flicking like gigantic rosy lightning bugs, and went up the front steps shoulder to shoulder.

The mosquitoes had driven Sam off the porch at last, and he lay stretched out on the couch with his head on one pillow and his feet in dirty blue and white socks on another. Dorothy sat at the table staring intently at the pictures of elaborately gowned and coiffured ladies in a Hollywood movie magazine.

Molly shoved her rocking chair back from the open door a little so that they could come in and then resumed her monotonous movement of chair and tattered palm-leaf fan. "Hello, there, the ball game over? Lord, if it don't seem good to have you boys both home here to once for one night!"

Carl found a chair and Kenny stretched out at her feet before the open door. "You oughta come down and see me play ball, Ma," he said.

"Lord," Molly laughed her full pleasant laugh. "Can't you just see me though a-walking way over there by the lake to that ball diamond and then a-standing there while I'm watching you."

"You get Ernie to bring you down in the car some time."

Molly stopped fanning. "Say, ain't neither one of you seen Ernie, have you? I kind of wanted to see Ernie tonight, I been thinking . . ."

"God, you oughta heard Smitty talking tonight, Ma," Kenny broke in. "That Smitty is a screwball if I ever see one. He's been hanging around Slim Rogers' wife a little and now he claims she's gonna get a divorce from Slim and marry him on account of this next kid she's having belongs to Smitty."

"Huh!" Molly sniffed. "There's always plenty a men hanging around that woman! That baby she's having is more likely to belong to a dozen other men than it is to Smitty."

Molly glanced suddenly at Dorothy, who listened to them absorbed, her magazine forgotten. "Say, Dor'thy, you wanta go out in the kitchen and bring Grandma a drink of water?"

Dorothy went scowling but without argument, perfectly aware of why she was being sent away.

As soon as the little girl disappeared Molly leaned down over her stomach and said in a low voice to Kenny, "I didn't want her to hear us talking like this, but somebody said the other day that young Henry Hotchkins had been seen up to Ashbury with that Rogers woman. Now don't that beat everything, him clerk in his father's bank downtown and everything, and then him chasing around with that Rogers woman just like all the common everyday no-goods around town?"

Kenny laughed hard, showing double rows of firm white teeth. "Hell, Ma, I don't believe it."

"Well, neither do I, Kenny. I said I didn't believe it right off I heard it. The Hotchkins' are one of the nicest famblys in this town. His father owns the bank and everything, and I don't believe Henry would do nothing like that . . ."

"That ain't what I meant," Kenny said. "I don't think a real, no-kiddin' she-woman like Myrt Rogers would ever take up with a little sawed-off pipsqueak like Hank Hotchkins!"

Molly said, "Shshshsh—" warningly as Dorothy came in with the water slopping indifferently out of the glass. Kenny and Carl shouted together, and Sam on the couch grinned weakly. The amusement danced in Molly's blue eyes, while she drank the water. "There," she said, giving the glass back to Dorothy. "That was just what Grandma wanted, a nice cold drink of water."

Jen came through the screen door then, letting it slam behind her.

"Hey, look where you're stepping, will you?" Kenny caught hold of her ankle as she stepped over him.

Jen squealed and tripped and caught at the arm of her mother's rocking chair for support. Molly brushed at her face with one stiffened finger. "If you're gonna use lipstick," she said, "I wish to Lord you'd put it on straight. You got a big gob of it smeared right there on your upper lip."

Jen licked at her upper lip, feeling tentatively along the full bright lip with the tip of her tongue.

"Where you been?" Molly said.

"Just walking around awhile with Fran Cope. We had a Coke uptown and then we come on home."

"Did you tell Franny I still loved her?" Kenny said, tugging at his sister's silk-stockinged ankle.

"No, I didn't," Jen said, making a pert little face at him. "If you want Franny to know you still love her you gotta tell her yourself."

Carl turned red suddenly at the mention of Fran Cope's name, and slouched down in his chair, twisting his hands in his pockets. The name of the girl, bringing with it the image of her plump body and shining dark hair, stirred vague desires in him, and left him choked and embarrassed and tongue-tied.

"So you won't tell her for me, huh?" Kenny pinched Jen's ankle in his fingers.

Jen sat down suddenly on top of him. "Well, if here ain't the angel of the family, spending an evening at home!" She tickled him until his big solid body squirmed and writhed underneath her, and ruffled his hair down into his eyes. "What's the matter, you out of money, or couldn't you hook a ride into Ashbury tonight?"

"Yeah, there's a good reason when you spend an evening in, toots," Kenny said as soon as he caught his breath. "You and Fran Cope hung around uptown looking for a date till it got so late there wasn't no chance of you getting one any more, and then you give it up and come on home. You're slipping, toots, you're getting old. Didn't brother Kenny tell you you oughta get married and settle down two or three years ago? But no, you wanta keep fooling around. And now you're slipping; you're old stuff; the boys are on to you and Franny now. They know you ain't nothing but a couple of cold-blooded little gold-digging chiselers, the both of you . . ."

Jen and Kenny enjoyed his harangue hugely, both of them grinning.

Jen sat comfortably on his stomach and examined a snagged place in her silk stocking carefully, spitting on her finger to moisten the rough spot on her knee. "Oh, you don't hear me complaining," she said. "Business is fine. I'm all dated up for the rest of the week." She ticked them off on her bright red fingertips. "Wednesday night, Thursday night, Friday night, Saturday night. How much better'n that you think I can do?"

Kenny pillowed his head on his doubled arms. "Why don't you quit that tearing around and act your age," he said conversationally.

"Anybody'd think you was a damn sixteen-year-old high-school kid, the way you're going."

"Land," Molly said, plying her fan energetically, "that ain't no way to talk. I like to see a young girl have a little fun before she settles down and starts raising her fambly. I got married when I was eighteen, and you kids started coming right away, and that's where all of my good times went to."

"Why don't you practice what you preach, mister?" Jen said poking her finger into Kenny's ribs again.

"Oh, sure," Kenny said, "go ahead and have your fun, but don't forget what Ma said, don't forget to marry and settle down before you start raising your family."

"Kenny!" Molly said disapprovingly, and Jen boxed his ears and said, "Wise guy, ain't you, handing out advice." She mimicked in a high singsong voice, "Do as I say, not do as I do."

An automobile slid to a stop out in front, the brakes squeaking, and the fine dust at the edge of the pavement rising up into the darkness. Kenny turned glum. "That's Ernie, and I guess he picked up Josie somewhere. God, what is this? Family reunion? Say, get up will you?" he said to Jen. "Where you think you're setting? You got my guts pasted to my backbone."

Jen got up and shook her skirt out and smoothed it over her hips and went across to the table and took the movie magazine away from Dorothy. Before Dorothy got her mouth open to scream, she threw it back onto the table again.

"That's last month's. I already seen that one."

Ernie shoved Josie in the door ahead of him. "Hi, folks. Look what I just picked up about a half a block away from Clarks' house. First thing you know we're gonna be breaking into the society news, running around with the Clarks."

"Why, hello there, Ernie," Molly said, holding her face up for him to kiss. "I been wanting to see you all day."

He kissed her warm big face, and stood bent down, his hands on either chair arm. "How are yuh, Mom? Still love me?"

"Go on with you," she said. "Sit down. Get up and give him that chair, Dor'thy. Where you been keeping yourself, Ernie? We ain't seen you in a coon's age."

"Why, I was just here Sunday night, wasn't it?" He pulled the chair around in front of the center table. "How's the rheumatiz, Dad?"

Sam sat up on the end of the couch and began his slow mild speech. "Well, now, I tell you, you'd think this hot dry weather would drive the rheumatiz out of me, wouldn't you? But I been having that ache through my back and legs all day, like the toothache. Course it ain't so bad like it would be if the weather was damp and cold, but . . ."

"Say," Molly said impatiently, "you see any nice red raspberries uptown, Ernie? I want some red raspberries to put up the worst way. They make awful nice eating sauce, and I wanta get hold of the berries while they're still nice. They ain't gonna stay nice long if this hot dry weather keeps up . . ."

"Ain't today been a scorcher, though?" Ernie said, crossing his legs comfortably. "Boy, and don't think it wasn't hot out there on that railroad! Them men like to sweat themselves to death. I had two gangs out the other side of Benton, laying rail. Talk about hot, you oughta be out there, the sun a-shining down on the steel. Little guy named Joe passed out on us. I see him just a-standing there, and all of a sudden he turned whiter'n a sheet and just keeled over and started throwing up. He kind of hit his head when he went down on the edge of a tamping machine. It bled like hell and we couldn't get him to, so I sent him into town to the doctor's. Why, they said the doc had to take seven stitches in his head and when he come to he kept talking crazy like. The doc said it was the heat. I tell you that heat is something awful."

The family sat quiet momentarily in solemn agreement.

Josette stood just inside the door listening to Ernie attentively and he reached out and pulled her over beside his chair. "Well, honey," he said, "how's everything coming up to school? Ma, how does it feel to have a daughter in college?"

"I think she's doing real well up there," Molly said.

Jen fingered the curls at the back of her hair. "I don't know when she has any time to study, chasing after Midge Clark all the while."

Josette stood in the circle of Ernie's arm awkwardly, her face bland and preoccupied. She scowled and said sharply, "If you don't like the friends I have you don't have to. Anyway, I'd a whole lot rather have people see me running around with Midge, than with somebody that's common town talk like Frances Cope is."

Carl catapulted himself into the discussion excitedly. "Yeah, you run around with that stuck-up Clark girl long enough and you won't even be speaking to nobody the way she does. It's getting so you think you're so damn good . . ."

Jen stood in the middle of the floor with her hands on her full hips. "You think you're too good for Pat Thompson right now, except when you want to go some place or something. Well, I just hope that Pat gets a belly full of you and leaves you cold, that's what I hope."

Molly shook her fan at all of them. "Now you kids hush up and quit your picking. We was all setting here talking nice, till you had to start picking."

"Don't let 'em kid you, honey," Ernie said to Josette fondly. The light shone on his even false teeth when he talked and on his dark sunburned face, with the thinning hair above, and on his light suit and on the big cameo ring on his finger.

Josette detached herself from his encircling arm and crossed the room with her face set and angry. She went upstairs, slamming the door hard behind her.

"God, ain't we something!" Kenny said, screwing up his face toward the ceiling in caricature of Josette's lifted chin. "Ma, you sure you didn't double the ante on Pa back there about war time, steppin' out some night with some society boy in a fancy uniform?"

They laughed, all of them, even Sam and Molly, laughed hard, and the sound of their mirth spilled out of the doors and windows of the house into the quiet dark night.

"Oh, go long with you, Kenny," Molly said at last, wiping her eyes and groping for her fan on the floor.

She fanned herself vigorously, her blue eyes still snapping with mirth, and turned to Ernie again. "Say, Ernie, I been tryin' to ask you. You see any red raspberries uptown today? I been wanting some red raspberries the worst way to . . ."

Mary came in suddenly and closed the screen door noiselessly behind her. She looked very tired. The golden-brown circles around her eyes were deeper and her crumpled lips seemed always on the verge of beginning to tremble.

"Why, Mary, what's the matter you home here, you sick or something?" her mother asked.

"I've got a headache," she said. "I haven't had any sleep the last week and a half. All I need is sleep."

The family shifted around finding a chair for her, silently.

Before she sat down she spoke to Molly. "Mom, how come you let Dorothy stay up so late? She needs to go to bed early regular, she's so skinny. Dorothy, you go on upstairs now and get in bed."

"Lord, I just forgot the kid was still up, we was all talking. Go on up there, Dor'thy, and go to bed, there's a good girl. Josie's up there to bed already, and we're all going to bed in a minute, it's getting late." Molly hugged the child to her and kissed her loudly, and Dorothy went, leaving the stair door open behind her.

Mary said to Ernie suddenly, "You fired Bill Dodge off the road last Saturday, huh?"

Ernie's face turned dark, and closed and cautious.

"Yeah. Bill Dodge has been needing firing for a long time. It was getting so he figured he knew more'n me or any other damn man on the road." His voice was defensive. "Why, hell, he got so he wouldn't take orders. You can't have no guy like that working in a gang of men."

"He's going to make trouble," Mary said.

"Hell!" Ernie said. "I ain't afraid of Bill Dodge. He's the biggest mouth there is. Any time he wants to start something, I'll knock his damn head off, and he knows it."

Carl behind the table looked up from his book, and watched the light shine on Mary's short hair. She blew a couple of smoke rings, and one of them drifted up above her head and enlarged and hung there for a moment like a halo.

"He's going to take it up with the head office."

Ernie's face turned dark with anger. "Why, the little son of a bitch. I'll knock his head off. He ain't got the guts to make no trouble. Besides," his voice turned flat and cautious again, "he ain't got nothing to report. He comes under insubordination, see, and I got a right to fire anybody I God-damn please under insubordination and . . ." His voice trailed off under her level eyes.

"You better watch out," she said. "Suppose he gets some of the other boys to start talking."

Ernie was bursting with rage. He got to his feet, his face flushed dark red. "I don't believe a God-damn word of it. Bill Dodge ain't got the guts to start nothing."

Mary did not answer him, and her quiet self-control seemed to infuriate him. "G'night, Mom," he said thickly. He went out and let the door slam behind. In a moment they heard the furious roar of his automobile motor as he shot down the street.

Molly looked after him, bewildered. "What you talking about to Ernie to make him fly off mad like that?" she asked Mary. "He ain't got into no kind of trouble, has he?"

"Now, Ma!" Kenny said. "Don't you start worrying. There ain't nothing for you to worry your head about."

"That Dodge ain't a-going to do something to Ernie, is he?"

"No, Mom, don't you worry," Mary said.

"Well . . ." Molly relaxed in her chair. "There, sir, now Ernie's gone and he never said nothing about getting me them raspberries."

Mary got up and shoved her chair back. "I ordered you ten quarts of red raspberries from Clark's. They'll deliver 'em in the morning."

Molly's face shone with pleasure. "Mary, that sure was nice of you. If you hadn't a-done it, no telling when I woulda got some. Most likely I never woulda got any at all, and I wanted to put some up for sauce the worst way."

Jen yawned with her mouth stretched wide for a long time, profoundly bored. "Going to bed and get some sleep," she muttered.

Carl followed her upstairs carrying the book with him, to read in bed if Kenny, his bedmate, would allow it.

In the kitchen, after Molly and Sam had gone off to bed, also, Mary and Kenny ate a snack of toasted cheese sandwiches over a corner of the kitchen table. They moved about on tiptoe, taking pleasure in the surreptitious nature of their snack, and smiling together, when Kenny dropped the cheese knife. Over the plate of warm golden sticky sandwiches between them, Kenny said, "You think they can get anything on old Ernie?"

Mary thought a long time before she answered. "No. Lew doesn't either. He gave Dodge the money to go to the head office in

Detroit and make the complaint, though. The boys could get Ernie fired all right if they'd stick together, but they won't because they're afraid they'll lose their jobs."

They sat together quietly after that. There was no sound anywhere but the busy insect voices, and the smack of small bodies on the window screens. One brown miller flapped around and around the electric light bulb over their heads. Far off a dog howled, and after that a rooster crowed.

"Listen to that damn rooster of Smith's," Kenny said idly. "That damn thing crows all night."

They were quiet again.

Mary moistened her finger and dabbled up the last crumbs of toast from the empty plate.

"Your head still ache?" Kenny said sympathetically.

She nodded indifferently.

"What you need is sleep. My God, you don't never sleep at all. You come on upstairs now and go to bed."

Kenny pulled the light out and they went upstairs in the dark together. They whispered good night in the darkness and Kenny closed her eyelids down gently with his fingers. "Get some sleep, kid."

She went into her room and closed the door. Two slits of light shone out into the hall, one from the twins' room and another from the room that Carl and Kenny shared. Kenny opened the door quietly and went in. Carl lay in the middle of the big white iron bed, propped on both pillows, sound asleep, the book dropped out of his hands. The humming sound of a mosquito filled the room. Kenny swore under his breath and pulled the light out and undressed in the dark. The bright moonlight shone in the window onto his big firm body clad only in brief shorts. He went to the bed and yanked one of the pillows out from under Carl's head. Carl half woke, stirred and then slept on with his mouth open, the pillow stuffed under his shoulders, his head hanging down from it against the head of the bed. Kenny prepared to shove him over, but he stopped and swore again under his breath. He took his pillow and doubled it under his head and lay carefully with his body hanging on the edge of the bed. He heard the sound of Carl's heavy breathing and the chorus of snoring from the room of his father and mother and the sound of faint voices from the twins'. His mind flittered a little: Mary's face, the feel of her eyelids under his fingers, a little squirt named Bill dead in Milwaukee. Smith's rooster crowed once more, and Kenny slept deep and dreamlessly.

In her room across the hall, Mary sat in the darkness, her filmy nightgown clinging to her soft full body stretched out in the deep chair by the window. She looked out the window, at the tree leaves shimmering in the bright moonlight. The tip of her cigarette turned red and faded out rosy again. Millions of stars huddled down over the house, and in the trees a night bird cried out and was still again.

From the twins' room the faint sound of voices continued. When Jen had come up to bed she had found Josette stretched out across the bed in her pajamas, with the window shades chastely pulled down to the sills.

"My God," she said, brightly, "but it's hot up here! How you ever expect it to cool off so we can sleep with them shades pulled down like that?"

She pulled them up noisily and Josette withdrew under the sheet and went on filing her finger nails.

Jen threw her clothes off in all directions, littering the tidy room. "You get your studying done?"

"No, I didn't," Josette said shortly.

"I don't see how you expect to do any studying running around with Midge Clark every night."

"I don't see how you think I could get any studying done around here, anyway. There isn't a decent quiet place in the whole house where I can study." Josette's smooth forehead wrinkled again into the familiar worry wrinkles under the light beading of perspiration.

"I know it," Jen said, unexpectedly sympathetic. "You can't study downstairs with everybody talking, and there ain't no place up here. And it's so hot."

"And you don't see anybody trying to help me find a place neither, do you? Nobody thinks of that. They seem to think just sending me up there to school is enough."

Jen rummaged through drawers and turned the neat top of the bureau into a shambles. "Couldn't you fix it up with Ernie to study over to his house?"

Josette propped the pillow up behind her back. "How could I study over there? He has a crowd in there drinking and tearing around every night. Besides, how could I study over there with Erma there?"

"Yeah."

Both girls thought of Erma silently. Ernie's present housekeeper, whose jealousy of him, and natural greediness for money combined with the inevitable precariousness of her position had developed in her a deep antipathy for all of the Veeches.

"Did Pat come over tonight?" Josette asked.

"I don't know," Jen said, wiping the cold cream off her face with a piece of tissue. "I wasn't here. You had a date with him for tonight, didn't you?"

"Yes."

Jen threw the tissue down and stood with her hands on her hips in front of her sister. "Jo, you oughta be ashamed the way you're treating Pat. Pat's crazy about you, and he's done an awful lot for you and then you treat him like that. First thing you know, he's going to get his belly full and leave you flat, and then where'll you be?"

"That's all right with me. Any time he gets sick of hanging around here, he knows what he can do. I'll get along. Pat Thompson isn't the only man on earth, and he doesn't need to act like he owns me. There are a lot better men than Pat Thompson."

"Not around here," Jen said. "He's got an awful good job in the shops. Going to trade school and all, he'll get ahead up there and make good money and you know it."

"Phooie!" Josette said. "Factory worker!"

"Phooie, factory worker, that's all right. You think you're so much that you got your pick of the best there is?"

"I don't want to discuss it." Josette tucked the emery board under her pillow and looked away.

Jen curled up on the edge of the bed, and began the evening task of rolling each lock of hair around a thin metal curler. After a little she said cautiously, "Say, Jo, you don't want a date with Clim Hawkins, do you?"

"No, I don't." Josette sat up straight in the bed with an indignant face.

"Shshsh, you don't have to yell, do you? I only asked you."

"You think I'd have a date with a man like Clim Hawkins? Why, he's no good. He drinks and chases after tough girls and . . ."

"Well, I only asked you. I told him you wouldn't."

"You mean Clim Hawkins asked you to ask me for a date?" Josette said incredulously.

"Yeah. Clim has seen you around and he thinks you're about the tops. Honest to God, I think he's nuts about you. He's always asking me about you, and stuff."

"Well, you tell him to mind his own business. I wouldn't have a date with Clim Hawkins if he was the last man on earth."

"Oh, I don't know," Jen said around the curler she held in her mouth while she combed out a curl on the back of her head. "There's a lot worse fellows than Clim, and he's kind of good-looking. He ain't half so bad as they say he is. I've dated him some myself."

"Hum!"

Jen dropped the curlers down on the bed suddenly and leaned toward her sister. "Jo, what's the sense you being so snotty to all the kids around here? It's getting so everybody, even Pat, thinks you're getting stuck-up. Where you think it's going to get you? It's all right this summer to tell 'em to go to hell and run around with Midge Clark if you wanta, but what you gonna do in the fall after Midge is gone away to school again? You're still gonna be here, and you're gonna be setting home by yourself night after night and you know that ain't no fun."

"I'm not getting stuck-up, and if I am I can't help it. You think I don't know what all the kids think of me?" Josette's mouth drooped but she drove the tremble out of her voice. "Well, let them think it. I hate this town, I hate everybody in it. What do you think I'm going to school up to Ashbury for? Do you think I like to go up there to school and try to study day after day after day in all this hot weather? Well, I don't. I hate it. But I hate this town worse. I'm going to get out and get a job; have nice clothes and a nice apartment and associate with nice people. I don't care what the kids think. I hate 'em. I hate this whole town!"

Jen sat quiet before her sister's intensity. After a little she got up and gathered up the rest of the curlers and put them on the bureau top. "Well, I don't know," she said. "I guess you and me ain't a thing alike, even if we are twins. But you hadn't oughta take things so hard and get so worked up. It don't help a bit, and it only makes you feel bad. There's lots of other places I guess I'd rather be than here, but as long as I am here, I don't see any sense in tearing myself to pieces wanting to be somewhere else, and treating everybody nasty and setting home by myself night after night."

"I don't expect you to understand how I feel." Josette settled down on her pillow on her own side of the bed. She felt a little ashamed of her outburst, so she spoke more sharply than usual. "For heaven's sakes turn that light out and come to bed. First thing you know this room will be full of mosquitoes and then neither one of us can sleep."

In a moment Jen turned out the light and crawled into the bed. She kicked the sheet down to the foot and pulled up the legs of her pajamas as far as she could. "My God, but it's hot!"

"If you'd lie still and quit thrashing around, you wouldn't be hot. I'm cooled off already."

Jen wriggled in the bed and pulled her pillow under her head. "Say, did you see those new dresses Mary brought home last night? I guess Lew must have got 'em for her in Chicago. You know he was in Chicago and he just come home last night. Boy, talk about clothes. I wish Mary wasn't so little. There's a black taffeta one that I'm crazy about."

"I haven't seen them and I don't want to."

"Oh, don't be like that. There's a blue suit among 'em, you oughta see it. Boy, Mary will be a knockout in that. It's a real bright blue just the color of her eyes. I wish I could wear clothes like Mary. She's the best-dressed woman in this town. I wish I looked like she does. She's the most beautiful woman I ever saw. Everybody thinks she's beautiful."

"Well, I don't," Josette said. "Mary hasn't done a thing for this family to be proud of. Everybody knows where her money comes from and her swell clothes. She doesn't look beautiful to me, she just looks cheap and common. Everybody in this town has talked about her for years, and they've had a right to, the way she's acted. The decent people in this town wouldn't even speak to her."

Jen's voice was drowsy and contented with sleep coming easily and unsought after. "You hadn't ought to talk that way about Mary, all she's always doing for us."

"She can keep her money," Josette said glumly. "She hasn't done a thing for this family, especially for us girls by being the kind of woman she is. She's just made it a million times harder for us to get in with the right kind of people and ever amount to anything."

Jen's voice rose and fell in the natural rhythm of her warm drowsy body. "I ain't never been ashamed of Mary. I'm glad she's my sister. I think she's perfectly beautiful. I wish I could be just like her. I never knew Mary to get mad nor spiteful, nor do one single damn mean or underhanded thing in all her life. She's always good to everybody and she never bawls you out, no matter what. She's a friend to everybody in this town that will let her be, and if you ever got in a jam she'd do more for you than anybody else on earth. She ain't the least bit stuck-up, but there ain't nothing cheap nor common about Mary. She's beautiful, and there's something else about her. She's got class, that's what, yes, sir, Mary's got class," Jen finished drowsily.

Josette sat up and leaned over on her elbow and stared at her sister's face in the moonlight. "There you are," she said. "You ought to be ashamed of Mary, but instead of that you want to be just like her. And the way you keep running around with that tough gang that you do, you're going to be, too. Somebody ought to talk to you good, the way you're doing. You're never home at night. You run around to tough beer gardens and dance halls with a tough crowd of people. You don't need to tell me you don't drink too much. I've seen you come in here to bed night after night when you were silly drunk and couldn't walk straight. You ought to be ashamed. You're old enough to know better. You ought to be looking for a job and thinking about getting some place, but all you want to do is run around all night and spend half the day with Frances Cope. Frances Cope isn't fit for anybody to associate with, and if you don't watch out you're going to be just like her, and, for all I know, you are right now."

Josette paused for breath. Jen was breathing deeply. "Jen, you hear me?" But Jen was sleeping quietly. Josette could not tell if she was shamming or not, but she lay back on her pillow in disgust and looked out of the window into the leafy tree branches.

She thought of lessons unstudied and the hot hard day before her and of Midge Clark's cool, well-furnished bedroom in the middle of a cool, well-ordered house and she began to feel miserable. She wanted things to be decent and clean and nice so desperately. She thought of the stack of bright gay letters on the top of Midge's desk, from friends scattered all over the country on vacation, the kind of gay amusing people that she wanted to know. A great lump came up in her throat and the tears pushed at her eyelids. She crowded the tears back, straightened her pillow and resolutely tried to sleep. But sleep eluded her. She heard the heavy breathing and the sound of snoring from all over the house. It seemed the last straw to her, that on top of everything else she must also be the only one in town cheated out of a night's sleep. She lay numb with misery. A strident noisy train went through and shook the bed. The room seemed shrunken and cluttered and stifling. Far away there was the brassy sound of a rooster crowing. Josette began to cry, choking her sobs into her pillow. She cried on and felt relaxed and wretched and hopeless, but the pain went out of her. Let her eyes be red and swollen in the morning, she thought, what of it, what difference did it make how she looked or what she did or what ever became of her. Her crying died down to a kind of tearless sniveling and suddenly she slept.

4

ON WEDNESDAY NIGHT THE HANDFUL OF GROCERY stores, the drugstore and the one untidy cluttered drygoods store that composed the town's business section stayed open for the country business. As an extra attraction to lure shoppers into the town, the high-school band offered a concert, weekly, on that night. After supper at Veeches, Sam and Jud and Dorothy drifted uptown that they might not miss any of the unwonted activity in the village. It was almost equal to a Saturday night when the stores also stayed open and even more people came in to shop or stand and talk along the store fronts on the sidewalk.

Molly piled the dirty dishes in the kitchen sink and went to change her dress. She had to buy some groceries, she said, and she kind of liked to talk to folks and hear the band play. Jen washed in the kitchen, with her hair done up on top of her head over two dozen or so tin curlers. She had no time to bother with dirty dishes either. She had a date, she told her mother, and she was expecting Fran Cope any minute. Fran was going to help her comb out her hair in this new style that she was experimenting with. In the midst of the ensuing argument, Carl took his book and went upstairs to his room to read. He was not fleeing so much from the face-to-face meeting with Fran Cope as he was from the anticipation of his mother's suggestion that he do the dishes. Upstairs, he closed the door and turned on the light. He sat hunched uncomfortably on the edge of the unmade bed with his book on his knees and a bent ash tray beside him. The night was hot and clear and already a stream of rattling old automobiles poured into town past the house. He finished the last pages of the book and sprawled on the bed, upsetting the ash tray on the sheets. The insipid romance had ended as he had gloomily predicted after reading the first dozen pages. While Carl was still scowling over the book, his mind lost in vague reveries and vaporous romances of his own making, Kenny came in whistling and slammed the door open against the wall. "What you doing up here?" he said to Carl.

"I been reading."

"God, you're getting as bad as Pa!"

Kenny turned the bureau drawers upside down, looking for a clean shirt, singing lustily a song the burden of which seemed to be that I can't give you anything but love, baby. "Where's that blue shirt of mine? Ma said she ironed it and put it up here in the drawer. You seen that blue shirt?"

"No, I ain't," Carl said sourly. He groped around for the ash tray with his cigarette stub.

"You're sure making a mess of that bed. Why don't you look what you're doing? You got ashes spilled all over."

"You should worry. You won't be home tonight to sleep in it, anyway."

Kenny found the shirt at last and spread it out over the foot of the bed. He took off his soiled one and threw it on the floor. "What's eating you?" he said to Carl. "You look as sour as all hell. Why don't you go on downtown with the rest of the boys and drink a little beer? Pick up a date with some of these little chickens running around town."

"To hell with it," Carl said.

"What's the matter, you think these females would be too much for you to handle?" Kenny leaned over and good-naturedly tousled Carl's straight black hair down into his eyes.

"Cut it out. Leave me alone, will you?"

"Okay, okay, don't get excited." Kenny started whistling again. He combed his hair in front of the cracked old mirror, and matched a tie to the blue shirt.

"How come you're all dressed up?"

Kenny cocked an eyebrow at his own reflection in the mirror. "I'm going to the big city, kid. I'm gonna see people and do things."

Kenny whistled again, and dusted off the toes of his shoes with his dirty shirt.

From below came a chatter of voices and laughter. Feet sounded on the stairs as Jen and Frances Cope came up to Jen's room.

Kenny went to the doorway and grabbed Frances Cope's arm as she went by. "Hi, Franny, you still love me?"

She stopped willingly. "Why, sure I do, Kenny. How's the boy?"

"I'm swell," Kenny said. "I'm feeling fine. I'm doing all right."

He put his arms around her and pulled her plump body up against him and kissed her. She put her arms around his neck and tipped up her face, her dark hair falling back from her olive-tinted brow.

Jen yelled at them from her room. "Kenny, for God's sake, get out of here and let Fran alone. I want her to fix my hair."

"Say, Fran," Kenny said, "you got a date tonight?"

"Jen!" she screamed. "What you think? Kenny's asking me for a date."

"There you are," he said. "Now if that ain't just like you chiseling nitwit kids. My God, I say have you got a date tonight and right away you start screaming about me asking you for a date. Look,

Franny, any time I want a date with you, see, I'll send you a telegram."

Fran laughed hard with the rich warm color coming up into her face and neck. "It's all right, Kenny boy. You don't have to yell for your momma, nor nothing. Wicked, nasty, bad old Franny ain't going to take advantage of you this time."

"Shut up, will you?" He cocked his fist at her. "Keep your little mouth shut and just answer questions like a nice girl. You got a date tonight?"

"Yes, teacher," Fran said meekly.

"Oh, hell," he said. "Here I was gonna fix one up for you."

"Ooooh, Kenny! How sweet of you! Who you gonna fix me up a date with?"

Kenny put his arm around her and led her into the bedroom, where Carl sat on the edge of the bed, red with a presage of embarrassment to come.

"Now, I'll tell you," Kenny said elaborately. "You know my kid brother Carl here, don't you, Franny?"

"Sure," she giggled.

"Well, now Carl's a real nice kid, see? But that's the trouble right there. He's just a kid, and you girls have all got him scared. Now, take you for instance, Franny. Carl's crazy about you, but you got him so scared he don't dare walk right up to you and say, 'How about a date tomorrow night?' Stead of that he just sits around here eating his heart out for you. I swear to God he's getting skinny all on account of you. You gotta be nice to the kid, Franny."

Carl recoiled on the bed with his face vermilion.

"Oh, Kenny," Fran said, with mock wide-eyed concern. "If you'd only told me sooner. Why, I never dreamed of such a thing. I just never thought of you having a bashful kid brother. I wouldn't have had him getting skinny on account of me for nothing."

"There, kid, you see?" Kenny said triumphantly. "Brother Kenny's got it all fixed up for you. There ain't nothing to it."

Carl felt choked and suffocated and their two faces ran into a blur. He wanted to crawl away under the bed. The odor of the cheap perfume that she wore was strong in his nose. He searched vainly for quick glib careless words to extricate himself with.

Kenny's eyes were dancing. "Why don't you say something nice to the lady, kid? Maybe you want me to go out in the hall a minute, huh?"

Carl's throat contracted and went dry.

"There Franny, you see how it is? You got him scared. He tightens right up. Why don't you give him a nice kiss? That'll loosen him up, you just see if it don't."

Carl heard their voices distorted through the blood pounding in his ears.

"You think that would fix him up, Kenny?" she was saying.

"Why, sure it would. That's all he needs. The first one always comes hardest; you know that."

"Well, if you say so, Kenny . . ."

She leaned down laughing, and reached her hand out to his face.

Carl turned chalky white beneath his straggling dark hair and jumped to his feet. The girl squealed and backed away at the unexpected transformation in him. Carl saw Kenny only as a multicolored blur that approached and receded in waves. His voice sounded hoarse and strangled to his own ears. "Why don't you leave me alone, you damn son of a bitching . . ." He swung out wildly at Kenny with both fists, his long arms waving.

Kenny held him off at arms' length and spoke sharply to him. "Shut up, kid, cool down. Can't you stand a little kidding? You cut it out or you're gonna get hurt."

Carl heard the sound of his brother's voice, but not one word of what he was saying. Kenny held him back and Carl went mad with fury at his own impotence before Kenny's strength.

Kenny said, "Why, you crazy little fool, you!" He could hold him back no longer. He dropped his arms and cocked his right fist measuring for Carl's face, indifferent to the rain of light blows Carl was delivering against his face and body.

Kenny moved suddenly, all in one piece, the muscles of his whole heavy body rippling, and struck Carl on the jaw. The impact of the blow knocked the boy back across the bed, and his head struck hard against the iron spokes of the foot board. A little cut gaped open above his left eye and spilled blood out onto his white face. His breath came in sobs.

Fran had disappeared and Jen stood in the doorway with her hair still half on curlers. "Oh, Kenny," she cried, "what made you fight with him? You hit him so hard. Look, his head's bleeding."

"You get out of here and leave him alone," Kenny said briefly. He closed the door behind her and stood with the knob in his hand. The blood trickled down Carl's face onto the bed sheets. His eyes were closed and his whole body was racked by his great heavy choking breaths.

Kenny went over to the bed. "I'm sorry, kid. Let me see your head." He took hold of Carl's head and turned it around to the light. Carl struggled under his hands, but he held him until he had looked at the cut.

Carl shook him free at last. "Leave me alone," he cried. "Why won't you get outa here and leave me alone?" He began to cry hard then, and rolled over smothering his face in the bed covers.

"Okay," Kenny said. "Your head's all right. The skin just broke open." He wiped a spot or two of blood from his hands on the dirty shirt, went to the mirror and smoothed his hair and straightened his necktie. He lingered a moment opening and shutting drawers noisily over the sound of Carl's crying. A train went through and drowned out all the sounds. Kenny walked back to the bed again and put his hand down onto Carl's thin shaking shoulder. "You'll be all right, kid. You put some styptic on your head in a minute and it'll stop bleeding." He dropped the white styptic pencil on the bed beside Carl, patted his shoulder again and went out closing the door softly.

After a while Carl stopped crying and lay still, limp and wet with sweat, his face still buried in the bedclothes. His head throbbed as if it would blow apart and he was too weak and miserable to move.

A car kept tooting out in front and he heard the girls come out into the hall. The footsteps, punctuated by spike heels, stopped opposite his door. He heard Jen speak to Fran, and one pair of the tall heels clicking down the stairs. In a minute Jen said softly through the closed door, "You all right, Carl? I'm awful sorry it happened. Kenny shouldn't have teased you like that. He feels awful bad about it too. Does your head hurt bad? I wish you'd let me come in and look at it. I'll go downtown and send Ma home if you want me to."

Carl spoke at last, his voice smothered in the bed. "You don't have to run and tell Ma everything, do you? I'm all right."

"All right, I won't tell Ma, if you don't want me to. I just thought maybe you'd want her to put something on your head."

"Well, I don't. I'm all right."

"Okay," Jen said. "I'm awful sorry, Carl. G'bye." He heard her footsteps on the stairs, and voices as she went down the porch steps. The car drove away and the house was quiet.

In a minute Carl sat up on the edge of the bed. He felt dizzy and sick, and there were strange noises in his head. He stared at his own image in the mirror over the bureau spiritlessly. Some of the color was coming back into his face beneath the blood smears, but his shoulders sagged with fatigue. The room was close and hot and the faint sounds of the band playing came in the window. He felt a great desire to get away from this room and out into the cool darkness where he could breathe and think. On the impetus of that desire he hunted the styptic pencil out of the tumbled bedclothes. His long slim hands shook and he started the cut bleeding again, but the styptic bit, and that sharp pain cut pleasantly through the dull roaring ache in his head. He watched the cut anxiously. Minute white crystals formed along the edges and the bleeding stopped. He slicked his hair back, turned out the light and started downstairs. Halfway down he remembered that the book he had just finished reading was due back at the circulating library. His father had spoken to him about it at the supper table. He went back upstairs wearily and found it on the floor, under the bed.

Out on the street the fresh air drove the sickness and dizziness out of him. He walked away from the blatant band music and the lights and the high wooden bandstand set up in the middle of the street, amid the clutter of automobiles and people. He walked along the dark quiet streets with his face lifted to the trees and to the clean sky overhead where the first pale stars shone. Beyond the railroad tracks the lake water shone a little among the weeds and the trees and bushes, and the frogs and crickets and all of the other voices of the night sang louder here. In spite of himself, Carl's nerves relaxed. There was a certain sensitive responsiveness to his immediate surroundings that he had long ago discovered in himself and vaguely resented. He walked on with his quick long nervous strides, cutting back and forth on the empty side streets, following the sidewalk. The tension and emotion went out of him so completely that he deliberately had to think back to the scene in the bedroom to unsettle himself again.

He let the humiliation of it etch into him again. He hated Kenny for his assurance, for his glib speech and easy strength. The very thought that Fran Cope had been a witness to his humiliation separated her from him completely. That is, if there was any such a person as Fran Cope. The Fran that left him tongue-tied when she walked down the street with a smile on her mouth and the sun shining on her incredibly dark hair and skin, and her full body moving rhythmically, had nothing to do, for him, with the slightly commonplace girl who had let Kenny kiss her in the hall. He felt spent and confused, and childishly eager to be with people again.

He remembered the library book under his arm and started off for the smear of lights and the distant band music at a swift eager pace.

Once he was downtown, he found the sidewalks clogged with people and he had to pick his way among them. The band was still playing discordantly and earnestly, twenty or so high-school students with sweaty serious faces playing away on the high bandstand under the bright lights, with the insects billowing over them like a swirling winter blizzard. Carl stood still a minute, frowning with annoyance. Miss Malott, their instructor, stood in front of them, her body rigid, a fixed smile on her face, jerking the slim baton up and down mechanically, in a way entirely unrelated to the music they were playing. Carl hated them all suddenly, with a deep and profound hatred, and he hated all of the gaping flat-faced people that lined the sidewalks to hear them. The street was roped off, and the traffic detoured, and the space in front of the bandstand was full of parked automobiles, full of people. Only the small children threaded back and forth through the crowd, intent on their own business and quite oblivious to the band. The young boys and girls, although they stood still in the semblance of attention, were staring at each other self-consciously, unaware also of the blaring music.

The band suddenly stopped playing, and Miss Malott turned around and began to bow and smile to the good-natured applause and confusion of appreciative automobile horns. Carl could stand no more of it. He bolted into the drugstore, and down to the back to the half-dozen shelves that held the county circulating library books. There he dropped the book he had under his arm into the basket for returned volumes. The stools along the soda fountain in the front of the store were full of high-school girls. He had noticed them when he came in. He was peculiarly aware of them now, their chatter and their laughter. He looked toward them out of the corner of his eye. Several of the bright faces were turned to him, and when they caught his eyes, they looked away again immediately, giggling and talking softly among themselves. Carl discovered he was in no mood to select a book. He went out the front door looking straight ahead of him and stood uncertainly on the edge of the crowd again. He fancied that everybody who looked at him must be speculating on his disfigured facial anatomy. He saw his mother across the street standing in a group of women, her arms full of brown sacks, her legs straddled apart to bear the weight of her heavy unwieldy body.

He dodged into the ice cream parlor. Some of the stools were occupied so he went down to one of the booths in the back. He sat alone over his cigarette and Coca-Cola. The continual throbbing in his head gave an unreality to everything. He listened to the slamming of the screen door, the voices and the sound of tinkling glasses. He stared at the faded linoleum and the big black stove, shoved to the back for the summer, at the pinball game half covered with canvas, waiting for the last anti-gambling crusade to blow over. He stared at the baseball schedule of the Tigers' games hanging on the wall, and at the picture of the beautiful recumbent blonde girl in the scanty bathing suit, on the calendar. He felt completely and terribly isolated, an unfulfilled need for someone congenial to himself that he might talk to. He had been alone all of his life, and with a rare swift insight he wondered whether he was not to be alone all the days of his life to come. He was frightened and his head pounded. The thought of one more year of high school terrified him. What was he going to do when that one brief year was over, and he was no closer to ways and means of extricating himself from this hateful life? He felt trapped and impotent and desperate. The Coca-Cola was forgotten. Inside of him a tiny hysterical voice was screaming over and over, "What am I going to do? What am I going to do? I've got to get out of this town. I've got to get away from here. But how and where, and what am I to do? There is no place in all the world for me except here, but I can't stay here, I can't, I can't. I can't live here. I can't live here another day, I can't live any more. How can I walk out of here tonight and go home and go to sleep and wake up here another day. I can't go on living, I can't. I've got to throw myself into the lake. I've got to throw myself in front of a train because I can't live any more, not another year, not another day, not another hour!"

He got up out of the booth and rushed toward the door, his long gangling body swooping, his eyes wild. At the door he ran against Pat Thompson and Josette. Pat spoke to him but Carl paid no attention. Outside on the street he stumbled over children and ran into people, their faces and bodies all a blur. His mother just crossing the street on her way home called to him to come and help her carry her groceries, but he neither saw nor heard her. In a moment the lights and people were behind him and he had room to walk and cool air to breathe. He tramped for an hour until his body ached with fatigue, and a sharp pain stabbed through his side from the exertion. Then he went home and through the dark house to his bedroom. He did not bother to turn on a light. He threw himself down across the lumpy unmade bed and that last jar seemed to split his aching head apart. He held his head between his hands. One cheek was pressed against the edge of the tin ash tray but he did not notice it.

5

WHILE THE VEECHES WERE FINISHING A LATE AND leisurely hot weather supper, Ernie stopped his car sharp out in front with the wheels sliding in the dirt. He came through the house and out to the kitchen hurriedly.

Molly hitched her chair around to greet him. "Why, hello there, Ernie, you're just in time. You had supper yet?"

"Yeah, I already et," Ernie said. He stopped just inside the doorway. His face was preoccupied. He was impeccable overdressed as usual in a light gray summer suit, the creases exact down the legs of the trousers. His white hat was shoved back on his head and he was freshly shaven. In the flare of light from his cigarette lighter, a little smear of white aftershaving powder shone along his heavy jaw.

"Well, you better set down and have a cup of coffee, anyway," his mother said comfortably. "We got lots of coffee left, and it's still hot. The coffee pot's been setting right there on the stove."

"No, I don't want nothing. Set still and finish your supper. I told you I already et." He spoke irritably, and the voices around the table thinned out. All of the family looked at him.

Ernie leaned up against the door jamb and crossed his feet. "Well, I'll tell you how it is. I got the tip-off tonight. It come straight from the head office in Detroit. I got friends down there and this come straight from the head office. Them sons of bitches is sending an investigator down here tomorrow."

"What they doing that for?" Molly said urgently. "Ernie, you ain't got into no trouble, have you?"

"Bill Dodge has been making trouble, huh?" Sam said mildly, setting his cup down in his saucer, and wiping off his mouth on the back of his hand.

"No, I ain't in no trouble," Ernie said. "That damn Dodge has been shooting off his mouth around the office, that's all. But there ain't a thing they can get on me. There won't be nothing to it. The investigator they're sending is a pretty right kind of guy. There won't be nothing to it."

"What'll he do?" Molly said. "They won't take you down to Detroit, will they?"

"Hell, no, Ma. There ain't nothing to it. The investigator will come into town some time tomorrow and start snooping around. You see, he won't figure on me knowing he's coming, nor nothing. He'll probably snoop around my place and he may come over here. He'll ask a lot of questions around quiet, see? And then he'll come out on the job just quitting time and ask the boys some questions and stuff. Hell, then I'll take him up to Ashbury and blow him to a dinner and some drinks and we'll talk it over and that'll be all there is to it. It ain't nothing for nobody to get excited about, nor nothing. They ain't got nothing on me."

Molly relaxed visibly, but a sort of tension still hung around the table. No one spoke, and Ernie spit a piece of tobacco off his tongue.

Jud broke the silence suddenly, grinning at Ernie. "Well, sir, I always said you'd get into trouble yet. I always said they'd find out about you stealing company gasoline night after night, and putting it in your car. You ain't never bought a pint o' gas since you got to be a foreman, and I always said they'd catch you." Jud nodded solemnly. "Yes, sir, that's just what I always said."

Ernie's face began to darken, and he spoke furiously to the old man. "Hell, I wish you'd shut up your yawping about that gas. There ain't nobody making no fuss about a few gallons of gasoline one way or the other. Every foreman there is around here has got a key to that gasoline tank and there ain't a one of them but what don't fill up his car once in awhile."

"Yes, sir, Ernie, but I always worried about you just going over there at night and helping yourself to gasoline," Molly said. "It ain't right, and you know it ain't. If it was, you wouldn't have to sneak over there after dark to get it. I always worried about you doing that."

"For God's sake, shut up talking about that gasoline, can't you?" Ernie said wildly. "There ain't nobody coming up here to check up on that damn gasoline!"

"Well, maybe they ain't," Molly said. "But you can't tell me that every little thing like that ain't against you."

"Oh, hell," Ernie said, with a gesture of disgust. The silence fell again, and Kenny scraped his chair a little tipping back in it. He ran his hands down deep into his pockets and watched Ernie with a half smile on his face.

"I tell you," Ernie said, "there ain't nothing to this. That damn Dodge has just been shooting his mouth off on account of his being sore after I fired him. Dodge is no good, and everybody knows it, and he's a born troublemaker. He just went down there to Detroit and did a lot of crazy talking and that's all it amounts to. I just thought I'd stop in and tell you what it was all about in case that investigator comes around here tomorrow, that's all."

"Well, that's all right, I'm glad you did," Molly said instantly.

"We're your family and we got a right to know when anything like this comes up. We ain't trying to stick our noses into your business, nor nothing, but we can't help being interested and worrying kind of about it."

"Why, sure, that's all right," Ernie said.

"No sense of us staying out here in the kitchen," Sam said, placatingly. "Come on in the other room, Ernie, and set down awhile."

"No, Pa, I can't stay. I gotta go right away. I got a lot of things I want to get tended to tonight."

Kenny laughed suddenly, but no one noticed it.

"Say, Pa," Ernie said casually, "you got some tools and stuff around here that I brung you, ain't you?"

"Why, yes, I guess so, Ernie," Sam said slowly. "There's some mallets and . . ."

"Sure, that's what I mean," Ernie said. "Just a few little things like that. The point is, there ain't no sense of that investigator happening to stop in here and the first thing him seeing is some of the company tools laying around."

"Why, no, if you want me to I'll . . ."

"I tell you, Pa, you can do just like I done myself around my place. You go on out tonight and hunt 'em all up and go out there behind the shed and dig a little hole and drop 'em in, and cover it up, and then none of us got a thing to worry about, see?"

"Sure, Ernie," Sam said. "I'll tend to it right away."

Kenny laughed again, softly, throwing his head back, and this time Ernie whirled around in the door toward him. "Shut up your damn laughing, will you? This ain't nothing to laugh at. The whole of you set around here taking every cent a money I got to pour in here and then something like this comes up, and you set around laughing. Go on and laugh, but where in hell you think you'll be if . . ."

"Hush up," Molly said. "There ain't none of us laughing, Ernie."

He was already gone and she got up out of her chair hurriedly and followed him through the house. "Now don't you worry your head about them tools and things. I'll see to it that your father takes care of them right away tonight." As he went out of the door she called after him, "Ernie, you come over here right away as soon as that man is gone tomorrow night, won't you? You know I'll be thinking about it and worrying and stewing all day long. You come, now, won't you, Ernie?"

"Yeah, I'll be over," he said, over the slamming of the front door. Molly stood and looked after him until his car was out of sight and then she came back to the kitchen.

"Kenny Veech," she said, "I'd like to turn you over my knee and give you a good whipping. Here poor Ernie was worried to death, and then you set there laughing at him, and after all he's done for this fambly."

Kenny was still grinning. "Ah, Mom, take it easy, will you?"

"Well!" she said decisively.

Carl leaned over the table toward them excitedly, his eyes alive with interest. "Hey, Kenny, what's it all about, huh? What's Bill Dodge got on Ernie, huh?"

"Lord, there ain't no call for you to get all excited," Molly said. "Nobody's got nothing on Ernie. You heard what he said. That Dodge is no good, and he just got sore at Ernie on account of Ernie firing him off his gang. Sam," she said authoritatively, "you go on out there now and pick up them tools and do with 'em the way Ernie said."

Sam went obediently, and Kenny stared a minute at his brother's intense excited face, with the little puffy red scab over the left eye. He spoke to Carl deliberately. "Bill Dodge ain't got a thing on Ernie that he can prove. Long as he can't prove nothing, this'll all blow over."

"Huh!" Molly said in disapproval. "The way you talk! How could that Dodge prove anything on Ernie when Ernie ain't done nothing wrong? That Dodge is just sore on account of Ernie's firing him the way he did. Lord, it ain't no crime to fire a man that's making trouble, is it?"

Jen got up and filled her coffee cup from the pot on the stove. Until now she had been bored with all of the talk, but suddenly she stopped dead still in the middle of the kitchen floor with her cup in her hand. "Say!" she said. "They couldn't put Ernie in jail or nothing, could they?"

"Why, sure they could." Jud stopped still with a fuzzy pinch of tobacco in his fingers. "You mark what I tell you. I always said Ernie would get into trouble. They'll put him in jail, that's right where they'll put him."

"Could they, honest?" Jen said, looking from her mother to Kenny.

"Why, of course not," Molly said.

The idea tickled Jen's fancy. She laughed merrily. "Can't you just see poor old Ernie a-pacing up and down and hollering to get to hell out of there, what in hell you think you're doing locking me up here in this damn stinking jail?" She laughed again.

"Such talk," her mother sniffed.

Jen turned on Josette suddenly. "Josie, this is sure going to be tough for you. They'll lock up poor old Ernie sure, and then how'll you get the money to go to school?"

"Jen, you talk like a little fool," her sister answered her. "Why don't you use your head? How can they arrest Ernie when he hasn't done anything wrong?"

"Not anything wrong they can prove, anyway," Carl said with a knowing look at Kenny.

"Why, sure, you're safe, Josie," Kenny said. "No sense you start worrying. Ernie's too smart for 'em. It'll be a long time before they ever get anything on Ernie. You'll have plenty of time to graduate before then."

The worry wrinkles began to fold across Josette's forehead. "Kenny," she spoke sharply. "You know something about Ernie that you aren't telling. There is something more to this than just firing that Bill Dodge, or taking a few tools or gasoline, isn't there? Why don't you tell us what you know; we've got just as much right to know about it as you have."

"Now take it easy," Kenny said, scowling. "There ain't no sense you getting all stirred up. Ernie fired Bill Dodge, see, and Bill Dodge got sore and went down to the office and did a lot of talking, and that's all there is to it."

"All right," Josette said. "That's all there is to it. You haven't got any business going around making funny remarks in front of people as if there was a whole lot more to it then."

"That's just what I say too, Josie," her mother added.

"Yes, sir, they're going to lock up poor old Ernie," Jen said gayly.

She laughed again and parodied a popular song in a squeaky baby-talk voice:

"Poor ole Ernie in a itty bitty cell—" Kenny took up her song from there:

"Hollering and yelling jus' like hell—"

Carl supplied the next words, his eyes shining, his voice far off the tune:

"No use for him to yell at all—"

"Tause he jus' tan't dit over the wall," Jen finished it up triumphantly.

"There we are," Kenny yelled. "Come on now, all together." They stood in a line in front of Molly, Jen in the middle and Carl and Kenny on either side, their arms intertwined, singing in mincing falsetto voices:

> *"Poor lil Ernie in a itty bitty cell*
> *Hollering and yelling jus' like hell*
> *Tain't no use for him to yell at all*
> *Tause he jus' tan't dit over the wall."*

They finished it together, with considerable volume, and Molly and Josette and Jud joined in their laughter while the child Dorothy lingered open-mouthed in the doorway.

"Well, it ain't no laughing matter, let me tell you," Molly said wiping her eyes. "But I guess it ain't no matter if you laugh." And so the discussion ended and the family drifted away about their own affairs.

Some time later in the evening, Ernie came out of the beer garden downtown and stood a moment on the sidewalk looking up and down the quiet street. Directly across the street from him was the shining shuttered front of the hotel, and to Ernie at this moment it took on the form of Lew Lentz's smooth impassive face with the pale quiet eyes shining beneath lowered lids. Ernie more than half suspected that Lew was somehow mixed up in this trouble Dodge was stirring up for him. There was no love lost between them. Lew Lentz had bettered him in more than one business deal. For a second now, Ernie thought of going over and talking to Lew, but he knew that he was no match for him in any subtle conflict of wits, so he decided against it. He cursed Lew viciously under his breath. He would like to beat that still pale face with his fists until it was bloody and swollen. Actually, Ernie was jealous although he never admitted it to himself, jealous of Lew's financial success and of the power he occasionally wielded unobtrusively over a number of people in the town. He'd give a hell of a lot to know where Lew Lentz got his money. He sure never got it running a hotel and beer joint in this little burg. It was common knowledge that Lew Lentz was involved in most real estate ventures both in the village and in Ashbury, but that had never satisfied Ernie's curiosity, nor that of a number of other townspeople, for that matter. The story ran that Lew Lentz had been a prohibition bootlegger who had saved the fortune he had amassed then, and increased it now by canny speculation and business ventures of all sorts, perhaps even investments in what was vaguely referred to as "the rackets." Ernie, at this moment, was quite sure that Lew Lentz had given what aid he was able to Bill Dodge to stir up this trouble for him, and he was infuriated because there was nothing in the world he could think of doing about it.

Ernie stood still on the corner and looked up and down the street carefully. The town was quiet and the streets were empty. The lights were still on at the Gates filling station, and at the beer garden, and the poolroom and a couple soda fountain places. There were only a dozen or so scattered cars parked on either side. The sound of radio music drifted out of the drugstore. Around the corner on the side street two small boys straddled their bicycles in the shadows, whispering together, and sharing a stolen cigarette. Something about the quiet infuriated Ernie; the subdued harmless idle tenor of the village was ominous and somehow foreboding of trouble to come, to him. He got into his car, backed it out and roared away in the darkness toward Ashbury.

Not long after that Bill Dodge was ushered into Lew Lentz's office in the back of the hotel. Lentz was a short thick man with thin blond hair. Tonight he sat in shirt sleeves before his desk in the path of a humming electric fan, his expensive suit coat draped over a chair back. He turned to Dodge the pale expressionless face that Ernie hated.

"Hello, Bill, sit down."

Bill Dodge slumped down in the chair at the end of the desk, rumpling his rusty-colored hair in his fingers. His face was sunburned, and there was a patient doglike look around his eyes.

"You talk to the boys, Bill?" Lew asked, gathering up some papers from his desk and snapping a rubber band around them.

"Yeah," Bill said. "But it ain't no use talkin' to 'em. Couldn't get a word out of a damn one of 'em. They just let me talk but they wouldn't say a word. Veech has got 'em all scared. They won't do a damn thing tomorrow."

Lew turned off the fan, got up and put on his coat. "I told you it was no use talking to them. They been working for Veech for a long time and he's got them scared. They think he's got a lot of pull down to the main office. They figure if they make a peep they'll lose their jobs and you can't tell them no different."

"Sure, I know, Lew." Bill's voice sounded thin and hopeless. "God, I hate his guts. He's been gettin' away with murder like this for such a damn long time. I tell you, it ain't right, the way he's doin', and if they'd just . . ."

His voice trailed off and Lew Lentz slapped him on the shoulder sympathetically. "Well, you've done everything you could. You're the only guy yet that had guts enough to stand up to him.

"Look, Bill," he continued, his voice changing. "I got to beat it up to Ashbury awhile. But you better stick around here. Don't go back to your room tonight."

"Huh? Why, I . . ."

"Now you do like I say, see. You got Veech jittery. Before tonight's over, he'll be tearing the town apart to find you, and if he catches up with you, the way he's feeling he'll beat hell out of you."

"Well, I ain't afraid of Ernie Veech, and I never have been."

"Hell, I know you aren't afraid of Ernie Veech, Bill. That isn't the thing. Use your head. What good is it going to do, letting him make a punching bag out of you? Let him look for you and wonder where you're at and what you're doing. There's a room upstairs you can sleep in tonight and I want you to do it, and I don't want you showing your face out front tonight either."

"Okay, Lew, I'll do like you say. I sure want to thank you, all you done for me."

"Forget it," Lew said as he closed the door.

Bill sat still, his head between his hands, crumpling his rusty hair between his stumpy fingers.

He sat like that for a long time, and suddenly the door at the other end of the office opened softly and Mary Veech came in. She carried two beer bottles under her arm, and glasses in her hand. She closed the door behind her softly.

At the sound, Bill Dodge looked up and got up out of his chair. "Lew just left. He said he wanted me to stay here tonight, so I just been setting here a minute . . ."

"Yeah, I know." She put the bottles and glasses down on the table in the middle of the room, and wiped the moisture from the bottles off her bare smooth arm with her handkerchief. She sat down in the chair behind the table and opened the beer expertly. "Pull up your chair and have a drink with me. I never like to drink alone."

Bill pulled up his chair, his sunburned face crinkled into a smile of pleasure at the friendliness of her voice.

"Don't mind if I do, ma'am. A nice cold drink of beer sure hits the spot on a night like this."

Mary shoved one bottle and a glass across the table to him. She filled her own glass carefully, pouring it in a thin quiet stream, and stopping at exactly the right moment, so that the foam rose to the top of the glass and no farther. She sipped a little out of her glass indifferently and leaned back in her chair looking very cool in a sheer white blouse with lace high against her throat, and her hair combed smooth to her head in shining waves. But the room was warm and the drops of sweat stood out on Bill Dodge's face. Mary got up and turned on the electric fan above the desk, directing it toward Bill.

"How's Lucy and the kids?" she asked.

Bill's face brightened at the mention of them. "They're all just fine. Lucy's got 'em over to her folks, you know. She's been living over there for about a year now. Her mother's kind of sick, and then since we got that last pay cut on the road, we just couldn't swing it. It sure takes a lot to feed and clothe four kids."

"It sure does," Mary said. "I've only got one, but she wants to eat all the time, and she grows out of her clothes faster than I buy them."

"They're awful nice kids though," he said. "I wish you could see that youngest one. He ain't quite two yet, and if he ain't one cute kid . . . He's gonna be dark, I guess, like Lucy. My oldest boy's a redhead, you know, and I guess one of the girls is going to be, too." He warmed under Mary's sudden brief smile. "Lucy's going to have another baby in October."

"She is! How's she feeling?"

"Oh, she feels just swell. She's doing all the work over there to her mother's and looking after the kids herself and everything. She says every one of 'em comes easier than the last one did." He grinned foolishly. "Lucy says she guesses it's just getting to be a habit with her."

He poured out the rest of his beer into the glass. "Well, I tell you how it is. I guess this is the only one of my kids that I ain't been glad it's coming. That's an awful thing to say, and when it comes I'll love it to death, but God, you know how it is. I guess that's about the main reason I been trying to make a fuss about Ernie and him firing me. Lots of folks think I'm just doing it to be mean, but I ain't."

"I know," Mary said. "The boys have been taking a lot from him for a long time. You didn't get anywhere talking to 'em tonight, huh?"

He shook his head. "I guess I didn't say what I had to say to 'em right. I ain't no good at talking, anyway. Hell, it made me sick to my stomach. All they gotta do is stick together and tell about the way Ernie has been doing, but they ain't a-going to do it. I can tell they ain't. God, I wish I coulda got Lew to go and talk to 'em."

He looked at Mary cautiously, but her face was expressionless and her eyes were fixed on the bright shining blades of the electric fan.

"Oh, I ain't blaming Lew. I ain't asking nobody to go out of their way to help me; it's the same way with the other boys. I wasn't trying to get 'em to squeal on Ernie so much to help me as it is to help themselves."

"You better finish my beer before it gets stale," Mary said pushing the bottle to him. Her glass in front of her was still half full, but she drank no more of it.

He took the bottle mechanically without stopping talking. "I ain't asking nobody to help me, but alone I can't do a God-damn thing. You know what this means to me. Ernie's got me blacklisted, insubordination. There ain't a foreman on the road now that would hire me. Well, I been railroading for fifteen years. That's all the kinda work I know. I just can't step out into another job. Jobs is scarce. I'm too old now to start factory working. I don't know nothing but railroading. This is gonna finish me, and it ain't only me I'm thinking of, it's Lucy and the kids too. Her folks ain't got no money either; they got a mortgage on their farm, and they're getting old. This is just going to finish me." His face turned drawn and taut as he talked.

"You know it's funny, this insubordination. I wouldn't mind it so much, if it hadn't happened like it did. If I'da come out on the job drunk some day and took a swing at Ernie with a crowbar when he told me to do something, you wouldn't hear a kick outa me now. But all I did in God's world was tell Ernie last payday, after we come back to the car house with our pay checks, that I'd be damned if I'd hand him over six dollars and a half like the rest of the boys did just because he said I had to. I've worked for guys up and down this track, I says to Ernie, I been railroading for fifteen years pretty near, but you're the first son of a bitch that I ever had to pay money to to hold my job. And that's all there was to it. I never worked another hour after that, and you can ask any of the boys that was standing right there and heard it all. You can ask 'em, yeah, but not a damn one of 'em would come right out and say a word that Ernie didn't want 'em to. That's what hurts."

The hurt was there, deep in Bill Dodge's eyes, as he spoke of it. Mary twined and intertwined her strong fingers on the table top.

Bill shoved his chair back a little from the table. "Oh, hell, I don't know. Maybe I'm a damn fool. I'm kinda quick tempered, and there's some things I ain't never took from no man as long as I lived. Maybe if I had it all to do over again, I'da stopped to think about Lucy and the kids and give Ernie his cut and never said nothing, I don't know. I just don't know." He mused a little, staring at the back of his stubby freckled hand.

He stood up suddenly and looked across at Mary apologetically. "Say, I guess I been doing a lot of talking about myself that ain't so interesting to listen to or nothing. I ain't had much of anybody to talk to. Lucy, she—well, she don't understand nothing about these things. All she knows is that I got fired for talking up to Ernie, and with the baby coming and all, and worrying like she is, she don't understand nothing about it."

Mary stood up slowly, and looked at him a moment out of her shadowed eyes, and then held out her warm strong hand to him. "You go on upstairs to bed, Bill, and get a good night's sleep. Tell Lucy I said hello when you see her. If you ever get a chance, bring Lucy and the kids in sometime. I'd like to see 'em. And don't worry, something will turn up."

"G'night," Bill said. At the door Bill stopped and rumpled his red hair again, awkwardly. "Thanks for the beer. I want you to know I appreciate you—coming in and setting with me like you did. You're, you're . . ." Bill Dodge ran out of words and he went out and closed the door quickly.

Mary stood by the table a moment and brushed a smear of cigarette ash from her skirt. She went over and shut off the electric fan, turned out the light and went through the door at the other end of the office.

Soon after midnight, Ernie Veech closed the garage doors behind his automobile wearily, and started across the dew-wet backyard toward his house. The liquor he had drunk in Ashbury an hour or so ago had worn off now and left him with a gnawing fear. He had just come from Bill Dodge's rooming house, to satisfy himself once more that Bill was really not there. He had driven up and down the deserted main street of the village and had seen no one more than the night watchman taking a leisurely survey of the store fronts. On the back porch a toad had hopped suddenly at the vibration of his feet and he had crushed the small insolent brown body underneath his foot.

He entered the back door noisily and went through the dark kitchen to the front room. There he found a blaze of lights. Erma, in pajamas, was curled up in a corner of the gaudy davenport, with candy, cigarettes and a confession magazine. The radio was turned on loud to cover up the night sounds that frightened her when she was alone.

"Tum tiss Mama!" she said, throwing down her magazine, and

holding her face up. She was a tall thin girl, still immature of figure, with dark permanent-curled hair tucked behind her ears.

Ernie scowled and threw himself down into a chair. "Turn that damn machine off. You can't hear yourself think in here, the racket it's making." He had reached the end of his endurance, he thought. He could stand no more. Something in his face told the girl that this was no ordinary fit of bad temper that he was in. Instantly and skillfully she went about her business of soothing and satisfying him.

"I bet you got an awful headache, ain't you?" she said. "You set right down here beside Erma on the davenport and let me rub your poor old hurtin' head . . ."

She held out her arms to him, her voice soothing and tender and the anger went out of him, leaving the misery and fear only. She flung her young hard body across him, one arm under his back, her face against his chin, and stroked his forehead gently. "Does that make your head feel better?"

"Yeah, I guess so." He put his arms about her and muffled his mouth in her hair. "I just feel so awful. I couldn't find that damn Dodge anywheres.

"I get so sick of this, I just can't stand it. I wasn't never cut out for railroading. I got brains. I could get some place if I got outa this town. The thing is, I never had a chance. I never even got a chance to go to high school. Soon as I got big enough I had to quit school and start working."

"Erma won't never leave you, never. Erma's going to stick right with you always . . ."

And so she wheedled and coaxed him to be silent and his nerves relaxed. Sleep came to Ernie that night quickly and unexpectedly, and dropped a dark curtain over the pattern of his living. Behind the curtain he dreamed sweetly of an office somewhere of his own, and Erma with a fur coat and diamond rings. Lew Lentz came and asked him for another chance, but he beat him until his face was a bloody mass, and when he fell down to the floor he was not Lew Lentz at all, but a little brown toad hopping up before his feet, and he put his foot down over him and felt the life and motion squash out beneath his foot. Suddenly Mary was there and she took a cigarette out of her flat silver case and smiled her brief lovely childish smile and a great deep solemn voice like a gong filled the air, saying: The living are the dead and still, and the days of living will pass away. Come to the fair! Come to the fair!

6

WITH THE SUNLIGHT ERNIE WAS AWAKE IN THE morning, and miraculously his fears were gone. He felt like himself again, and even unusually good-humored. The mood carried over after he arrived at the depot. His voice on the wire was cheerful while he made contact with the road-master for the day's orders and he exchanged unusually friendly words with foremen on the wire all up and down the line. Ernie, as foreman of the extra gang, was the hub of the greatest activity on the road during the summer months, as well as boss of the largest crew of track workers on the division. Ernie's good humor held, and he felt the familiar glow of power and superiority. When his gang of twenty or twenty-five men assembled at his temporary car house, he gave them a little lecture.

He leaned against the corner of the shed, carelessly, with his hand full of yellow order sheets, and the cigarette wabbling in his lips.

"Now listen here, you guys," he said, tersely. "We're gonna have company today. Some of my pals down to the Detroit office called up and told me. If you're smart, you're gonna keep your God-damned traps shut. Nobody works for me that don't play ball with me, and I'd just as soon as not fire every God-damned one of you sons of bitches tomorrow morning. And don't think, damn it, that I couldn't do it. You know what happened to that big-headed bastard, Dodge. Think it over. While I'm bossing this gang, what I say goes. Don't forget it. Now get moving!"

The men listened to him impassively, while the sun shone down on their faded blue overalls and sunburned faces; on the shiny humming steel rails and the billow of smoke from a freight train coming around the curve far down the track. When he was through talking they moved apart, glancing at him admiringly out of the corners of their eyes. They did not like him; most of them feared him. But they all admired his surety and conscious wielding of power, his toughness that made him the most feared and talked-of foreman on the division.

Ernie shuffled the orders in his hand and flung his cigarette spinning into the cinders. He felt better and better. He doubted the loyalty of his boys no more. Let the office send out a dozen investigators if they chose. His position, he felt, was secure.

The investigator arrived as expected soon after dinner, a very hot, bored and disgruntled man. He did the greater share of his investigating at a table in the beer garden, while he killed time waiting to interview Ernie's gang at quitting time. He loathed all people who made complaints in hot weather, and he loathed small-town beer gardens. He came to loathe every one of the ten records on the record-playing machine after he had inserted a steady stream of nickels.

He did not go to the Veech home at all, but he was expected there all day.

By afternoon Molly complained that the worry and strain fairly made her sick to her stomach, so she went to bed, draping the curtain back from the window that she might look out to the street in front of the house.

Sam put on a clean shirt for the occasion and sat patiently in the porch swing all day long, secure in the knowledge that the tools were safely buried in the edge of the garden.

But while the Veeches watched and worried, Ernie and the Detroit man were sitting together under the soft lights in one of Ashbury's most expensive taprooms, where they had been drinking steadily since dinner. The Detroit man was very sad, tears sometimes ran down his beefy face. His was the worst job in the world, he insisted, everybody disliked and distrusted him. Ernie protested vigorously that it was not true. But his heart wasn't in it. Ernie was feeling sad too, but only because he was not so drunk that he could not still calculate just how much those drinks were costing him.

It was three o'clock in the morning before Ernie slid his car to a stop in front of the house, with a great squeaking of brakes. He got out unsteadily, talking to himself in a loud voice. He stumbled up the porch steps and found the front screen hooked. He shook it a little and then came down the steps again and out across the yard.

"Hey, Ma," he shouted. "Hey, Ma, where are you? What in hell's the idea of going to bed witha chickens? Hey, Ma, wake up. Hey, Ma!"

Molly pulled her heavy body up out of the bed and went to the window. She draped the lace curtain back over the head of the bed carefully, removed the ragged ventilator screen and leaned out over the window sill on her elbows, her hair hanging around her face.

A little soft wind was stirring the tree branches, and shimmering the green leaves to silver in the moonlight. Ernie stood below, a stumpy figure in the middle of the little grassy space between the sidewalk and the house. He was still yelling at the top of his lungs.

"Shshshsh . . ." Molly said, her voice ridiculously soft. "Ernie, for Lord sakes, cut out that yelling. You want to wake up the whole town?"

At sight of her, Ernie burst out into incoherent speech, unrecognizable words wedged in between unfortunately recognizable vile profanities, all of it yelled at the top of his lung capacity.

Molly listened attentively, pulled her head in the window and said to Sam who was raised on an elbow in the bed, "Lord, you can't tell a word he's saying, but I guess he means that everything's all right." Her own voice was warm and uneven with relief.

Ernie was riotously happy. He waved his arms and yelled faster and louder. Dorothy bounced out of the cot at the foot of the bed and ran to join her grandmother at the window, unwilling to miss the uproar.

Molly spoke placatingly to Ernie out of the window. "Well, Ernie, we're all awful glad to hear that everything's all right. You go on home now and come back tomorrow night and tell us all about it."

But her voice was drowned out in the noise he was making.

Carl and the twins, sleepy and in various stages of undress, came in to join the group at the window.

Molly maintained her position square in the middle of the window. She lost her patience completely.

"You cut out that yelling, Ernie!" she screamed at him.

The twins wedged in on either side of her.

"Ernie," Josette called to him. "You hear me, Ernie? You stop that racket! If you want to wake up everybody in your end of town yelling like that it's all right, but you go on away from here." Her voice was hopelessly lost in the noise.

"Attaboy, Ernie, you tell 'em!" Jen screamed.

Molly gripped her hands on the edge of the window sill, took a great deep breath, and screamed at him in a terrible voice, loud and distinct over his babbling. "Ernie Veech, you go on home now. You oughta be ashamed of yourself. You cut out that racket and go on home. You're going to wake up everybody in town. You're crazy dead drunk, that's what you are, and you ought to be ashamed. You cut out that racket, you hear me?"

Ernie undoubtedly heard her. He stopped dead quiet for a moment, and then he gave a yowl of delight. He started yelling again, incoherently, waving his arms.

"Stop it, I say," Molly screeched. "You stop that noise Ernie Veech and go on home."

Josette turned away from the window and began to cry, rocking back and forth on the edge of the bed.

Dorothy began to scream too, hopping up and down in her bare feet and shrieking like a banshee.

Molly pulled her head in the window again. "Well, sir, I don't know what we're going to do with him," she said, her voice hoarse from her yelling. "I just don't know. Lord, I wish Kenny was here. If Kenny was here he'd shut him up proper."

Carl was quiet, his eyes snapping with excitement. "You suppose we oughta call the night watchman, Ma? I'll go get the night watchman if you want me to."

Molly ignored him, and leaned out of the window again, helplessly. She took another great breath, and screeched again, her voice a wail. "Ernie Veech—you go on home."

Just then a long shiny car stopped in the street. Mary got out and stood a moment beside the open door.

"Mary!" Molly wailed, at sight of her.

Mary walked quietly across the lawn and took hold of Ernie's arm. He had not heard her come, and her touch startled him into abrupt, ear-splitting silence. Mary spoke to him without raising her voice. "Go on home, Ernie," she said. She turned her back on him and walked around the house to the back door.

Ernie stood still swaying a moment in the middle of the front lawn. Then without another word he went to his car and drove away. When he had gone, the long black car, the motor purring idly, drove off toward town.

Molly pulled her head back in the window, and sat down heavily on the bed. "Lord, oh, Lord," she said. "Josie, you cut out that sniveling. Go on, get outa here. How you think a body can sleep, you all standing around? Dorothy, you hear me? You go back to bed this minute. I don't know what your mother'd say, if she saw you awake this time-a night."

The family dispersed silently except for Josette's whimpering.

7

IT RAINED ALL DAY IN ASHBURY, A CONTINUOUS effortless drizzle. At five o'clock Josette wrapped newspaper around her books and her accounting exercise sheets, and walked the six blocks to the parking lot stoically in the rain. Since she had been in school, she had arranged to ride with Nina Warren, who worked in an office in Ashbury. Miss Warren was a crabbed, colorless little woman, her life divided between the clerical work she had done for the last twenty years, and the care of her aged invalid mother. Josette detested her for her peculiar bloodless quality, and for the way her drab ill-fitting clothes hung carelessly upon her lean body and for her sulky bad tempers upon all occasions that Josette was not ready and waiting in the parking lot at the time that she arrived at five o'clock.

It made Miss Warren nervous to drive in the rain. She crept along the edge of the pavement all of the ten miles to the village, complaining continually, until Josette was ready to scream.

By the time she got home, Josette was seized with another agony of fear over the accounting examination. She went to her room immediately, refusing to eat supper, and changed into dry clothing hurriedly. Then she barricaded the door with a chair and prepared to work. She made a temporary desk in front of the bed, with two chairs, and two pasteboard boxes out of the closet on top of them, and then a table leaf that she kept under the bed for this purpose balanced between the boxes. She unwrapped the accounting sheets and went to work desperately.

She worked until her eyes smarted so that all the figures ran together, and her head throbbed dully. She worked until every one of the sheets was in a hopeless unbalanced muddle. She stopped then and lay back across the bed, weak with panic, and a great lump choking in her throat.

While she lay there, she heard suddenly the familiar honking of an automobile horn out in front. She jumped up, knocking over the table leaf and spilling the papers over the floor, and flew down the stairs.

Midge Clark sat at the wheel of her father's automobile, her chin pillowed on her clasped hands dejectedly. Josette got in beside her.

"Say something cheerful to me quick," Midge said. "This has been the most foul day. I hate this town when it rains. My folks went out tonight and I thought I'd go crazy alone in the house. Come up and talk to me for awhile."

"Well, I don't know," Josette said. "I'm in the terriblest mess, Midge. I've got an exam tomorrow and I know I can't pass it. I've been studying ever since I got home and . . ."

"Oh, forget it!" Midge said impatiently. "It never does any good to cram the night before an exam. Anyway, you can study better if you leave it alone for a couple hours."

"Well, I don't know, I've simply got to study," Josette wavered.

"Oh, come on," Midge said, rimming her hands around the steering wheel restlessly. "I've been waiting for you to get home all day. You're the only person in this town I can talk to."

"Well, all right," Josette said. "I'll come. I don't think it is going to do me any good to study, anyway. If you'll wait, it won't take me but a minute."

"Okay, but hurry," Midge called after her.

Inside the house, Molly came in from the kitchen, wiping her hands along the sides of her dress. "You ain't going up to Clarks' are you, Josie?" she asked. "I thought you had to do a lot of studying tonight."

"I'm only going up there for a little while," Josette said as she went up the stairs. "Midge is alone tonight, and I've got my studying just about done, anyway."

"Well," Molly said, "just so's you don't neglect your studies. After all that money Ernie's spending to send you up there to school, seems like you could stay home one night and study."

"I told you I had my studying done," Josette called back to her. In the bedroom, she stripped the faded cotton dress over her head, glancing in the mirror at her disheveled hair. She put on a dark suit skirt, and a clean blouse that belonged to Jen, tidied her hair, and retouched her lipstick. She felt wildly happy and carefree, and kicked at one of the papers on the floor as she put the light out. She ducked through the rain to the car.

"What did you do, take a bath?" Midge Clark said, racing the motor impatiently.

At the Clark house, the girls climbed the stairs to Midge's bedroom. Josette sat down on the bench before the dressing table and Midge prowled around the spacious room, turning on soft rose-shaded lights. The wind blew the rain hard against the windows, and Midge shuddered at the sound. "I can't stand this rain. I don't know what's the matter with me. I feel simply foul." She jerked the venetian blinds down to the window sills, and closed the shutters. The rain sound was muffled then, except for the noise on the roof and the roaring in the eaves.

Josette looked at herself with pleasure in the mirror over the dressing table. The rose light was becoming to her, and she thought that she looked quite as if she belonged here. The room was warm and comfortable with the rain shut out; there was a soft scent in the air from the perfume bottles on the table, and then the bitter tobacco smell cutting through it, as Midge lighted a cigarette.

Midge turned away to the windows again, restlessly twitching at the drapes. She was a small, well-formed girl with dark-blonde hair pinned back in smooth curls from her attractive pert face. Tonight there were shadows of discontent at her mouth and eyes, and Josette prepared herself to listen to whatever tale of boredom and dissatisfaction Midge had to tell her. Josette did not mind; she made an extraordinarily good listener. She was not fond of Midge really, but Midge held a fascination for her. Through Midge, Josette caught glimpses of the kind of life that she wanted to make for herself.

Midge walked back and forth by the window. "Oh, I can't stand this," she said. "I'd like to go downtown and get drunk! I'll never spend another vacation at home. All I do is sit here, day in and day out!"

Josette laughed, and then hurried to say penitently, "Oh, I know how you feel, Midge. It isn't funny. This town is terrible. It's the deadest place on earth. I ought to know, I have to live here all the time."

It seemed to Josette somehow childish and amusing of Midge to talk like this. I could sit right here in this room day in and day out, she was thinking, and I wouldn't go crazy. I'd think it was heaven.

"You must get awfully lonesome," Josette added automatically. "Why don't you invite some of your friends out here to visit you?"

"Oh, I have," Midge said. "My mother made me. There is a whole gang of them coming out next month. I'm sick to death of them before they get here. I wish they weren't coming."

Josette felt a shiver of pleasure and excitement through her. More than anything else, she had hoped that some of Midge's friends would come to visit her, and that she might have the opportunity to meet those amusing fascinating people from whose letters Midge had been reading snatches to her all summer.

But Josette still found it somehow amusing and unbelievable that Midge should feel like this. She spoke impersonally, without sympathy. "Well, never mind, they won't be here so very long. By the time they go, the summer will be just about over and then before you know it you'll be going back to college."

Midge stopped at the foot of the bed and laughed mirthlessly. "That's just the trouble. I'll be going back to college before I know it. I can't stand to think about it. I've had two years of college and that's enough!"

"Oh, Midge, don't be silly!" Josette said, half laughing.

"You think I'm just talking," Midge answered, her lips thinning.

"Well, I'm not. I'm sick to death of college. I go because my folks make me go. I'm sick of it. The same old thing over and over, football games and fraternity dances and sorority dinners, and rushing, and the same bunch of smug people, going the same places and doing the same things . . . My God, Josette!"

Josette shook her head incredulously. "I don't see how anybody could get sick of that. You don't know how lucky you are. I'd give the world if I could go away to a real college this fall."

"You can have it," Midge said. "I'm sick of it, and I'm sick of myself. Oh, I'd like to go downtown and get drunk tonight, or—or— have a love affair over the weekend with the first man I could pick up off the street."

"Midge, what an awful thing to say!" Josette was really shocked and somehow angered at Midge.

"Well, I mean it!" Midge said defiantly over her shoulder. She stared into the slats of the venetian blind broodingly, with her back hunched disconsolately and her hair falling around her face.

Josette kept looking at Midge, her hair shining fresh from a beauty shop, and the expensive rose linen sports dress that she wore; and the odor out of the great crystal perfume bottles on the dressing table suddenly seemed to suffocate her. She spoke stiffly and coldly. "That's a terrible thing to say, just the same. I think it's—it's—wicked for you to talk like that. You don't know how lucky you are. You've got everything, a nice home and nice parents, and money and beautiful clothes and a chance to go to college and meet nice people . . . Why, I'd give the world if I . . . You just don't know what it is to . . ."

Midge whirled around from the window with anger in her face too. "Yes, I've certainly got a lot, haven't I? I've got the world done up in cellophane and ribbon, haven't I? Why, Josette Veech, I'd trade places with you right this minute, if I could."

Josette could only stare at her incredulously.

"I would," Midge said. "You don't know how lucky you are. You've got freedom! You can do what you want to. Your parents don't ride you to death every minute not to do this and not to do that. You don't know what it means either to have a mother that the only thing she cares about is to have you meet the right people and make just as good a marriage as you can."

The rain came down hard against the windows, a loud continuous sound in the still room.

"You don't know what it means," Josette said at last. "It's all right for you to talk, but you just don't know what it means."

But suddenly and inexplicably, without warning, Midge's mood was broken. She laughed and threw herself across the satin-covered bed. "Oh, let's skip it! I don't know what is wrong with me. I think it's this town. I never get as bad as this any place else. I think this town is bad for people. You just sit around here until you start getting violent or something. If I don't take a vacation from here in another couple weeks I'll explode."

Josette accepted a lighter conversation willingly. "I haven't exploded here yet," she said, "and I've been here quite awhile."

"Oh, you just wait!"

Midge sprawled on her back comfortably. "What's your brother Kenny doing these days?" she asked lazily. "Honestly, Josette, he's the most gorgeous man I ever set an eye on. Do you suppose you could put in a good word about me to him?"

At that very moment, while the wind blew the rain before it in the darkness, Rita Sibley at the wheel of her automobile was threading back and forth through the traffic in the busy downtown section of Ashbury. Rita loved to drive. She loved to feel the power of the soft-voiced, perfectly coordinated engine under the shiny long radiator and to guide her automobile through the maze of rushing traffic that surrounded it on the streets. She loved the intricacies of stop lights and traffic regulations of the city. Tonight she loved the rain beating on the car windows, the cleavage of the wiper across her windshield, the policemen in shiny wet black raincoats, the splash of the water on the pavement, the reflections of the city lights on wet cement. And she loved the automatic ease with which she guided her car; it left her mind free to think. The only time that she really could ever be alone and think was when, on nights like tonight, she guided her car back and forth through the traffic, with the radio humming soft music.

But the skill and precision that made her an expert driver were not present in her thinking. Her thoughts, tonight, scattered in all directions and then turned back on themselves, bumping and colliding and clogging up the channels of her brain.

It was not good for her to be idle, she reasoned, for surely it was out of idleness and boredom that she was becoming so discontented and morbidly egocentric and introspective. For several summers now, she had traveled from spring to fall. She thought listlessly of all the places she had been: New York, New Orleans, Yellowstone, California and Mexico, but none of them seemed inviting to her now. She needed work, she kept telling herself. She needed to be so busy that she would have no time to think. She needed to be so tired that she could sleep at night. There were some people who were not meant to relax and do nothing, and she must be one of them.

Tonight she would not be alone. Instead she would go to the movie that she had told herself an hour ago she was driving in to Ashbury to see. Robert Taylor, wasn't it, and Hedy Lamarr? And after that she would stop in at Alice Clinton's apartment, have a drink, talk to Alice for awhile, then drive directly home, take a sedative and go to bed and sleep. But even while she was planning these things she knew perfectly well that she would do none of them. She turned a corner suddenly, her automobile tires skidding a little on the wet pavement.

She realized that there was a dissatisfaction in her she could not run away from. It was a real thing, nothing imagined, no mere product of an idle summer month. She acknowledged it because she believed that it was better to look at it squarely and examine it for causes and remedies than to try to hide it from herself or to rationalize it away.

Rita Sibley possessed what she, at least, believed to be a logical mind. She wanted order in her thinking and living. She wanted to categorize things and list them in neat columns under appropriate headings. She had made mistakes in her living before, she told herself, and she had carefully analyzed them, methodically trying to rectify them. This, she told herself, was the only sensible way to live. If she had made another mistake in the last few years she must discover what it was, and correct it, as she had done before.

She turned her car resolutely back uptown, against the stream of traffic, enjoying the inventory which she was taking of herself. Age, thirty; health, perfect; attractive, and better than average intelligence. She had taught school for eight years. She taught easily and competently and enjoyed it. She liked the village where she worked and lived. She had been born in Ashbury, and educated there. Her first job was in the near-by village where she had taught ever since. There had been one time in her life which she barely remembered when she wanted to go away, but that was during that troubled uprooted period immediately following her graduation from teachers' college, and the death of her father. It was then, she reminded herself, that she had made one of her greatest mistakes—her marriage to Ernie Veech.

As always, she felt relief that she had terminated her marriage when she did. Looking back to it now, she reaffirmed her previous conclusions that she had married Ernie only because he had loved her so much and wanted so desperately to give her security, to have her for his wife, to climb all sorts of visionary material heights and make a new life for them both. She prided herself on being cynically analytical of that first marriage of hers. The trouble came because Ernie loved her as an ideal, as some sort of mythical hazy goddess on a pedestal. Once he really became acquainted with her, he found that they had nothing in common and that she was completely beyond his understanding. Nor had she loved Ernie. She had wanted the imaginary security of his clumsy incoherent adoration. It seemed silly and adolescent to her now. She could even laugh over it. She had been very wise to divorce him. The one small doubt she always had about her first marriage came to her now in the suspicion that Ernie had found her cold and lacking in passion, sexually unsatisfying. However, she stepped deftly away from this thought by reminding herself that if she had ever been cold to him, it was only after she subconsciously realized their incompatibility.

She thought then of those bright empty years between her first and second marriages, when she had been very happy in a brittle superficial way. She had gone many places and done many things, had met many charming and amusing people. She had worked hard, and played harder. She had seen herself at the edge of a physical breakdown; she had seen herself come to a reckoning day, when she had had to face the fact that she had nothing in her life that was real or satisfying. She had become sobered and frightened. Then she had met Joe Sibley.

Now, she told herself abruptly, her second marriage was a failure. She smothered the thought instantly, but the wretched feeling that it had induced remained with her. At any rate, she had married Joe with her eyes open. Joe had seemed infinitely worthy to her. She liked his quiet strength, she had liked the aim and direction of his living. She had known about his political and economic views and the large share of his life that they occupied. She did not understand or care for his convictions but she had admired them in Joe. And she had loved him.

She believed that Joe had loved her. They had met two years ago and married very soon. She thought that she had found lasting happiness. Then came the big factory strikes all over Ashbury last year when she saw those same political and economic ideas that she had admired in Joe Sibley absorb more and more of him. She saw his activities after working hours leave him no time for her. She began to feel herself a stranger to him, separated from him by a great barrier that he had neither the time nor inclination to surmount. Then a whispered rumor attached itself to Joe in the village. She had come to be afraid that that rumor might touch her also, and rob her of her position in the local schools. The only reason that it had not, she believed, was because the people of the village knew her and liked her too well. They were more apt to pity her for what they considered her unhappy choice of a husband than to question her suitability as a teacher for their children.

Well, she had lost Joe, she told herself with tears against her eyelids; she had lost Joe to a political philosophy, of all things. Not that Joe seemed lacking in affection. He simply had no time for her. The nibbling doubt as to her physical capacities to hold a man nagged at her again, but she turned it aside. Joe had no time for himself, any more than for her. He was lost, hopelessly immersed in secret and dangerous activities that she did not know about and did not care to know about. There was another strike hanging in the air; she knew that, and it sickened her. But, she told herself, she still loved Joe for this very selfless idealism that set him apart from every other man that she had ever known.

At that moment her eye fell upon the big illuminated clock dial in a jewelry store window. Five minutes to ten o'clock. She turned her car down a side street quickly, and her heart beat faster. She knew suddenly that she had been driving her car around Ashbury all evening waiting for ten o'clock, the hour of her date with Kenny Veech. She was to meet him at the parking lot near the theater on Mechanic Street. Her heart beat fast and she could hardly breathe. She was frightened. She must be out of her mind, she thought. What was she meeting Kenny Veech for? She must go home immediately, or, better still, go to Alice Clinton's, and let Kenny wait for her in the parking lot. The quick visual image of Kenny, slouched in the dark parking lot in the rain waiting for her, peering eagerly at each approaching car, made her weak and miserable. She put all of the thinking and analyzing out of her mind willfully, and sped toward Mechanic Street. She had done too much thinking and analyzing all of her life, she told herself wildly. Now she was simply going to do the things she wanted to do, without thinking any more about it.

She slammed on her brakes at the edge of the parking lot before she knew it. Her car skidded to the curb. She stared out into the dark bleak expanse of dirt, with a car parked here and there. She could not see Kenny anywhere. She opened the door of the car on that side that she might see better, and the wind blew the cool rain in on her face, and on her hands upon the steering wheel. She thought that he had forgotten, and she was astonished at how great her disappointment was. Just then the door of the office shanty opened, and the warm light shone out into the darkness. Kenny came out and slammed the door carelessly behind him and ran through the rain to the car. She laughed out loud, because she had thought of Kenny waiting for her in the rain and darkness.

She was still laughing when he slid onto the seat beside her. He grinned at her, his white teeth shining, and his curly blond hair glistening with water drops. She liked the smell of him, tobacco and wet clothes. "Go on laughing," he said. "I like to hear you laugh."

She slid the car away from the curb. "Shall I tell you why I'm laughing?"

When she turned to look at him, he was staring at her.

"God, you're pretty when you laugh like that," he said. "Sure, tell me what you're laughing about if you want to, then maybe I can laugh too."

"Well," she said, "maybe you wouldn't think it was funny. You see, I never intended to meet you tonight. I was at the apartment of a friend of mine. She was having a party and I was having an awful good time. All of a sudden I looked at a clock and it was almost ten. I thought of poor you, waiting for me out in the cold and rain. I saw you soaked to the skin, your teeth chattering, and going to the hospital with pneumonia. I felt so sorry for you that I decided to come over and tell you that I wasn't going to meet you tonight. Then I leave the party, drive way over here, and find you warm and dry, enjoying a nice little chat with the man in the office."

She laughed again and Kenny watched her attentively.

"You aren't going to ditch me on a damn nasty lonesome night like tonight, are you, and go back to that party?" he said dolefully.

"Well, I don't know," she countered. "It was such a nice party. There were a lot of very amusing people and some very good liquor."

"Oh, hell, if that's all! Now look, I'm awful funny, and we can stop in anywhere and have a drink."

She laughed some more. She felt ridiculously carefree, and happy. "Kenny, you don't need me to cheer you up on a rainy night. You must know three or four dozen girls in Ashbury who would love to go and have a drink with you."

"I'd rather be with you," he said seriously.

"I don't see why. I'm a staid settled old married woman, and . . ."

Kenny put his hand out suddenly and covered one of hers on the steering wheel. "I guess you know the way I feel about you," he said with his voice still grave. He felt the quick tension through her body at his touch. Kenny was an expert in such matters. He congratulated himself that he was handling this very neatly and that his timing was perfect. He waited for her next move; he anticipated it to the very words she would speak.

"You mustn't say things like that, Kenny," Rita Sibley said carefully.

They were silent. Kenny sighed audibly, shrugged his shoulders and took his hand off hers. The wind blew the rain in great gusts, and the windshield wiper slowed and labored against the streaming wash of water.

Rita spoke at last with her voice gay again. "This is a night fit for nary man nor beast. I couldn't possibly desert anybody on a night like this. You start being amusing, and we'll go have a drink."

Kenny laughed, relaxing his heavy body comfortably on the seat close beside her, their shoulders touching. "Well, the funniest thing I can think of right now is that I'm broke. I'm so broke that I can't buy you a drink. Hell, I couldn't even buy myself a drink."

Rita laughed again. Laughter came easy to her she had discovered when she was with Kenny. "Kenny Veech," she said, "you are irresponsible and you're crazy. You know perfectly well that I wouldn't drop you out broke on a night like this. You know I'll buy you a drink. Now I see it all plain. It isn't me that you want, it's my money."

"Rita," he said, "don't say that."

"I'm sorry, Kenny. I have a rotten sense of humor, haven't I?"

"Well, I don't know about that," he said. "All I know is sometimes you're laughing and wisecracking, and you don't mean it, because inside you are feeling low and blue. You don't have to keep up no front for me."

"Kenny, you know too much about women. You must have had a great deal of experience with them. After this, I'm going to believe all the stories that I hear about you."

"See, that's what I mean. There you go again, wisecracking and saying things you don't mean just to be funny and keep up a front."

"If you don't quit talking like this you are going to be boring instead of amusing. Where shall we go to have a drink?"

"Well," Kenny said. "I don't like to see you do it, anyway. I don't like to have to see you feeling blue and trying to laugh on the outside. Where do you want to go?"

"Well, let me see." She thought a moment. "Oh, I know just the place. I can't think of the name of it. It's just a little place. It's quiet, has soft music and cozy lights—a few tables scattered around. It's perfect for a night like this, and the liquor is good too."

"It sounds swell." He hesitated a little. "Look, Rita, I'm not very dressed up or nothing, you sure you want to . . ."

"Don't be silly, you look perfectly all right. I'm not dressed up either. The people who come to this place never dress up."

Inside the door an alert waiter took them to the only empty table left, a secluded one back in a corner by a window. "Oh, I'm simply soaked," Rita whispered to Kenny. "I look terrible."

"You look gorgeous," he whispered back. Rita felt a choking acceleration of her heartbeats. I'm thirty years old, she thought, there won't be so much longer that men will think I'm beautiful. Well, I'm beautiful tonight, and Kenny Veech is in love with me. I can see it in his eyes. It has been a long time since a man has looked at me like that. I wonder what there is about Kenny Veech that fascinates me and makes me want to be with him?

In fact, Rita *was* almost beautiful. She was tall and slender. Her smooth skin was tanned an even golden brown from years of careful exposure to the summer sun. Her hair was delicate blonde, light against her skin, and her eyes were a light clear gray. She wore a trim dark suit tonight that set off this unusual contrast of skin and hair to the best advantage. But for one feature, Rita would have been very lovely. Her mouth was thin, quiet and cold, even when she smiled.

Rita concentrated on the liquor menu while the obsequious waiter stood beside the table. Kenny ordered a whiskey and soda, and she chose a wine. When the waiter was gone, she carelessly laid a dollar bill on the table corner.

"This is a nice little dump," Kenny said speculatively, studying the room, and then looking back again to Rita's sleek blonde hair silhouetted against the dark rain-tracked window. She laughed again. The word "dump" jarred in so harmonious a spot.

When he saw the waiter walked off with the dollar bill, and leave no change, Kenny whistled softly between his teeth. "Class, huh?"

Rita sipped her sweet wine and studied Kenny out of the corner of her eye. "This is nice," she said. "I'm really very glad that I didn't desert you now."

"It's a lot nicer than you know," he said.

The calculated intimacy of the room drew them closer together. "You know, Kenny," she said, her eyes lowered to her wine goblet, "I'm a terribly funny person. I lied to you tonight for no reason."

"Sure," he said readily. "About the party. I know you did. There wasn't any party. I could tell. Something's bothering you, isn't there? You're unhappy about something, and you're feeling blue tonight."

"Kenny, you frighten me. I have a feeling sometimes that you know more about me than I know myself."

"I guess maybe I do." Kenny was elated. The game he played was progressing somewhat faster than he had anticipated. Rita Sibley, he decided, was exactly like any other woman, for all her education and her habit of constantly evading things by talking around them in empty high-sounding words. But he must be cautious. He must get the timing exactly right; one false word now would destroy everything he had achieved.

"What's the matter?" he asked casually. "You and Joe having trouble?"

"Oh, no, nothing like that. If there's any trouble, it's all with me. Tell me, Kenny, you know Joe, don't you? What do you think of him?"

Kenny grinned because he had been certain that she would ask him that. "Well, I don't know. I don't know Joe. I've seen him around, but I don't know him. He seems like a nice quiet guy. He always acts to me like he's got something on his mind that he's thinking about all the while, that don't leave him no time for nothing else—not even you," he finished deliberately.

Rita flushed a little and kept her eyes on the tall stemmed goblet that she turned in her fingers. "They talk about him a lot around town, don't they?"

"About him being a Communist? Yeah. Well, I don't know and I don't care. I figure that is his business. It don't make no difference to me, one way or another."

"That's exactly the way that I feel about it." She lifted her cool clear eyes to Kenny as she spoke. He felt a glow of sensuous pleasure at the way her pale eyes came up from under her lashes in her tanned face.

"I wish you knew Joe," she said. "He's a fine person."

"Maybe he is, but I wouldn't like him. I wouldn't like any guy that was married to you."

She smiled faintly. "You don't feel that way about your brother, do you, and he used to be married to me."

"Ernie's a damn fool," he answered. "He never knew how lucky he was."

"I think he did. Ernie's the lucky one; he got rid of me."

"I know better." He put his hand over hers on the table. Her hand underneath his was cool and perfectly still. "Kenny, you mustn't."

"My God," he said, "what do you think I'm made of, setting here with you and can't even touch you."

She felt a warm excitement. As if I was a schoolgirl, she thought. She drew her hand away and rested her chin on it. "We've talked too much about me," she said lightly. "Let's talk about you now."

"Oh, me," he said easily. "Everybody knows about me. I'm a bum. I don't work and I don't want to. I mooch money and cigarettes and drinks off everybody I know."

She laughed at his words. "Well, I'm sorry about the cigarettes. I can't offer you one. I don't smoke, you know. I used to, but I gave it up when I found out that people in a small town don't want a schoolteacher that smokes cigarettes. I never smoke at all now. But, if you're out of cigarettes, I'll get a package."

"No, I don't want you to."

"Don't be silly. What good is money unless you spend it? All I've got is money."

"You got a hell of a lot more than that, don't kid yourself."

"Signal that waiter over there. We want more drinks, anyway."

After the waiter had gone away again, Rita resumed the conversation. "No, I really want to know about you. I know that you don't work, but I can't understand you. Ernie wasn't like that. He wanted to get ahead terribly."

"Sure, he still does. He's after every cent he can get."

"I know, that's why I can't understand about you. Don't you want to marry and settle down and work really?"

"I guess the right woman just never came along."

"That's a silly thing to say. It's no excuse. You're different from all the rest of your family. Ernie works and keeps a home. Your brother Carl works at the meat market. Josette is going to business school. Jennine helps your mother at home."

"Sure," he said, "I guess I'm just the black sheep in the family."

"Well, of course there's Mary," she said carefully. "Mary is different too."

He scowled at the mention of his sister's name. Rita was curious about Mary, and she went on probing delicately, hoping to bring him into a discussion of his sister. "I think Mary is the most beautiful woman I have ever seen. I can't understand about her. I wish I knew her."

"God, did you see it lightning just then," he said. "This is the worst storm we had all summer."

Rita was puzzled at his reticence. "I don't think anybody really knows Mary, though. She seems to live a life of her own, separate from the village and most everybody in it. I wish I was more like her in some ways. I think perhaps you are more like her than anybody else in your family, but still you are a different type of personality."

He moved restlessly in his chair. Rita saw that he did not wish to discuss Mary with her. She thought she understood his reticence, but still he was not conventional in his thinking about anything else and she could not understand why he should maintain a conventional attitude toward his sister. Her curiosity increased and she decided suddenly to put her thoughts into words. "You don't want to talk about Mary, do you? I can't understand why you wouldn't. You're not the kind of person that would condemn her or be in the least ashamed of her."

He spoke in sudden anger. "Hell, I ain't ashamed of Mary. Why should I be?"

"That's just it. I know that you aren't. That's why I can't understand why you won't talk about her."

"Hell, I don't mind talking about her. Mary . . ." he began, and then he stopped. His face puzzled her, she had never seen him look or act like this. He was completely detached from her now, lost in himself and his own thoughts. The image of Mary came up with sudden startling clarity into Rita's mind, her strange face with the peculiar dark brown shadows around the eyes, her shining hair, her exquisite body. Rita was disturbed and a little frightened. There was something here, she realized, that she did not understand, and that she did not want to understand. She wished now that she had never spoken Mary's name.

"I'm sorry," she said. "I seem to be an awfully crude, unpleasant person tonight. I've had a headache all day, and tonight I felt so lonesome and unhappy. I don't know what's wrong with me. I haven't been sleeping well lately. I think that I'd better go."

Kenny was himself again; she knew him instantly. "I'm worried about you," he said. "I can't stand seeing you blue and not feeling good. You ought to laugh and feel good all the time. You're so gorgeous when you laugh."

At the look in his eyes, Rita was content and forgot completely the strange mood of his that had just passed.

"I'll be all right. It's sleep I need more than anything else. I'll go home and take a sedative and get a good night's sleep. In the morning I'll be a new person."

"Don't do that," he said softly. "Don't be a new person."

"There's no danger; sometimes I wish I could be though."

"Why don't you wait a little?" he said. "Maybe this rain will kind of let up after awhile. I hate to think of you driving home in a storm like this."

"You don't need to worry," she said. "I'm the world's best driver. It's the only thing in the world that I can do really well."

"Just the same I hate to think of you alone driving in this storm."

"Well, then, why don't you ride back to town with me," she said lightly. "I could drop you off at your place as well as not."

He started to say something, and then he changed his mind. He almost got his timing off that time, he thought. With a woman like this you had to take it slow and easy. "No, thanks," he said. "Hell, the night is just beginning. What do I want to go home now for? I tell you what, we might ride around or something for awhile though, and then you could go over and pick up Joe when he gets out of work over to the shop."

She shook her head. "Goodness, no. Joe would be astonished if I ever went after him at the shop. Besides, he wouldn't be ready to come home for hours after he gets out of work. He always has all kinds of things to do after he gets out of work nights."

"Well, we could ride around for awhile, anyway."

"No, I don't think I'd better. Not tonight, Kenny. I think I'll go straight home and go to bed."

He shrugged his shoulders. "Okay. When am I going to see you again?"

"Why, I don't know, Kenny. You're liable to see me around most any time."

"I don't mean that. When are you going to meet me again?"

"Well, I don't know. Perhaps I'll come up here some night next week, and if you should happen . . ."

"No, I've got to see you again before that. I can't wait till next week. I couldn't stand it that long."

"Kenny, you have to stop talking to me like this. You have no right to say such things."

"Why not?" he said coolly. "I got the best right there is."

Rita felt fear again at his words. The ground seemed to be slipping from under her feet. "Perhaps I won't ever meet you again. I shouldn't; I don't think I will." The words were incoherent.

"Okay," he said. "Then I'll come down to your house to see you. Hell, it don't make no difference to me. I'd just as soon see you down there as any place."

"No," she said. "You wouldn't do that."

"You know I would and you know if I come down there you wouldn't slam the door in my face neither."

Because she could not be sure that she would, she weakened. "Well, I can't come up here tomorrow night," she said.

"How about the night after?"

"All right," she agreed weakly. Rita, she kept telling herself, you are a fool, you've gone stark raving mad, you don't know what you're doing. You are playing with fire with this man. But underneath that she was pleased and excited, because Kenny Veech, who was a very attractive man and one who had his choice of many women, was in love with her and desired her passionately. She had to have more of his passion and desire for her, she thought; it was the only tonic that would ever help her.

"Okay, that's settled," he said. "Day after tomorrow night, same time, same place."

She nodded. The eager, frightened young look on her face elated him. He decided to be daring, and went on to the next move with consummate artistry. He took her hand again and spoke softly and tenderly to her. "Don't fight against things so hard, darling. You only hurt yourself, fightin' so hard against things that you can't stop, anyway."

She looked at him oddly, her face flushing a little, and got up from the table. They went out into the cool wet street, and Kenny unlocked her car for her. Neither one of them had spoken a word.

She slid in under the wheel, and looked at him standing by the open car door. "Can't I drop you off some place?"

He lifted his head and apparently took bearings. "Uh-uh, thanks just the same."

"Where are you going?" she said before she thought.

"Oh, I'll just make the rounds and see what all the boys are doing for awhile," he answered.

She slid her hands back and forth on the steering wheel. "I hate to just drive off and leave you standing in the rain."

"Do you?" he asked, smiling suddenly. "Well, I tell you what, if you want me to, I'll walk off and leave you. How's that?"

She laughed.

"Okay," he said. "I'll be seeing you. Don't forget." He looked at her for a moment more and then he turned on his heel and walked off down the street without looking back once. He walked easily with a sort of free pleasing rhythm through his big wide body. He held his head up to the soft rain, and once a streak of light from a neon sign caught his wet blond hair and made it sparkle.

Rita Sibley sat at the wheel of her automobile and watched him go until he was swallowed up in the darkness and mist. Then she slammed the door shut and shot her car away from the curb. She drove furiously, but with a reckless precision, the city speed regulations entirely disregarded. The task of getting out of the city traffic at that speed left her no time for thinking. Once she was out on the empty wet and narrow strip of pavement that led back to the village, she shoved the accelerator down until the speedometer wavered above sixty-five, and held it there. The car leaped and skidded under her. She drove in the middle of the pavement, straining her eyes ahead into the receding puddle of yellow light from her headlights.

Where the road went between two marshes, a thick fog drifted like a blanket across the road and shut off her vision for a foot ahead of her. She only slackened speed a little, and blindly drove the skidding, careening car from memory of the road. And when she came to the sharp, unbanked curve just north of the village, she lost control of the car momentarily, and slid around the curve sideways. She righted the heavy automobile just before the wheels struck the muddy shoulder on the wrong side of the road. She twisted the steering wheel, her face set and her lips still, while the tires shrieked on the wet asphalt. She tore down the middle of the pavement again into town. The speedometer still ticked at sixty-five, and her foot was numb from holding down the accelerator.

8

THE NEXT DAY OLD JUD DISAPPEARED. HE WAS already gone when the family gathered for breakfast in the morning. He did not appear at dinnertime. By late afternoon Molly became concerned about him. She made haphazard preparations for supper, worrying audibly about where in the world Mr. Higgins could be. Kenny was impatient to be off to a baseball game, so at last Molly abandoned her supper preparations temporarily and gave him a lunch of sandwiches and cookies, promising to have supper later after the game was over. She followed him out onto the porch and called after him up the street. "Kenny, you come right straight home now when that game's over, 'cause I'll have supper all on the table waiting. If you want to hang around uptown, you come home and eat your supper first. And Kenny, you ask the boys if anybody's seen Mr. Higgins today. You be sure and ask, won't you?"

When Kenny was out of earshot, she turned to Sam in the porch swing. "Move over," she said, and sat down heavily beside him. The sun was falling out of sight rapidly in the sky to the west, casting strange splotches of bloody light on the porch. Dorothy sat on the top step with the old cat on her lap. The cat sprawled across her thin knees on his back, relaxed and unafraid, with his legs sticking out stiffly. Dorothy was preoccupied with exploring his bony ribs and his hip joints with her spidery, sharp little fingers. The air was close as if there was more rain to come.

"Dor'thy, I wouldn't handle that cat all the time if I was you," Molly said absently over the placid creaking of the swing. "This hot weather makes him kind of sick and he don't like to be handled; besides he's just covered with fleas. Lord, I wonder where Mr. Higgins has gone to."

"I wouldn't worry about Jud," Sam said, looking up from the folded paper that he was straining his eyes to read in the dim light. "Wouldn't be surprised if he got up early this morning and beat it over to Centerville to see that old man that lives over there that he used to be so thick with. You know that old man—what's his name now? Jud used to go over to see him real often a couple years ago; he's the one that used to . . ."

"You mean that old Moses Hathaway? Lord, he's been dead and buried three years. Don't you remember Ernie took Mr. Higgins over to his funeral? It must have been three years ago."

"Well, I wouldn't worry about Jud, anyway," Sam said. "He's just gone off somewheres. He'll be back when he's ready to."

"That's all right," Molly flamed. "You don't have to worry about him none if you don't want to, but I can't help worrying. Mr. Higgins is getting along in years and I can't help but worry, his bumming off somewhere all by himself. Suppose he had a bad spell walking along some place, and just toppled over in the weeds and is laying there right this minute so sick he's like to die and no way of calling nobody or getting to no help?"

Sam was silent. Dorothy listened to them attentively, while she tried to pry the old cat's mouth open in order to count his teeth.

"Like enough Jud hiked out to some farm around here," Sam said at last, "to see if he couldn't get a job in the haying. Jud always gets restless in the summer."

Molly was angry now, and anger loosened her tongue. "Sam Veech, you know just as well as I do where Mr. Higgins has went to. He's gone off on another of them drinking spells of his, that's where he's gone, and you know it. And he's getting too old to go out and drink like that. Two or three days at a stretch. He can't stand it no more. It makes me so mad, that cussed drinking . . ."

They were both silent then. At last Sam said, "Tell you, I could step uptown while you're getting supper on and ask around and see if anybody seen him, or if anybody up there sold him any liquor today."

"Well . . ." Molly said doubtfully. "All right, but you get right back here. I ain't gonna have you hanging around up to that poolroom with that good-for-nothing Marv Roberts half the night when Mr. Higgins is gone like this and I'm all upset."

"Supper's ready!" Molly called up the stairs. "You kids come on down here right away before everything gets cold."

Carl opened the door and went down the stairs in three great bounds, stumbling against Josette at the foot.

"You big lummox," she said. "Why don't you look where you're going?"

"Yaa, yaa, yaa," he answered cheerily, with singular inappropriateness. "Why don't you?" he rumpled her hair airily, as he had seen Kenny do.

"For heaven's sakes!" she said sharply, striking at his wrist.

Sam and Kenny were already seated at the table in the kitchen. They had just returned from town together. Jen took up round, hard, fried patties of hamburger from a sizzling hot frying pan, and Molly sat down last of all with the coffee pot.

The light poured down on the family around the stained oilcloth table top, and outside, beyond the open kitchen door, the lightning flickered in the darkness uneasily.

"Lord, if it's going to rain, I wish it would go ahead and get it over with," Molly said, wiping at her fat perspiring face. "I hate this thundering and lightning. Did you hear it thunder right then, kind of rumbling, far off? I always been afraid of lightning."

Dorothy laughed loudly and uncontrollably, and Molly stared at her. "Being scared like that ain't nothing to laugh about," she reproved. "It's a terrible thing, I tell you."

"Seems like the wind's coming up a little," Sam said soothingly.

"I'm always so 'fraid of windstorms this time of the year too," Molly said.

That time Kenny laughed, between great healthy bites of food.

"Poor old Mom! Looks like you're just in for a good scare no matter what happens."

"It seems so funny, eating without Mr. Higgins here," Molly said. "I can't bear to think of it raining tonight and him laying out somewhere, for all we know."

"Rain oughta sober him up, and then the old boy would come home a-running," Kenny said.

"Well, it's like I told you," Sam said to her. "Nobody uptown has seen him around today. I asked all around up there."

"I seen Jud today," Dorothy said suddenly, mashing the warmed-over potatoes on her plate with her fork, and looking up to see the effect of her words on the family.

All eyes were turned to her. "You did!" her grandmother said. "Why in the world ain't you said nothing about it when you heard us all talking about him and wondering where he went to? When did you see him? Where was he at? What did he say when you saw him?"

"Well . . ." Dorothy closed her eyes and tipped her head to one side, apparently attempting to remember the details connected with her having seen Jud. Her audience waited for her impatiently.

"You think hard now, and tell Grandma all about it."

"Well . . ." Dorothy said finally, "I was playing down by the lake, I guess it was before dinner, and I see Jud coming and he was acting kind of funny, and kind of talking to himself kind of . . ."

"You little liar!" Jen said cheerfully. "You never played down by the lake in your life. You know you'd get skinned if we ever caught you running off down there."

"I was too down there," Dorothy said. "I play down there lots. You don't know where I play. An'—I see Jud coming and he was looking awful funny-like, and I got scared something awful, and I hid in the bushes, and Jud went right by, walking right along close to the water, and he had a whole lot of bottles, about a dozen of them. He was carrying them. They was full of something, I guess it was whiskey bottles," she finished brightly.

The family stared at her in consternation.

"You're a little liar," Jen said.

Molly for once was at a loss. "You suppose she really seen him?" she asked.

"Naw!" Kenny said.

"I seen Jud down by the lake," Dorothy's eyes were closed, and she talked, her voice singsong in a kind of ecstasy. "And he had a lot of whiskey bottles, and he was drinking out of one of them, right while he was walking, and he walked right along by the water, and all to once he fell right over, right in the water, and he just laid there, right in the water."

"For Lord's sakes," Molly said solemnly.

"What did you do when Jud fell in the water?" Kenny said casually, still busily eating.

"Why, nothing," she said. "He just laid in the water all still, and I was scared and I run away, and I looked back and he was awful sick, like to die, and he was hollering something awful, but nobody could hear him and he was drinking whiskey right out of a bottle."

"He was, huh?" Kenny said. "Drinking whiskey right out of a bottle. Did you get a real good look at the bottle he was drinking out of, the whiskey bottle?"

"Why, sure," Dorothy opened her eyes in surprise. "I see him drinking whiskey out of a bottle, just as plain . . ."

"Sure," Kenny said, "I know you did. Did you see what color whiskey it was he was drinking out of the bottle?"

"Sure, I did," she said promptly. "It was blue, bright blue. Some of the bottles he had was red and green and yellow, but the one he was drinking outa was blue, I seen it real plain."

"There you are," Kenny said. "Looks like Jud's took to drinking soda pop in his old age."

"You think she was just making it all up?" Molly said, round-eyed.

"Hell, yes."

"That doesn't prove a thing," Josette said earnestly. "She might have seen him just the way that she said she did, but you wouldn't expect her to remember the color of the bottles. And when you asked her about the colors, any child her age would make up all the colors she knew when she couldn't remember."

"Dor'thy," Molly said sharply. "I want you to tell Grandma the truth now. You been lying or did you really see Mr. Higgins down there by the lake like you been telling about?"

"I seen him right down by the lake drinking whiskey, and he fell right over in the water and it splashed up something awful, an' a great big fish flew right up outa the water . . ."

"You're the worst little liar I ever heard," Jen said. "You oughta be spanked for telling stuff like that till you couldn't set down for a week."

The first big drops of rain rattled on the roof and on the porch steps.

Molly pushed her plate aside disconsolately, and drank coffee instead. "Well, sir, you boys'll just have to swallow your supper and go down there by the lake and look. I couldn't sleep a wink tonight unless you did."

"Oh, for God's sakes!" Kenny said, holding out his cup for more coffee. Later he leaned over toward the little girl and drew her close to him. He whispered in her ear, running his fingers along her sensitive bony little back, as he talked. She listened to him attentively, and then she nodded and both of them laughed loudly.

"There now," Kenny said winningly. "Now you tell your grandmother about how you was just playing a joke when you said you seen Jud down by the lake drinking whiskey. You was just having fun and teasing everybody, wasn't you, Dorothy?"

"Sure," she said, readily, nestling against Kenny's arm. "Sure, I was just fooling everybody." She laughed immoderately until tears shone in her large blue eyes.

"Lookit here, young lady," Molly said. "You tell the truth now. Did you see Mr. Higgins the way you claimed you did, or didn't you? You tell the truth."

Out of the protecting circle of Kenny's arm, Dorothy spoke, clutching his shirt tight in her hand. "Sure, I was just fooling you. I never seen Jud at all. I just made it up. I never seen Jud. I wasn't even playing down to the lake."

"Oh, you make me sick," Josette said to Kenny. "You know very well that that child will say anything you tell her to. She's crazy about you and anything that you want her to do she always does. Ma, don't you pay any attention to what she just said. Kenny just put her up to saying that to get out of going out in the rain to look for Jud."

Molly dealt with the situation decisively. "Well, I don't know. You boys better go on down there and take a look around anyway. It won't do no hurt, and I ain't gonna sleep tonight unless you do. Dor'thy, you listen to me. I catch you lying any more, and I'm going to tell your mother on you proper, and she'll straighten you out, young woman, don't you forget it."

The rain was blowing hard against the window, and it came in through the screen door and made a puddle on the warped boards of the kitchen floor. Carl watched the rain blow in apprehensively. "I ain't going out in no storm like this chasing after old Jud. If he don't know enough to come in out of the rain, he can stay out in it, for all I care. I ain't got no raincoat nor nothing, and I won't go out and get soaked looking for him."

"You'll do as I tell you," Molly said. "You oughta be ashamed to talk like that about Mr. Higgins, him just like a grandfather to all of you kids. He was the best man alive, except when he was on one of his drinking spells, up to a few years ago when he started getting kind of funny as he got older. Lord, many's the night he used to walk the floor half the night with you, Carl Veech, when you was just a little tiny baby and had the three-months' colic. You got a raincoat, ain't you, Kenny?" she queried. "I guess there's an old umbrella around here, somewheres, you can take, Carl."

"I don't want no umbrella," he said sourly. "Getting wet can't no more'n kill me. I'll go on out and get soaked. I don't care."

"Why can't Kenny go? He's got a raincoat," Jen said.

Molly evaded the question neatly. "You boys hurry up and go on down there by the lake and look around before it rains any more. Lord, if that old man's laying out in all this rain, it's enough to give him pneumonia, sure."

Carl got up immediately with a scowl creasing his forehead. He went over to the clothes hooks hanging in the corner by the stove and selected an old dark gray suit coat, and put it on. It was too broad for him in the shoulders, but he buttoned it up and turned the collar up high around his neck. "Come on," he said to Kenny, "we might just as well get it over with."

"You won't just go downtown and fool around and then come back, will you?" asked Molly earnestly.

"Ah, take it easy, Mom. We'll go down to the lake and look, don't you worry no more about it," Kenny said.

Both of them steeled themselves for the plunge out into the rain. Molly stood in the doorway and watched them go down the street together until they were out of sight.

They walked close together, with their heads down. "Hell, what a night," Kenny said. The water ran over the sidewalk in a thin stream, wetting their feet before they had taken a dozen steps. The water ran out of Carl's dark hair, and plastered it over his forehead in a heavy bang.

Carl found suddenly a sort of pleasure, walking beside his brother, intimate with him, while the cold rain soaked through his clothes to his skin. He breathed deeply and found an exultation in it. He felt excited and alive to be walking with Kenny in the rain, and sharing a mission of importance with him.

When they reached the corner under the lights of the downtown area, Kenny said, "Hell, let's stop in to the beer garden for a minute. Ain't no sense us trying to keep moving out in a rain like this. We can have a beer, and maybe it'll let up and then we can take a look around for Jud. Ma gets all excited over something like this. I knew damn well the kid was just lying when she claimed she seen Jud down there by the lake."

"Okay," Carl said casually. He felt excited and good. Kenny had never offered to take him with him to drink a beer before. But now it was different, he was thinking. He and Kenny were both grown up, the men of the family.

Kenny dodged in the door of the beer garden, with Carl behind him. They stopped inside the door and wiped the water from their faces. The room was warm and brightly lighted, and smelled pleasantly of beer and tobacco smoke and perspiration. The tables were about half filled, and the room was full of the sound of voices and the music from the record machine standing in the corner, the front of it shining with bright green light.

Once he had the raindrops brushed out of his eyes, Kenny gave a wild yell, because there just inside the door stood Ernie. The brothers swooped down on him on a run, and Kenny threw his arms about him. "Ernie, old kid, old scout, old brother, how's the boy? Damn, are we glad to see you. How's everything in heaven, old angel, old kid, old Ernie?"

"Hey, leggo, you're choking me," Ernie said. His voice was good-humored, but his face remained impassive.

"Ernie, you're just the guy we wanta see."

"Hey, Joe, gimme two packages of Camels, will you? Whose bail you trying to raise now?" he said to Kenny.

"Ernie, how'd you like to take us for a nice little ride, huh?"

"Maybe. Where you wanta go, Ashbury?"

"Well, we was figuring on Detroit."

"Sure, anywhere you say."

The brothers went out together and dodged across the sidewalk to Ernie's car. Carl crawled into the back seat, and sat hunched forward, his elbows on the back of the seat between Ernie and Kenny.

"What's up?" Ernie asked Kenny.

"You seen old Jud today?"

"Hell, no. What's the matter? He gone off on another drinking spree?"

"Yeah, he sneaked off sometime last night, and we ain't seen nothing of him all day. Dorothy was telling a lot of bull about seeing him laying around down by the lake, at the supper table. You know how Ma is. She's worrying herself sick about him. She wanted us to go on down there and take a look around, just to make sure."

"I could tell Ma where he is," Ernie said.

"Sure, I thought I could too. But Horning's outa town. His wife don't allow no drunks hanging around down there when she's running the place."

"Yeah. God, I don't know where else he'd be, unless he just figured on laying outdoors some place. He sure picked nice weather for it."

"Yeah," Kenny said. "And you know Jud when he's been drinking whiskey. He wouldn't even know it was raining even."

"Well, we better go down and take a look around the lake." Ernie started the motor and turned the car in the direction of the lake. As they neared the shore, the houses thinned out and the street became narrower and more winding. The brothers were silent, straining their eyes ahead through the rain. Ernie drove slowly, and the heavy car slid a little in the soft mud of the road. They came to the end of the road abruptly, and Ernie stopped the car. The powerful headlights shone out along the overgrown lake front, and onto the dark, weed-infested lake itself, where the rain hung over it like some malignant vapor.

"I don't know how you'd find him if he was down here," Ernie said.

"I'll get out and take a look around," Kenny said.

Kenny opened the door and put his foot out on the running board.

"You can't see nothing in this rain," Ernie said. "Wait a minute. I got a flashlight around here some place." He hunted in the glove compartment and on the floor between the seats. Carl searched the back seat thoroughly. "You never can find the God-damn thing when you want it," Ernie grumbled.

"Never mind. I can see all right. I got eyes like a cat's. I can see in the dark." Kenny jumped down and slammed the car door. He went toward the lake, running easily, his hands in his pockets, leaping and zigzagging through the puddles of water and the underbrush. The rain seemed to fold in around him. He stopped right at the water's edge and looked both directions up the lake shore. The trench coat made him a vague, light-colored figure silhouetted against the water. Carl felt chilled; something about the lake and the deserted uneven shore line in the darkness and rain impressed him as being peculiarly evil and sinister. He could not bear to think of his brother alone there, separated from the world of warm human beings by an air full of water and darkness. He jumped out on the running board. "Hey, wait a minute! I'm coming with you."

Kenny whirled around and looked into the blinding car lights. His voice floated back to them, weakened and distorted by the rain. "Go on, get back in the car, you crazy little fool. Won't take me but a minute."

Carl stood uncertain, and Ernie hauled him back into the car by his coat tail. Kenny looked up the lake shore as if he was smelling the very air for directions. Suddenly he turned off short to the right, trotting along at the very edge of the water, in the sand, beyond the low underbrush, leaving great black water-filled tracks behind him. He passed beyond the range of the auto lights and was instantly swallowed up in the darkness under the great willow trees that leaned over until their trailing fronds lay along the water.

Ernie talked musingly, while both of them strained their eyes into the darkness at the point where Kenny had disappeared from view. "He sure was a funny little kid that way. Never scared of nothing. Used to drive Ma crazy running off alone around the lake at night. Hell, I can remember, when he wasn't more'n eight or nine years old, the damnedest thing. They still had prohibition them days, you know. Some big bootlegger from Detroit used to run liquor in here by truck. Had a cache where he used to hide it down here by the lake some place. Then he used to put it on motor boats and take it across the lake and through the channel into Big Goose Lake, and God only knows where from there. Most likely he got it right over the state line by boat before he ever had to load it onto trucks again. Anyway, Kenny was just a little kid then, but he was the only one in this whole town that knew where the cache was, or ever saw the guys that was handling that liquor. He used to be friends with all that crowd, called 'em all by their first names and everything. They used to give him money and candy and stuff. It used to about drive Ma wild. Funny thing though how close-mouthed he was about it. You couldn't get nothing outa him about the cache or where the liquor went from here, nor nothing. Kenny even claimed he knew the big boss himself from Detroit. Ma couldn't keep him in the house at night. It was the damnedest thing I ever heard of."

Ernie was silent again, and the two windshield wipers cut double swaths through the water. The story he had just heard stirred Carl's imagination. The atmosphere here became charged with sinister potentialities and dangers for him. He felt gooseflesh all over his body. He worked his hands together nervously and strained his eyes for some sight of Kenny.

They waited together, while the rain drummed down on the car roof and beat against the windows. Ernie lit a cigarette, and Carl thought that his hands moved nervously too, as if Ernie also felt this curious tension.

"God, I don't know what he wants to chase around the whole damn lake for," Ernie said at last.

They both kept their eyes on the darkness under the willows where Kenny had disappeared. But when he came back again, he came up out of the underbrush from behind the car. He opened the car door before either one of them saw him, and when the door opened they both jumped.

Kenny was laughing and out of breath. He peeled off the dripping raincoat and wadded it up under his feet. His face was shining with moisture and his wet hair was curled into tight dark ringlets.

"God," he said, "I like to drowned. Somebody gimme a cigarette."

Ernie handed him a fresh package. "What was you doing? Walking clear around the lake?"

"Well, old Jud ain't nowhere around this side of the lake, and I don't figure he'd be apt to be over on the other side." Ernie turned the car around, the motor roaring, and the mud and water flying up from under the wheels.

"This place is enough to give you the creeps on a rainy night," Ernie said, when they were back on the street again headed for town. "I don't suppose you saw nothing of your old pals from Detroit that used to handle liquor outa here, tonight."

"I hadn't thought about them guys in a long time," answered Kenny. "Remember, Ma and Pa used to live in that house up on the hill by the point, that burnt down, then. Them sure was the days, all right."

"All I gotta say is you sure used to pick yourself a nice bunch of little playfellows," Ernie said.

Kenny laughed softly. "Say, Ernie, did I ever tell you about the time that that Detroit mob had a gun fight with a bunch of hijackers right down here by this lake? I was right there and seen it all. Two guys they killed right here by this lake on a rainy night, must have been fifteen, sixteen years ago. I seen the whole thing. And you know what they did? They filled them bodies fulla lead and tied some weights around their necks and took 'em out in a boat and dropped them right in the middle of the lake, in the deep part over the drop-off."

"The hell you say," Ernie said derisively, but Carl's chest became so tight that he could hardly breathe.

"Okay, you think that's nothing but bull. Well, anytime you want to do some big fishing, you just get some hooks and do some dragging around in the mud bottom the other side of the drop-off and see what you find."

Ernie was sobered into half-belief by the tone of his brother's voice. "I don't believe it. If you'da ever seen 'em do anything like that, they'd a drilled you full of holes and sunk you right over there in the middle of the lake with them hijackers."

"Like hell they woulda," Kenny said shortly. "Them guys was smart. I was a local kid. What you think they was gonna do? Have the whole town out dragging the lake looking for me, and tipping the whole thing off?"

"Well, I don't know nothing about it, and I don't want to," Ernie said. "Any more stories like that you got about your pals you can keep to yourself. You always thought you was pretty smart playing around with guys like that and always keeping in the clear. All I gotta say is, you can't do stuff like that forever and get away with it. Some day some of your pals are gonna get kind of nervous with their trigger fingers, and then I'll be taking a little trip into Detroit where you'll be laying all nice and quiet on a cold marble slab down to the morgue, shot so fulla holes you'll look like a sieve."

Kenny laughed again and Carl was afraid. Kenny suddenly was no longer the simple, warm, lighthearted brother whom he thought he knew so well. He was shocked to realize how little he really knew about this brother of his with whom he had shared a bed as long as he could remember. He was afraid. He wished that he had never heard them talking this way. He thought of the lake, and believed that he would never go near it again. He remembered how boys who were unwise enough to go swimming in its waters always broke out in a rash over their bodies, and fishermen said that the fish in this lake were poisoned and no good. He shuddered at his own thoughts.

Ernie stopped the car in front of the house. "Rain don't seem to be letting up none. We better run for it. Don't forget your raincoat there on the floor."

They clattered up onto the porch together and Molly met them at the door.

"Didn't you see him anywhere down around the lake? Ernie, you ain't seen Mr. Higgins today, have you?"

Molly's gloom spread a damper over all of them. Ernie stayed but a few minutes, and when he left she followed him out onto the porch and stood there for a few minutes peering up the street into the drizzle of rain as if she expected to see the bent figure of Jud Higgins coming along the sidewalk. When she came in, she said, "We better leave the front door unlocked in case Mr. Higgins comes home sometime before morning." The family trooped upstairs to bed, and the last thing before she put out the lights and climbed the stairs Molly went out to the little bedroom off the kitchen and looked at Jud's empty bed. Not quite empty, for tonight the old cat slept there undisturbed. She moved to put him out, and then she thought better of it. The skinny old cat, sleeping peacefully there with his mouth open, and his legs sprawled stiffly, seemed to her symbolic of old Jud himself. She decided to let him remain there, warm and comfortable against the storm, just as she was hoping that Jud himself had found a refuge this night against the weather. She sighed a little, switched off the kitchen light and went up the stairs slowly to her own bed.

In the room at the end of the hall, Kenny sat on the edge of the bed and smoked a cigarette while Carl undressed silently. It was far too early in the night for the prospect of sleep to appear inviting to Kenny. He felt peculiarly alert and wakeful, but it was no concern over Jud Higgins that kept him so. Carl climbed into bed on the other side, and turned his back on his brother, pulling the covers up over him. Kenny sat still with his elbows on his knees and wriggled his toes in his socks, watching their busy agile movements appreciatively.

Carl tossed the covers back suddenly and flopped over on his back in the bed, shielding his eyes against the light, in the crook of his elbow. "For God's sakes, you coming to bed, or are you gonna set up there all night with that light on?"

"Well, I'll tell you. I ain't decided yet, see?" At the coldness in his brother's tones, Carl nearly relapsed into the fit of nervous fear that he had experienced earlier in the evening. He repeated the words that Kenny had just spoken over and over in his mind, studying his brother's strong back while he did so. After the fifth or sixth time that he recalled them, he found something hard and sinister in the words, something quite to be expected in the way of conversation from a man who consorted with murderers and mobsters. The sudden vivid thought image of the two limp bodies slipping over the side of the boat and sinking silently to the bottom of the very lake that he had looked at every day of his life gave him a nasty start and turned his mouth dry.

Kenny turned around to him suddenly. "What in hell's the matter with you tonight, anyway? Your eyes look like a scared cat's. You look like you got the jitters right."

Carl stared back at Kenny fascinated. It seemed to him that Kenny's half-closed blue eyes had a power to look into his very mind. He was not at all surprised at Kenny's next words. "What's the matter? You still thinking about that stuff Ernie and me was talking about tonight, are you?"

Carl's mouth sagged open foolishly, and he never took his eyes off his brother's face.

Kenny appeared slightly bewildered. "Look," he said helplessly, "what you worrying about stuff like that for? It ain't nothing for you to worry about. It happened a long time ago when you was just a little kid. It's all done with now. There ain't been no mob around this town since repeal."

But the fear was still there before his eyes, plain on Carl's face.

"You ain't worried about what I said about a couple of stiffs sunk over there in the middle of the lake, are you? You been living here next to that lake ever since you been born and they ain't never hurt you yet, have they?"

Carl worked his lips a little, but he did not speak. He kept staring at Kenny, fascinated and horror-stricken.

Kenny was completely baffled by something soft and sensitive in his brother that was beyond his understanding. "You ain't thinking about that stuff Ernie was feeding me, about me getting hurt some day and ending up in a morgue some place? It's a lot of baloney. Ernie just likes to hear himself talk. There ain't nothing to it. I got lots of different kinds of friends. It never made no difference to me what a guy did so long as I liked him, but no guy is gonna shoot me full of holes or nothing else, so long as I don't give him no cause to."

Carl licked at his lips and listened to his brother attentively, his eyes still bright and distended in his face. He was making a vast effort to comprehend the logic of Kenny's words and drive this weak senseless fear out of himself. But time after time the image of those bodies sliding down over the side of the boat into the black rain-flecked waters came up into his mind, and each time it was as if it were a motion picture projected against the raw sensitive nerve tissue throughout his body.

Kenny closed his fingers over Carl's ankle in the bed. "What's on your mind, kid? Spill it," he said kindly.

Carl made another great effort to put into words this groundless fear that tortured him, and made him afraid to be in the room with his own brother. He spoke with his voice toneless, and the words disconnected, hanging in the air. "Them bodies—out there in the lake . . ."

Kenny was silent, closing and unclosing his fingers around Carl's ankle. "I don't know what to say, kid. I can't seem to get the way you feel about it. I can get how it is to be afraid of some guy that's crazy mad at you and out to get you, but stiffs is something altogether different. When a man's alive, he's apt to get mean and ugly or crazy and hurt people. But once a guy is dead, that's all done with. A stiff—hell, I don't know, and I been around plenty of 'em in my time—a stiff ain't a person no more. It ain't nothing. It ain't a thing more'n a stone alongside of the road, or a heap of dirt, or a puddle of water. You see what I mean? It ain't nothing to be scared of."

Carl nodded his head a little and licked his lips again.

Kenny was aware that there was much more to this feeling of Carl's than he had touched upon. But he could not understand. He closed his fingers tight around the boy's ankle under the bedclothes and groped for understanding and for the right words to say to him. There was actually only one thing outside of death—which he rarely thought of in terms of himself—that Kenny was afraid of, and that one thing was fear, fear in a human being, or in an animal. Kenny was abnormally sensitive to fear around him, and it always frightened him. To be aware of it in anyone knotted and chilled the muscles in his abdomen and made him feel sick. He was afraid of fear. It seemed unclean to him, contaminating and disgusting. He wanted to say something to Carl to make him feel better, but the words would not come right for him.

"The trouble is, kid, you take things too hard. You let everything get you. Of course you're young, but you're getting older and you gotta get hold of yourself. It's something nobody can do for you, or tell you about. You gotta quit letting every little thing get clear through to you. You see what I mean?" Kenny was floundering down hopelessly in his own words, but he went on again.

"The only way to keep living is to be hard and at the same time to take things easy. You see what I mean? There's a hell of a lotta things you run up against living along from day to day that ain't pretty and pleasant, but you can't let 'em get you down, nor you can't let 'em scare you; you can't even feel sorry about 'em. You just gotta take 'em easy, and not let 'em get through to you. You can't even think about 'em, or try to understand about 'em. You just gotta forget 'em and keep moving. You see what I mean?"

The words he spoke were only so many inexplicable words to Carl and Kenny realized it. He got up from the bed abruptly. "Oh, hell," he said. "Forget it. You go on and get some sleep. I don't feel like sleeping. I guess I'll go downstairs and see if I can scare up something to eat, or something."

He went out of the room into the dark hallway, and closed the door softly behind him.

He crept down the stairs noiselessly and turned on the light on the sitting-room table. He was not hungry, but he felt a restlessness. He rummaged through the books and papers on the table, but found nothing among them that caught his interest. The big old-fashioned radio set was dark and silent on a stand beside the wall. He idly turned the dials and snapped the buttons. It had been broken for almost a year. Ma liked a radio, he thought. Maybe Ernie would buy the folks a new radio for Christmas. He made a mental note to speak to Ernie about it. He walked through to the kitchen and snapped on the light. The room was empty and forbidding. Just as he reached to turn the light off again he saw his shoes resting on the oven door of the stove where he had put them to dry when he came home. He picked them up and turned the light off and went back into the sitting room. He sat down in a chair and put his shoes on. They were warm and dry, but they felt stiff and bumpy from the soaking. He felt better now and stretched his legs, sitting slumped in the chair, listening to the rain. He realized suddenly that he was lonesome for Mary, that he could not sleep without seeing her.

He relaxed in his chair and listened to the drowsy sound of the rain, with the thought of Mary warming and soothing him. He heard the car stop out in front and he thought that it was Jen coming home. But when he heard the soft light steps on the front porch he knew better. He got out of his chair and to the door just as it opened. Mary smiled at him as she closed the door quietly behind her. "You holding down the fort alone?"

He nodded. "Yeah, everybody's in bed but Jen, I guess. She's still out, chasing around somewhere. God, ain't this an awful night? I was just setting here wishing I could see you. You're home early."

"Lew's going into Detroit for a couple days tonight, and I'm going with him. I just come home to pack some things."

"I heard the car. That Lew out there now?"

"No. One of the boys drove me home to pick up my things."

"Oh, hell, then you ain't in too big a hurry." Kenny relaxed visibly.

"I gotta get right back, though. Lew's just finishing up some business and then he'll be ready to leave."

"You know Jud's gone?"

"Yeah, so I heard. Look," she said, "you come on upstairs with me while I pack, if you want to."

They went up the stairs quietly together and Kenny closed the door of Mary's room behind them. She turned on the light, and Kenny sat down in her big chair in front of the window. She knelt down by the bed and drew out from under it a trim overnight case and put it on the bed.

"Yeah," Kenny said. "Jud beat it outa here sometime last night, and we ain't seen nothing of him since. Tonight Ma got to feeling nervous, so the kid and me and Ernie took a look around, but hell, you don't know where to look for him."

Mary put silken underwear and cosmetics in the bag swiftly. "He wouldn't be down to Horning's this time, because Horning isn't home," she said.

"Yeah, I know it. There ain't no place else he'd be; must be he just figured on laying out outdoors some place till he got sobered up. This rain is gonna raise hell with him, if he's out in it."

Mary stood still reflectively with a delicate negligee draped over her arm. "I don't like the looks of it. If he isn't back here by morning, or nobody's seen him, you better get moving."

"That's what I figured," he said. He was silent a moment while she went on with her packing. "State Police?"

She nodded to him from the clothes-closet door. "By noon anyway, tomorrow. Ma won't want to, but you better."

Mary stripped the limp linen dress she was wearing over her head and hung it on a nail in the closet. She took a blue suit down from the wire hanger and threw it across the bed, and pulled a sheer white blouse down over her head. She fumbled with the buttons in the back and gave it up and put on the blue skirt. Kenny went over to her and she stood still with her arms at her sides while he buttoned the blouse. There were five tiny pearl buttons, but Kenny poked them through the little holes at last with his big brown fingers.

When he was through he returned to the chair, and she put on the blue jacket. "How's everything?" she asked him.

"So-so," he said with the familiar weary gesture of his hand. "I got a date with Rita Sibley tomorrow night."

She stood still with her hands at the last button at her throat. "Yeah?"

"Yeah."

Mary laughed then, as she had laughed once before when Kenny had spoken of Rita, a quick mirthless laugh.

"She may be an iceberg," Kenny said, smiling, "but there's a way to melt her down."

Mary went to the mirror and combed out her short silky hair, and set her hat at the right angle. She powdered her nose quickly and retouched her lips. She kicked off her shoes, inspected her hose seams and put on the pumps that matched the purse and gloves, laid out by the closed bag on the bed. Then she turned to Kenny. "I guess I'm ready."

"You look beautiful," Kenny said. He cupped her face in his hand and moistened one finger to his lip and ran it along her dark, shining, winged eyebrows, wiping away the tiny flecks of powder. She smiled at him, her rare childish sweet smile. He picked up the suitcase from the bed and followed her down the stairs.

At the door he gave her the suitcase, and she hesitated a moment with her hand on the door knob. "Have a good time, kid," he said. "Go buy a half a dozen new hats. They say it always makes a woman happy to buy hats. Go buy a dozen of 'em."

"I think I will," she answered. "They're showing fall hats in Detroit already. I think I'll buy a lot of hats. How do you think I'd look in a pill box with a snood?"

"I don't know what in hell a pill box with a snood is, but go ahead and get one. You'd look swell in it."

"I'll be back in a couple days," she said. "Three days at the most."

"You better."

She opened the door a crack, and looked back to him once more. "You can sleep in my bed," she said.

Kenny grinned across his face. "Thanks. I was gonna, anyway. Well, up at 'em, kid!" He caricatured a boxer's feint, with a slight motion of his body, and cocked his doubled fist at her chin. From outside the door, she ducked her head slightly and duplicated his gesture, but touching his chin briefly with her small doubled fist. She turned then and walked down the steps briskly, the suitcase in her hand, her back straight and her head up. The door of the long black car was opened for her. Hands reached out and lifted the suitcase over into the back seat. When she got in, the car drove away toward town.

Kenny closed the door, switched out the light and went back upstairs. He closed the door of Mary's room behind him and turned the bed down. He undressed leisurely and then tidied her dresser back into its usual order, wiping off the dust of powder along the edge. On the bed he found one of her filmy stockings. He crumpled it up in his hand, his face suddenly serious. He loosened his fingers carefully so that they might not snag the sheer chiffon and laid it gently down on the corner of the bureau. It did not look right to him there. He opened several drawers exploringly until he found one with a stack of silk hose piled neatly in a corner. He laid the lone chiffon stocking in on top of them and started to close the drawer. But still the stocking was out of place because there was only one of them. He searched the room for the mate to the lone stocking but he could find no trace of it. At last he gave it up. He took the stocking out of the drawer, closed it and stood helplessly with it in his hand. On an impulse he bent down and peered under the bed, as if he was making a last effort to produce the mate to that baffling lone stocking of Mary's. Then, as if disgusted at his own foolishness he suddenly crammed the stocking under the pillow on the bed and turned off the light.

9

THE RAIN WORE ITSELF OUT IN THE NIGHT, AND IN the morning the sun shone clear and hot. The air was close and unbreathable with the steam that rose from the wet ground.

Dorothy sat on the top stair step hunched over with the little tin box in her hands, the tin box that had contained her savings and that she had kept hidden away among the box of toys at the head of the stairway. The box was empty. She had found it empty when she came this morning to put in a nickel that Ernie had given her the night before. She was angry in hot and cold flashes, and she was wise enough to know that she could not complain about her loss to anyone without giving away the secret of her little hoard. She put the one lone nickel in the bottom of the tin box.

She was so angry that she sat there for nearly an hour, holding her breath from time to time until her heart pounded and she felt faint and sick. She suspected each of the family in turn. Most of all she was angry because she could not know for sure which one of them had done it and because she could think of no adequate way of getting even with anybody that did not involve telling her grandmother of the loss.

She got up finally and sneaked downstairs and out of the door, the little tin box hidden in her hands. She went down among the weeds in the back of the garden where she would be all to herself, and sat down. She wanted to writhe on the ground and scream with hatred. She wanted to hurt people, break things to pieces and set things on fire. She sat swaying back and forth with her eyes closed, her mouth wide open, shivering all over. She gripped the tin box so tight that it cut into her hands.

The bony old cat came ambling up out of the cool weeds headed in the general direction of the kitchen door. He stared at her out of his oblique, wise, old eyes, then went up to her and rubbed against her bare arm. The touch of his mangy fur startled the little girl and she opened her eyes.

A perfect scream of fury came up into her throat, but she did not make a sound. She dropped the tin box on the ground, grabbed the old cat by the neck with both hands and squeezed with all the strength that she had. The cat struggled for his life, twisting and clawing with his feeble strength. She threw her thin body on top of him, careless of the scratching claws that drew blood along her arms and hands, never releasing her fingers from around his neck. The motion went out of the cat's body finally, leaving it still and limp, but for a long time the child did not release her fingers from his neck. She let go at last and sat up. She did not look at the cat. She stared at her tiny, numbed fingers curiously and at the blood running down her arms and hands. She was tired and worn out. The heat seemed oppressive to her. She hid her face on top of her knees awhile, conscious of the stinging pain in her arms and of the ache in her head. She sat up at last, and this time she stared at the twisted limp body of the cat beside her on the grass. She took hold of one of his feet experimentally, and then she put her hand along the prominent rib bones where so many times she had felt his feeble old heart pounding. She stared at the body of the cat for a long time, her face impassive. Some of the blood from her scratches had dried on her arms and hands. A long smear of it along the side of her face and up into her pale hair had dried also. She got up on her knees and peered out through the weeds to the back of the house.

Then, still kneeling, she dug a little shallow pit in the ground with her hand, put the tin box in it and covered it over again. She picked the tender green tops from a couple of weeds above her, and laid them over the spot where she had hidden the box, crossing them carefully to make an X. Then, looking toward the house again, she furtively crawled through the weeds, dragging the cat's body behind her by his hind legs. By keeping to the weeds of the vacant lot she came out on the sidewalk about a block from the house. She picked up the cat then, carrying the body carelessly over her arm, as she had carried him many times before. The street was deserted in the heat. There were no cars along the pavement. She crossed the pavement and crawled under the fence to the railroad track. She walked up the track, in the deep grass beside it, until she was directly behind a large billboard that faced the pavement. Securely hidden by the billboard she climbed up the bank onto the railroad track. She looked cautiously in all directions to see that there was no train coming, or anybody watching her. There were three or four tracks together here. She studied them carefully and finally decided on one of the middle ones. She looked again in all directions, and then she squatted down and draped the limp body of the cat directly over the hot shining steel rail. She arranged the body carefully, the head hanging down inside the rail against the tie. She stood up breathing a deep sigh of relief. The creosote on the ties had melted in the sun, and stuck to her shoes, a black sticky substance. She wiped her shoes carefully in the thick grass and darted back across the pavement onto the sidewalk and ran toward home. As soon as she came in sight of the house she began to cry. The tears ran out of her eyes and streaked down her dirty face. The crying and the tears were genuine enough. She wept at the top of her voice, her whole body shaking. She ran up the front steps, past her startled grandfather into the house, and straight to Molly in the kitchen.

Molly caught the weeping child in her arms. "For Lord's sakes, what in the world you been doing? Why, child, you're all covered with blood. Did you fall down? Tell Grandma how you got hurt. Here, let me see. Why, something just like to scratched you nearly to pieces. Tell Grandma what happened to you, Dor'thy."

She went to the sink and wet a cloth with water and began to wipe the dirt and blood from the child's face, hands and arms.

Over her sobbing Dorothy talked incoherently. "The cat done it. The prettiest black and white cat, and it scratched me something awful. I just picked it up and wanted to pet it. I wasn't going to hurt it, and it scratched me something awful . . ."

Molly got the turpentine bottle out of the cupboard. "This is gonna smart just a minute, but then it will make you feel all better. There, hold still and let Grandma put it on your arms." She applied the turpentine liberally, and Dorothy danced and shrieked with the smarting of it, over the kitchen floor.

She gathered the weeping child into her arms again, pressing her against her big soft bosom. "There, there, now. Don't cry no more. You'll feel all better in a minute. Next time you see a strange cat don't you pick it up, 'cause some cats is ugly. You just don't want to have nothing to do with 'em. There, don't cry so. Why, I swear to Lord, she's just shaking something awful. There, there, don't cry so. Why, the poor little thing!"

10

THE STATE POLICE DID NOT LOCATE JUD HIGGINS after all, just as Kenny had suspected when he notified them. It was Mike Setlowe, or rather his dog, Pat, that found Jud lying under some bushes by the drainage ditch the other side of town that night just after sunset. The old man was unconscious, and Mike picked him up and took him home.

The family were gathered in the sitting room—Molly, Sam, Carl, Josette and Dorothy—when he arrived. Mike got out and Pat, the Irish setter, jumped out ahead of him, her beautiful tail pluming the air. Mike carried the shriveled body of Jud Higgins up the walk to the porch steps. They heard the sound of his feet on the steps, inside the house. All of them looked up nervously and stared, fascinated by what they saw. Pat came first to the screen, pressing her soft muzzle against it, and behind her came the great towering figure of Mike Setlowe carrying old Jud in his arms. The old man's head rolled limp against his chest. For a moment they were all perfectly still, staring in horror at the picture before their eyes.

Setlowe broke the silence irritably. "Will somebody please open the door, or do you want me to stand here and hold him all night?"

Carl moved first and opened the screen, his knees weak and shaking, staring furtively at old Jud's face.

"Oh, Lord, oh, Lord," Molly said, utterly bewildered.

Pat bounced through the door ahead of her master and shuttled back and forth from one to another of them, sniffing inquiringly.

Molly stumbled up out of her chair and stood helplessly by, her eyes on Jud's shriveled pinched face with the mouth hanging open, and the breath coming through it hoarsely.

Mike Setlowe looked at her irritably. "I think we had better put him in bed, Mrs. Veech, if you'll show me where to take him."

With the first shock over, strength and energy were coming back to Molly. "You can bring him right out here and put him in his own bed," she said. She led the way and Mike Setlowe and Pat followed her to the little bedroom. Molly switched on the light and hesitated, undecided whether or not to turn down the covers. While she was still wondering about it, Mike lay the old man gently on the blanket spread over the top of the bed. Molly pulled the pillow from under the blanket and put it under his head. She could not take her eyes off Jud's face. "For Lord's sakes, what's the matter with him?" she said tremulously to the big man.

"I think you had better call a doctor, Mrs. Veech. Do you have a telephone?"

Molly did not answer him. She picked up Jud's limp hand between her own and was rubbing it briskly, anxiously watching his face.

Mike Setlowe came out into the kitchen where the rest of the family stood aimlessly by, looking into the bedroom. He singled out Carl and walked over to him. "Do you have a telephone?" he asked.

"No," Carl said awkwardly.

"I was just saying to your mother that you ought to have a doctor right away. I think you better get one. I can take you on my way home."

"No," Carl said. "You don't have to. I'll go over to Doctor Biessels'. It's only about a block, I can run and be there in just a minute."

"You better tell the doctor to come right away; the old man's unconscious."

Carl nodded, and bolted out of the front door into the twilight.

He felt resentful toward Jud for all the trouble he was making and a little ashamed because he felt resentful. He wished fervently with the careless selfishness of the well and strong that if Jud was going to die he'd hurry up and get it over with.

This was the first time in his life that Carl had come in contact with illness, and he found it disgusting and upsetting. He foresaw that the whole house was to take on this new atmosphere.

The pompous little doctor came and went, leaving his envelopes of pills and labeled bottles behind. There seemed to be a number of things wrong with Jud Higgins. The doctor mentioned alcoholism vaguely, and shock, a fever from exposure, poisoning from insect bites, sunburn, possibly a sunstroke, and a high-blood-pressure condition. There was no cause for alarm, however, he said. He predicted that Jud would be delirious for several days, and then might very possibly exhibit some kind of temporary mental derangement for a few weeks, before he made a complete recovery.

In the days that followed, the entire household pivoted around Jud's sickroom, just as Carl had anticipated. Molly gave up all pretense of doing housework and remained in constant attendance upon him. The burden of the work therefore fell upon Jen, who complained about it bitterly. Meals became even more irregular than normally, and were generally scanty and ill-prepared.

Jud remained unconscious for several days, and then one morning he woke up in a more normal state of physical health, cheerful enough, but also, as the doctor had predicted, in a state of mental derangement. The family had had no previous experience that could prepare them for this. The old man's delusions made it a constant task to keep him quiet and in his bed. His constant rich and varying hallucinations crowded his bedroom continually with all manner of unexpected objects, people and animals.

Molly accepted his condition more readily than did any of the rest of them. Neighbors and townspeople that she had known all her life came to call on her in a steady stream offering their sympathy and assistance and bringing gifts of food. Molly came to enjoy it all. She talked with them for hours, basking in their interest and in the sense of her own affliction, entertaining them with long detailed accounts of Jud's latest exploits and aberrations.

* * *

Carl's birthday was approaching, and he was secretly excited about it. He had retained a childish delight in the anticipation of a cake and gifts. Furthermore, it was to be his eighteenth birthday, and for some reason it seemed to him to be a momentous occasion. It did not seem possible to him that the family could overlook it, but as it drew nearer he began to have a suspicion that they had forgotten it completely. And he was right. Not one of them thought of it.

The morning of his birthday confirmed his suspicions. There were no teasing references made to the date, no congratulations offered, and no veiled hints of secrets to come later. His feelings were deeply hurt. He was sure that they had forgotten about it only in the preoccupation over Jud, and that if they only knew that this was the day they would be only too anxious to celebrate it. But his pride forbade him to make any mention of the day to them.

He was so morose that Mr. Sneider teased him unmercifully all day. He had an impulse to confide his troubles to Sneider, but pride again interfered. The butcher was a kindly man. He would have undoubtedly given Carl the afternoon off had he but known the occasion and possibly would have handed him a dollar out of the cash drawer as well. But Carl was determined to suffer this out alone.

Kenny came home from Ashbury that morning and while his mother regaled him with a belated breakfast in the kitchen, Aunt Maggie Hoyer waddled in bearing a somewhat squashed four-layer cake covered with smeared sticky white frosting, and a great bouquet of flowers. Aunt Maggie had been in attendance upon Molly when every single one of the Veech children was born. They were just like her own children to her, she often proclaimed, and they had accorded her since childhood the courtesy title of Aunt Maggie.

Molly sank down into her chair in astonishment. "For Lord's sakes," she said. "Would you believe it, I clean forgot everything about today being that kid's birthday. I just had so much on my mind here, I never give it a thought. Why, sure enough, today's Carl's birthday and he's eighteen years old. Well, sir, none of us thought a thing about it. We ain't baked him a cake or bought him a present nor one single thing. You know, he was acting kind of funny at the breakfast table this morning. He kept scowling and you couldn't get a word out of him. I'll just bet you that's what was wrong with him. He could tell that we'd all forgot about this being his birthday."

Aunt Maggie was delighted. "You know, that was just what I was afraid of. I got to thinking about it last night and I says to myself, Now ten to one, Molly's so busy with Jud sick and all, she ain't never give it a thought. So I got up this morning and got a fire started in my cookstove and hustled around and made him a cake and picked him a big bouquet outa the garden and come on over here with 'em."

Kenny was inordinately concerned about it. "Damn it, Mom, we gotta have a party. We always have a big supper and stuff everybody's birthday. The kid's gonna take it something awful if we don't kind of make a fuss over his birthday."

"I know he is," Molly said. "But what we gonna do about it? I ain't got no time to fix no fancy supper nor nothing, and there ain't a soul of us that's bought him a present. You can't buy nothing here in town. I don't know what in the world we can do but just explain it all to him and kind of postpone things for a day or two!"

"Oh, hell, Mom, you can't do that. It ain't no fun having a birthday after it's all over with."

"Now that's just what I say, Kenny," Aunt Maggie said. "You know how kind of sensitive Carl is about things. It'll just bust him all up, telling him you forgot about today being his birthday."

"Well, I know it," Molly said, unwilling that anyone else should show more concern over one of her own children than she did. "But I just don't see what in the world we are gonna do about it."

"Mom, don't you give it another thought," Kenny said. "You just leave it to me and Aunt Maggie and we'll see to it that the kid has the best birthday today he ever had. How about it, Aunt Maggie?"

Aunt Maggie was only too glad to be taken into the Veech family affairs and Kenny was a particular favorite of hers. "Why, sure we will. You just say the word, Kenny, and anything I can do, you know I'm only too glad to do it."

"Well," he said, "suppose you get the dinner, huh? I'll get Jen home here to help you, and you do the cooking and fix up a fancy spread for tonight. I'll go downtown right away and buy everything you want. Then I'll kind of tip off everybody to be home here for supper. Ernie'll come all right, and Mary can get away if she knows about it."

"But what about the presents?" Molly asked.

"Oh, hell, that's easy. You can all give me the money and tell me what you want to get and I'll beat it up to Ashbury and buy everything all to once. Then I can get a ride home with Josie and Nina Warren at five o'clock."

His enthusiasm was contagious. Aunt Maggie started to roll up her sleeves. "Well, that's just what we'll do. I can cook up something nice for tonight easy, and we got the cake all baked. Why don't you have chicken, Molly? Chicken always cooks up nice and Carl likes it, and maybe we could have biscuits and gravy. That'd be something Jud could eat too."

"Atta girl!" Kenny said approvingly, getting up from the table himself.

The women planned the meal together, and Kenny went off downtown with a list of groceries to be bought. He talked to Ernie at the depot and collected money from him for an order of ice cream from the drugstore. He called Mary on the telephone from the beer garden, instead of going to the hotel to see her, and received an ample donation of money from her, sent over to him by a waiter from the hotel. He discussed the matter of presents with her over the telephone, and with his mother back at the house, and then he departed for Ashbury.

When Carl came home from work that night he found a bustle of activity around the house, and tempting smells from the kitchen floated out to meet him on the front porch. Inside the door, Aunt Maggie met him, enfolding him in a great warm embrace. She kissed him heartily and called him her baby, to his great embarrassment, and wished him a happy birthday. After his first spontaneous pleasure and relief to find that the family had not forgotten his birthday, as he had thought, his embarrassment at being so unwontedly the center of all attention grew. He began to wish fervently that the family had seen fit to ignore the occasion.

He was not used to so much attention. He did not know what to do with himself. In the kitchen, extra leaves had been added to the table and, considering the occasion, Molly had insisted that her best white linen tablecloth be used on it. Aunt Maggie put her bouquet of flowers in the middle of the table triumphantly, and the birthday cake beside it. During the course of the afternoon eighteen pink candles had been added to the slightly lopsided top of the cake.

Carl knew that he was in for a general family celebration when he saw Mary arrive. He was thankful that she had the decency to omit the beaming and kissing and hugging. She went immediately to the kitchen, donned a big apron, and went to work. A few moments later he saw Kenny and Josette arrive, mysteriously carrying a load of parcels through the back door.

By the time that Ernie arrived, he was as weak as a rag, and his dark eyes were distended in his pasty white face. He had reduced his conversation to the minimum, because he was afraid to trust his voice, which in times of embarrassment was apt to play tricks on him, wabble and waver, and cut off entirely. He wondered what would happen if he should faint right at the supper table.

In the kitchen Kenny was treating Molly to surreptitious peeps into the various packages while going about the task of painstakingly labeling each one of them. "Carl from Mother," "Carl from Father," and so on through the family. He whispered into her ear the details concerning the delivery of the ice cream, and he confided to her that they had better eat as soon as possible because he had to be back in Ashbury by seven-thirty at the very latest.

When Ernie arrived Kenny went out immediately and lugged in the two sacks of bottled beer that Ernie had brought for the occasion. The men all drank beer while they waited for supper, Carl slopping his down the front of his shirt in his anxiety to drink carelessly out of the bottle the way the rest of them did. Then, of course, he had to go upstairs and put on a clean shirt before they could go to the table. During his absence the packages were all smuggled in and deposited according to family tradition on Carl's chair, at the place of honor, just behind the birthday cake.

When they all trooped out to the table, Carl stood helplessly by his chair, staggered at the array of parcels, while the family beamed on him. It was Mary who suggested that he stack them on the floor and wait to open them until they were clearing the dishes, before they ate the cake. Carl was only too glad to postpone it. Once they began to eat the attention veered away from him, to his great relief, but even so he had no appetite at all for the meal that Aunt Maggie had prepared so painstakingly.

The bedroom door had been left wide open, and Jud, propped up on two pillows, so that he might look out on the festivities, took no notice of them whatsoever. He mumbled to himself occasionally and made strange motions with his gnarled old hands along the cover-let, completely occupied with the exigencies of this peculiarly engrossing mental life of his.

Molly, at the table, was mourning the disappearance of the old cat vociferously. "It's the funniest thing. I ain't seen hide nor hair of that cat since Mr. Higgins has been sick. He was getting to be such an old cat, it was getting so I was kind of afraid. This hot weather had been awful hard on him too. Lord, he wasn't nothing more'n skin and bones. I thought maybe he took sick and died out in the weeds somewheres, but Dor'thy's been looking for him all over. Course, he mighta got run over. You think he mighta got hit by a train, Ernie?"

"Hell, cats and dogs getting hit out there on that track every day."

"You ain't seen nothing of his body out there, have you?"

They roared all up and down the table at Molly's innocence.

"Hell, Mom," Ernie said seriously, "you can't tell one of them from another. If the train goes right over a cat like that there ain't enough of it left to tell what color it is hardly."

"Well, don't let's talk about it," Molly said. "Especially right at the table when we're eating."

Over the babble of voices Kenny spoke to Mary, beside him, softly, "I guess our party's going off all right, kid."

"Yeah," she said. It was the first word she had spoken since they sat down to the table.

Keeping her voice down under the other voices around the table she asked, "You going back up to Ashbury tonight?"

He nodded, "Yeah, I gotta. I'll have to be beating it outa here pretty soon, too."

"Dutch is going up from the hotel at a quarter of seven. Why don't you get up there and ride in with him?"

"Thanks," Kenny said. "I was just wondering where I was gonna hook me a ride."

He spoke again in a moment as if he were reluctant to let this intimate moment with her end. "I haven't been home enough to see you hardly at all. How's everything?"

"So-so, same old thing." She turned her shadowed eyes on his face. "You staying up to Ashbury?"

"Yeah."

"Mechanic Street?"

"Uh-huh."

She looked at the watch on her wrist. "You better not stay for cake, if you're going up with Dutch."

"I'll sneak out right now, nobody ain't gonna miss me."

Molly and Aunt Maggie and Jen were already clearing away the plates and food, and there was a great deal of confusion as Carl lifted his packages up onto the table.

Kenny lingered a moment by Mary's chair.

"Have fun," she said, looking up at him.

She made the familiar half motion of her body imitating the boxer's feint, cocking her fist at his jaw. Kenny smiled with her, and replied in the traditional manner. Then he slipped out of the kitchen door.

Carl unwrapped his packages with trembling awkward fingers, while the family looked on delightedly. Most of the gifts were the ever-practical ones of shirts, socks, handkerchiefs and neckties. Ernie's gift, when opened, excited so much interest and comment that Ernie felt called upon to demonstrate its peculiar virtues on the spot. It was a mechanical pencil complete with a new package of leads. It was made of glass, which revealed all of the inner workings of its mechanics plainly to the astonished eye. The most unusual feature about it, however, was that by the pressure of writing the amazing pencil shed a little pool of light around its point. It was a pencil, Ernie explained, to use for writing in the dark. Only Jen was unable to conceal her bewilderment. "What in God's name would anybody ever want to write in the dark for, anyway?"

Ernie gave her a withering look, and let her question go unanswered as being too stupid even to notice. But everything that came after this extraordinary gift of Ernie's was bound to appear anticlimactic.

Of the three packages yet unopened, two large ones and a small one, Carl opened next the largest one of all. It was marked with Dorothy's name and it contained a carton of Mary's own expensive and mild cigarettes. Mary's own gift was contained in the small package. It was a fine leather wallet, and in the pocket for bills there was enclosed a five-dollar bill.

The last package of all, marked with Kenny's name, contained a cheap camera, a roll of film and an instruction book on the art of camera angle shots.

After that, the candles on the cake were lighted, and Jen led them off in singing "Happy birthday to you."

With the meal finally over, Molly divided the family and suggested that those who were to be excused from doing dishes should play cards. Ernie, Sam, Mary and Carl started a game of rummy around the center table in the sitting room.

11

SEVERAL HOURS LATER KENNY FOLLOWED RITA SIBley out of the cheap hotel on Mechanic Street in Ashbury where he had kept a room for the last couple of weeks. He was at that moment somewhat weary of Rita. They had ordered liquor several times in the course of the evening and he suspected that Rita had by far exceeded her capacity. Furthermore, one of her baffling, difficult moods had come over her. When she had proposed leaving he had been frankly thankful, looking forward to a good night's sleep, with her out of the room and away from him. But she had insisted that he come out with her for a ride before she returned home. Rita, after the course of recent developments in their relationship, was becoming far too possessive to suit him. He was weary of her now. She no longer retained anything that could interest him. He wondered why it was that women never could see when something was played out and over with; or was it that they never would admit it to themselves, even when they did see it? Why should any woman ever want to prolong a relationship from which the zest and pleasure were completely exhausted? That problem was too much for him, and he abandoned it. His own mind, he admitted, was not quite as clear as it might be. He was not used to these expensive liquors that Rita ordered.

Out on the street, Rita linked her arm through his, and walked with her body close up against him. "Oh, it's such a beautiful night," she said. She stopped still and raised her face up to the sky. "Just look, Kenny. Oh, it's such a beautiful night!"

There was a dry hot wind that seemed to have blown bright more stars in the dark sky than he had ever seen before. But Kenny was preoccupied instead with finding her car and getting Rita into it. The ambling, incurious passers-by who frequented the sidewalks in this area of the city moved out around them, with no more than a glance at them. Rita was wearing a white silk suit, and the reflected electric light turned her hair as light as the suit, bringing out a startling contrast with her smooth dark skin.

He closed his fingers on her arm and started her walking again. "Come on, there's the car right over there."

"Kenny," she said solemnly. "You have no soul at all in you, have you? Do you know what the trouble with me is? I've got too much soul. All my life I've had too much soul."

They came to the car then, and she stood and waited while he unlocked it, with the strong wind billowing her skirt. He held the door for her to get in and said, "Why don't you let me drive, honey?"

"No, I want to drive. I love to drive. It's the only thing in the world that I can do really well. It's so neat, driving; all precision and no mess."

Rita never seemed less appealing to him than when she talked around things as she was doing now, circling continually, and covering things over with wordy artificial language.

"You don't want to drive tonight," he urged. "You just want to sit side of me with the wind blowing your hair, and look at the stars."

She laughed. "You are so simple, Kenny. The only time that you ever say poetic things like that is when you want something. You think I'm drunk, don't you? Well, I'm not. I'm cold stone sober. I wish I were drunk. But I'm not, and I'm going to drive myself."

"Okay," he said. "Go ahead and drive if you want to." She stepped by him to get into the car. "Wait a minute," he said deliberately. The zipper fastener on the side of her skirt was gaping open, unfastened. He zipped it up, with a smooth rippling sound. Rita watched him do it and a flush of color came up in her face.

He got in beside her and slammed the door. As she started the car she said, "Do you know what Bill Saroyan says about love, Kenny? He's right about it, too. He says that love is a lot too good for people. It's all right for the birds and the bees, he says, but it's a lot too good for people."

Kenny was in no mood for philosophical discussion about love. "Where you gonna go?" he asked her, as the car slid away from the curb.

"I don't care, any place, but out of the city. I don't want to go any place. I just want to drive."

He was somewhat relieved to see that she handled the car with her usual adeptness. The cool air evidently wasn't going to have the effect on her that he had anticipated.

She crisscrossed through the city toward the outskirts, and neither one of them said anything for a long time. At last she said to him, "Kenny, what do you think about when you just sit still and quiet like that?"

The wind was blowing hard through the car, because Rita had rolled the windows down on both sides, and it blew the smoke from his cigarette back into his eyes, smarting them.

"I don't know. I guess I wasn't thinking about nothing. I was just setting here watching the lights shine on the road and feeling the wind blow. I always get a kick outa riding. I wasn't thinking about nothing."

"I might have known it," she mourned. "You are the luckiest person I know of. It's just natural for you to feel always, instead of think. As for me, I can't help myself. I have to think all the time, so that I hardly ever have time to feel."

He did not understand what she was talking about, and he liked her less when she talked. She looked very attractive though, at that moment. She was smiling, her eyes on the road, the wind lifting her hair. On an impulse he reached out to her forehead and gently brushed the hair back from her eyes.

She turned to him immediately at his touch. "I think I can come in again tomorrow night," she said lovingly.

Immediately he regretted the gesture that had made them suddenly more intimate. "Well, I don't know," he said. "I don't think I'll be in tomorrow night. I got some real important business to attend to that's gonna keep me tied up till real late. You hadn't better come in tomorrow night." This was the first time he had ever refused an offer of hers to see him. Kenny disliked this stage of the game particularly: the tapering-off process, for now all of the zest was gone. He felt only impatience to get to the end of it, and when you are bored and impatient it requires a great deal of skill to keep the timing right, he had learned long ago.

He was not prepared for the effect that his words were to have on Rita Sibley. They were driving along a wide gravel road with the outskirts of Ashbury behind them. She stepped on the accelerator hard, sending up a hail of gravel stones against the sides of the car. Her speech became less controlled; it was rapid and fluid. "Kenny, don't say that, don't, don't. Don't change your feeling about me. Don't get tired of me, Kenny, because I can't stand it if you do. I tell you I can't stand it. You loved me, Kenny, you know you did, and I gave you everything I had to give, more than I've ever given before in my life. Don't say now that you're sick of it, and tired of me, because I can't stand that, I tell you."

She was driving the car too fast, the wheels sliding in the loose gravel, and from her sudden burst of uncontrolled speech he thought that the liquor was beginning to show its effect on her at last. "Now, Rita honey," he said. "Don't get so excited and talk like that. Why don't you let me drive awhile and we'll talk this over?"

"Don't touch me," she said. "Take your hands away from me." She was driving the car like a crazy woman down the middle of the road while the speedometer ticked steadily upward.

Kenny felt no fear, but he had an intuition of danger. He

searched for words to placate her. "Look, Rita, there's no sense you acting like a fool about this. I just said I was gonna be busy tomorrow night. I had some business to see to, but if you're gonna take it like this, why, I can let it go. You can come tomorrow night if you want to."

"Shut up," she said. "Don't go on talking; you only make it worse."

Her face was stretched taut, like a mask, and her eyes were half closed against the wind that rushed through the car, blowing her words back into her mouth, so that her voice was twisted and unrecognizable. She hunched down over the steering wheel talking loudly and wildly. "Kenny what's the matter with me? Tell me, just tell me, why don't you? Why am I different than other women? Why do all men get tired of me? Men fall in love with other women and keep right on loving them all of their lives. But what is the matter with me? Why am I different? What do I lack that other women have? Why don't you tell me? All my life I've wanted somebody to love me and keep right on loving me, but they never do. They get tired of me."

"Stop talking rot," he said angrily, "and look where you're driving. If you don't slow down you're gonna turn this car over."

"It isn't rot; it's the truth and you know it. There's something wrong with me. I married Ernie and look what happened. He got tired of me and started going to other women. I divorced him and after that I met a lot of men, but what happened? After two or three months they went on to some other woman. I married Joe, and I thought that was different, but Joe got tired of me too. He's tired of me right now. He doesn't care whether he's married to me or not. He stays away from home all the time, hanging around up there in Ashbury. I hardly see him for days and days."

"Damn it," Kenny said, "will you stop the hollering and look what you're doing?" His mind was moving swiftly. He wondered if he dared risk trying to get the steering wheel away from her. Her hands were clenched on it with all of her strength, and at the speed the car was traveling he did not dare take the risk of struggling with her for the wheel. The same problem faced him if he attempted to pry her foot loose from the accelerator. Any struggle at all at the speed they were traveling would be fatal, and to touch the brake was out of the question in the loose gravel. She was a good driver, and perhaps she would have sense enough to keep the car in the road herself, but it was a long-shot gamble, but a long shot either way. He tensed his body and kept his eyes on the road ahead and weighted the comparative odds desperately.

"And now you, Kenny Veech," she said. "Now you've got sick of me too. Well, there's one thing I want you to know right now. I never loved you, don't ever fool yourself. You're nothing but a crude, uneducated, rotten bum. Do you think I'd ever love a man like you?" She laughed bitterly. "I was just playing with you, all the time. I was just using you for an experiment. I wanted to prove to myself that I had what it takes to make a man want me and keep on wanting me. Well, I found out all right, didn't I?"

Her words roused an anger in Kenny that temporarily quelled his anxiety over whether or not she would be able to keep the car in the road. "You bet you, you found out, all right!" he shouted at her, over the roar of the wind and the clattering gravel stones. "And don't you ever fool yourself that I ever was in love with you either. I wanted to make you, that's all, and I did. And it was easy, so God-damn easy. You ain't got a God-damn thing to make any man love you. You don't never think about nothing on earth but yourself. You never loved no man in your life. All you love is yourself. You're all the time wanting men to love you just because it makes you feel good, that's all. You think you can get something for nothing, but let me tell you right now you can't. You gotta pay for every damn thing you get in this world and give something right back. That's what's the matter with you. Why, hell, you ain't no kind of a woman at all."

"Stop it," she screamed. "Stop it, I won't have you talking to me like this. Why, who do you think you are, you low-down, good-for-nothing . . ."

"You shut your mouth and listen. You kept asking me what's the matter with you. Well, I'm gonna tell you. You ain't no kind of woman at all. You never give nothing to no man in your life. Remember when Ernie wanted you to have a baby? But you didn't want no kids, and you seen to it too, didn't you, that you didn't have any? Sure, you did. You want something for nothing all the time. You want some man to love you just so it makes you feel good, but you want to cheat outa paying for it. And you can quit your bellyaching to me about Joe Sibley, too. Joe Sibley is so God-damn much better than you are that it ain't even funny. Joe Sibley is working his heart out up to Ashbury every day of his life, trying to get a break for a lotta guys workin' up there in them factories. He ain't setting around all the time thinking about himself. You ain't no kind of woman at all. Why, hell, you ain't even as much a woman as a common whore in a whore house, because even they know they gotta give something to get their money."

He stopped for breath and Rita Sibley screamed incoherent words at him in her rage. And then she stopped talking and just screamed, holding her breath and shutting her eyes tight.

Kenny tensed his body to lunge for the wheel, but it was too late. He saw all kinds of kaleidoscopic things in that second after the car slid crazily in the loose gravel along the edge of the road. He saw the cement abutment on the bridge over the dry stream bed; he saw the stars blown bright all over the sky; he saw the wide white gravel road that they had left winding away among the dark hills and gullies under the stars. And just as the great crash came that shut all other sounds and sights and feelings out of his consciousness, he opened the catch on the door on his side of the car and said Mary's name like a prayer, and then everything was gone from him. The car broke and folded together against the cement abutment, and catapulted over like a child's toy thrown carelessly aside. And as it rolled, the door on Kenny's side came open and his limp body was hurled aside into the darkness and the car rolled on, and came to rest at last at the bottom of the bank, the two rear wheels of it that were still intact, spinning and spinning in the darkness.

At home the birthday party was breaking up. The rummy game had given way to general conversation, and after that Molly had insisted over everyone's protests on making coffee and eating the remains of the cake. Ernie had offered to take Aunt Maggie home and she and Molly went to the kitchen to find her empty cake plate. Mary and Dorothy climbed the stairs. Dorothy did not know her mother very well, and she was silent and suspicious when she was with her. Mary herself did not vary her manner with her daughter from that which she showed any adult in the family, outside of Kenny. In silence she assisted the child to undress and, just as she was tucking her into her bed, quick footsteps sounded on the front porch and someone knocked furiously on the door.

At the sound, Mary turned and ran down the stairs, stopping midway to listen to the torrent of words that an excited boy was pouring out to the family. "Say, Mrs. Veech, Central just called our house on the telephone and wanted us to come over here and tell you folks quick. They just telephoned down here from Ashbury to get hold of some of you folks. Kenny's been in an awful automobile accident and he's up to Ashbury in Receiving Hospital right now. They said he was awful bad hurt and there was some woman with him and she's terrible bad hurt and gonna die, and they don't know who she is, and they thought maybe you folks would know if she was anybody from town or not because they want to get hold of her folks quick too, but they can't tell who she is. They said some of you folks better come up to the hospital right away."

Molly's face crumpled up and she began to sob before the boy was half through talking. "Oh, Kenny, Kenny! What are we going to do? What are we ever going to do?"

Mary on the stairs heard the news with an expressionless face, only her hand on the guard rail clenched tighter for a second. Then she turned around and ran up the stairs to her room where she tidied her hair mechanically, powdered her nose and slipped on a coat and hat.

Downstairs she found a babble of sound. Molly was weeping and Sam was trying to quiet her. Jen also was crying noisily and Josette, white-faced, was saying over and over to Carl, "I always knew that something like this would happen to Kenny. I wonder who the woman is. I wonder if it could be anybody here from town. I'll bet you anything they had been drinking. I'll bet you anything."

"Carl," Molly sobbed. "Go get Ernie quick, go on and get Ernie. Somebody's gotta go right up there to that hospital right away."

Mary shook her head at Carl. "Don't cry, Mom. You can't help Kenny any by letting yourself get all upset. Ernie will be back here in just a minute and then he and I will go right up to the hospital."

"Well, why don't Ernie come?" Molly sobbed.

They all waited together nervously for Ernie to come back. Molly began to cry louder as the minutes dragged by. "Oh, why did it have to be Kenny? I could stand it better if it had been anybody else but Kenny. I just couldn't stand it if anything should happen to him."

"Shshshsh," Sam said nervously. "You don't want to talk like that. You don't want to say anything now you'll be sorry for later. You'd feel just like this if anything happened to any of the kids."

"No, I wouldn't," Molly said angrily. "Not the way I feel about Kenny."

The disturbance woke up old Jud, and for once the sounds about him seemed to penetrate his consciousness. He began to yell at the top of his voice and pound on the head of the bed with his fists.

In the midst of the clamor, Ernie arrived, but none of them heard him. He opened the door and stopped in astonishment. "For God's sake, what in hell has gone wrong around here?"

"Ernie," Molly called to him wildly from Jud's bedroom. "Kenny's been hurt terrible bad. He's up to Ashbury in a hospital. You got to go up there right away."

Ernie's face turned sardonic for a moment and the look of it chilled Carl through. "So Kenny got hurt, huh?"

"Automobile smash," Mary said. "Let's get going." At the door she called back to her mother. "Now, take it easy, Mom. Just as soon as I can I'll telephone back here to Jones' and the kid can run over and tell you."

Ernie and Mary went out to the car together. "Well, I don't know as I'm surprised any," Ernie said. "If ever a guy was heading for trouble Kenny was the one."

"I want to go back to the hotel a minute first," Mary said briefly.

When they reached the hotel, she got out of the car and ran in the front door. The taproom was deserted except for a couple of waiters. She went directly to the door of Lew Lentz's office without speaking to anyone.

Lew was at his desk when she came in, his coat neatly draped over the back of a chair, and the electric fan humming. She came up to his desk. "Kenny's been badly hurt in an accident. He's up to Ashbury in the hospital."

Lew Lentz's pale blue eyes gleamed a little, but his face and voice were impassive. "Well, isn't that too bad," he said softly, looking straight into her face.

They looked at each other quietly. The brown shadows were deeper around Mary's eyes, but her soft pink crumpled lips were quiet. She looked straight at him, without moving, only the little pulse in her throat moving quickly in and out. But Lew Lentz returned her look without flinching, and his eyes did not turn away before hers.

"Did you expect me to bust out crying?" Lew said. "Hell, I hope he dies. If it wasn't for him hanging around here and the way you feel about him, we'd be married now."

After a moment she spoke softly without taking her eyes from his face. "There are other places where I can get the money I need, if I have to."

Lew Lentz's eyes became expressionless, and he got to his feet. "Oh, hell, I'll give you all the money you want," he said. "But if he's hurt as bad as I hope he is, all the money on God's earth won't save him."

He went to the safe in the corner and twirled the combination dials while she waited. He came to her with a packet of bills, and she put them into her purse without looking at them.

He stood close to her. He was a short thick man, only several inches taller than Mary herself. "One other thing," she said. "I wish you'd get on the phone right away and see if you can get hold of Joe Sibley in Ashbury. You wouldn't get him at the shop now, but if you call Jimmy Martin's I think his wife would know where you could get hold of him. Tell Joe to get over to Receiving Hospital right away. They don't think that his wife is going to live."

"Oh," Lentz said, "so that's how it is. Isn't that just lovely? Maybe we can hang a drunk-driving-manslaughter charge around his neck before we're through with this."

"Don't worry about it," Mary said. "I imagine Rita Sibley was driving her own car, all right."

"Well, we'll see," Lew said. "Don't worry, I'll have Joe over there by the time you are."

He put his arms around her and kissed her on the mouth lingeringly. She disengaged his arms from around her and walked to the door. As she went out he said to her caressingly, "Don't hurry so, Mary. I hope you'll be too late."

She ran out of the hotel and back to Ernie's car. "Step on it now," she said as she got in.

Ernie needed no encouragement. He sent the car hurtling over the road toward Ashbury. "Receiving's the big hospital this side of the city, ain't it?"

"Yes," Mary said.

"They tell you anything about the accident?" he asked.

"No, just that it was an automobile accident, and that Kenny was badly hurt. There was a woman with him that they don't think is gonna live. They haven't identified her yet, and they thought maybe she was somebody we knew."

"Damn, I hope Kenny wasn't driving the car," Ernie said. After a moment he asked cautiously, "You got any idea who the woman is?"

"Yes," Mary said quietly, looking at him as she spoke. "The woman is Rita Sibley."

Ernie's face did not change expression at all, nor did his voice. "Then I figure she was driving, all right. She drives something awful. It's a wonder she hasn't got smashed up before this."

He kept his eyes straight on the road ahead of him. "You know, I been hearing some talk around about Kenny and her, but I never believed there was nothing to it."

"It's true, all right," Mary said briefly.

Ernie laughed his dry unpleasant laugh. "Well, what do you know! So old Kenny made Rita, huh?"

Mary did not answer him and neither one of them spoke until they were at the hospital.

They left the automobile in the parking lot and went in the door of the big hospital together. In the vast cool efficient interior, Ernie was plainly embarrassed and out of place. Mary went to the information desk and stated her name and business directly. The crisp, white-garbed woman behind the desk consulted her cards and looked at Mary curiously while she talked. "Your brother's condition is not really serious, Miss Veech. He was unconscious when he came in here, of course. He has some smashed ribs and a broken collar bone and a bump on his head that we can't be sure about until after the X-rays."

"Thank you," Mary said coolly. "Is there a telephone around here that I could use, please?"

"Right over there," the attendant said with her brisk smile. Apparently she enjoyed an opportunity to talk. "Your brother is a lucky fellow, Miss Veech," she said. "The automobile, they say, is smashed to pieces and the young woman with him is in a very bad condition. Would you be able to give us her name and address? Unless you have some idea who was with him, you couldn't, of course, her face was cut so badly. Anyway, your brother can tell us as soon as he comes out from his anesthetic."

Mary evaded the question that had been asked her, but she walked back to the information desk at a sudden thought. "I wonder if you can tell me how my brother was identified?" she asked.

"Certainly," the woman said. "From a hotel-room key in his pocket. It's easy to identify a hotel-room key in a city the size of this one. It was from a small hotel on Mechanic Street. The proprietor came over here and he identified your brother, and from the clothing that was on the woman when she came in he was able to identify her as a woman who visited Mr. Veech often at the hotel. They had left the hotel together earlier tonight."

"I suppose all that was reported in plenty of time to make the morning newspapers," Mary said softly.

The woman's bearing changed perceptibly and her voice became much crisper. "Miss Veech," she said, "both our records pertaining to accidents such as this and the records of the police are available to the city newspapers. I hope that you did not mean your remark the way that it sounded."

"I am not responsible for the way I sounded to you," Mary answered. "I just asked you a question."

She turned away with Ernie following her and walked across the marble floor with her high heels clicking.

"This is sure gonna make a sweet story for the papers, all right," Ernie said as she entered the telephone booth.

After she had sent a brief message to her mother reporting

Kenny's condition, they went to take the elevator to the second floor. But before they got to the lift they saw Joe Sibley come in the front entrance and stand a moment, uncertain in the large interior.

Mary called out to him instantly. "Kenny's on the second floor, Joe," she said meaningly. "You can come up with us, if you want to."

Joe Sibley looked at her oddly, a flush of color over his thin face. Then he stepped into the elevator behind Mary and Ernie.

"How is she?" he asked.

"I don't know," Mary said. "I guess we can find out up here. She hasn't been identified for sure yet. I'm afraid the papers are gonna make kind of a bad story out of this, and I don't see what we can do about it."

Joe Sibley's face was expressionless. "How did it happen? How bad a story?"

"I don't know, except that it was a bad automobile crash." She looked at him hard for a moment. "The man that runs the hotel over on Mechanic Street where Kenny had a room, come over here and identified him, and shot off his mouth a lot."

"You mean . . ."

She nodded. "Yeah, he identified Rita by her clothes as a woman who had visited Kenny at the hotel. I know the papers have got hold of that much for sure."

"Then I don't see as we can do anything about it," Joe Sibley said. "I'll have to identify her and the papers will have to go ahead and print what they want to."

They stood together talking in front of the elevator on the second floor and Ernie kept staring at Joe Sibley covertly as he talked to Mary.

Mary touched Joe Sibley's arm. "If I had only got up here an hour sooner," she said.

"It isn't your fault," Joe said. "There isn't a thing you could have done."

"Will this be bad for your work?" Mary asked him.

Joe Sibley looked at her with gratitude on his face. "It won't help it none," he said. "It'll give the papers a big chance to print a lot of dirt about me. They just wait for chances like this to get in a lot of dirty digs, that's what the papers are like in this town."

Mary and Joe walked up to the supervisor's desk and faced the kindly, gray-haired woman.

"I'm Mary Veech, and I want to know how my brother Kenneth Veech is, please. He was hurt in an automobile accident tonight."

"Oh, yes," the woman said. "Your brother is coming along fine, Miss Veech. His injuries weren't serious and he is resting comfortably now. He has been asking for you. You may see him for a few minutes if you like."

"If you please," Mary said.

As Mary turned back to Ernie, she heard Joe Sibley say in a loud clear voice, "I would like to know how my wife is. Her name is Rita Sibley, and she is the woman that was in the same accident as Kenneth Veech."

The supervisor hesitated for just a moment. "Ah, yes, Mr. Sibley. We have been trying to locate you. Mr. Veech gave us your wife's name and address just a few moments ago. Her condition is very grave. You see . . ."

"I am going to see him for a minute," Mary said to Ernie, and then she followed the nurse down the dimly lighted corridor between the clean closed doors. The nurse's rubber soles made no sound at all, but Mary's heels made a sharp decisive clicking. The air was saturated with a strong antiseptic smell. Mary looked at all of the doors along the corridor, plain closed doors, with so much suffering behind them.

The nurse opened one on the left side of the hall and stepped aside for Mary to enter. The room, little more than a cubicle, was clean and cheerless. "Here is your sister to see you, Mr. Veech. But you mustn't try to talk to her too much."

Kenny was lying slightly propped up on a high narrow bed. One of his arms was in a sling and there was a bandage around his head. His eyes were closed when they entered, but he opened them wide immediately and grinned at Mary. "Hello, kid," he said.

Mary went to the edge of the bed, stood close to him and touched her hand against his cheek. "How do you feel?"

"I feel swell. I got a little headache, that's all. I musta bumped my head—and I'm as hungry as all hell. You oughta see all the adhesive tape they got on me. I'll leave it to the nurse they got about two yards of that stuff on me."

The nurse, hovering in the doorway, smiled slightly at his words. "Can I have a cigarette?" he asked her. "Just one, please?"

"I think you might, if you want one," she said. She withdrew from the room and as she closed the door she said to Mary, "I'll come for you in a few minutes. We want him to go to sleep as soon as possible."

Kenny grinned at Mary dolefully. "And they always tell stories about beautiful nurses!"

Mary struck a match for his cigarette silently. "Tastes good," he said.

"You're doing all the talking," she said. "I'm the one that's supposed to do the talking."

"Okay, shoot."

She smiled at him and lit a cigarette for herself.

He looked away to the wall for a moment and at last he asked quietly, "How is she? They wouldn't tell me nothing about how she was."

Mary hesitated. "I don't know."

"Spill it," he said. "Is she dead? I don't see myself how she could still be living after that. If I hadn't got throwed out before the car quit rolling I wouldn't be here. That's the last thing I remember, getting throwed out."

"She's still alive," Mary said, "and I guess that's about all."

He moved his head a little in a half nod, and inhaled his cigarette deeply. "Musta rammed that steering wheel right through her. Car musta struck hardest on her side too."

"She was driving then?"

"Hell, yes. If she hadn't a-been driving, I wouldn't be in the hospital. We'd been drinking some, just enough so they probably will give it a nice drunk-driving write-up in all the papers."

"She was drunk then," Mary said slowly as if she was trying to reconstruct what had happened. "And she lost control of the car."

"She might have been drunk, but she wasn't that drunk. She was mad, that's mostly what was wrong with her. She was mad at me and driving like hell. She had a regular temper tantrum and she run the car into a cement bridge abutment. Because she got so mad she started screaming and shut her eyes. Shut her eyes, right at the wheel, driving eighty-five, ninety miles an hour. She went nuts. You can figure out yourself what was burning her up."

Mary nodded.

"Now look," he said, hunching up a little on his pillows. "We gotta talk fast. That damn fool of a nurse is gonna be back here chasing you out in a minute. How come you got up here so soon? How come they got me identified so quick?"

"Hotel key," she answered significantly.

Kenny whistled a little. "Oh, my God! What a story for the newspapers!"

"Yeah. They'll smear it all over the morning edition. If it tore the car to pieces they'll even have pictures."

"Then there ain't nothing we can do. Hell, when they asked me who she was I told 'em right away. I figured it would be worse if I didn't. Besides, I didn't know that damn son of a bitch from the hotel had been over here shooting off his mouth about her."

"It isn't your fault," Mary said.

He looked at the door anxiously, as if he expected to see the nurse coming in at any moment. "How about Joe?"

"He came up in the elevator with us. The trouble is they'll give this a big smear in the papers on account of Joe being mixed up with the labor unions and stuff here in Ashbury. They'll throw a lot of dirt just because she is his wife."

"Damn it to hell!" Kenny said. "When the papers get done with this if she ain't dead she'll wish she had died."

Mary took hold of his hand and squeezed it hard, and just then the nurse opened the door. "I think you had better go, Miss Veech. Your brother needs rest and sleep."

Kenny clung to Mary's hand and talked fast. "Don't you worry about this none. It's all over and done with, and it's too late to do anything about it now. Me! I'm not worried. Hell, it's too good to be alive to worry none about nothing. Tell Joe—you know what— and . . ."

"Mr. Veech!" the thin light-haired nurse opened her prominent blue eyes even wider. "You must not talk so much. You mustn't let yourself get so excited."

"Yeah, I know. Take it easy," he said to her impatiently, "and I'll be outa here and home tomorrow afternoon. The doc said if everything was all right I could come home tomorrow. Just gotta tote my arm in a sling on account of a crack in my collar bone."

"Mr. Veech, I insist," the nurse said. "If you aren't quiet and get some rest you won't be going home tomorrow."

"And don't forget to tell Joe, and listen, maybe you better save all the morning papers for me, and . . ."

Kenny and Mary smiled together while the nurse made ineffectual shooing gestures.

Mary rocked back on her heels, and slid into the old familiar gesture, cocking her fist at Kenny in the bed. Kenny in return clasped his two hands together and shook them at her gently and solemnly.

Mary was gone then, and while the nurse fussed around the bed, Kenny sighed deeply, still smiling, his eyes on the door through which Mary had disappeared. "No wonder you were so anxious to see your sister," the nurse said conversationally. "She seems to be a charming and beautiful woman. I hope that her visit hasn't tired you too much though."

"Oh, hell," he said. "I feel fine. I can sleep now."

The nurse smiled at him warmly. "You really look better. I think seeing your sister was good for you."

She slid a thermometer into his mouth and while she waited she said, "You know, having a sister like that must make it hard for a young man. Finding a wife, I mean, that could measure up to her."

Kenny looked up dumbly at the smiling, simpering nurse with clouded eyes.

Mary joined Ernie in the corridor again. "How is he?" he asked.

She smiled shortly. "He seems to be feeling pretty good. He says he's coming home tomorrow."

"He does, huh?" Ernie smiled appreciatively. "Well, it takes a lot to kill a Veech."

They walked toward the elevator and Mary hesitated a little. She saw Joe Sibley suddenly coming up from the other end of the corridor and she went to meet him, while Ernie waited.

"How is she?"

Joe looked at her wonderingly, his clear brown eyes looked more unbelieving than suffering. "God, she's just broke all to pieces. The doctors say she hasn't got hardly any chance at all. She's broke up through here," he passed his hand over his chest. "Even her jaws are broken—they're going to wire 'em—and her nose was broken. She got cut awful bad too, all over her face and neck and head. She's still unconscious. They just let me look in at her. Her whole face and head is covered with bandages. I don't see how she breathes. No skull fracture, though. They say that she is strong and young and she's got a better chance than lots of people would have. But I don't see how she can."

Mary said nothing.

After awhile she said, "Joe, Kenny wanted me to say something to you. I think you already know most of what he wanted me to say, yourself."

Joe's face was strained and expressionless. "How is he?" he said briefly.

"Pretty good. He says he's coming home tomorrow."

Joe made a funny noise in his throat that might have been a laugh.

Mary looked down to the shiny toes of her shoes, very black against the plain white floor. She stood there silently beside Joe Sibley. At last she looked at him again and her eyes were dark in the dim light. She put her hand out to his arm. "Joe, I'm sorry. That's all I can say. I'm sorry."

"Thanks," Joe Sibley said. "You're all right, Miss Veech. I'm not blaming you; none of this is anything you could help. Your brother, a man like your brother . . ." Joe's face showed anger suddenly, and more than anger, a kind of helplessness. "I don't know what to say about him, a man like your brother. Why, it seems like he's no good to society or himself or anybody. Oh, you needn't worry. I'm not gonna beat him up, or anything; it wouldn't do any good. He isn't even worth that . . ."

Mary closed her fingers tight on Joe's arm, and then she turned away. She walked into the elevator with a sleepy and disgruntled Ernie. "Hell, I thought you was never coming," he said. "I gotta get home and get some sleep. I'm a working man. I ain't used to staying up all night."

He nearly drove the wheels off the car going back to the village, yawning deep and wide from time to time. When Mary got home, as she expected, she found a sleepy anxious family waiting up for her. As soon as she came in the door they bombarded her with questions. "How is he? Did they let you see him? Did he tell you how it happened? How does he feel? Who was the woman with him? Is she going to die? Was he driving the car? When can he come home?"

Mary took off her hat, threw it on the center table and loosened the hair back from her face. She selected some of the questions and answered them, speaking wearily, like a child reciting a piece that she has repeated too many times already. "He's feeling pretty good. They let me talk to him for a few minutes. The accident didn't seem to upset him much. He says he is coming home tomorrow, and I guess he can all right, unless he gets worse."

Molly noticed the fatigue in Mary's face and she said, "Why, you look all tuckered out. It's been hard on you going up there, and everything. The rest of you all keep still and quit asking her questions all at once. You set right down here, Mary, and let me get you a cup of hot coffee. That'll make you feel better right away."

Mary sat down obediently and Molly bustled out to the kitchen, returning in a minute or two with a cup of steaming black coffee. Molly had a cup of coffee for herself too, and she sat down in front of Mary and said to her, "Now tell us just what's the matter with him? He didn't get nothing broke did he?"

"Well, Lord, I'm glad it's no worse," said Molly, after Mary's recital.

"He wasn't driving the car, was he?" Sam asked anxiously.

Mary shook her head.

Josette could not curb her curiosity any longer. "Who was the woman with him, Mary? Is she going to live? Have they got her identified? Is she anybody from town?"

Mary hesitated a little before she answered. "Well, I guess there isn't any use of trying to make a secret of it. Everybody in town will know it by tomorrow morning anyway, after the papers come out. The woman was Rita Sibley."

Molly caught her breath with a sharp whistling sound.

"You see," Mary continued, "the newspapers will make an even bigger story out of it on account she is Joe Sibley's wife. Joe isn't very popular up to Ashbury right now, because he's mixed up in the labor trouble. The newspapers are bound to take this up, make it a kind of left-handed dig at Joe while they're at it."

Molly stated her opinion conclusively. "Well, sir, I'm awful sorry for Kenny mixed up in all of this, but I ain't a bit sorry for her, not a bit sorry. The way she was doing, she oughta get smashed up like this. She had it coming to her. Her, a married woman, and older than he is, and then chasing after Kenny like that, and going right up to the hotel where he was staying to see him and everything. She oughta been ashamed. She never was extra what you'd call good for anything. Lord, I'm glad Ernie got rid of her when he did. She deserves every single bit of this, getting hurt, and the talk there'll be about her and everything. Her a-chasing after Kenny, going to his hotel to see him, and carting him around in her automobile and smashing it up and about killing him. Don't nobody need to expect me to feel sorry for a woman like that."

"Well, I think Kenny's just exactly as much to blame for it as she is," Josette flared. "I suppose you think she did all the chasing. You oughta know Kenny better by this time. If there was any chasing done, Kenny Veech did his share of it. I feel sorry for Rita Sibley."

Molly was very angry, but the argument finally wore itself out and the family trooped off to bed, Molly going to her cot in the kitchen outside Jud's door.

And so it was that Carl's eighteenth birthday was not destined to be a day set apart for him after all. It went down into the annals of family history not as "the day that Carl was eighteen years old, and we had the party for him when Jud was sick," but instead as, "the day that Kenny got hurt in that automobile accident."

12

THE MORNING PAPERS THE NEXT DAY DULY DEVOTED as much print and as many pictures to the accident as had been anticipated. Rita herself was well known in Ashbury, and there was a certain news value in her very name. Nor did they neglect Joe in the reports of the accident. Several of the more outspokenly prejudiced newspapers in the city referred to Rita openly as the wife of a labor agitator who was stirring up trouble in the city.

The Veeches read all the newspapers and went about their affairs. It was not the first time that one of the family had been a central figure in an unsavory story running all over the village. Mary had always figured in the town gossip. Kenny's record had not been clean previous to this, nor Jen's either, not to mention Ernie. The Veeches were not as annoyed by the situation as might have been expected. Although the village talked avidly and disapproved, in the main they did not condemn.

Molly had a singularly busy day of it. She had a steady stream of callers all day long, well-meaning old friends who came ostensibly to inquire after Jud Higgins' health, but who were eager for Molly to discuss the accident with them. In most cases Molly did discuss it freely and told everyone exactly what she thought of a woman like Rita Sibley, whose misdemeanors placed her beyond the range of anybody's sympathies.

The afternoon passed and while the family was at supper Kenny came in the front door unnoticed. He appeared suddenly before their eyes.

He coughed a little, a dry hacking little half-cough in his throat, and they all turned around and looked at him. "Hi, everybody," he said smiling. He was looking much as usual, except that his right arm was doubled up in a sling. He was a little paler than normal perhaps, his mouth was a little pinched, giving his features a finer cast than they usually had. But his grin was wide and genial, his hair was tousled up over his eyes in blond curls and at the moment there was a pronounced odor of alcohol about him.

Molly got up from her chair and went to him immediately, half-laughing, half-crying. "Kenny boy, are we ever glad to see you, mister? How do you feel? How are you? You sure it's all right for you to be up around?"

"Hey, Mom, go easy, will you," he said as she embraced him heartily. He coughed again, the little dry tentative cough down in his throat.

"You good-for-nothing old bum, you," his mother said caressingly. She hurried to pour him some coffee and set a chair for him at the table.

"Don't fuss around getting any supper for me. I ate before I left town. All I want is some coffee."

"Well, darling," Jen said merrily, "we read about you in the papers."

Molly shook her head disapprovingly, but Kenny said genially as he sat down, "Say, wasn't those papers fierce though!" He coughed again as he spoke.

Jen cupped her chin in her hands and stared at him across the table curiously. "Say, what's the matter with you, anyway? We thought you busted a collar bone. You're coughing like you got T.B."

"Oh, hell," Kenny said. "It's the damnedest thing. The doc says my ribs where they got smashed are irritating on my pleura or something, whatever in hell my pleura is. He explained all about it to me. It's got something to do with my lungs. He claims while the ribs are healing they keep kind of tickling on there. I keep feeling just like I gotta cough all the time. But the doc says I gotta be careful. If I ever coughed real hard once, he says I would bust loose all of them ribs again." He coughed again after he got done telling it.

"Well, I tell you," Molly said. "You're lucky to be here, that's what you are. Why them pictures in the paper just made my blood run cold. That car was just smashed clean to pieces. I never see nothing like it."

Kenny laughed softly, and relapsed into his cough.

Sam, who'd been silent all the while, suddenly burst out indignantly at Kenny. "Damn it, I don't know how you can set there and laugh with that woman dying up to the hospital right now. Let me tell you, young feller, if I'd ever pulled anywhere near the stunt you just pulled when I was your age my father would have took the horsewhip to me right. And then you come in here tonight acting big and smart like nothing happened and laughing right in our faces, and smelling of liquor right this minute. Why, hell, it would seem to me that you'd drunk enough liquor lately to last you for awhile."

Molly flew to Kenny's rescue. "Sam Veech, you shut up your mouth, talking to Kenny like that. He's a sick boy, just come home from the hospital."

"It's true," Josette said with her face set. "Every word that Pa said is the truth. He ought to be ashamed. He hasn't got any shame, or he couldn't look us in the face after all that printed right in the papers . . ."

Kenny banged his fist down on the table before Molly could speak again. He coughed a little before he started to talk, and his voice was tight with suppressed anger. "Now just a minute, all of you. There's a few things I want to get straight around here, and then I ain't gonna say nothing more about it, so you better listen now." He looked around at all of them with his face grim and set and coughed delicately. "Rita Sibley wasn't drunk when she crashed that automobile. We'd been drinking all right, but she wasn't drunk. If she hada been she wouldn't have been driving that car, I'd seen to that."

"She wasn't drunk!" Molly breathed. "Then how . . ."

"Rita Sibley was having a regular temper tantrum when she crashed that car. She was so mad at me she couldn't see straight, because she got it in her head that I was giving her the gate. She got so mad she like to went crazy. She did a lot of yelling and talking and driving faster and faster. She got so mad that she didn't know what she was doing, and then she lost control of the car in the gravel and run it smack into the cement abutment of that bridge over the gully. When the car hit, I opened the door on my side and if I hadn't of, I wouldn't be here. You know more about the rest of it than I do. You been reading the papers." He had to stop talking then, his voice was strangling out, to cough.

"There, sir," Molly said triumphantly. "How anybody can feel sorry for a woman like that, I don't know. It'll be better for her if she dies, because I don't see how she could ever hold up her head in this town again. Why, she liked to have killed Kenny, busting his collar bone and his ribs . . ."

Sam was almost crying with his helpless indignation. "You can talk all you want, you can't change it a bit. You was chasing after some other man's wife, or you wouldn't have got into all this trouble."

"Sam Veech," Molly said warningly. "You heard what Kenny said. He don't want to talk about it no more. You just shut up your mouth, right now."

Sam got up and fled away from the table back to the front porch.

Josette gave Kenny a look of perfect loathing, and also left the table. A silence fell in the kitchen. The wind blew around the house, raining down crab-apples onto the roof. Kenny scowled moodily into his coffee cup. Jen got up and stacked the plates together. From some place a clock was ticking in noisy unconcern. From the bedroom came the sound of Jud's voice, talking incessantly, holding a conversation with someone or other visible only to himself.

Dorothy hung around the back of Kenny's chair, fascinated by his arm in the sling, the attention he was getting and particularly by his continual soft coughing. Finally Kenny got up from the table. His mother said anxiously, "Kenny, you ain't going uptown or anywhere tonight, are you? You hadn't oughta go out. You can't tell me you feel good enough to . . ."

"I'm going to bed. Where you think I'm going?"

Carl heard his brother coming up the stairs, the drag of his feet, the sound of his gentle coughing. Carl was in a panic at the thought of being alone with Kenny. He wondered what he should say to him, whether he should say that he was sorry he was hurt, or what.

Kenny opened the door and came into the room morosely. The wind outside was still blowing hard, driving the lace curtains out straight into the room. The green wormy crab-apples from the tree outside kept up a continual fusillade against the roof. There were no billion stars blowing in the sky tonight; the night pressed close against the windows was black and full of mysterious unseen motion before the wind.

"If you ain't ready to sleep this early, you better take that book and go on downstairs," Kenny said to Carl. "I'm going to get some sleep."

Carl laid aside his book obediently and put the other pillow, doubled beneath his head and shoulders, over on the other side of the bed. He watched Kenny while he took off his shirt. He had to take his arm out of the sling, holding it carefully doubled in the same position, and work the sleeve down from it. He was awkward with it, left-handed, and Carl wanted to help him, but he did not dare to offer. He suddenly became afraid of having to share the bed with Kenny. Suppose he should roll against him in the night . . .

"Listen," he said, fighting the embarrassment out of his voice, "don't you want me to sleep downstairs on the couch? I can, just the same as not. It don't make no difference to me. I just thought that maybe you . . ."

"Hell, no, you're all right where you are. I'll sleep on this side of the bed, though, then my shoulder and my banged-up ribs will be to the outside of the bed. You always stay on your own side the bed, anyway."

Kenny took an envelope from his shirt pocket, and spilled out a couple of white capsules. "Go downstairs and get me a glass of water," he said to Carl. Carl resented his peremptory tone of voice but there was something definitely sinister about his brother, he thought. He remembered a movie he had seen once in which an exceedingly tough gangster coughed all through the picture—just like Kenny did.

"You have to take medicine?" Carl asked tremulously when he brought the glass.

"Sleeping pills," Kenny said laconically. He lay back on the pillow, settled his body and closed his eyes.

Carl listened to Kenny's deep breathing and thought about the possibility of Kenny's having taken an overdose of the medicine. He shuddered to think that Kenny might quite conceivably die in the night, and that he should sleep for hours in the same bed with a corpse and never know it.

While he was still dwelling on this morbid thought a little screech owl close to the window emitted its peculiar cry. Carl jumped, then held his breath, fearful that he had awakened Kenny. Carl's attention was turned now to the outdoors, the rustling of the leaves, and moan of the wind, the windows shaking in their frames.

The very blackness, unbroken by any alien star or beam of light, was soothing. He discovered suddenly that it was a comfort to have Kenny home in bed with him. His fears of Jud were allayed; he was safe because Kenny was here. With his mind so completely at rest, he turned in gratitude to the thought of the girl, the ideal girl, that he was going to meet some day. He fumbled with the skeins of his fancy, ready to weave himself a dream of her. The moment had become infinitely pleasant, infinitely precious to him. While he still fumbled for his dream he fell asleep and the moment was lost forever. The crab-apples rolled over the roof ironically and plunged off into the deep thick grass below.

Book Two

1

THE CARNIVAL MOVED INTO TOWN FOR THE WEEK, and Kenny's accident was relegated to ancient village history. The street carnival was an annual affair, sponsored by the American Legion Post for the purpose of raising funds. The main street of the downtown area was roped off and a cheap carnival company brought in its trappings: the rickety Ferris wheel; the merry-go-round which had lost its popularity with a more daring and enlightened genera-tion of children; canvas booths containing a fishpond, shooting gallery, balloon and dart gallery; ball-throwing concessions; penny pitching, roulette, refreshments, beer.

From the moment that the first truck arrived, the village children fairly lived there, never tiring of running back and forth among the booths that transformed the quiet village street into something alien and exciting.

The Veeches were pleasurably excited about the show and attended it in shifts in the evenings, since someone always had to remain at home to look after Jud. The responsibility fell more or less upon Sam and Molly, so they worked out a sort of agreement between them. Molly went up first, early in the evening. She never varied her procedure. Immediately upon arriving she went to the refreshment booth and drank a bottle of lemon pop, stopping to talk with everyone that she knew. Then she went directly to the large bingo concession, a table in the form of a hollow square with benches all around, and a long table in the middle where the prizes were displayed and the callers conducted the game. Molly would hoist her heavy body down onto the bench and scoop up a handful of corn off the table to use for counters, and play steadily sixty or seventy cents worth of cards, one after another. She never won. She always demanded a new card each time and lamented the fact that if she had kept the card that she had had the last game, she would have been able to bingo this game.

Kenny went down the first night, and, surrounded by a group of his friends, his circle of friends in the village particularly solicitous and admiring of Kenny at this time, he made a rapid circuit of the carnival, pointing out its obvious defects and deficiencies. He encountered Jen and Fran Cope wandering through the crowd arm in arm, smiling pertly at all and sundry, obviously out for whatever game they might encounter, and he good-naturedly admonished them to beware of riding on the merry-go-round with carnival men, at the top of his lungs over the heads of an appreciative crowd. The shooting gallery was the only concession that he would condescend to patronize. Although his right arm was still doubled in the sling he was able to handle one of the light rifles. He was a good shot and he was proud of it. He ignored all of the numbered boards and single cigarette packages and fired continually at a package of cigarettes with a dollar bill wrapped around it and secured by a rubber band. Each time he aimed at it, he hit it, and although, as he pointed out, he hit low, it simply fell over backward on the shelf instead of being knocked off the shelf as by all the rules of fair dealings it should have been. He knocked the package over six times, pointing out each time to the crowd gathered around the concession that there was obviously something crooked about it. To prove his point he fired at an ordinary package of cigarettes the next time, and knocked it well off from the shelf and received its equivalent in fresh cigarettes. Then, over the protests of the man in charge of the gallery, he fired at the package with the dollar bill again, and it gently fell over backward on the shelf. The man in charge gave him a fresh package of cigarettes and a dollar bill, and Kenny departed in triumph, and was seen at the carnival no more.

Josette had taken an unusual interest in the carnival from the beginning, to the surprise of her family. The cause of her interest dated back to a conversation with Midge Clark. Midge had informed her that several friends of hers from the East were coming to visit her at about the time that the carnival began, and she was sure that the carnival would amuse them. Josette must certainly meet her friends, Midge assured her, and she added that according to the last letter she had received there was a possibility that there would be an extra man in the party. Josette was excited by the prospect. She made plans for inveigling money out of her mother and Ernie with which she intended to buy some new clothes. But as the carnival drew nearer she saw and heard nothing from Midge. She worried about it, but she finally decided that Midge would naturally be busy making preparations and would have no time to see her until her friends arrived.

The first night of the carnival, Josette defiantly told Pat Thompson that she had another engagement, and dressed with great care, checking and rechecking each item and detail of her toilet until she was certain that she was suitably and attractively garbed for the occasion. Although she had heard nothing from Midge, she departed for the carnival alone in high spirits. Once there the crowds and lights and the cheapness of it wearied her; there was nothing about it to interest her. She walked alone among the crowd watching for Midge Clark and her friends. Josette made a rather attractive figure, tall and well formed, her head with the neat brown curls carried high. She was wearing a yellow dress with clean white accessories, stepping daintily in her high-heeled white sandals. Several men in the crowd attempted to approach her, but Josette met their loose-lipped inviting smiles with a stony face and hurried on. She walked back and forth past the various concessions without speaking to anyone, looking anxiously among the crowd. After a half-hour of it her head ached and her feet hurt, and she was angry with herself. She should have waited at home for Midge to come after her, she thought, and she should not have come down here so early, anyway. She went over to the refreshment stand at last and ordered a bottle of pop and sat down on the bench to drink it. While she was still sitting there sucking on her straws dispiritedly and contemplating the stains and smudges already dirtying her white shoes, she saw them: Midge, another girl and three boys noisily buying tickets for the merry-go-round. Josette stared at them. The girls wore slacks and sweaters and bright jackets that matched the bright sandals on their feet. They were all disheveled and talking too loudly, screaming with laughter as the slow old merry-go-round chugged around and around with them, the little horses bobbing up and down jerkily. The three boys were all tall and good-looking. They were all smoking, and one of the boys sprawled across his horse waving a bottle while Midge and the other girl screamed protests at him to be good. They were the center of all eyes, and the village was frankly disapproving. Josette studied the girl with Midge, a short, dark-haired person, and decided that she herself was much more attractive-looking. Although Josette did not approve of their loud and conspicuous behavior she was longing to be one of them. The merry-go-round stopped at last and they came tumbling off it, toward her, and Josette steeled herself, smiling already a cool pretty smile. They passed by her so near that the full swinging legs of Midge's slacks brushed against Josette's knees, but they did not stop. For one terrible moment, just as they passed, Midge looked squarely into Josette's face, smiled and said "Hello." They went on up the line, shouting and laughing, crowding together into the booth where photographs were taken for a dime and developed while you waited.

Josette was stunned. She sat still on the bench with the crowd surging around her and the blare of music and voices in her ears. A child carrying a great wad of pink spun-sugar candy stumbled against her feet and smeared the candy over the front of her dress, but she hardly noticed. Her mother, and Jen, and all of them had so often prophesied that this would happen, but she could not yet believe it. The hurt and disappointment were welling up in her and Josette got up and fled for home. She ran away and left the light and noise of the carnival behind her. She ran all the way to the house until a stab of pain shot through her side. She went straight up the stairs to her own room and threw herself across the bed and cried into her pillow. The sound of insect voices filled the room, and, over it, the muffled sound of the music and laughter and shouting from the carnival up the street.

Saturday, the last night of the carnival, was bound to be the biggest night of all. The concessions opened long before dark and they would remain open until very late.

When Jen went upstairs, she was surprised to find Josette already dressed, putting on make-up before the mirror. Except for the few minutes that she had spent there the night that it opened, Josette had not been near the carnival, but today she had promised Pat Thompson to go down with him in the evening.

"You going down to the carnival?" Jen asked her.

"Yes."

"You going with Pat?"

Josette nodded.

"Atta girl. You know I figured you was going with Pat. I see him about six when I went downtown after the groceries, and he was ·grinning from ear to ear. I think it's a shame the way you been treating Pat lately. Pat is just crazy about you. I wish some nice steady fellow like Pat was that crazy about me. Why, you can't get Pat Thompson to date another girl but you."

"If you didn't tear around so much, maybe some boy like Pat would get crazy about you, maybe Pat would even. You can't expect any nice boy to get crazy about you, the way you run around all the time with everybody in town."

"I know it," Jen said seriously. "You know, it's funny. I wouldn't like nothing better than to have somebody like Pat, some steady fellow with a good job, get crazy about me. I'd like to get married and have a house of my own and start having babies, and everything. I been wanting that ever since I can remember. But, my God, while I'm waiting I can't help but run around with the kids and have a good time, can I?"

"But that's just the trouble," Josette said severely while she combed her curls over her finger. "You do so much playing and tearing around that no nice boy will ever get crazy about you. You ought to make up your mind what you want; you can't have both."

"I'm going to stop running around so much some of these days. I been thinking about it for a long time." Jen slipped a bright flowered print dress with a full swinging skirt over her head, and pulled it down smoothly over her hips.

"How come you're putting on your good dress to wear down there tonight?" Josette said, looking at her in the mirror.

"Oh, tonight is special," Jen said, posing before the mirror and twisting so that the full skirt swung around her legs. "This is gonna be the last date I'll have with Dick."

"Dick?" Josette asked. "For heaven's sakes, who is Dick?"

"Dick Meyers, a guy that travels with the carnival. This will be his last night in town. I've got a date with him for until the carnival closes. Then they're going to pack right up and move out. So after the carnival closes I'm going out to Greenings Lake for the end of the dance out there with Clim Hawkins."

"There you are," Josette said disapprovingly. "You claim you want the nice boys in town to like you and then you pick up one of those carnival men and go running off out to Greenings Lake at twelve or one o'clock with Clim Hawkins."

"Well, any time you want to save me from Clim you know what you can do," Jen said. "Honest, Clim is just dying to have a date with you. Clim thinks you're the smartest and the best-looking girl in this town. I've heard him say so lots of times."

The compliment did not please Josette. "Well, Clim Hawkins doesn't have to go around talking about me at all."

"Aw, don't be like that," Jen said. "Say, Jo, where are those chiffon stockings of yours with the black heels and seams up the back? I want to wear my black pumps tonight and them stockings would look swell."

"You can't have them," Josette answered promptly. "You have been wearing my stockings all the time, and you've ruined them, wearing them down to that carnival."

At that moment Molly called up the stairs, "Hey, Josie, you ready yet? Pat is setting down here waiting."

Josette picked up her purse and a clean handkerchief and went downstairs.

With her sister gone, Jen sang softly to herself while she rummaged through the drawers of the bureau. She found the stockings with the black seams at last, done up carefully in tissue paper and hidden away under a stack of underwear. She put them on carefully, and then tipped the mirror down and swung her skirt around her knees, admiring her well-shaped legs in the sheer chiffon hose with the startling black seams going straight up the backs.

Ever since the carnival had been in town Carl had been attracted to the tent of the gypsy fortune teller. He had never had his fortune told, and more than anything else in the world he wanted to have this gypsy woman forecast his future. But as much as he wanted to consult the woman, he could not get up enough courage to walk boldly into her tent. He realized that if any of the family ever heard about his going to see her he would never hear the last of it.

The trouble was that there were always some of the Veeches in evidence. With the idea of evading them, he had gone uptown right after supper. As he approached the tent, nervously, he came face to face with Dorothy. She looked at him hard, as if she was able to read his secret. He continued to walk past the fortune-telling tent.

Next he came upon Josette and Pat Thompson. They had paused before a concession where baseballs were thrown at pyramided wooden milk bottles. Pat was earnestly throwing balls at the bottles while Josette stood by, cool and detached, carrying a particularly gaudy and befeathered doll, a large Scottie dog covered with brilliants, and two canes trimmed with bobbing monkeys on rubber bands, the rewards Pat had already earned for her by applying his strength and skill at various prize-offering concessions on the midway.

The sight of them completely unnerved Carl. If there was one member of the family he especially wanted to avoid when he went to the gypsy woman, it was the cool and superior Josette. Carl turned away directly and went to the refreshment stand for a Coca-Cola, feeling that he had had a narrow escape.

By the time that Carl dared leave the refreshment booth, Jen, too, had appeared. She was walking arm in arm with the dark and fascinating carnival man, Dick Meyers, deeply engrossed in conversation with him. Jen was looking very lovely; even Carl stared at her. Her hair was done up with a mass of curls on the top of her head, and the bright lights toned down her make-up to a becoming color. The flowered print dress that she wore showed off her figure to the best advantage, her full breasts, slim waist, and full hips, and every step she took the wide skirt swung becomingly around her very lovely legs with the triumphant startling black seams up the back.

Dick Meyers was being appropriately sad as the hour of parting drew nearer. He was pouring out to her the story of his life, and all the misunderstandings that he had encountered until he had met her. And he was also pointing out the terrible hardships and disappointments and unstable features of the life with a carnival that made it utterly impossible for a man, out of fairness to the girl he loved, to marry and take a wife upon his travels. Jen was being appropriately reasonable and sweetly understanding about the whole thing. The point was that these lengthy conversations involved a great deal of walking up one side of the midway and down the other. Carl abandoned his project temporarily and went into the drugstore and dipped into the county library books.

When he came out into the street again it was much later and the carnival was in full swing. After a few more family encounters, he headed straight for the fortune-telling booth, looking neither to the right nor the left. He fingered his fifty-cent piece and walked in, stooping to enter through the low door. Inside, the tent was more brightly lighted than he had anticipated. The old woman sat on a chair and motioned Carl to sit in another close in front of her. He sat down and mutely handed her his fifty-cent piece. She was smoking a cigarette, and she threw it down, stepped on it and took his hand in both of hers. She looked incredibly old under the bright, unshaded light bulb. Her voice was full and rather sweet and she spoke with no accent at all in spite of her dark skin. "So you want to know the things that are going to happen to you in your life to come, my son," she said to him, fixing him with her bright beady eyes while she stroked and smoothed his hand. Carl began to feel embarrassed and he wanted to run away.

"You must not be afraid," she said gently. "That is the most important thing in all your whole life, you must not be afraid." She read his face rather than his palm expertly. "You are not happy. There is a great unhappiness and sorrow always in you, here," she touched his chest gently. "But not forever. You must not be afraid, then this trouble will go away." She branched out into a more set pattern now. "I see an interesting life for you, a long happy life, with success. Things will not come easy, but you must work and not be afraid. Now you may ask me two questions. Whatever you want to know, I will tell you."

Carl was baffled and self-conscious. Any questions that he could think of, he could not bring himself to ask.

She went on deftly, working on what he himself revealed to her so plainly. "You see, you keep things inside of you always, and that is bad. You must learn to let out the things that you carry inside of you, the things that make you unhappy. Speak them in words, do them in deeds, and then you will be happy again. You are not like other people, my son, you are soft, here," again she touched his chest gently. "The things that other people forget about, you remember and they make you sad. But you will have a very interesting and successful life far away from this town." She studied his long slender hand carefully. "You are not made for hard work," she said. "You are never to work hard with your hands. You are an artist. I see great talent in your palm, it is—" she hesitated—"yes, I see. It is music. You have a great talent for music, is it not so?"

Carl, who could never carry a tune, and who had not even learned to dance, shook his head at her stupidly.

"Ah, yes," she insisted. "I see it there in your hand, a great musical talent. Maybe you have not discovered it yet for yourself, but I see a great talent for music in your hand, and the hand tells everything and never lies, you know."

She changed over to another line of approach where she was more sure of her ground. "You are very lonely, aren't you? Tell me, am I not right?"

Carl nodded to her as she fixed him with her bright small eyes.

She nodded her head too. "Yes, you are very lonely. You have very few friends. You have not found any girl that you care for. There have been maybe one, maybe two, girls that you have met and at first you thought that you cared for them, but you found out you were wrong. They did not understand you. I am right? You will meet another girl soon, but she will not be the one for you either. You must beware of her. You do what your heart says, but your heart is wrong. Your heart will be wrong many times, I see it in your hand. You must beware of the things your heart says to you. This girl will make you very unhappy. But some day, not so long, maybe two years, maybe three, you will meet a girl that you will really love, and she will love you. I see it in your hand. She will be a very beautiful girl, a blonde-haired girl. I see a long and happy marriage.

"You would like to ask a question of me, now, maybe? No? Well, then, I can tell you no more. Good-bye, and God bless you." And for the interests of her business, she added, "Do not discuss the things that I have spoken to you with anyone."

Josette and Pat Thompson had left the carnival somewhat earlier than Carl did. Josette had been bored with it all. She had been thankful also that she had not had to encounter Midge Clark and her friends there. Pat had gone about doing the carnival methodically, as he always did everything. He had started on one side of the midway and worked down from concession to concession, urging Josette to participate in everything, which she usually refused to do. He loaded her arms with his winnings. At the end, he began again on the other side and worked his way up to where they had started. They rode the merry-go-round stolidly, and Josette consented to go on the midget automobile ride and the Ferris wheel. She had declined to ride the "tilt-a-whirl," however, and she had not allowed Pat to stop at the roulette wheel. They did not talk much, nor have a conspicuously merry time of it. After they had covered all the attractions the carnival had to offer, Pat gravely escorted Josette into the drugstore and bought her a chocolate soda. They ended the evening with playing bingo again, and Pat won a blanket. He presented it to Josette, but she declined to accept it, saying that he should keep such a valuable prize for himself. Pat folded the blanket, put it on the seat beside him and ordered three more cards. After spending about a dollar for bingo cards, he was able to win Josette a blanket of her own. They got up then, collected their various prizes and Pat walked Josette home.

They sat together in the creaking old porch swing, rocking placidly back and forth in the darkness.

Pat apparently was at a loss for words.

"I haven't seen you so much lately," he began.

"I know," Josette said. "I've been awfully busy. It isn't easy to keep up all the school work I have to do this hot weather."

"I know it," Pat said. "It's the same way with me, and the work I'm doing in the trade school. How are you getting along in business college?"

Josette did not dislike Pat. She rather admired his obvious good qualities, industry, steadiness, neatness, orderliness and good character. His interest in her and her affairs touched her. At the moment she felt kindly toward him, and she was seized by a desire to confide in him.

"Oh, I'm not getting along at all. I don't know what's the matter with me. I just can't seem to get any of it right. I'm pretty good at typing, and business law, and things like that. But I'm not a bit good in shorthand, and bookkeeping, and accounting. I just don't know what I'll do, if I don't start doing better work pretty soon. I haven't got nearly enough credits to be admitted to the second class, and the time limit that you can stay on up there in the first class is just about over. I worry about it so, but I just can't help it."

Pat nodded in the darkness, but the ready sympathy that she had expected was not forthcoming.

"Well, I tell you," he said hesitantly. "I don't believe you were ever cut out to be a business woman anyway, Josette."

She was stung by his lack of sympathy and understanding. "I don't see why you say that. I don't see what you mean. Why am I not cut out to be a business woman? But anyway, I've simply got to make good up there. I've got to do something. I've got to get some kind of a job, and I'd rather work in an office than almost any other place."

"Why have you got to get a job?" Pat asked baldly.

"Oh, that's a silly question. I've got to get a job some place and be self-supporting. I want to get out of this town and away from here."

"Why, Josette?"

"Because I just can't stand it to live here another day, that's why."

Pat weighed her words carefully, and interpreted them after his limited understanding. "I know what you mean, Josette. I know how you must feel. It isn't pleasant for you living here at home. And then your family—the way they are, they . . ." He hesitated, floundering out of consideration for her. "Your family—always—getting into trouble and everything. It makes it hard for you."

Although Josette often criticized her family to herself, and blamed them entirely for the unfavorable position she held in the town, she did not like to hear Pat Thompson speak of them disparagingly. She instantly switched off, cold and distant. She was sorry that she had confided to him her difficulties at school.

Pat went on talking awkwardly. "You know I got another raise, Josette. I told you about it. It don't amount to much, of course, but I'm going to get a better job up there to the shops. I'm bound to. The foreman talked to me just the other day. I'm to be transferred again the last of next month. That'll mean another raise. I won't be making so much, but every little raise like that counts up. In another year, I'll be making pretty good money."

"That's fine, Pat," Josette said automatically, without thinking of what he was trying to say to her, only wishing that he would go away so that she could go to bed.

"What I mean is," Pat went on doggedly, "as long as I am all set the way I am, I don't see what you have to worry about. If I were you, I'd just quit up there to business college and come on home here for awhile. I think you're working too hard, you look so tired and worried. I'd a lot rather that you just stay home here and rest. I hadn't really planned on anything before next year, but if you can't stand it to stay home here, why, we could do it sooner. We could buy all the furniture we want right away, and pay for it on the installment plan. I wouldn't like to do that so well, but we can, if you want to. I've got quite a little money saved up in the bank, besides. We could get married any time you say, just as soon as you want to."

Josette listened to him in astonishment, calmly going ahead with his plans, speaking to her possessively, taking their marriage as a matter of course, when never once had he openly asked her to marry him.

She was so astonished that she spoke more sharply than she meant to. "Well, I won't do any such a thing, Pat Thompson. I won't give up going to school. I'll get along up there, somehow. I'm not going to quit and come home here. And I don't care how much money you're making, nor how much money you have in the bank, nor what you are planning on doing next year."

"You see," Pat said. "You're so nervous and worried all the time you don't talk and act like yourself any more."

Josette searched her mind for anything that she had ever done or said to Pat Thompson that gave him the idea that she was going to marry him. The whole thing seemed ridiculous and unromantic to her. "Pat, you just better get such ideas out of your head," she said angrily. "I'm not tired and worried, or, if I am, it doesn't change the way I feel about things. I don't know where you get such ideas about me. I wouldn't marry you if you were the last man on earth." Once the words were out of her mouth, she was a little sorry. She had not meant to be so open and abrupt about the whole matter. She had not meant to make Pat feel hurt and angry.

Pat got up out of the swing. "Well, there's no use of us talking any more about it tonight. You're just all tired out and upset from worrying. I won't bother you about it any more, Josette. But you know the way I feel about you. I don't think you'll be able to stay up there to school very much longer, and when they won't let you stay up there any more, why, you know that all you have to do is say the word to me. You don't have to worry, because I'll take care of you then." He touched the side of her face timidly with his hand, and then he walked down from the porch and up the street. He had left his blanket from the bingo game in the porch swing.

"Pat, you forgot your blanket," Josette said mechanically.

After he was gone, Josette sat still in the porch swing. There was a sprinkling of rain coming down, rattling on the leaves, and a cool breeze touched her face. She leaned back in the swing and closed her eyes. For a moment she felt bewildered and close to tears. She would not admit the gratitude she felt because he wanted to take care of her and make things easy for her. But the anger, the bright blind anger came afterward. She hated Pat Thompson, she thought, she hated him for the smug way in which he disposed of her. He simply took it for granted that she would flunk out of business college, and then, regardless of how she felt about him, she would be only too glad to marry him to solve her problems. And the worst of it was that in all probability she would flunk out of business college just as he prophesied. Well, whatever she did in that eventuality, Josette told herself grimly, the very last thing she would do would be to marry Pat Thompson. She made the resolve over and over again. Never, never would she humble herself to him and come to him and say, "Pat, it is all as you expected it. I flunked out of school and I can't get a job and I can't stand it to live here, so please will you marry me right away?"

2

SUNDAY WAS TRADITIONALLY A DAY GIVEN OVER TO sleep and rest at the Veeches'. Although Molly was forced to rise at her accustomed hour to care for Jud, the rest of the family remained in bed until almost noon. Sam came downstairs early and got the Sunday paper off the front porch and a handful of crackers and went back to bed again.

Josette awoke early and passed the time away studying in bed. The bright clear morning lightened her mood considerably. She decided to get up and go to church, and take Dorothy along with her for the Sunday school hour. She dressed quickly, went downstairs and unfolded her plans to an approving Molly. At least once a month Josette was in the habit of attending church, accompanied by a silent, uncomplaining Dorothy.

Molly went about preparing the usual elaborate Sunday breakfast of eggs and bacon, coffee, cinnamon rolls, molasses cookies and orange marmalade. When she had it on the table she called the family down. There was still another convention connected with Sunday morning breakfast. It was the one meal of the week when it was permissible to come to the table in almost any stage of undress that might suit the mood or the temperature. This morning, Mary appeared in a negligee and mules, and Kenny and Carl did not bother to don shirts.

As the meal drew to its leisurely close, Josette and Dorothy came in, carrying Sunday school quarterlies and papers and cards.

Molly got up to pour hot coffee for them, and to fry more eggs and bacon. Kenny and Mary lit cigarettes over second cups of coffee and the whole family lingered at the table.

"Well, where you been so early in the morning?" Kenny asked Dorothy affectionately as the little girl slid into her chair beside his.

"Church," she said.

"Well, ain't that something," Kenny said, sharing his amusement with Mary across the table. "Ain't that something. Did you pray for me?"

Before the child could answer Josette spoke sharply. "Now don't tease her like that and make fun of it. It's nice for her to go up there and be in the Sunday school class with the other children. She ought to go to church every Sunday."

"Well, listen to who's here," Kenny said sneeringly. "I suppose all Dorothy's gotta do is go to church and grow up like her aunt and then she'll be a regular angel with wings."

But Josette was in a rare good humor this noon. She did not bother to reply to Kenny. To his astonishment, she only laughed at him.

Carl's reaction was different. Josette had the power to make him feel choked and suffocated with helpless rage. He could not endure her flaunted superiority over the family. He sought around in his mind for something to say to her that would hurt her.

The words sputtered out of his mouth. "Well, I hear Midge Clark dropped you cold now she's got friends visiting her from east."

"That's all you know about it," Josette said triumphantly. "Midge is not the kind of a girl that drops anybody. I was talking with her just this morning when I came out of church. She stopped and talked to me for a long time. She invited me to meet her friends and go over to a dance at the Westbridge Country Club next Wednesday night."

The family was properly surprised, and Josette smiled triumphantly at all of them.

"For Lord's sakes," Molly said. "Are you gonna go?"

"Certainly I am."

"Well, I don't see how you can," her mother said practically. "You ain't got no clothes swell enough to wear to such a place as that."

"You have been promising me the money all summer for a new dress," Josette said, talking rapidly. "And I don't see why I can't have the money now. I can get me a dress to wear, some afternoon up to Ashbury. I've got to have a new dress, anyway. I haven't had a single new thing to wear all summer. Jen got a new dress, but I haven't had a thing. I don't see why I can't get a new dress now."

"Well, I been intending to give you the money to get you a dress," Molly said, "but I don't see no sense in letting you go buy a swell fancy party dress just to wear over there, and then hang it away and not wear it again."

"I don't have to buy any fancy party dress, just to wear to a dance in the summertime," Josette said. "I'll just get an ordinary pretty dress that I can wear when I go out all the rest of the summer."

"You can't go to no place like that in just any ordinary dress," Molly said. "Why don't you wear that dress you had for the prom when you graduated from high school? It's just hanging up there in the closet rotting away. You ain't never had it on since that prom. If you want a fancy party dress why don't you wear that one?"

The vision of the peach-colored dowdy organdy infuriated Josette. "Why, I wouldn't be seen in that dress any place. I don't want to buy a long dress. I just want to buy an ordinary dress-up dress. You don't have to have a formal just for a dance in the summertime."

"Well, I guess you'll find out," Molly said.

At that moment Jen burst into the kitchen, all out of breath from running. She sat down immediately and began to cry loudly.

"For Lord's sakes, what is the matter with you?" Molly demanded crossly. "Mr. Higgins is sleeping. You want to wake him up? What you bawling about?"

"Franny's awful sick," Jen sobbed.

"She is! Why, what's the matter with her?"

"I don't know." Jen sobbed. "She was awful sick this morning. They took her up to Ashbury to the doctor right away and her father just phoned back and he said they took her right over to the hospital."

"Huh!" Josette said. "I guess there's just about one thing likely to be wrong with a girl like Frances Cope."

"Shut your mouth!" Jen screamed at her.

"Now, damn it, Jo," Kenny said. He turned his chair around to Jen and put his hand on her shoulder. She sat doubled up in the chair with her face hidden in her hands. "There, now," he said. "Quit crying so, honey, and tell us about Franny. I didn't even know there was nothing wrong with her. I seen her running around downtown pretty near every day."

Jen nuzzled her face against Kenny's bare arm, smearing off the tears, gratefully. She stopped crying and sat up straight in the chair. Her lips and her wet eyelids were still twitching a little. She had not bothered to put cosmetics on her face, and her hair was still pinned tight to the top of her head uncombed. She looked sad and wretched and altogether pathetic.

"Franny hasn't been feeling right for a long time," she explained. "She's been having the awfulest headaches, and everything. I could just tell she was feeling rotten, but I couldn't get her to go see a doctor, or nothing. Last night we went to the dance after the carnival and Franny wasn't feeling good then. We come home late and went to bed and when we woke up this morning, Franny was bad sick."

"Well, how did she act?" Molly asked impatiently. "What was

wrong with her? She wasn't broke out or nothing, was she? I sure hope she ain't got something that's catching, you over there all the time and sleeping with her."

Jen's eyes widened and she spoke in a horror-stricken voice. "She was swelled up just terrible. All swelled up, her face and her neck, and her arms and legs and hands. It was awful, she looked just terrible. She was just about scared to death, and her father took her up to Ashbury right away. And he just phoned back and said they took her right to the hospital, to put her under observation, he said."

Jen's words called up a peculiarly sickening vision to Carl's eyes. He saw in a flash Fran Cope's beautiful face and body bloated up like balloons. He thought it was monstrous that something like this should happen to her.

"Oh, well," Molly comforted, "it probably ain't nothing very serious. It sounds to me like she's got some kind of kidney trouble. There ain't no sense you letting yourself get so upset over it. Come on here to the table and eat some breakfast before you get sick yourself."

Dorothy stared at Jen. She too had a bright mental image of Fran swelled up into a grotesque balloon. She found it very interesting. It was on the tip of her tongue to ask if Fran had been drinking whiskey, as Jud had, the only cause of illness she knew, but the presence of her mother silenced her. Dorothy was afraid of her mother. She was afraid of her mother's long silences and of her infrequent scoldings. She thought of it, and kept her questions to herself.

Jen began to eat listlessly and Josette reverted to the topic of the discussion that Jen had interrupted. "Well, are you going to give me the money for a new dress, or aren't you?" she asked her mother baldly.

"Lord, you still harping about a new dress? Well, we'll see. We got lots of time to talk it over yet. There ain't nothing that has to be settled right this minute I guess."

Josette was uneasy about the matter of her new dress being shelved by her mother. She left the table and went up to her room, her mind still busy with various ways and means of raising money to buy the dress. Just at the moment that she was considering selling, or at least pawning, the wrist watch that had been her graduation gift from the family, she heard a tap on the door and it opened. Mary stood in the doorway. Josette stared at her in surprise. The light from the hall showed the outlines of her body through the filmy negligee that she wore, a beautiful garment, beige and topaz in color, almost the color of the unusual shadows around her eyes.

"I was thinking about you going to that dance out at West-bridge," Mary said, in her low even voice. "Ma's right; you couldn't wear an ordinary afternoon dress out there. All the other girls will have summer formals."

"Will they?" Josette said in a spontaneous surprise. The next moment she was covered with confusion. It was never easy for Josette to be trapped into admitting that she did not really know all about everything that concerned her. In her confusion she said, "I didn't know that. Of course, then, I hadn't better go. I'll tell Midge. I didn't understand. I've heard about Westbridge, but I didn't know it was a place like that. I'll let Midge know right away."

"No," Mary said surprisingly. "I think it would be a good idea if you went. But don't say anything more to Ma about getting a dress.

"Do you have classes tomorrow afternoon?" Mary asked then. Josette shook her head.

"Well, then, tomorrow afternoon you go over to the Julia Forbes shop. Do you know where it is? It's a dress shop."

Josette shook her head again stupidly.

"Well, it's in the first floor of the Willis Hotel Building. You go over there tomorrow afternoon and tell Julia that I sent you, and she'll help you pick out a dress. Maybe it will have to be fitted, so that's why you better go over there tomorrow afternoon."

"But, Mary . . ." Josette said, bewildered.

"Tell Julia to charge the dress and the alterations to my account there. You can call it a birthday present from me," Mary said gently. "I guess you'd rather have a birthday present now than in November."

She went as quickly as she came, and Josette sat down weakly on the edge of the bed. Mary was the last person she would have thought of turning to in a crisis such as this. She was touched and pleased by Mary's understanding and generosity. She could not explain how it happened that Mary was able to understand just how much it meant to her to be able to go to the dance with Midge and her friends appropriately clothed. Josette took it as a good omen. The fates were with her, she thought. Perhaps this was to be some momentous turning point in her life. She wondered which one of the three young men she had seen with Midge would be the one that she was to be paired with. But as she thought about Mary's unexpected generosity further, Josette was characteristically displeased with the turn of circumstances that compelled her to accept aid from Mary. It was nice of Mary to get the dress for her, Josette admitted, but it did not change what Mary was. She could not like and accept Mary. She supposed that Lew Lentz paid Mary's bills and the thought sickened her. Her dress was not to come from Mary at all, but from Lew Lentz. She was somehow making herself a party to the unholy alliance between that man and her sister. Josette raged at the circumstances that left her no choice. But the dance was more important to her at the moment than was her pride.

3

THE NEXT DAY JOSETTE SELECTED HER DRESS FROM the shop Mary had sent her to, and after that the time crept by slowly.

The day of the dance, Wednesday, turned out to be a busy one for the Veeches. Jud woke up early in the morning and insisted that he was dying. He poured a stream of abuse upon the family because they would not call a doctor and accord him the proper sympathy and respect. He kept it up all day long, refusing to eat, lying with his eyes closed, and panting for breath occasionally, when he thought of it. By afternoon he began to demand a minister. He had never been baptized, he said, and with death at hand it was well to take care of things like that. Molly at last became unnerved by his performance. She telephoned the doctor from the neighbor's, and the doctor assured her curtly that Jud was not dying. He suggested that it would be better for Jud if the family left him alone until his tantrum had spent itself.

But Molly was a little doubtful.

By suppertime her mind was made up. Jen had gone up to Ashbury to the hospital that afternoon with the Copes and had not yet returned. Molly got supper herself, and while she moved silently and heavily around the kitchen, Jud continued to splutter and rage in the bedroom. When the family gathered at the supper table, Molly announced her decision to them. "I'm going to call a minister over here," she said.

After a moment's silence Kenny turned to Josette. "Well, so tonight's the night we step out in high society with all the swells, huh?"

Josette, of course, ignored him completely.

"God," Carl said, "we won't be able to live with her for two weeks after this."

"Well, sir," Molly said. "I think Josie is an awful lucky girl. Mary bought her a beautiful dress, and shoes and a little spangled pocketbook and everything to go with it. I should think she'd be awful nice to her sister after this. If it hadn't been for Mary she couldn't even have gone."

"Mary bought her a dress, huh?" Kenny said interestedly.

"Well, I'll say she did," Molly answered. "The swellest dress I ever laid an eye on in my life."

Jen came into the kitchen so silently that they never noticed her until she pulled up a chair to the table.

"Lord," Molly said to her. "It's about time you was coming home here. I tell you, you're gonna have to turn over a new leaf around here, young woman, gone all day long and every night, too. If you're just going to sit around and expect us to feed and clothe you, you're going to help do the work around here. If that's the way you're going to do business, you might just as well take your clothes and go on up to Copes' and stay there."

Jen put a spoonful of cold, greasy warmed-over potatoes on her plate silently, and a piece of bologna beside it. She was strangely quiet. She did not seem to hear a word that her mother had spoken to her. Her face looked pale and pinched under her bright make-up and there was a sort of frozen stillness all through her. She handled her fork clumsily, as if she could not even feel it in her fingers, and her eyes were set on nothing straight ahead of her.

"Say," Kenny said with concern in his voice, "how's Franny?"

She turned to him listlessly and her voice was a low monotone. "They're going to operate on her tomorrow afternoon."

"Operate!" Molly said. "Why, what in the world's the matter with her? Has she got to have her appendix out?"

"They're going to operate on her head," Jen said slowly. "They cut every bit of hair off from her head. They thought maybe they was going to operate this afternoon, but they had to send away for a special doctor, and he can't come till tomorrow afternoon."

"Her head," Molly said in horror. "What they got to operate on her head for? It ain't a mastoid, is it?"

Jen looked at her mother, and her voice and face were expressionless and numbed. "They say she's got a tumor growing in her brain some place."

"Oh, God!" Kenny said.

"For Lord's sakes, I never hearda such a thing," Molly said. "You mean they're going to cut her head right open and go cutting around in her brain?"

Kenny put his hand over Jen's. "Oh, hell, them surgeons can do anything nowadays. You read about brain surgery all the time. I know a guy right up to Ashbury myself that's running around just as good as ever with a great big silver plate up there in his head."

"They don't think she can live through no such a thing as that, do they?" Molly asked.

"They say she can," Jen said wearily. "They say she can't live at all, if they can't get that tumor out of there quick."

"Poor little kid," Kenny said. "They ain't told her about it, have they?"

Jen nodded. "They explained it all out to her, them doctors. She knows more about it than her folks do, even."

"How's she taking it?" Kenny asked curiously.

For the first time Jen seemed to come alive and there was real feeling in her voice when she answered him. "She's being just wonderful about it. I don't see how she can be. If it was me, I'd just die right there thinking about it. If she's scared, she ain't letting on. She says she wants to get well so bad that if this is what they got to do to fix her up, why, it's all right with her. Today she was even joking about 'em cutting her hair all off. She was laughing about that when we come away tonight. She says that it's a good thing them baby-style hair-do's are in style now, 'cause then she'll look all right when she gets out of the hospital while her hair's growin' back."

"Atta girl," Kenny said in admiration. "You sure gotta hand it to her. That takes a lot of guts. Franny's a swell little girl. You tell her tomorrow what I said. Tell her I'm betting on her any time."

Jen's face was softer and living again. "I'll tell her. She was talking about you today, Kenny. She said that if you could go through an awful automobile smash like you did and walk out of it, why, she guesses no little old operation is going to get her down."

"Why, sure," he said. "You just watch, she'll come through this a-flying. They couldn't kill off folks like Fran and me if they tried."

"Only the good die young," Josette said hollowly from across the table.

Kenny burst out into warm spontaneous laughter, throwing his head back, and resting his hand on Jen's shoulder in a comradely fashion. "Well, you said a mouthful that time!" Jen joined in his laughter with some of her old animation coming into her face.

Kenny made an effort to draw Jen out of herself. "Boy, will you look at your kid sister over there with her hair all done up on curlers, so's she'll look pretty. She's stepping out in high society tonight, right."

He turned to Jen and spoke in a squeaky simpering voice with an exaggerated accent. "Oooooh, Miss Veech, may I have the next dance?"

Jen stuck her chin up high in the air, pursed her lips, and answered him elaborately. "Well, I think that you might, Mr. Rockefeller, seeing that it's you."

They got up and danced stiffly and sedately around the kitchen, Kenny holding her away from him at arm's length, and Jen dancing with her head up high in the air and her eyes tight closed.

Amid the laughter, Josette got up from the table, banged her chair back and walked out of the kitchen.

"Hey, Josie," Kenny yelled after her, "you want to be careful none of them society boys don't put knockout drops in your liquor tonight!"

A car stopped out in front and they all straightened up in their chairs nervously. But it was Ernie who came in.

"Why, hello there, stranger," Molly said to him affectionately. "Where you been hiding? We ain't seen you in a coon's age."

"Oh, hell," Ernie said gloomily. "I been having the damnedest toothache, last couple of days."

"Toothache!" his mother said attentively. "For Lord's sakes, why don't you lay off work and go on up there to Ashbury and have it out?"

"Well, I been meaning to, but we been so God-damn busy out there on the road."

"We got some oil of cloves around here, ain't we?" Sam said. "Why don't you put some of that on it? That'll cure a toothache quicker'n anything I know of."

"Hell, I already tried that," Ernie said. "I like to burn the whole inside of my mouth out, and that tooth just kept right on a-jumpin' and tearing right through my whole head. I never seen nothing like it."

"Well, it's a shame," Molly said. "I don't see how you can stay out there and try to work with a tooth a-going it like that."

Immediately after supper, Molly went over to the neighbor's telephone and called up the Reverend Mr. Bradley, who told her that he would come over right away, that in such circumstances he was only too glad to do what he could.

When Molly came back to the house with the news, the group still around the kitchen table disintegrated rapidly. Kenny left the house on the spot. Jen slipped away to her room.

Upstairs Josette turned and posed before the mirror over the bureau while the light sparkled down the length and breadth of her long full skirt. Jen sat hunched on the foot of the bed staring at her sister in sincere admiration. "Gosh," she said tremulously. "That's the swellest dress I ever saw in my life outside of the movies. Honest, Jo, you look swell. I mean it."

Josette was warm and vibrant and softened with excitement. She turned this way and that, moving her arms, admiring her smooth bare back, admiring her skin and hair, admiring the slim well-fitted lines of her gown. "Does the skirt hang all right?" she asked anxiously, preoccupied only with her reflection in the mirror. "Is the skirt even all the way around? It isn't too long, is it? How does the skirt look?"

Jen stared at the skirt obediently. "Turn around, no, the front again. The skirt's all right."

Josette turned back to the mirror, and promptly lost herself in her own reflection, spreading out the skirt with both hands, and standing on tiptoe, as if by so doing she would be able to bring the hem of her skirt into the range of the short mirror hung above the bureau.

"Gee," Jen said forlornly from the bed, "I wish to God Franny could see you. Honest, she'd go nuts if she ever saw a dress like this. She was always crazy to buy a formal. She used to always say she wanted one just so she could put it on and look at herself wearing it in the mirror whenever she wanted to. Don't it seem just terrible to think that maybe after tomorrow Franny won't never be . . . I just can't stand thinking about it."

"Look," Josette said abstractedly, "are you sure the skirt's all right? It feels just like it's longer in the front. Are you sure it's all right?"

Jen sighed a little and got up from the bed. "Jo, will you take it easy? I told you, that skirt looks perfectly all right. The whole dress looks swell. You look just beautiful, your hair, and everything. You're gonna make Midge and that little half-pint gal friend of hers look sick. So for God's sake, take it easy. You're so nervous and excited you're just about ready to fly to pieces."

"Don't be silly! I'm not the least bit nervous," Josette said rapidly, peeping at her skirt hem. "I never felt better in my life. Why in the world should I be nervous? Look, I'm positive this skirt is just a little bit longer right in the front."

Jen stuck her hands out in front of her, palms upward, and rolled her eyes to the ceiling. "Baby, I'm glad you don't get invited out to Westbridge every night." She brought the chair from across the room and put it in front of the bureau. "Here, Jo," she said wearily, "if you stand on this you can see the bottom of the skirt. Be careful with your dress climbing up there."

Josette lifted her skirt carefully, and Jen steadied the chair. Once on top of it Josette let down her skirt again over the gleaming golden-bronze slippers.

"Now are you satisfied?" Jen said.

"It does hang all right, doesn't it?" Josette marveled. "It fits just perfectly, doesn't it?"

The sound of an automobile motor in front of the house sent Josette skipping down from the chair.

"For God's sakes," Jen said. "Be careful! You want to rip that dress before you ever get out of the house in it?"

"Who's out there?" Josette said nervously, peeping around the window shade. "I heard a car. Is that Midge already?"

Both girls listened attentively. As a matter of fact, the automobile that they heard was that of Reverend Bradley who was just making his departure. In the excitement of Josette's toilet both of them had forgotten all about his visit.

"No, it just must have been some car going by. Hear it going?" Jen said.

Josette looked relieved, and went to the bed and fingered again her sequined evening bag and the fluffy golden-colored angora wrap that she had laid out in preparation for her departure. Then she returned to the mirror restlessly and dabbed powder onto the tip of her nose. "Don't you think my hair looks awfully plain?" she said to Jen anxiously. "Do you think I could comb it any different? You know I've got that gold-colored artificial flower that was on that brown dress I had last winter. Do you think I'd look better if I pinned that in my hair, right here—or here, maybe."

"No," Jen said decisively. "You don't want to go sticking nothing in your hair. Your hair looks just right, all plain and soft and shiny. You leave it alone."

"Lots of the girls wear something in their hair though, a velvet bow, or flowers or clips or something."

"With this dress, you don't want nothing in your hair, honest," Jen insisted. "You know how I can tell? It's like I always do when I'm dressing up for some special date or something myself. I always try to figure out what Mary would do if she was wearing what I got to wear. It works every time. I can just see Mary wearing this dress and I know she wouldn't go sticking nothing in her hair."

Josette was not pleased by Jen's words. She had a swift vision herself of Mary wearing this dress, and the comparison that she instinctively made was not too flattering to herself. She wished suddenly that she could possess, just for tonight, Mary's beautiful quiet poise. She was nervous, she admitted suddenly, and afraid. She made a great effort to steady herself. She deliberately pushed the throbbing, quivering excitement out of her voice.

"Do you suppose he'll buy you a corsage?" Jen asked.

"I'm sure I wouldn't know," Josette said coldly. She was herself again, she thought. This was far too important an occasion to indulge in nerves.

"Why don't you come on downstairs and show Ma and Ernie your dress and everything?"

"No, I don't want to. They can see me when I leave." This recaptured calm of hers was too precious to Josette for her to risk losing under the battery of family admiration or criticism.

Josette folded her hands together and stared at herself in the mirror until her reflection blurred before her eyes.

Jen took up a position at the window where she could look out to the front of the house. And as they both waited the two cars drove up together at last, tearing the soft summer darkness apart with blaring horns.

"I guess there they are," Jen said, her own voice trembling with excitement.

Josette's face paled a little, and the worry lines etched deeper across her smooth forehead. Her hands were clumsy and icy-cold.

"Here," Jen said, "let me help you with that jacket." Josette straightened it across her shoulders and grabbed her bag off the bed.

"Josette . . ." Molly called up the stairway in a strange and artificial voice.

The sisters exchanged amused glances of comprehension, and giggled together involuntarily. Jen squeezed Josette's hand tight in her warm one as Josette flew toward the door. "Josie, you look swell. Be careful of your dress going downstairs. Have a good time, won't you?"

The family down below caught only a glimpse of Josette, the half-dozen steps or so from the stairway to the front porch where Midge

Clark and Johnnie Meredith waited, only a glimpse of the color and sheen of her gown and of her eager smile, and then she was gone.

"Josie's sure all togged out like high society tonight, ain't she?" Ernie said, incoherently, packing the cotton tighter around his aching tooth with a toothpick.

"She sure is," his mother said. "Lord, if she didn't look funny all dressed up like that! Them long dresses make the girls so much older and grown-up, like. I think it was awful nice of Mary to buy her that outfit. Her heart was just set on going to that dance tonight right away she got asked, but if it hadn't a-been for Mary she never could a-gone."

Ernie grunted a little, his eyes shut and his mouth open wide to facilitate the work with the toothpick around his tooth.

Molly glanced at him quickly and went on talking over the leisurely squeak of her rocker. "Josie's an awful lucky girl to have a sister and a brother to help her like she's got. Sending her up there to business college is going to be a great thing for her, all right."

"Oh, hell," Ernie said modestly, snapping the toothpick between his fingers. "Josie's a smart kid; she's got a right to go to school. It ain't nothing special for me to send her up there."

"Yes, it is too, Ernie," Molly insisted. "It's an awful fine thing for you to do for her."

"Well, I'll tell you." Ernie leaned forward in his chair close to Molly. "I figure it this way, Ma—some day me and you are gonna be real proud of Josie."

"You bet we are," Molly assented.

Sam moved the sheets of his newspaper noisily. "Say, where's that feller from, that Josie's gone out with tonight?"

"Well, sir," Molly was saying, "I think Josie made a whole sight prettier and trimmer-looking girl than that Clark girl did in that blue dress without no shoulder straps she had on."

And in the corner, Dorothy walked up and down slowly, the full skirt of her imaginary gown trailing behind her.

Once settled in the front seat of the roadster at Johnnie Meredith's side, Josette relaxed a little. Johnnie Meredith was no terrifying person after all, she decided, studying his profile covertly. He was just an ordinary, average-looking young man, but of course you could tell that he came from a good family, and that he had money. He did not seem inclined to be talkative. He looked almost as if he were sulking, Josette thought. She attributed his mood to the fact that Midge was going to the dance with his cousin Philip, instead of with Johnnie himself, and that Midge looked particularly desirable and beautiful tonight. She felt a little sorry for Johnnie Meredith. She felt suddenly strong and sure of herself, and superior and poised. Tonight she was not just Josette Veech who was trying to run away from a down-at-the-heel existence, but instead she was just any girl meeting any man, just any girl like Midge or Sally, pretty and well dressed, a girl for a man to admire and respect.

"You're from the East, aren't you?" she said to Johnnie Meredith, in a polite, well-modulated voice.

"Uh-huh, Massachusetts."

Josette tried another tack, experimentally. "Are you going back to college in the fall?"

"Sure!" He took his eyes off the road and stared at her, surprised that even for conversational purposes she might doubt that he would attend his college in the fall again. When he looked at her, Josette smiled at him encouragingly. "You're lucky to be having a vacation," she said to him. "I go to business college, you know, and I've been having classes all summer."

Johnnie Meredith seemingly found her smile attractive. He smiled back at her and said, "Yeah? Tough having to go to classes this weather, all right. I know. I took summer school the year I was a freshman." He flapped open his cigarette case in front of her. "Cigarette?"

"No, thank you," Josette said gaily. They were off to a good start, she thought. She had made him look at her and talk to her, and he was interested, she could tell. She felt excited and confident.

He was looking at her, and Josette looked straight back at him and then let her eyes drop along the breadth of his wide shoulders. "Do you play on the football team at college?" she said.

Johnnie Meredith was obviously pleased. "No, I never went out for football. That's one game I don't care so much about. Of course, they're always after me trying to get me to go out for the team, but I don't care a thing about it. They have awful strict training rules, anyway."

"I imagine they do," Josette said politely, wondering what the nature of training rules could be. She tidied her hair down, as the wind blowing in over the low windshield and the back of the roadster disarranged it. She liked the motion of the car. She had never ridden in a roadster before. She liked the looks of Johnnie Meredith in a white coat behind the wheel, in the soft summer darkness. She liked to think that she, Josette Veech, in a gold-colored dress, was on her way to a dance at the Westbridge Country Club. Oh, this, she told herself, was just a sample of the kind of life she had a right to, the kind of life that she was going to have. This was the preview of the new world that she was to have; the world where people had money and wore good clothes, and where everybody was good and decent and had nothing to be ashamed of, the world where there was love and romance, and where life moved easily and smoothly.

Because she felt so good, Josette did something that she had never done before in all of her life. She tipped her face up into the rush of air over the car, to the sky above, and pointed with one hand. "Oh, look," she said in a warm glad voice to Johnnie Meredith, "there must be a million stars!"

"A million trillion," he said cheerfully. He took his eyes away from the bright strip of highway between the dark hills for a moment, but he looked at Josette instead of the stars. Josette felt his eyes on her face, and before her eyes all the stars flared up into victory torches, and bleared together in a flaming sky. What if Johnnie Meredith should fall in love with her, Josette asked herself excitedly. It had been known to happen before; love at first sight. Suppose that he should really fall in love with her, why, then, tonight would be the real turning point in her life. She thought of Pat Thompson suddenly, with scorn. The joke was going to be on Pat, who thought that she belonged to him, that she would marry him because she could do no better. The bright scorn for Pat went through her as bitter and sharp as rusted needles.

"Come a rain storm—put your rubbers on your feet,
Come a snow storm—you can get a little heat,
Come love—nothing can be done . . ."

Johnnie Meredith was chanting over the smooth sound of the motor, driving with one eye on the will-o'-the-wisp of red light that was the taillight on Clark's car, ahead of them.

When Josette and Johnnie returned to the car several hours later, Josette was in a different mood. The dance was a blur in her mind, a blur of a crowded, shining dance floor, several score of dresses at least as lovely as her own, muted rhythmic music. She had danced nearly every dance, most of them with Johnnie. She had found him the best dancer she had ever danced with, but he shifted continually from one new step to another, most of them unknown to Josette. It had required a great deal of concentration on her part to follow him. She had given up conversation altogether and concentrated on her dancing, with the worry lines deep in her forehead. Several times they had traded dances with Ted and Sally. They had not, however, traded any dances with Philip and Midge, because after the first couple of dances Philip and Midge had disappeared from the floor and did not reappear. Josette hardly noticed their absence at first in her anxiety over her dancing. But as she became more accustomed to Johnnie's erratic style, so that she was free to observe and to think again, she began to wonder about their absence. Josette felt momentarily much older and wiser than Midge in the affairs of the world. She wished that she dared suggest to Johnnie Meredith that they go to look for Midge and Philip.

Whenever Josette and Johnnie had not danced, they sat at one of the little tables in the crowded bar. Josette ordered ginger ale each time, or merely sat and waited while Johnnie drank his cocktail.

As the trips to the bar increased, Josette began to feel slightly apprehensive. It did not once occur to her that Johnnie might become drunk. She was aware that he was becoming very silent, very taut and contained, that his dancing was becoming more precise and complicated, that he had taken to holding her much tighter as they danced, but Josette did not think of attributing that to the liquor he had been drinking. She thought at first, romantically, that he was worrying about Midge some place alone with Philip. Then she came to the conclusion that, after all, she did not know Johnnie Meredith very well; this might very possibly be his more normal personality. She was somewhat disappointed by the transformation in him, but at the same time it interested her.

When Johnnie had suggested to her some time later that they go outside where it was cooler, Josette had consented gladly. They left the loud music and the lights behind them. They strolled down the length of the long verandah slowly, and down the steps into the shining white sand of the beach along the lake front.

The country club was set on the very edge of the lake. It was a large lake with a wide strip of sandy beach and many trees behind the beach. The bright moon this night turned the gentle limpid water luminous. Josette saw none of this beauty before her; she was conscious only of Johnnie Meredith who walked at her side. When he reached out and took her hand in his, she closed her fingers on his hand gladly. They walked together aimlessly in the thick sand, along the edge of the shining water of the lake. Here and there they caught glimpses of other couples who, like themselves, had deserted the blatant efforts of the sweating orchestra inside. They heard their voices, sudden words, low spoken, broken off, saw the rosy tips of their cigarettes. The air was soft and warm, and filled with the sound of the waves on the beach, and the insects of the night, the leaves of the trees stirring in the breeze, the faint sound of the music from inside.

"You don't want to get sand in your shoes. Let's go over to where the car is, huh?" Johnnie said suddenly, his voice tuned low, blended into the humming muted harmony of the sounds around them.

"All right," Josette said.

There was a path from the beach to the top of the hill where the roadster was parked under the pine trees. They climbed together, hand in hand, and Josette found great emotional satisfaction in it: the atmosphere of the night, the warm clasp of his hand, the uneven earth under her high heels that made her lose her balance and stumble against him, quick casual contacts of their two bodies; the feel of her silken skirt in her hand as she held it up carefully so that she might not catch it on any of the underbrush along the path, and the thought constantly in the back of her mind that this place was Westbridge Country Club, and that she, Josette Veech, had come to dance here, in a golden dress down to the floor, like other girls did.

Johnnie opened the door, and Josette got in, sitting carefully, so that her skirt would not wrinkle. He slammed the door, and went around to the other side and sat on the deep leather seat beside her.

From the hill under the dark shadow of the pines, they could look down across the roof of the club building, across white sand, across water that was shimmering light, to dark wooded hills beyond the lake, and the great moon over them.

"God!" Johnnie Meredith said softly. "We're sitting on top of the world."

Josette did not know exactly what he meant, and everything before her eyes was a blur, waves of blur in rhythm to her heartbeats, and so she only nodded.

Johnnie took his eyes away from the lake down below them and looked at Josette—looked at her for a long time.

She stirred a little under his gaze, half uncertain, half embarrassed by his steady, unwinking eyes.

He said to her softly, "What's the matter? I'll bet you did get sand in your shoes, didn't you?"

"A little," Josette said. "It doesn't matter." As a matter of fact she had no idea whether or not the sand had crept up into her sandals; she could not tell.

"Can fix that," he said. He leaned down, his head and shoulder against her knees, and loosened the narrow straps around her ankles and took the sandals off her feet.

Josette sat quite still and let him do it, and felt his fingers, cool and delicate, against the arches of her feet. And, strangely enough, she thought again of Pat Thompson with bitter scorn. Never once in a million years would Pat have thought of sand in her shoes, or cared enough to take them off for her. She felt an unspeakable tenderness for Johnnie Meredith. Her thoughts turned into rhetorical theatrical phrases. She kept saying to herself over and over, "This night, this moment must never end. This night is love."

Johnnie sat up again in the seat and put his arm around Josette and drew her firm up against him, bent her head back against his shoulder gently with his hand. His words were disjointed peculiarly. "Poor feet! All tired out after all that dancing. Now you can rest. Just relax and rest here, and shut your eyes, and listen to the waves down there on the beach, and the music . . ."

Even with his words in her ears, and his arms around her, Josette knew perfectly well what she should do. She knew that she must sit up straight and push him away, and smile at him and say some bright clever words, and then put on her shoes and go back to the lights and the music. She knew it quite well, but she had no will to do it. There was no harm in this, she told herself bewilderedly. There was a hunger and eagerness in her body that she had never before experienced. She felt in his arms a kind of warmth and security, a fool's snatch at security that gave her release in these moments from the gnawing worries that made her life unbearable. And, besides, there was no harm in this, she kept repeating to herself, no harm at all.

She let her body go limp and relaxed against his, and unconsciously her fingers fluttered against his chin, her hand along the side of his face, up into his hair, crisp and fine to feel. Johnnie shifted his body in the seat, and kissed her on the mouth and on the face many times. And Josette clung to him tightly while her whole world picked itself up and gyrated around her. Her body knew the beginnings of an ecstasy, her breathing came quick and deep, and the voices of warning in her mind were strange voices, voices only, for she did not listen to the words that they were speaking to her.

All in one deft motion, with his mouth still against her face, Johnnie bent her over on her back along the seat, with his heavy solid body half on hers, and half upon the seat edge. The feel of the cool seat leather along her bare back came to Josette like electric needles crowding through her veins. And absurdly enough it was her dress that she thought of first now, her beautiful golden dress that must not be soiled or crumpled or torn. "No, don't!" she said to Johnnie Meredith.

She struggled to sit up, but if he heard her or felt her struggling he gave no sign of it. She felt his breath against her throat and the pressure of his moving body.

"Stop, please stop," she whispered to him fiercely. She flung out her arms and legs desperately, one leg loose, from under him, her skirt doubled back, the moon shining along a long expanse of shining chiffon hose. And then his fingers on her leg, quick hot fingers like mice scurrying, at her knee, up her thigh, flesh that was quivering under his touch. She got hold of his wrist with her one free hand, but she had no strength to hold him. She did not scream. Oddly enough, she listened carefully to the music they were playing down below for the dancing, and she dug in all five fingernails into his wrist with all of her strength.

He jerked his hand away then, and he laughed, the strangest laugh, Josette thought, that she had ever heard, and it terrified her. She struggled desperately, and he kissed her again all over her face, her throat, her shoulders, and then the fingers again, the scurrying mice inside the bodice of her gown. She twisted and turned underneath him desperately, and at last she pushed his hands away from her, and when his hands came free there was a ripping sound, and the golden gown was slit in the front down to the waist.

With that sound in her ears, Josette dug her free hand into that short crisp hair along the back of his head, and pulled. She lifted him up with the pulling, and once the pressure of his heavy body was gone from her, she opened the car door and slid down from the seat onto the ground. She walked a few steps from the car to the tree, and looked down to the blur of shimmering light that was the lake with the moon on it, unseeing. She was shivering a little, one of her arms felt as if it had been jerked out of its socket, and under her shoeless stockinged feet she felt the sharp, hard gravel stones. And then the shame came, and the anger and the disappointment. Josette did not cry; she only stood quite still. At last she reached out her hand blindly and pathetically against the rough cool bark of the pine tree, the fingers with the delicate, manicured nails over which she had spent so much time a few hours ago.

Behind her in the automobile, Johnnie Meredith sat still for a few moments, and then he ran his hand down over his face, and shook his head sharp and hard. He sighed a little, smoothed his hair back with a comb, arranged his tie, and brushed at a little sand sticking along his trouser leg. Then he picked up Josette's sandals from the floor and got out of the car and took them to her.

"Come on," he said gently and wearily, "let's go back to the dance. Here are your shoes."

Josette did not turn around or speak to him. He touched her

carefully upon the shoulder. "We better go back now. Here are your shoes."

Josette turned on him suddenly, with her voice choked and angry. "You go on back down there if you want to. I'm not going. I can't."

She motioned to the crumpled soiled skirt, some of the gathers at the waist ripped loose. With her other hand, she was holding together the slit bodice of her gown.

"I'm sorry," Johnnie Meredith said.

Josette's face was dark and furious with anger. "You ought to be."

His face darkened in the bright chromium of the moonlight, but he answered her smoothly. "What do you expect," he said, "when you wear something like that to a wrestling match?"

Josette looked out down the hill again and did not speak.

"I'll take you home," he said at last.

He was still holding her sandals, and she turned around suddenly and snatched them from him. "No!"

"Come on now, get in the car like a good girl and I'll take you home."

"Do you think I'd get in that car again with you?" she said without turning around.

He was quiet a minute, and then he said rapidly, "Look, you stay here and put your shoes on, and I'll go down and get Ted. You'd let Ted take you home, wouldn't you? It wouldn't take him but a minute, and I could stay and dance with Sally. That would be all right, wouldn't it?"

Josette did not answer him. She walked by him and sat down on the running board of the car and began putting on her sandals.

Johnnie started down the path, and he turned around with the moonlight shining on his white jacket and called to her. "You stay there now. Ted'll be up in just a second."

Josette watched him down the path in silence, and tightened the straps of her shoes around her ankles. She wanted more than anything else to run away, and never see any of them again, and walk the way home by herself. But she also knew that she had to wait and accept the ride home that was offered. So she sat still on the running board with her head tipped back, resting against the side of the car, and her hands folded quietly in her lap.

Ted came then, and found her like that. He hurried up the path out of breath. "Hello!" he said. "I didn't see you for a minute. You scared me. I thought you'd run off some place."

He handed her her wrap with the inner pocket sagging under the weight of her evening bag. She took it silently and climbed into the car.

Ted closed the door, and got in beside her and backed the car out into the road.

"Sally said to tell you good-bye," he said to her at last, scowling ahead of him over the steering wheel.

Josette gave no sign that she heard him.

In a minute he tried again, prefacing it with an awkward laugh. "Haven't seen a thing of Midge and Phil since we got here. Guess they pulled a real vanishing act."

Josette sat quietly beside him, a million miles beyond his reach.

He slid the heavy car around a curve expertly. "Look, I'm awfully sorry this had to happen, about your dress and everything. I know Johnnie feels bad about it. Johnnie's an awful good guy, but when he's been drinking a little too much, why sometimes . . ."

"He can't use drinking for an excuse," Josette said suddenly. "He wasn't that drunk."

It was Ted's turn to be quiet before her words.

The white road wound away in front of the car, between dark swelling hills with every leaf of every bush and tree silvered by the moon. The little hard gravel stones splattered continually against the fenders.

He scowled and wet his lips with the tip of his tongue, and Josette shivered beside him in the seat.

He spoke again over the rushing sound of the wind through the car, and the steady roar of the motor. "I mean it. Johnnie wouldn't have had this happen for anything. I tell you what, when you get home you change your dress and powder your nose and stuff and come on back with me. I'll wait, and then you come on back to the dance. Johnnie was hoping you'd change your mind and come back; he said he was. I'll wait and you come on back with me."

Josette smiled a little, grimly. As easy as that, change your dress and go back to the dance, put on another dress and put powder on your nose and comb your hair and smile and go back and never miss more than three or four dances, as simple and easy as that.

"You will come back with me, won't you?" Ted said to her.

"No."

"I think you're taking this too serious. I don't see why you want to let it ruin your whole evening." There was a shade of anger in his voice as he spoke.

"Oh, don't you!" Josette said.

"No, I don't. Johnnie's a good guy. Maybe he'd been drinking a little too much, but . . . ."

"Don't talk to me about him!" Josette said furiously. "Don't try to make excuses for him. I never want to see him again as long as I live."

"Okay," Ted said, and there was real anger in his voice now. "Okay, if that's the way you feel about it. But I don't see why you should get so mad about this. What did you expect? Johnnie's just human, and he's been drinking a little. What did you expect?"

"What did you expect," the words dinned themselves over and over against Josette's ears, hundreds of voices, all kinds of voices, all saying to her loudly and softly, urgently, insistently over and over again, "What did you expect? what did you expect?" And what was it that she had expected, Josette wondered. How could she say, "Why, I expected that Johnnie Meredith would fall in love with me, and that this would be the beginning of a whole new life for me, that he would marry me and take me away to the kind of a life I want to live." "What did you expect?" the very motor of the automobile took up the chant, and Josette said wildly, "Please keep still about it. I'm not going back. I don't want to talk about it."

Ted said no more, and in a few moments they saw the lights of the village ahead of them. When he stopped the car in front of the Veeches', Josette went weak with relief. The house was completely dark. The whole family must be asleep. She said a little prayer of gratitude.

"Don't get out," she said to Ted hastily. "I'd rather you wouldn't."

"Okay," he said coolly. "I'm sorry things had to go to smash like this. But it looks like this is the way you want it. If it isn't, you better get wise to yourself."

"Good night," Josette said politely. She almost added, "I had a very nice time," because the words came mechanically from some spot in her bewildered brain where order and conventionality remained. She turned away toward the house, and heard the roar of the motor behind her as he drove away.

She tiptoed up the steps, into the darker shadows of the porch, past the porch swing to the door. She tried the screen experimentally, and found that it was not hooked. She took her sandals off, holding the straps firmly in her hands and slipped through the door. At that moment her whole consciousness was absorbed by the idea of getting up the stairs and into bed without encountering a single member of her family. Inside the living room, the moonlight lay along the faded rug and touched the glistening tinsel trimmings on the dolls and Scottie dogs on the piano top, the prizes from the carnival. Josette saw them and thought of Pat Thompson, and put the thought of him out of her mind.

Two of the steps of the stairway squeaked loudly under her weight, and each time Josette stopped dead-still with her heart pounding, but there was no sound from above to show that anyone had heard it. Josette was not so expert at avoiding the creaking places of the stairs as Jen had become after years of experience.

But at last Josette shut her bedroom door behind her, and leaned her back against it in the darkness. Her head ached, and her stomach was sick, and she felt weak, but most of all there was a vast hurt in her that as yet she had had no chance to analyze, only a great aching hurt, too great for tears.

The light came on suddenly, glaring into her eyes. She could only see the vague outlines of Jen sitting up in bed, with her hair wound around a dozen or so metal curlers all over her head. "My God," Jen said. "You're home early. I didn't think you'd be home for a long time yet. How come you came home so early? Don't tell me your society boy has to go to bed early."

Josette did not answer. Jen stared at her curiously, her own eyes gradually accommodating to the bright light in the room.

"What's the matter with you? What are you standing over there for?" Jen sat up straighter in the bed. "Can't you say anything? You look awful, and you musta ripped . . . Oh, Josie, your dress! For God's sakes, what happened to you? It's all wrinkles, and there's some dirt on it, and the front's all ripped open and . . ."

Josette walked over to the bureau stiffly and laid down her evening bag. She slipped her arms out of the fluffy brief angora wrap. She was very careful not to catch a glimpse of her reflection in the mirror.

Jen hopped around to the foot of the bed and leaned over the footrail, wide-eyed and silent. Josette stood rooted to the floor with her arms at her sides, as if she were loath to take the dress off.

"Josie, tell me what happened to you!"

Josette began to pull the long bedraggled skirt over her head without answering.

"Gosh, that dress is sure a mess," Jen said in an awestricken voice. "You better put it back in that box it came in. If Ma ever gets a look at it, she'll raise the roof, after Mary went and bought it and everything. I wish you'd tell me what happened. Please, Josie, tell me."

Josette put her dress away in the box without bothering to fold it, and jammed the cover down over it.

"Come on and tell me," Jen urged. "I always tell you everything that happens to me, don't I? You know I'm just dying to know what happened."

Jen was becoming impatient. "Look, you don't need to act like there was any secret about it. I could tell what happened the first good look I got at you. Your swell high-society date turned out to be pretty hard to handle, didn't he? I bet he'd been drinking too." Jen's voice turned soft and warm with sympathy. "Aw, you poor kid, and you get all dressed up swell, and go out there to have a good time and then . . . Aw, Josie, I'm so sorry, honest. . . ."

The sympathy and understanding in her sister's voice broke down barriers for Josette. She was too hurt yet for her pride to erect defenses. The weak tears welled out of her eyes.

"I never want to have another formal as long as I live," she said oddly, in a tremulous voice. "Never. I never could put one on again without thinking about what happened tonight."

"Aw, Josie! Honey, I'm so sorry!" Jen pulled her sister down onto the edge of the bed and put her arm around her. "Come on and tell me everything that happened. What did he do? Gosh, it musta been something awful to make you feel like this. Come on and tell me."

Because there was more hurt in her than pride at this moment, Josette told the whole story, briefly and honestly, in a low, monotonous voice, leaving the dance hall, the walk on the beach, climbing the hill to the car, the removing of her shoes, the brief happiness she had felt in his arms, his kisses, and then the disastrous end of the affair, omitting, of course, the things that Ted had said to her on the way back to town.

Jen listened to her story attentively, and, as she listened, she gradually leaned back upon her pillow on her elbows, with a curious puzzled expression on her face.

As Josette talked, her tongue loosened and the color came back into her face, and she grew angry. "And I never want to see Johnnie Meredith again as long as I live," she finished. "I hate him. I won't speak to him if I meet him on the street. After doing a thing like that, the idea of him expecting me to go back to the dance like nothing ever happened, or to get into that car with him again and let him bring me home. I don't see how anybody could be so . . ."

"Yeah," Jen said reflectively. She leaned back along the pillows, her eyes lowered to the white bedspread, and tapped her teeth carefully with one long crimson fingernail.

"Well, don't you agree with me?" Josette said. "Don't you think it was a perfectly rotten filthy thing for him to do to me?"

Jen was silent, her eyes still following the intricate woven thread that made up the design of the thick worn old bedspread.

"Oh, of course you wouldn't," Josette said bitterly. "You'd have stayed right there in the car and let him maul you and that would have been all right with you, but I'm not that kind of a girl, and I . . ."

Josette got up from the bed abruptly and went to the bureau and began to comb her hair, jerking the comb through it fiercely over and over again. Jen sat silent in the middle of the bed and studied her manicure with rapt attention.

Suddenly, Josette threw the comb down and turned around with her hands braced along the edge of the bureau. Her face was flushed with color now, and she spoke a little incoherently out of the very center of her hurt and her bewilderment. "How could he do something like that? What made him do it and spoil everything? How could a man like that do something so—so—cheap and common and nasty? That's what I can't understand. What made him do it?"

Jen stroked a red nail with a fingertip and carefully studied its hue and symmetry. She spoke softly without looking at Josette. "Well, I guess it just proves society boys ain't no different than anybody else. It just proves men are all alike, that's all; whether they run around in tuxedos or overalls—it don't make no difference."

"That isn't so," Josette said angrily. "Just because that tough gang of men you go around with all the time all make passes at you is no sign that all men are like that. Do you suppose the men that Midge and Sally go around with in college all act around them like that? Of course they don't. You just say that because you don't know any better, you never had a date with a decent man in your life. You and Frances Cope and girls like you don't know what it is to have a man respect you."

All in one motion, the covers flying, Jen jumped up onto her knees in the middle of the bed, her eyes dark and wide with anger. "Okay," she said, "you asked for this. You make me sick enough to puke, always thinking you're so damn much better'n anybody else on earth. Maybe Franny and me don't date with the four hundred, but you never see us coming home with our clothes half tore off, and yelling bloody murder about why in God's name could Johnnie be such a louse, anyway. The trouble with you is you're dumb, you don't know any better. You better go to college for a couple years more, that's what I say."

"Shut your mouth!" Josette said. "Stop yelling at me. Do you want to wake up everybody in the house? I won't listen to anything you say, anyway."

"Oh, you make me sick!" Jen said. "You're so dumb! You betcha Midge and Sally and girls like that don't get pawed over on a date unless they want to. That's because they got brains, and you ain't. And then you make cracks about poor Franny when she's laying up there in that hospital right this minute." Jen hesitated over tears, but she choked them back and went on talking, with her voice rising higher and higher. "You come home here tonight, howling about this all being Johnnie Meredith's fault. Well, the hell it was! It was your fault, that's whose fault it was!"

"Shut your mouth!" Josette was pale with anger, and her fingers were splayed out pale and flat as she gripped the edge of the bureau. Her own voice rose out of control into a scream. "Shut your mouth!"

But there was no stopping Jen now. She crouched at the foot of the bed, hanging onto the chipped iron footrail with her two hands, looking straight up into Josette's face. "When this guy says 'let's go take a walk,' you say 'okay.' When he says 'let's go sit in the car,' you say 'okay.' My God, you was either looking for trouble right then, or else you was leading with your chin. He kisses you a couple of times, and that's plenty okay with you. Sure, you liked that. Well, then, what in hell did you expect the guy was gonna do next—take his knitting out of his pocket and start crocheting himself a pair of socks? Oh, sure, blame it all on him! You started something and then you get sore as hell because he tries to finish it. Oh, you make me sick, and all the nicey-nice girls just like you. You like kissing and you like mugging around, every chance you get with any nice-looking guy that comes along, but then you want to stop right there. You play around and get a guy all worked up and then the game's over and you give him hell if he don't stop right on the dot. Aw, you make me sick! God, there oughtta be a name for girls like you . . ."

"Stop! I won't listen to you," Josette said in a strangled voice. Her face was white and she was shivering, gooseflesh all over her body, clad as she was only in brief brassiere and step-ins. "You don't know what you're talking about. You think that all girls are—are . . ."

"Shut up, shut up, shut up!" Jen shook at the footrail like a demon. There was the sound of bedsprings squeaking from adjoining rooms, but they were unheard here. "You was talking about respect a minute ago. Do you think Johnnie Meredith's got any respect for you right now? The hell he has! Respect! That's funny!"

Josette grabbed the box of Kleenex tissue off the dresser and threw it at Jen, and Jen laughed and ducked, and Josette sent her books and pad of typewriting paper spinning at her.

Jen kept laughing. "He thinks you're a cheat, that's what he thinks of you; a common little cheat, that's been cheating around for years. Only he don't know the half of it about you. You give him all the go-ahead signs; he don't stop just the minute you're ready to, and then you come home here and holler like he'd raped you!"

Jen dodged the heavy glass cold-cream jar, and it rolled crashing over the floor. Josette emptied the bureau top in her fury, and then Jen dove at her over the footrail. The cracked old mirror caught them in the flat two dimensions. Jen's full young body in the thin nightgown topped with the weird metal curlers on her head, suspended in the air, and Josette pushing her away, leaving red scratches in soft white flesh, and all the while her face white and detached and disgusted, as the face of an onlooker rather than a participant.

Molly flung the door open and stood blinking in the doorway. "Well, for Lord's sakes, what's going on in here?" Molly was out of breath from her hurried ascent up the stairs. Her big white nightgown billowed around her, and her big bare feet, solid on the floor, and lumpy with corns, stuck out below the hem. The space around her, in the doorway, was filled by bobbing heads, suspended against the darkness of the hall like balloons on strings, Sam and Kenny and Dorothy and Carl.

Kenny, clad in shorts only, crowded into the room around Molly. "Cat fight," he said cheerfully, with his delicate cough. He picked Jen off the bed, and stood her down on the floor, holding her struggling body in his arms. At his touch, the fight went out of her, and she put her arms up around his neck like a small child and began to cry. Josette stood alone in front of the bureau, in the midst of the havoc that they had created out of the bedroom.

"Well, I should say it was a cat fight!" Molly said indignantly. She turned on Josette as the more composed and responsible of the sisters at the moment. "You oughtta be ashamed, a-hollering and yelling and throwing things and digging each other, right in the middle of the night, when everybody is trying to sleep, and sickness in the house and everything. It's a disgrace, two great big girls like you a-fighting. You oughtta be ashamed."

Kenny looked at Josette coolly over the top of Jen's head. "From Ritz to roughhouse," he said. But Josette paid no attention to any of them. She stood quietly in front of the mirror with her shoulders drooping and her eyes fixed and far away.

"What was you fighting about?" Molly demanded.

Josette did not speak, and through her crying Jen answered incoherently. "All my fault . . . We got to arguing, and I got to talking nasty to her. But I don't care. I'm just so jumpy and nervous tonight I'm like to going crazy, just thinking about Franny up there in that hospital and that operation tomorrow, because if anything happens to Franny, why, I don't know what I'll do, or what will become of me. I just don't know."

"Sure, we know it's hard on you, but take it easy, honey," Kenny said to her tenderly. "You gotta keep your chin up. You wouldn't find Franny a-crying and taking on like this. She's laying up there braver'n a soldier. You wouldn't get a peep out of her."

"There's no sense you getting all upset like this," Molly said sensibly. "It don't look like to me that Cope girl's got much of a chance, and you might as well start getting used to it. Ain't no call for you to let yourself go all to pieces. Lord, and Mr. Higgins so sick downstairs and everything, it would seem like you'd think of things like that."

She whirled around suddenly on the interested audience in the hallway around her. "Well, are you gonna hang around here all night? Why doncha git back in bed and let somebody get a little sleep? Dor'thy, you're coming downstairs with Grandma and sleep on the couch, and then Jen can sleep in your bed. There now, hush up your crying, never come anything yet that sniveling helped it any," she finished as she led Jen out of the bedroom.

All of them melted away, and the door closed, and Josette was alone in the room, under the merciless stare of the light bulb. Her bewilderment and her shame were complete; she had done the one thing that she would never be able to forgive herself for, allowing herself to sink to the common level of the family, and indulging in a brawl, there was no other word, screaming and throwing things, and scratching and clawing. Never would she forgive herself for this, or Jen, for making her do it. But this thinking that she did was only perfunctory and superficial. Her mind and emotions seemed to be clearing out into a vacuum preparatory to the coming of a momentous realization, just as the stage of the theater is cleared before the entrance of the protagonist to deliver his greatest monologue.

Josette turned the light out, ignoring the litter over the floor, and slipped out of her clothes into her nightgown. She went to the window then, and put the shade up. The night was still, the insect voices were soft. The leaves over the limbs of the great tree against her window stirred a little with their breathing, in the moonlight. No automobiles, no trains, no people in the streets, no one left among the alive and the wakeful but herself, truly the time for great decisions. She stood stiff and still by the window, looking out with blank unseeing eyes, and her mind was still also, and waiting. And after a while it came to her, and when it came it was like a great deep solemn voice speaking within her, a voice so deep that she could not hear the tone of it, but rather felt it, in a series of great vibrations like the tolling of a bell into the empty quiet air of a summer day. And what it said to her was short enough, and irrevocable and final.

There was still another world, it told her, the gay good clean world, the world to which people like Midge and Sally and Ted and Johnnie Meredith and Philip belonged, the world where no one ever had anything to be ashamed of, and where life moved easily and charmingly, the world where things like tonight never happened. Oh, yes, there was such a world, all right, but it was not for her. And the reason was so amazingly simple; so strange that she had never realized it before. That world was not for her, because, fundamentally, she was no different from any of the rest of her family. Their blood was her blood; she was of them and like them. She was no better than Mary was, or Jen, and this steady inexorable voice of her own logic told her that there was something about her, some mark, some stigma, unseen perhaps, but easily perceived, by which people could always find her out, as Johnnie Meredith had found her out this night. There was no such thing, the voice reminded her, as escaping your own destiny, running away from your own fate, avoiding your own doom; it lay beyond your power of circumvention.

And then the voice stopped, and the last vibrations of it went on and on inside of her. Josette left the window, and crawled into her bed. She did not cry. She did not question her logic, or the premises upon which it was founded. She only thought in a pathetic wash of self-pity that it was too bad that she had not discovered this sooner. Incredibly she found no incongruities in her logic. Weird as her thinking had been, it satisfied her. She contemplated the tragedy of her life. She felt transcended, uplifted, rapt on her tragic heights, the breather of the rarefied thin air of arid peaks.

She lay stiff and alone in the middle of the big iron bed, and the moon shone in the window, and sketched a jagged shadow from the footrail of the bed, across the smooth white bedspread.

And there was her pride.

4

THE NEXT MORNING JOSETTE GOT OUT OF BED, dressed and went to school. It was a day that seemed never to end for her, a torment and an agony. She went about classes and books and Ashbury streets all in a haze. There was a strange feeling always with her, a strange gnawing persistent feeling, a feeling of unreality, uncleanness that could not be dispelled. The day was for her a caricature of a nightmare of a day. But it ended at last, and she got out of Nina Warren's car and walked into the lowering sun, up the uneven wooden front porch steps at home. She went through the house to the kitchen and there she found Molly bent over a cake on the oven door. Molly held the broom in one hand, and broke straws off it and jabbed them down through the cake intently. She straightened up from the hot oven as Josette came in, her face streaming with the heat.

"Lord," she said crossly, "I swear this is gonna be the last baking I do till the cool weather comes. It ain't no sense in me baking this kind of weather. Hanging around this hot stove just tuckers me all out. It's just exactly as cheap to buy your knickknacks from the bakery as to bake 'em here to home this weather. Besides, there ain't enough of you to home here for meals to pay me the trouble."

"I saw Jen up to Ashbury this afternoon," Josette said, filling a water glass out of the pail of warm brackish drinking water, indifferently. "She said to tell you that she wouldn't be home till late, maybe not till tomorrow."

Molly shoved the cake back into the oven, closed the door on it gently, and then mopped her face. "Well, for Lord's sakes, what is she . . ." Molly sat down hard on the old wooden chair by the door.

"Why, say, how did that Cope girl come out with her operation anyway?"

"Not so good," Josette said. "Jen said they couldn't remove the tumor. When they got in to it they found out they couldn't remove it, so they just had to sew her up again. The doctors said she probably couldn't live over a week or so."

Molly shook her head and sighed deeply. "Well, it ain't nothing more than I expected right along. You can't tell me that them doctors can go fooling around with the inside of somebody's head and them still alive. It sure is a terrible thing though, when you stop to think, her just a little young girl like that, and nothing they can do for her. Lord, I'll bet her folks are just all broke up over this."

Josette set the water glass down, and looked out of the kitchen door to the garden, and the trees and the sky. Somewhere in the neighborhood, a radio blared music into the quiet of the day's end.

Molly continued conversationally, "And, you know, they say now that that Rita Sibley is a-going to pull through up there to the hospital. It sure beats all, don't it, how somebody like that that ain't no good to nobody will keep on living and somebody like that little young Cope girl with her life all ahead a-her has to go. Yes, sir, it beats all."

Josette felt a shadow of the familiar rage that she always felt when her mother referred to Rita Sibley in this fashion, but only a shadow of it. She was too bound up in herself and too apathetic tonight to argue with her mother.

"You want some supper now?" Molly asked presently.

"No," Josette said. "I don't want any supper. I don't feel like eating; it's too hot. I'm going upstairs and study awhile and as soon as I get cooled off I'm going to bed and see if I can't get some sleep."

"Well, there you are!" Molly said crossly, fanning herself with a corner of her apron. "It sure is the limit! Here I build up a fire and heat the oven, and like to stew myself to juice, a-baking and a-fixing stuff for supper and everything, and now I'd like to know who's gonna eat it?"

She stopped for breath, listening to the sound of Josette's feet on the stair steps.

"What kinda cake you cooking out there?" Jud called querulously out of the bedroom.

"One of them black ones with cocoa," Molly said indifferently, as she hoisted her bulk up out of the little wooden chair, scraping it along the warped floor boards.

"Why, sure ye are," Jud said bitterly. "You know as well as anything I ain't never been no hand at all for them cocoa cakes. Oh, hell, what I wouldn't give for a hunk of one of them real old-fashioned molasses cakes right hot from the tin. I tell you, it's an awful thing when folks won't give a dying man the things he likes to eat."

"Mr. Higgins," Molly said, "you just hush up now. They ain't no sense you being mean like this. Every time you open your mouth, seems like you're trying to say something meaner than you did the last time. I swear you just lay in there in that bed a-thinking up mean things to say to us. Lord, didn't I bake a molasses cake last week and you wouldn't eat a crumb of it, and you kept a-harping about what you'd give for one of my cocoa cakes."

"That's a lie," Jud quavered. "Every word of it, nothing but a God-damned lie!"

"Oh, pshaw!" Molly said softly. She broke off more broom splinters, and stabbed them into the moist brown cake on the oven door, viciously.

Dawn cracked the sky to the east, and a strange unreal gray light crept through to herald the sunrise. It was a peculiar time of the day, darker than twilight, but more luminous. There was a profound quiet every place, punctuated only by the distant sounds of cocks crowing. A breeze came up and ruffled the dark gray trees, turned the leaves inside out, like a flock of silver birds flying, and gone.

Mary Veech lay very still in the middle of her white bed, and watched the dull light crawl over the floor from the window. It was a time of day when it is not good to be alone, half light, half dark, half day, half night. Mary Veech got out of bed abruptly, put slippers on her feet, and wrapped a robe about her. In the mirror she was as gray and ghostly as the dawn itself. She combed her hair briefly, and went to sit in her chair by the window. The air that came in was damp and thick and mistlike. She shivered a little. She sat still then, and waited.

She heard feet at last, shuffling carelessly along the sidewalk.

Then the sound stopped, and in a minute she heard them again, now cautious and soft, on the back porch. She heard the sound the door made, giving a little on the metal hook, as he tried to open it. She even heard the sound of the porch boards squeaking as he threw himself down on the porch; and then the sound of his delicate little hacking cough.

In the silence again, Mary got up and secured her robe around her. She held a match flame to a cigarette. The flame flickered small and pale. It was as if the still gray air swallowed it up, it was gone so soon. She slipped out of the door and down the stairs, without a single creaking of a board. She went out through the kitchen to the screen door, and lifted the hook in her hand.

Kenny was sprawled out face down across the porch boards, his head pillowed on his arms. He heard the faint click of the hook lifting, and he sat up and twisted around to the door. Neither one of them said a word, Mary in the door with the cold damp metal hook still in her fingers, nor Kenny on the porch. Kenny kept looking at her. He sat up very straight and made a futile weary gesture to smooth his hair back from his eyes. His eyes were bloodshot, his face pallid in the strange light. He was not drunk any more, but at the intermediate stage just before a hangover.

"Hi," he said at last, softly. "It was swell of you to come down. I was freezing out here. It's funny . . . It's funny . . ." But his thoughts and his words and his voice all got away from him and went off on tangents of their own. He made a familiar weary gesture of the hand.

Mary opened the screen door and came out onto the porch. "It's funny how cold it is early in the morning," she said dispassionately.

Kenny stood up beside her, with one hand against a post for support. He shook his head a little to clear it, and pressed his hand hard over his eyes and down the side of his face. And then he laughed silently. "Bum liquor," he said. "Makes you feel like hell."

Mary pulled out the flat silver case from a pocket in her robe and stuck a cigarette into his mouth. She found a match while he was still fumbling, and struck it deftly. Then she steadied his cigarette in his mouth with her fingers, and lit it.

"You must be cold," he mumbled. He closed his big hand over her shoulder.

"I'm all right," she said. "I want to talk a minute."

"Here, you better have my coat . . ."

"No. Leave it on. This robe is warm. We can't talk here."

They went down the steps together and, as if by common consent, they walked across the little backyard to the used-car lot wedged in between the filling station and the house. The car lot was almost empty, except for occasional ancient, denuded wrecks of automobiles. It was a great expanse of hard-packed damp sand, littered with the matches and cigarette butts of many days, and on two sides the great catalpa trees, immense green leaves and immense white flowers, unreal in the dim light, like stage-prop trees.

They walked across the car lot together, to a position out of sight and out of the wind behind two old cars at the back. Mary leaned against the body of the car, and the wind ruffled her hair around her face. Kenny stood close in front of her.

"How's everything, kid?" he said to her gently.

"So-so; the same old thing."

She threw her cigarette down and took hold of his wrist tightly. "Ken, you know a mug named Gitlo." She didn't ask as if it were a question; she said it quietly and flatly.

Kenny waited a moment before he answered. He closed his hand over hers, closed it tight and warm in his. "Sure, I know Gitlo. Great fellow this guy Gitlo. Gitlo's the guy that bought me drinks tonight. Lousy drinks, but a great guy, Gitlo."

She wadded up a handful of his shirt tight in her hand. "How long you known Gitlo?"

"Oh, I dunno—quite a while . . . I know Gitlo. Great guy, Gitlo."

She shook him suddenly. "Ken. Listen. How long have you known Gitlo? Years, months, days—what?"

Although her voice was cool and quiet as always, something in it seemed to sober Kenny. He pulled himself together visibly, and made a great effort to concentrate on what she was saying to him.

"Weeks," he answered. "Maybe two, maybe three, I dunno. Why?"

"How did you run into him?"

Kenny thought about it hard. "Robotelli. Robotelli does jobs for Gitlo sometimes. I've known Robotelli hell of a long time. Last week, week before, I dunno—Robotelli says to me, 'How would you like to meet the boss?' I says sure, and then Robotelli takes me over to Gitlo's place. That's how I meet Gitlo, must have been two, three weeks ago."

Kenny looked at Mary expectantly, but she did not speak. She leaned back against the car, away from him. She said at last, "So you know Gitlo."

Kenny found a meaning beyond the words that she had spoken. He took hold of her shoulders and spoke to her urgently. "Mary, listen. You know me. I know Gitlo, so what about it? I know a lot of guys. It don't mean nothing. There ain't a racket going they can get me into, you know that. Gitlo knows that. He's a good guy."

Mary looked away over the top of Kenny's head to the bright sky to the east. He kept his hands on her shoulders and watched her face, coughing a little, quiet in his throat.

When she spoke her voice was soft and flat as if she were talking only to herself. "Once Gitlo got in a bad jam. Lew got him the money to get out of it. Gitlo wouldn't be around here today, if it hadn't a-been for Lew."

Kenny laughed exultantly, with his head flung back. "Now I know what you got on your mind," he said. "But you ain't got a thing to worry about. You can take it from me."

She looked at him full in the face. He was still laughing. When he laughed he looked younger than Carl, young and strong and confident of everything and himself.

He kept laughing and he doubled his fist and touched it gently to her chin. "I'll tell you a secret," he said. "Hell, I know all about the deal Gitlo made with Lew. Gitlo told me himself. But that don't mean nothing. This is the secret. Gitlo hates his guts. He's got it in for Lew right. Gitlo don't go around telling that to everybody, see, but he told me all about it. He hates Lew's guts."

Her face was expressionless.

"I wish you knew Gitlo," Kenny said. "You oughtta meet him. He's a great guy, all right."

"Ken, watch him and go easy, will you?"

The mirth went out of his face. "Why, sure, if you say so. But you got the wrong idea on Gitlo. If Lew thinks Gitlo is still his errand boy, Lew's nuts. I know."

"Yeah, sure," she said wearily.

They stood together, and the leaves on the big catalpas rustled over them in the wind. The light to the east suddenly blotted out of the sky, as if the sun had changed its mind about another dawn.

Kenny's face was dark and brooding, and he said at last, "I see what you had on your mind, all right. God, ain't Lew Lentz never gonna rest till I'm put away somewheres?"

"No," Mary said.

He laughed unpleasantly then. "That's fine. I don't care what in hell he's got up his sleeve. He can't get at me. He ain't gonna get rid of me, the dirty son-of-a-bitching scheming old spider . . .

"Mary!" his voice changed, rose higher, thin and high and clear. "Mary, my God, I can't stand no more! You can't go on living with him. You gotta leave him!"

Mary drew her breath in sharply, and then her face was suddenly weary and still as if the breath and life had gone out of her altogether.

His hands were hard and rough on her shoulders. "Why, Mary . . . Why do yuh stay with him? You been with him longer now than you ever been with anybody before. Tell me why?"

She did not look at him, and after a little she moved her lips with an effort. "Lew needs me," she said tonelessly.

Kenny laughed and coughed all at once, an odd, tragic, broken sound. "Sure. Sure he needs yuh, but what about you? My God, Mary, what about you? Don't you ever think a yourself? Don't you want nothin' for yourself?"

She did not look at him or answer him, and he shook her hard by the shoulders. "Mary, what about me? I need you too. What about us?"

Then she did look at him, but her eyes were as lifeless and weary as her face. When she spoke it was as if the words she said had been repeated so many times that they were meaningless.

"Us, Ken? What about us? This is all there is for us now. We both knew that a long time ago!"

His hands dropped from her shoulders to his sides, and his voice was still unnatural, high and thin. "Oh, Mary!"

Mary closed her eyes, and sat down on the running board of the car abruptly.

The sky had clouded over, it was almost as dark as night now, except for that strange unearthly luminosity even in the gloom. The wind blew, and sent papers scudding across the used-car lot, tossing the catalpa leaves about like the ears of wild elephants on stampede, and the great white petals of the flowers rained down over the two below.

Kenny swayed over her uncertainly in the gloom. He said her name again, "Mary! Mary!" with his agonized voice mixing into the wind.

And then he dropped to the ground at her feet and stretched his arms tight around her. He buried his face in her lap, pressing his lips tight against her body, so that when he spoke his voice was muffled. "Mary! Oh, Mary, sometimes it don't seem like I can stand any more of this!"

His whole body twisted against her knees; he held her with all of his strength.

Mary did not move. She held her cigarette case raised up in her hands over his head. Not a muscle of her face moved.

The gloom deepened around them. The wind chased great dark-brown mottled clouds across the sky. Still Kenny clung to her, and, after a little, he began to cry.

Mary lit another cigarette. She carefully avoided touching him with her hands; she kept her eyes carefully averted from him. She leaned her head back against the side of the automobile and closed her eyes. She smoked the cigarette slowly. Gradually, his crying stopped. He still held her, his body twitching with nervous tremors. She threw the cigarette down onto the hard-packed sand. Her hands hung idly at her sides; her eyes were still closed. And when the tremors went through him her eyelids fluttered each time.

Suddenly her body doubled over. She put her arms around him with her hands flat against his back, and pillowed her head down on his like a tired child. The wind blew and rattled a wooden signboard some place inside its wooden frame. The wind blew and swept the scraps of paper up and down the lot, and lifted the full skirt of Mary's robe around her feet.

The wind blew and tangled Mary's hair, caught full of the big creamy petals flung down from the catalpa trees above them.

5

THE WIND WAS STILL BLOWING WHEN JEN CAME home at the end of that gray day. She came into the house and the wind banged the door shut behind her. She stood still inside the door smoothing her hair and skirt. Her father was lying on the couch with his shoes off and a sweater buttoned over his blue shirt, reading a book in the glare of light from the overhead bulb.

"Where's Ma?" Jen asked him.

He closed the book over his finger, and blinked his eyes at her.

"Why, your mother's out there with Jud, doing something for him. I dunno."

Jen fidgeted on her tall heels uncertainly.

"Say, it's chilly out, ain't it?" her father said conversationally. He yawned deeply with his mouth stretched wide for a moment. "Sure is crazy weather we're having. Hot enough one day to roast eggs, and cold enough to freeze 'em the next."

"Yeah," Jen said. She moved into the room, laid her purse down on the table, and ran her hands through a pile of magazines.

"Say," her father asked her carefully, "how's the little Cope girl, anyway?"

Jen shook her head and studied the cover of the magazine intently.

"I'm just as sorry as I can be," Sam said awkwardly. "She was the prettiest, liveliest little girl around here. She wasn't never in too big a hurry to stop and talk and joke and laugh a little. I guess everybody's gonna miss her."

Jen walked around the room restlessly while the wind rattled every window in the house. She stopped before the big upright piano, closed and thick with dust, and shoved the gaudy carnival prizes on the top into a precise straight line.

"Where's Kenny?" she asked.

"Kenny?" her father repeated. "Why, let's see. He musta went quite a while ago. Why, he ain't been here since . . . Yes, he was too! No, that was Carl. Carl come in just a minute ago, right after he got done working, but he went out again somewheres. That was Carl that come in though. No, I ain't seen nothing a Kenny, he musta went quite a ways back . . ."

Jen shoved the glittering carnival toys back and forth, and Sam searched his mind comfortably and leisurely.

"Funny, now you come to speak of it, I can't recall right off a-seeing Kenny today. His Ma was telling something though that she said Kenny said when he got home this morning, so he musta been home here early for a little spell. But I can't just recall, he musta been here when . . ."

"Oh, Lord," Molly roared out of the bedroom where she had been listening to the entire conversation. "Anybody'd oughta know better than ever ask you anything about nothing. Kenny's right upstairs in his bed a-sleeping right this minute, that's where he is. That's where he's been all day long."

"Well, I knew I hadn't seen him around here today," Sam insisted.

"Say," Molly called, drowning Sam out, "I was supposed to call Kenny to get up before suppertime. I promised him I would and then I went and forgot all about it. You wanta run upstairs and wake him up? You tell him I forgot and he better get right up. It's suppertime right now already."

"Okay, I'll tell him," Jen said. She moved toward the stair door, and Molly called after her out of the bedroom, "Say, what did you want to know where Kenny was for? There ain't nothing the matter, is there? How come you was asking . . ."

Jen banged the door shut loudly on the sound of her mother's voice. And at the bang of the stair door, as she started up the stairs, another door was slammed shut above her. It was the door to the room she shared with Josette, and it was a warning that Josette was studying and did not wish to be disturbed by Jen coming into the room unless it was absolutely necessary.

At the top of the stairs, Jen went directly to the room that Carl and Kenny shared, and pushed the door open. The room was dark and cheerless. One of the windows was half opened, the ragged curtains were blowing out straight into the room, and the window jiggled back and forth in its frame with a continual rattling sound. The wind tugged the door away from Jen and slammed it shut.

She came into the room, and pulled the string that was tied from the chain below the electric-light bulb to the head of the bed. Kenny slept doubled up in the middle of the bed. The room was chilly and in his sleep he had pulled the sheet and light quilt up over his head, so that his bare feet stuck out below. Jen closed the window carelessly with another bang, and plucked the covers down from his face. Kenny slept peacefully, oblivious to banging doors and windows and the incessant rattling of the wind. His face was flushed and his hair was tousled over his forehead in ringlet curls.

Jen perched beside him on the edge of the bed. "Hey, wake up," she said. She dug her fist into his chest a couple of times. "Wake up!"

He stirred a little and fumbled for the covers. "Hey, cut it out!" He was trying to pull the covers back over his head again, but Jen kept tight hold of them.

"You gonna sleep all day? You're a lazy bum. It's suppertime. You better get up if you're goin' to."

Kenny gave up the struggle and relinquished sleep regretfully. He opened his eyes and grinned at Jen with drowsy good nature. "Hi!" he said.

"You're a lazy bum," she scoffed.

"The hell you say," Kenny marveled lazily. He stretched his arms out wide over his head. "Don't know where the time goes to . . ." The cool air of the room struck his bare arms, and he pulled them back under the covers again hurriedly and hunched down farther in the bed. "Hell, what kinda weather is this? It's cold!"

"It's been cold all day," she said.

"We have winter enough, without having it in the summer too," he complained. "Jeeves, turn on the heat, will you, and draw the marster a nice hot bawth, and while you're at it chase the moth-balls out of my red-flannel underwear."

Jen smiled briefly, and pulled her jacket sleeves down on her wrists and tucked her legs up under her skirt.

"How's everything?" Kenny asked her, and then, his face sobering, "How's Franny?"

Jen shook her head again, as she had shaken it before when her father asked her that question. "Kenny," she said desperately, "I wanta talk to you."

"So Franny ain't got a chance, huh?"

Jen shook her head. "They say she just can't get well. It's terrible, I can't hardly stand to talk about it."

"Oh, it's tough!" Kenny patted her knee, and then jerked his hand back out of the cold under the warm covers again. "Damn, but it's cold!"

"Listen. It's about Franny I want to talk to you."

Kenny was peering around her out of the window. "Listen to that wind blow, would you! What a night! And what I wanta know is how in hell I'm going to get up to Ashbury without freezing my ass off?"

"Kenny, will you listen to me, please?"

"Take it easy. I'm listening, ain't I? Go ahead, shoot, say something."

"Well, pay attention and I will." Jen wrinkled her forehead, and wadded up a handful of the sheet in her hand, searching for the words to use.

"Sure, now that's just what I always say," he mocked her. "Thanks for telling me. I sure appreciate it. You don't mean to say so."

"Kenny, please!" her eyes were wet with tears suddenly.

"Okay, okay, I'm listening. Spill it."

"Kenny, Franny wants to see you," Jen said in a rush of words.

He was silent awhile before he spoke. Jen twisted the sheet up into a knot in her hand, without looking at him.

"How come Franny wants to see me?"

"You should ask," Jen said angrily. "You know damn well why she wants to see you."

"I don't know nothing about it," he said shortly. "You're telling the story, ain't you? How come Franny wants to see me?"

The wind blew around the house in gusts and Jen yanked the knot out of the sheet so hard she tore a slit along the top of it. "You know the way Franny feels about you. She's always been crazy about you."

"Oh, hell!" he said. His face darkened. "I don't believe it. How could she be crazy about me, I ain't had . . ."

"Go on and say it—you ain't had nothing to do with her for two or three years. Sure, I know. Well, Franny's just funny that way, that's all. I don't mean she set to home and cried her eyes out over you all this time, but you know damn well how she felt about you. There wasn't nothing she wouldn't have done for you, any time. She was running around with lots of different guys all the time, but she'd have thrown 'em all over just like that, any time you'd a-wiggled your little finger at her. Don't say you didn't know that."

"Okay," he said sharply. "So what? I couldn't help it, could I?"

"I'm not saying you could," she answered him angrily. "But you coulda been a lot nicer to her. I wish to hell you hada been, now."

"Sure, Boy Scout. Make all the little girls happy."

"Well, you coulda done a lot worse'n Franny."

He burst out laughing, suddenly and uproariously.

The tears shone over the rouge on Jen's cheeks. "I don't see what you got to laugh about. None of it ain't funny."

"I was just laughing to think about me and Franny. What you figure I oughtta done, married her?" He laughed again.

Jen stared at him wonderingly. "I can't make you out," she said. "I never could make you out. You're the funniest guy I ever knew. You're my own brother and I don't know nothing about you that matters. I never met a guy yet I couldn't tell pretty soon what makes him tick. Well, I don't know yet what makes you tick."

He coughed delicately before he answered her. "Just so's you won't worry about it, I'll tell you. I don't tick. My wheels all run backwards. I buzz."

She made a little gesture of exasperated resignation, with her palms upward and her shoulders hunched, but the next moment her face was downcast again. "You will go to see Franny, won't you?"

"Oh, hell! Sure, I guess so, if she wants to see me."

"When are you gonna go?"

"Oh, I don't know," he said. "I'm kinda busy. I can't just tell. First-a the week maybe. Her folks think it's all right for me to come to see her? How you know they'll let me in up there?"

"You talk like you think you'd have to sneak into the hospital to see her," Jen said. "She already said to her folks she wants to see you, and they asked me to ask you to come. They left word to the hospital, any time you go, you can see her."

"That's fine," Kenny said. He sighed profoundly.

"When you gonna go?" Jen insisted.

"I told you. I don't know. I'm busy. First of the week maybe."

Jen compressed her lips and began to knot up the sheet again.

"Now what's-a matter?" he asked. "God, you look just like Josie when you pull your face down like that. Cut it out. What's-a matter now? I said I'd go, didn't I?"

"You ain't said a damn thing yet," Jen burst out. "You can't just say maybe you'll go the first of the week. You ain't got forever to get there. The doctors say maybe any day, maybe tomorrow. How can you tell? If you're going, you gotta go."

"Okay, okay, take it easy. I'll go tomorrow. I'll go the first thing tomorrow afternoon, how's that?"

"That's swell," Jen said. "And don't let nothing make you put it off."

Kenny's good humor had all vanished. "Listen," he said sarcastically, "if it ain't asking too much of you, would yuh mind unloading your carcass offa my bed, and getting outa here so I can dress? It's dark already, and I gotta date to see a guy up to Ashbury, and it's gonna be one hell of a cold night to fool around looking for a ride."

Jen got up obediently, but at the door she hesitated, sliding the knob in her fingers. "Kenny," she said carefully, "what are you gonna say to Franny when you go up there tomorrow?"

Kenny sat shivering in the middle of the bed. "What in hell you mean, what am I gonna say to her tomorrow?"

"I mean . . . You're—you're gonna be nice to her, aren't you?"

"Oh, hell!" Kenny lay back in the bed, and pulled the covers up to his neck and groaned. "She asks me if I'm gonna be nice to Franny. What do you think I am? You think I'm going up there and have a fight with her or something?"

"You know what I mean," Jen said. "It ain't gonna cost you a thing, and it's gonna mean a lot to her."

Kenny sat up in the bed again. His face was impassive, all of the easy careless mirth and banter was gone out of him. He looked older and harder, and like a stranger to Jen. His voice was soft and impersonal, and prefaced with his coughing. "I had enough of this. Shut your mouth and get outa here."

Jen scurried out the door and ran into Carl at the top of the stairs. She brushed past him and ran down the hall to her own room. She burst in and closed the door behind her and leaned upon it. Josette looked up from her studying and stared at her disapprovingly.

Jen's eyes were big and round. "You know," she said wonderingly, "the screwiest thing, but sometimes I get scared to death of Kenny."

"Humm!" Josette said.

"No, honest, I mean it. You'll be talking to him or something. He'll be talking along, just as natural, like he always is, laughing and wisecracking, and then, all of a sudden he gets different, just like he's some other guy. It scares yuh. Kenny's an awful funny guy. He's different from anybody. I wonder what'll ever happen to him."

"Humm," Josette said, wiping her red chilled nose efficiently with her handkerchief. "Kenny doesn't scare me. He isn't anything to be afraid of. He just thinks he's smart. Nothing that amounts to anything will ever happen to him, because he's no good."

"No, sir," Jen said determinedly. "There's something about Kenny you can't get. Until you can get that, you can't add him up and make him come out even."

"I can add him up and make him come out even," Josette said. "He's nothing more or less than a lot of other good-for-nothing fellows in this town. He's lazy, he won't work, he swears, he drinks, he gambles, and he chases around with women all the time, married women, and tough women, and little young girls, or anything that will look at him. And that's all there is to Kenny Veech."

And in the room at the other end of the hall, just as Kenny got out of the bed, Carl came stumbling through the door.

"What is this," Kenny said bitterly, "a bedroom or a railroad station?"

But Carl did not hear him. He walked past him and sat down on the edge of the bed, cradling carefully in his arms the worn volume of poetry that he had taken out of the county library. Carl had just found a poet who, he believed, understood him. His face was removed and rapt and ecstatic.

Kenny stopped in the middle of his dressing to stare at his brother. "What in hell is the matter with you all of a sudden?"

Carl did not answer him, and Kenny laughed. "You know, you look just like a guy I used to see around, tall skinny guy, name of Guts. Guts was a screwball, if there ever was one. Somebody hit him on the head with something once years ago, and Guts acted funny ever since then. It made him wrong in the head, kinda. He used to hear voices, he claimed. Funniest damn thing, you'd be talking along to Guts, same as I'm talking to you, and Guts would be nodding his head back and forth and pulling out on his lower lip like he always done when you was talking to him, and then alla once, just like that, he'd be gone. He'd hold up his head kinda funny like he was listening, and his mouth would go like he was talking back to somebody. Give you the creeps to see him do it at first. In a minute, though, he'd be all right, and start talking to you again. Guts sure was a screwball, but he was a kinda nice guy at that. Never heard a word what ever become of Guts. Somebody said he had an accident. I dunno."

Carl was not listening to Kenny. His eyes were far away. He cleared his throat noisily.

Kenny stopped with a comb in his hand. "Oh, dear God," he pleaded of the empty air. "They're all nuts; this whole family is nuts. If I don't get away from here pretty soon, I'm going nuts too." Carl did not move or look at Kenny or indicate in any way that he knew that he was in the room.

Kenny cocked his head, watching him attentively, and then he went quietly across the room and opened the window up high so that the wind blew in a gale. He came back and stood close in front of Carl. He stood there so long and so quietly that Carl's attention was diverted at last and he stared at Kenny wonderingly. At that precise second Kenny emitted a blood-curdling scream and hopped up from the floor waving his arms from the sides of his head like enormous and elongated ears. Carl was so startled that he shrank back upon the bed, his precious book tumbling onto the floor at his feet. The moment that Kenny hit the floor again he bounded across the room to the window. He sent the window screen spinning away with one straight jab of his right arm, and then he dove head first after it out of the window into the darkness. As his hands closed over the limb of the big tree close outside the window Kenny emitted his mad banshee howl once more. He swung from the limb, and then dropped down to the grass underneath. With earth under his feet once more, he settled his shirt collar, and walked around the house to the kitchen door. He walked into the kitchen with a jaunty swagger and said, "Hiya, Mom. Whatcha having that's good for supper?"

Molly stopped dead still in the middle of the kitchen floor with a stack of cups and saucers in her hands, and her big moist face flat with wonder. "Kenny Veech!" she said. "For Lord's sakes, where did you come from?"

Upstairs, Carl sat stunned upon the bed, clutching the iron foot rail with both hands so tightly that the knuckles paled. The great dark wind roared in the open window, impatiently whisked the curtains aside, and encircled him.

Kenny's laughter filled the house.

6

KENNY CAME OUT OF THE THIRD AVENUE POOL Room in Ashbury into the sunshine, and let the door bang behind him. He was grinning, and back in the pool room everybody was laughing at some wisecrack he had made. Kenny felt good. He walked slowly with a slouch and a swagger. The sun was warm and full-bodied. The streets were full of people drifting along like himself. At the corner by the combination newspaper and fruit stand, there was the strong rancid smell of overripe bananas and plums, with a little cloud of fruit flies hanging in the air. Kenny ambled across the street with the traffic light. He felt a languor and contentment. He had eaten, he had a fresh cigarette in his mouth, and it was too early in the afternoon to have a thirst. There was nothing on his mind, nothing more than a teasing unidentified melody of some song or other, tum te tum te tum—tum te tum tum tum te tum. He felt fine. He had learned the value of times when he felt completely good and satisfied as he did now. So he savored this moment like a connoisseur. He had a faculty for being able to shut unpleasant things completely out of his consciousness at times. He did not think now about where he was going, Receiving Hospital on the other side of the city. He had promised to go to see Frances Cope. He had not particularly wanted to go, but he had promised that he would go, and he was on his way and that was all there was to it. He would not think about it again until he walked up the wide white steps to the front entrance of the hospital. He had given himself over to a sensuous, contented enjoyment of the day and the crowded streets of the city; he let it all come in to him at every pore. At the moment he was a man completely satisfied and happy. He ambled along jauntily with the little crescent metal heel plates pounded into the edges of the run-over heels of his shoes clicking against the cement. One of his shoes was untied, and the metal tips of the laces over the sidewalk made a complete orchestral arrangement of the sound of his walking.

"Tum te tum te tum," he hummed under his breath, "tum te tum tum tum te tum . . ."

He came around a corner like that, and suddenly he stopped still on the street, and froze back flat against the brick wall of the building. It was a hotel building and at the end nearest him there was a cocktail bar, probably the smartest and most expensive rendezvous in Ashbury. The entrance to the bar was not three feet away from Kenny, and just as he came around that corner he saw them. They got out of a car drawn up before the entrance—Lew Lentz and Mary. Lew assisted her out of the car and she crossed the sidewalk on his arm, and they went in the door into the glittering interior, so near to Kenny that he caught a subtle hint of her perfume in the air as she went by. The door closed behind them after emitting a blast of air-conditioned coolness and soft music, and they were gone. Kenny remained where he was for awhile, perfectly still, flat against the wall, with his face blank and expressionless. His mind was quiet and empty too, but time after time he saw them go into the bar again as vividly as the first time. It was like a series of explosions in the quiet twilight of his mind. He saw them again and again, Lew Lentz impeccably dressed, his blond heavy-lidded face under his hat brim; and Mary, beautiful and cool and remote, another woman in another world. She was wearing white that day, a full very short white skirt swirling about her knees, and a tight-fitting high-buttoned jacket, and some sort of tiny ridiculous hat with a great bow of white net in the back, but her pumps were a warm rosy color, the exact shade of the big shiny leather purse that hung from a long strap over her shoulder. Seven steps or so those small shiny rose-colored pumps took across the sidewalk to the door, over and over again, seven steps or so, with a full white skirt swirling around her knees, and her white gloved hand tight in the crook of Lew Lentz's bended arm, and her face turned to his face with a faint smile on her lips as he said something or other to her. Kenny was so angry that he did not know that he was angry; the agony of desolation was so great in him that he could not recognize it.

All that he recognized in himself was an old familiar and relatively easily satisfied need. Automatically he fingered the money in his pockets and estimated the amount, kind and brand of liquor best suited to his immediate financial condition. He started walking again, left the hotel behind him, and cut back down side streets into a less polished section of the city. He stopped in at a dreary restaurant and liquor place, and spent what money he had on whiskey and soda, neat small glasses, one after another rapidly, getting no pleasure out of it. He drank in solitary splendor at the front table, and the proprietor himself, a man with a dirty white apron, waited on him. The proprietor was a taciturn thin-faced man with a prominent Adam's apple and no taste for conversation. He read a detective-story magazine behind the counter, and Kenny brooded silently over his row of glasses. As the glasses marched across the table, and he began to feel the glow of the liquor in him, Kenny marveled that he could feel so disjointed and useless and unreal. Moods of deep melancholy were not common with Kenny. So now an excited hysterical voice inside of him kept chattering incessantly, "Pal, for the lova Mike, take it easy, why don't you? What's getting into you lately? For God's sakes, Pal, this ain't no way for you to feel. You better snap out of this, please, Pal, please . . ."

Kenny got sick of listening to that incoherent voice, so he drank down the rest of his liquor and left. His feet seemed to be heading for a definite destination, so he allowed them to take whichever way they willed. Although the sun still shone, he did not feel it now. He began to walk with a swift purposeful stride, and the perspiration came out on his face.

When he found himself suddenly climbing the broad shallow steps to the front entrance of Receiving Hospital, he was completely surprised, and stopped and stood still and wondered what had brought him here. He remembered Franny then, in that hospital some place in a bed, lying there and waiting to die, and that she wanted to see him, and that he had promised to visit her today. On his first impulse, he turned and started down the steps again. To hell with promises and to hell with Frances Cope. If she was going to die, she was going to die, and it was the same as being dead already, and who wants to go and pay visits to corpses that lie in beds and talk? And why must it be he that she wanted to come to her? She had been with a lot of other men since she had been with him. And he remembered Jen's story about it, that Franny was in love with him. He stood still and thought about that, and it seemed extraordinarily funny to him. He laughed silently and his raw bloodshot eyes danced in his face. He stopped laughing and coughed a little. Then he walked back up the steps rapidly, and straight in the front door to the information desk. He stated his business clearly and precisely, keeping himself in the meanwhile rigidly under control. From that desk a whole chain of motion was begun, involving several nurses, into elevators and out, and much walking down narrow, bare, unending corridors.

The nurse brought him at last to a plain wooden door, exactly like so many other doors. They stopped there, and the nurse held a conversation in a soft voice with another nurse who was just coming out of the room. Kenny stood and waited, holding his body carefully erect and painfully still. In his mind he still saw them, again and again. Lew Lentz and Mary walking together across the sidewalk from the automobile to the door, smelled her perfume, felt the rhythm of her body, saw her smile into that smooth sleepy face. Kenny was tensed like a spring. He could not wait to get through that door into that room, with the nurses gone. Slow and dreadful music passed through his mind. He was damp with sweat and the palms of his hands prickled. There was a fierce sort of happiness in him now that cut away the smothering web of that indecisive melancholy. He felt now as he did sometimes when he was fighting with someone he did not like, and felt the soft yielding vulnerable flesh of his opponent under the bones of his hands.

The nurse turned and spoke to him, rattling the doorknob in her hands. Her face was a swimming blur before his eyes. She spoke to him crisply, and she eyed him somewhat disapprovingly. "You may go in and see her now, Mr. Veech," she said. "But remember, you mustn't stay too long and tire her, nor must you say anything to excite her or upset her. She's a very sick girl, you know."

"Yeah, sure," Kenny said. He kept his eyes on the door, fascinated, like a cat waiting to pounce on a mouse.

The nurse opened the door then and he walked into the room.

White bare walls, and a window that the sun shone through, and a chair and a table beside the high narrow bed. Franny Cope looked at him with bright dark eyes from the pillow. "Hi, Kenny," she said. "I was afraid that you wasn't coming . . ." Her voice was low-pitched and unnatural, as if her lips were so stiff that she could not move them. Her face looked puffy and swollen, and the whole top of her head was wound with white bandage.

Kenny did not answer her. He pulled the chair back a little with a scraping sound on the floor and dropped into it. He sat sprawled out with his legs extended and his hands shoved deep in his pockets. He looked beyond her to the window, with his face relaxed and sullen and lowering. He coughed a little, but he did not speak.

"Poor Kenny!" Fran said tenderly, in her stiff unnatural voice. She even tried to laugh, an odd little broken sound. "You sure hated to come up here, didn't you? It musta took a lot of beers."

He curled his lips apart over his teeth, but he still did not answer her or look at her.

She looked at him fondly with her great dark eyes, studying him feature by feature, as if she photographed him now that she might always have the image of him.

She laughed again, that peculiar soft broken sound. "You know, I never woulda had the nerve to ask you to come, even feeling the way I do about you, if Jen hadn't told me about the way you felt. I guess I musta been dumb or something. I never used to figure you cared nothing about me."

She watched him with her eyes liquid and soft and gentle with emotion. "It's just about worth it, all this, to find out you cared about me."

He moved his body suddenly and impatiently in his chair.

"I mean it," she said. "I guess I wouldn'ta cared much about living anyway, if I couldn'ta had you. It makes it kinda hard now though, sometimes . . ." Her voice fumbled and broke over the words, ". . . thinking about all we coulda had together if I didn't have to . . ."

He sat up straight in his chair as if he was going to speak to her, and so she hurried on.

"No, Kenny, I don't mean that. I don't want you to think I feel bad, I just wantcha to know how much this means to me. I know they done everything they could for me here, and it ain't no use. But I ain't worrying, and I ain't scared much. You know why? The doctors and all, around here, they're all the time hollering about how brave I am and stuff. You know what makes me brave? It's because I'm so happy I got you. I been wanting that so long. Now I know the way you feel about me, I ain't scared of—kicking off. It ain't gonna be like I'm—dead—and—all alone some place. I'll have you, so I won't be alone, never. And having you care about me—don't you see—I'll still be living—all the while you are, and after that I wouldn't want to anyway . . ."

"Oh, Jesus, God, oh, Jesus, God!" Kenny said wonderingly.

"You mustn't feel bad about me, honey," Fran said to him tenderly. "I don't want that you should. Don't take on bad or nothing—after—it's over. I want you should be happy, and after awhile marry some other girl and settle down and get a job and have kids and stuff. That's the way I want it, Kenny, honest. And it's always gonna be like I'm . . ."

Kenny got up out of his chair suddenly and let himself off leash, and felt all the savage joy of it.

"Listen," he said, "will yuh shut up that yawp, for God's sakes?"

She stared at him wonderingly, her mouth a little open.

He came nearer to the bed, coughing a little. "Look," he said, "Jen musta been feeding you a lot of crap about me being crazy about you. Well, she was lying, see? And if you believed all that stuff you're even more nuts'n I figured you was."

"I don't get it," Fran said in an empty voice. "Jen said—she told me how . . ."

"Oh, sure," he said, "I know. She give you the works. She told you just what you wanted to hear. Some folks believe in doing that, lying to folks before they die to make 'em feel good. Well, I don't, see? And I don't want you shooting off your mouth up here all the while about me being in love with you. Hell, I don't care nothing about you. I never did. I never woulda, so shut up your trap about it, see?"

He stopped talking then, breathing heavily, and watching her face on the pillow.

She shut her heavy lids down over her eyes for a minute, and then she looked straight up at him with her eyes swimming in tears she did not shed. "Kenny, I'm awful sorry about this," she said to him in a low voice. "I wouldn'ta had it happen for nothing. I was a sucker, and all those things I said to you and . . . You don't wanta blame Jen though, she was just trying to . . . I'm awful sorry, honest. Just—just—forget about all this."

"Oh, sure, no trouble at all," Kenny said. He turned his back on her and swaggered toward the door.

But at the door she stopped him. Her voice was sharper and more uneven with her effort to restrain her tears. "Kenny! I wanta say—good-bye—an' wish you good luck an' stuff. I—I wish you'd remember me sometimes. We—useta be good friends, we useta . . ."

Kenny turned and propped his arm against the doorjamb and laughed magnificently. His voice was slurred and careless, and he chose each word with a calculated cruelty. "Hell, if you ain't one screwy dame all right. You think I can remember back to them days? Maybe you can; I can't. Hell, it was too long ago and I had too many dames since. What you think? I can't even remember what it was like, having you . . ."

She winced in the bed, and he struck a posture of elaborate thought. "Naw, I can't remember. I guess you wasn't nothing special. The only ones I ever remember are the ones I like or the ones that are real hot . . ."

Fran Cope shut her eyes tight. "Good-bye, Kenny," she said, "good-bye."

"Oh, I ain't in no hurry," he said. "I ain't got nothing special to do. It sure is a swell day outdoors. That sun feels swell. Lots of people out, running around the streets. I guess I'll go drink a little beer and then take in a good movie or something. Yeah, I guess that's what I'll do. There's a couple real good movies on, and then tonight, let's see, tonight I guess I'll pick up a dame and go dancing some place. I hear they opened up a new dump out here the other side a town. They say it's real classy, colored orchestra and everything. I guess I'll go out there tonight." He watched her face, with a smile on his own. "Yes," he said, "it sure is too bad, ain't it?"

Her voice was higher, and broken apart. "Go on, get outa here! I can't stand no more of this! Oh, God, I ain't never done nothing to you. Why you wanta come in here and . . . go on, get outa here, get out!"

"Oh, skip it," he said impatiently. "Save that for the angels!"

She began to scream then, and as he opened the door the nurse was twisting the knob from the other side. Once the door was open the nurse dashed by him to the bed, and he walked away, with the sound of the screaming and the confusion echoing in the corridor. He took the wrong turn in the corridor, and he walked a long way looking for the elevator, and all he came to was a blank empty wall at the end of it. He cursed a little under his breath and retraced his steps the long length of that corridor, listening to the echoing clatter that his feet made. He found the elevator at last, and went down in it to the main floor, and got out again into the bright sun and air. He started to walk fast, to get away from that big quiet hospital building. He walked fast without knowing where he was going. His hands were clammy and his lips were dry, and his stomach was icy-cold and twisting.

And behind one of the closed doors, along the corridor, Rita Sibley, swathed in a cocoon of bandages, had heard those sharp slow footfalls outside her door. She analyzed them. A man who moved lightly on his feet and wore heel plates on his shoes and walked in a definite individual rhythm. She tried to visualize what the walk was like, a slow stride, with a swagger in it, a catch that broke the evenness of the rhythm almost as if he limped on one leg. And suddenly all in a flash she knew that it was Kenny Veech who walked thus, Kenny Veech and no one else in the world. She knew that Kenny Veech had passed just now by the door of her room.

She put the thought of him away from her unhurriedly, as if

Kenny Veech was only a name that she had read once in a book, and nothing more than that. Her mind just now was content, as her body was content in its warm swath of bandaging, now that the pain was almost gone.

7

I T WAS A WARM PERFECT SUMMER NIGHT, WITH bright moonlight over everything while the sky was still rosy to the west. The air was slumberous and sweet-smelling. Birds chittered in the trees. The village was still. Faint sounds of radio music drifted on the light breeze, and faint sounds of doors slamming, and children's voices, and whirring roller skates, and dog barks, and the rasping sound of automobile starters, all of it stilled and muted, elusive and unreal as the unnaturally bright moonlight.

The squeaking sound of the porch-swing chain that needed oiling sawed rhythmically through the evening quiet on the front porch at the Veeches'. Sam and Molly sat in the swing in the darkness side by side. A train roared through along the tracks across the street, shaking the whole house, strings of bright windows, rushing along to the tune of grinding wheels and a shrieking whistle.

It was gone as suddenly as it came, and Molly spoke after the red and green lights on the back of the observation car had disappeared, spoke leisurely in a rich contented voice. "Well, sir, there goes the Limited. Got so now I look for it every night. It sure beats all how fast the days go. Don't seem like no time at all since I seen it go tearing through here last night and the night before." She yawned prodigiously and leisurely. "Sure goes tearing through here all right. Ernie says it's the fastest train on the whole railroad. Lord, you remember when that man got hit out here westa town last year by the Limited. Why, they said there wasn't enough of that man left to tell who he was. What was that feller's name, worked out there on a farm for somebody just westa town? I remember hearing what his name was at the time, but I can't speak it now to save me. Why, what was that feller's name, anyway?"

She puzzled over the elusive name, and Sam said, "Can't remember what that feller's name was. A kind of funny name, nobody I ever heard of, he was some feller from away somewheres." Sam yawned, and kept his eyes on the tireless spiraling of the airplane beacon at the edge of town. Tonight the sky was so bright with the moon that the beacon light appeared pale and yellowish and sickly. Sam wondered for at least the thousandth time what the beacon looked like from the air.

"Where's Dorothy?" he asked after awhile.

"Huh?" Molly said preoccupiedly. "Oh, Dor'thy. Lord, I dunno. She went uptown a spell back to buy an ice cream cone and I ain't seen hide nor hair of her since. She'll be coming home in a minute. Most like she ran into some kids she knew uptown and went off playing with 'em."

"Her Ma don't like to have her chasing around the streets with the kids after dark," Sam said mildly.

"Lord, her Ma don't want that poor little young one to do nothing," Molly said cheerfully. "I guess it ain't gonna hurt her to play with the other kids. The trouble with Dor'thy is she don't get out and play with the other kids enough. She's always going off by herself like a regular little old woman. Her Ma was just the same way though, when she was little, just the same way. Why, I remember once when . . ."

"Where's Josie?" Sam said suddenly. "She out with young Thompson somewheres?"

"Naw, she's upstairs there a-studying. Last few days she's like to studied her head off. Won't go out nowheres with Pat. Funny thing, course you can't never get a word out of her about nothing, but she's acted awful kind of funny ever since she went over to that dance with that Clark crowd. She ain't never said a word about 'em or gone near Clark's since the night a that dance, and they ain't been none of them hanging around here after Josie, neither. I figure she didn't get along with them, that's what I figure. Course, you never could get Josie to admit nothing like that, but that's what I figure, she ain't used to going around with swell people like that, and everything, and . . ."

"Well, I don't know," Sam said defiantly. "I guess Josie is just as nice and pretty-looking as anybody. I guess she's just as good as . . ."

"Why, sure she is," Molly said. "But you know what I mean. I wasn't a-saying! No need you taking my head off."

Sam yawned peevishly.

Molly switched to another topic of conversation without pausing for breath. "Lord, I thought I never would get through the day today. I never seen nothing like it the way Mr. Higgins acts. Why, it just seems like he lays in there all day long just a-thinking up new ways to torment me, till I can't hardly stand it. Why, I tell you . . . For Lord's sakes," she broke off, "ain't that Kenny comin' up the road?"

They both of them strained their eyes into the checkering of deep shadow and moonlight that marked off the sidewalk in black and white as it stretched away under the great trees. They watched the slouching dark figure as it approached.

"Why, sure that's Kenny," Molly said with the warm pleasure in her voice. "For Lord's sakes, what's a-bringing him home here so early?"

She never took her eyes from him, and when he turned in and crossed the thick grass to the porch, she called out to him fondly, "Well, sir, look who's coming here! I must be dreaming."

"Hi yuh, Mom," he said abstractedly.

She waited with her face lifted for his kiss, and he kissed her briefly and sat down on the top porch step at her feet.

"You had your supper?" she asked him.

"Sure, I et a long time ago. Don't you bother, Mom."

"'Twouldn't be no bother," Molly said brightly. "Wouldn't take but a minute to make some fresh coffee and set out what we had left from supper. You want some coffee, Kenny?"

"Naw. I already told you I et. I don't want nothing, honest."

"When I was his age," Sam said bitterly into the darkness, "if I'd-a come home a-smelling of whiskey enough to suffocate you, I'd have found a horsewhip waiting for me, instead of petting and cuddling and extra meals, and . . ."

"Oh, hush up," Molly said impatiently. "Kenny, you tired? Ain't you feeling good? You look like you're just all tuckered out tonight.

I bet you ain't feeling good. I keep worrying about you all the time, the way you keep up that coughing. I wish to Lord you'd . . ."

"I'm all right," Kenny said. "I'm just tired, that's all." He rubbed his face, and shoved his hair back impatiently, and rubbed his face again and left it there in his hands. He sat still then, with his shoulders hunched over and his head in his hands.

Molly shifted her bulk ponderously in the porch swing and leaned out over her stomach, and touched her coarse red big-boned hand to the back of Kenny's head.

"There now," she said tenderly with almost a catch in her voice. "You're just feeling tired, that's all. You let me fix you something nice and hot to drink, and then you take a couple aspirin tablets and go upstairs to bed and in the morning you'll be feeling fine again."

Kenny did not answer her, but the muscles in his back knotted and tensed.

Molly rubbed her knuckles gently up and down against his head. "Lord," she said tenderly, "it'll be all right tomorrow."

She took her hand away from his head then, and leaned back again in the squeaking weaving swing. She kept watching him anxiously, the forlorn hump to his shoulders, the beaten-down droop to his head. She spoke in a voice calculatedly bright and gay. "Say, somebody was telling me downtown today that they're gonna have some kind of a contest for playing golf up to Ashbury and Henry Hotchkins from downtown here in the bank has signed up to play in it. Don't that beat all? That skinny little white-livered feller getting mixed up in something like that! Must be a kind of a sissy game, but just the same . . ."

Her voice trailed off as the car drew up out in front of the house. "Is that Ernie?" Molly asked.

"No," Sam said. "That ain't Ernie's car, looks to me like it's Copes', stopping to leave Jen, on their way home from the hospital."

At his words, Kenny sat up straight and looked out to the harsh blaring light of the headlights. Jen's slim legs and light skirt came into view as she got out of the car, and the sound of their voices mixed saying good night, above the sound of the motor.

Kenny started to get up from the porch, and then he dropped back onto the step.

"Where you goin', Kenny?" Molly said. "My, I wonder how that Cope girl is tonight. They claim it's just a matter a time now. If that ain't an awful thing, though, when you stop to think of it, a little young girl like her . . . It sure has got Jen all broke up . . ."

Kenny fumbled through his pockets and found a cigarette at last, and lit it nervously.

The car drove away and Jen came up the walk to the steps.

"Say," Molly said, as she climbed the steps, "how is she tonight? She ain't no better, is she? The doctors don't claim there's any chance for her, do they? Seems to me like they could . . ."

Jen stopped dead still in front of Kenny, and Kenny looked away from her, to the burning tip of his cigarette, and knocked away from it the ash that was not there.

Jen stood still in front of him.

"Well, come on up and set down," Molly said. "You're enough to make a body nervous standing around like that."

Kenny shifted his eyes away from the red cigarette tip, and looked to the white splotches of moonlight on the pavement and on the grass, and then at last, slowly, very slowly, he raised his eyes to Jen's face.

Her face was set, and stony white, in the bright moonlight. "Kenny Veech," she said in a choked intense voice. "I hate you. I don't care what you do or say, as long as you live, I'm always gonna hate you."

Kenny did not answer her, but Molly flew to his rescue. "Well, for Lord's sakes," she said. "Now, if that ain't a fine thing to say to your own brother. You just hush your mouth now; you've said a plenty. You oughta be ashamed of yourself, that's what you oughta be, talking like that. You come on away now and leave Kenny alone. Get away from him. He ain't feeling extra good tonight anyway, and then the first thing you do, the very minute you get home, is try to pick a fight with him. Come on away now and leave Kenny alone, do you hear me?"

Jen flounced up the steps.

Sam said, "What's the matter? What's he done now?"

But the sound of his voice was drowned out in the slamming of the screen door behind her.

"Well, the little spitfire," Molly whistled shrill and prolonged. "Now don't that beat the Dutch! I tell you, that kid's just about crazy since that Cope girl got so bad up there to the hospital. She don't even know what she's doing, pitching right on to you like that outa a clear blue sky."

"I'll bet he's been doing something he hadn't oughta," Sam said warningly. "Jen wouldn't be turning on him unless she had a blamed good reason. I'll bet you anything he's been doing something he hadn't oughta, and that's what's wrong with him. Why, it's as clear as the nose on your face."

"You shut up, and quit your picking on Kenny," Molly said a little uncertainly.

Sam was triumphant. "Well," he said, "you ain't hearing him deny it, are you?"

Kenny was off the steps in one bound. He sent his cigarette spinning in a long arc out onto the pavement. He stood in the thunderous bright moonlight, with his legs braced apart, and looked up to his father on the porch. His voice was quiet and deadly. "You shut your yap, you God-damn old drizzlepuss!"

He turned on his heel and started toward town.

"Kenny, where you going?" Molly wailed after him. "They didn't mean nothing. They didn't mean to make you mad. Come on back, nobody ain't gonna pick on you no more."

Kenny walked fast without looking back, the blood pounding in his ears. He came down into the quiet deserted store section of the village.

The night watchman was already on duty. The early part of the evening, when there were still people about to observe him, he managed to keep very busy, and very much in evidence.

Kenny bumped against him now, and he stopped gladly with the prospect of a few moments' conversation ahead of him to break the monotony of his evening.

"Well, Kenny Veech," he said. "You old son of a gun you. I ain't seen you around this town in a coon's age. How you doing anyway? How's . . ."

But Kenny brushed by him, and by his proffered hand, and by his proffered friendliness. Kenny brushed by him and crossed the street and walked directly up to the entrance of the hotel, and went in the door.

"Damnation!" the night watchman stared after him in popeyed astonishment. "Damnation! That's the first time I ever know Kenny Veech to set a foot inside of Lew Lentz's hotel. And he's hopping crazy mad about something. It sure looks like trouble for somebody. I wonder . . ."

The night watchman kept his eyes on the quiet façade of the hotel. Nothing happened, nothing at all, but he would not have been surprised if the entire building had burst into flames, or if the walls of it had burst apart and scattered bricks over the town, or if he had heard the sudden leaden patter of machine guns from inside it.

As a matter of fact, although he kept his eyes steadily upon it and strained his ears, nothing happened, nothing at all.

Kenny burst in the front entrance of the hotel, and stopped dead still inside the door, and looked around the large room curiously. Lew Lentz had built the hotel six years ago, but this was the first time that Kenny had ever walked in the door. There were a few last late drinkers at the scattered tables, and they turned around from their bottles when the door slammed, and the hum of their voices died out instantly, leaving a heavy living silence in the room. Kenny rocked a little on his feet with his hands stuck deep in his pockets and surveyed the room at his leisure, with his face expressionless, and only his eyes alive and glittering. The waiter in a white jacket was leaning over the combination bar and information desk, reading a newspaper, and he too turned his face toward Kenny, a tipped-down white blob of a face with the lower jaw revolving up and down rhythmically as he chewed his gum. And the dark man behind the counter was wiping a glass with a grimy towel. For a moment he stopped and then he went on wiping it, twisting a wad of towel around and around in the inside of the glass without stopping, and never taking his eyes off Kenny.

Kenny stepped over to the bar suddenly in two quick catlike strides. "Lew in?" he said.

The waiter and the dark man looked at each other. They were

quiet and looked at each other. The waiter kept chewing gum, and the dark man behind the bar kept polishing the glass. At last the dark man said, "Maybe he is, and maybe he ain't. What's it to yuh?" But he didn't look at Kenny when he answered him, he kept looking at the waiter.

Kenny leaned over close to the man behind the bar, bending sideways over his arm. He spoke very softly but very distinctly. "Can the funny stuff. Is Lew in?"

The dark man looked at Kenny momentarily, but his eyes flicked away to the waiter again. "Whatcha want with Lew?" he said.

Kenny did not answer. He leaned close to the dark man. He did not move, he did not even seem to breathe, and waited. The dark man stopped wiping the glass suddenly, and set it down with the other glasses, and fidgeted the towel in his hands nervously. "You better get outa here!" he said to Kenny, and his voice was a whole tone higher, and sounded as if he was out of breath. He was still looking at the waiter behind Kenny, and he jerked his head a little almost imperceptibly.

Kenny did not move, but his body tensed, his eyes slid away down the bar.

The dark man yelled suddenly, "Hey, Gus! Watch it!" and the waiter stopped just in front of the little door at the end of the bar. But Kenny was already there, before the man could turn, he whirled him around, the white frightened blob-face rolling under the bright light. Kenny put his hand up against that face and pushed, and the waiter fell over backward against a table. The table slid away from him and up against another table, and he fell down onto the floor flinging out his arms wildly, together with two or three tables and a lot of chairs.

Kenny opened the small door and went through it and closed it all in one beautiful swift co-ordinated motion. When the door closed behind him, Lew Lentz turned around from his desk. Lew was working under a desk light, the rest of the room was dark and shadowy. "Why the hell don'tcha . . ." he began, looking out into the shadows. And then his voice stopped, not sharp and abrupt, nor trailing off either, it just stopped and was gone uncannily in the middle of what he was saying. He looked harder into the darkness, and then, still keeping his eyes on Kenny, he pulled open the drawer to the desk and put his hand inside and did not take it out.

"What do you want?" he asked, with his voice soft over the drone of the electric fan. Kenny walked toward him slowly, step by step, and Lew Lentz leaned back in his chair and let him come on.

"You little rat!" Kenny said softly. "You dirty little rat!" There was no anger in his voice, only wonder. "I'm going to take you apart, see, so that . . ."

Lew Lentz's hand came up out of the desk drawer then, balancing easily the blunt-snouted gun. "Get back," he said to Kenny. "I don't want to have to smell the liquor on you. You must be plenty drunk to get the nerve to walk in here. Go on, get back there by the door. You know I mean what I say when I talk with one of these."

Kenny stepped back then slowly, with his eyes on the shiny winking metal cradled so expertly in Lew Lentz's hand.

Lew Lentz smiled then. He sat perfectly relaxed in his chair, smiling, with both himself and the situation well controlled. Lew Lentz smiled at Kenny, all except his eyes, and his eyes were dry and deadly with hatred.

"That's fine. That's just fine. Now what can I do for you, sonny? Whatever you want, just say the word."

Kenny relaxed his body easily against the door casing. "Sure," he answered Lew Lentz. "It's all in the family, ain't it?" He began to laugh then. He laughed uproariously, good great belly laughter swelling the room apart with the noise of it. Not forced laughter or hysterical laughter or unnatural laughter, just the easy spontaneous full-bodied laughter native to him.

Lew Lentz might have been angry, but he did not lose control of himself. The smile disappeared from his face, and he shifted the gun a little in his hand. He did not lift his voice over the noise Kenny was making, he spoke as if to himself. "I don't like you," he said patiently. "I don't even like the looks of you, drunk or sober. I don't like you, so you better get to hell outa here."

But Kenny was not done yet with his laughter, and he made no move to go away.

Lew Lentz went on talking quietly and meditatively and patiently. "And I don't want you hanging around here, see! You come this once and that's all right, see, because you never been here before. But now you know the way it is, and next time it wouldn't be all nice and sociable the way it is this time. But there ain't going to be any next time."

It was then that the door at the other end of the room edged open a crack, quietly, slowly. And Kenny did not see it, because his face was hidden in the crook of his arm as he held it doubled against the wall. But Lew Lentz saw it, and for a moment his face was as if he were amused. And then it was smooth again.

He waved the gun back and forth, pointing it at the door. "Go on, get outa here," he said wearily. "I can't stand having folks I don't like hanging around me. Go on home. Sleep it off. I haven't got any job for you, and I wouldn't hire you if I did have. Go on, scram!"

Kenny opened the door suddenly and went, still laughing, and his laughter died away with his footfalls across the floor, mixed in with the slam he gave to the door.

Lew Lentz laid the gun down on his desk then and slid back in his chair, with his eyes still on the door at the other end of the room. And the door began to waver shut as slowly and silently as it had opened. Lew smiled, and just as the door closed he said. "Come here!"

The door opened instantly and obediently, and she came into the room. She slipped into the room primly and demurely. She wore a long blue housecoat but she had only zipped it down as far as her knees. When she walked it split apart, showing her bare legs, and the rose-colored shiny pumps on her feet. Her hair was combed out loose and fluffy.

Lew kicked the chair at the end of the desk around, so that it faced him. Mary sat down without a word.

He watched her with heavy-lidded amusement, but her face was quiet and unperturbed.

"Listening," he said. He made a little clucking noise in his mouth.

He waited for her to speak, but she didn't. He smiled then, and fiddled with the swivel shade on the desk light with his hand. He looked at her out of the sides of his eyes, and suddenly flipped the shade on the lamp around so that the bright hard light glared into her face. She didn't flinch from it; she did not even wink her eyes. Her face was as quiet and imperturbable as ever. She opened her eyes wide and looked at him, the startling blue eyes out of the brown shadows.

He smiled some more. "Your hair always shines in the light," he said absently. "The first time I ever saw you, remember. A party at Bill Macatee's, and I turned the light on for a joke. I saw your hair first, shining just like this, and then you turned around slow and looked at me, with your eyes just like this." He laughed silently, and turned the shade down again, so that her face was in the shadows once more.

He stuck his hands into his pockets and leaned back in his chair, balancing it on two legs. His shirt was immaculate, his gray vest hanging open. "God, how drunk he was!" His voice was reminiscent, full of pleasure.

"He wasn't drunk," Mary said.

"Of course he wasn't," Lew Lentz said.

"He didn't come here for a job either."

"Of course not," he said. He laughed again silently, and turned his head around to look her full in the face. "Nor he didn't come here to laugh."

"No," Mary agreed.

Lew laughed some more, silently under his breath, with only the muscles of his chest moving under his shirt.

"It makes you feel good, doesn't it?" Mary said to him.

"Sure," Lew Lentz said. "Makes me feel fine. Last laugh. Poor bastard!"

She blew smoke from a cigarette out of her mouth.

"Now, I mean it, honest. I feel sorry for him. Jesus, why shouldn't I? The poor bastard!"

She was silent and Lew Lentz went on laughing. "The last laugh," he said again.

Mary picked up the gun off the desk top idly. She held it easily in her hand, as if the feel of it there was not foreign to her. Slowly and idly she swung it around so that it pointed straight at his chest.

Lew Lentz stopped laughing. She held the gun steady and level. They looked at each other, and he smiled. They sat quietly so, for a moment.

Then suddenly Mary laid the gun down again on the desk top. She smiled too, her curious lovely childlike smile. Lew reached out his hand with the big amethyst shining on his finger, and picked up the gun and put it back in the desk drawer and closed it.

"Scram!" Lew said to her softly. "I can't work with you here. I'll be up in just a minute."

She got up, and as she walked past his chair, he reached out his arm and pulled her tight up against him. He kissed the little hollow of her throat, and then nuzzled his face down inside the low loose bodice of her gown. Mary leaned down a little over his head, and snubbed out her cigarette in the ash tray. When he released her, she walked out of the room,

Lew Lentz leaned far back in his chair with his hands clasped behind his head. He knew that he would do no more work that night. He found a pleasure in keeping himself there in his chair a moment or so, instead of going to her immediately. He reached out his hand with the heavy amethyst ring on it and turned off the electric fan. He cradled his head again in his clasped hands and stared at the ceiling. He chanted softly under his breath,

"Her name was Lil and she was a beauty
She lived in a house of ill-reputey . . .

"Well, what the hell," he said out loud, with his voice exultant. He turned out the light abruptly, and stumbled over the chair in the dark because he was in such a hurry. "Well, what the hell I wanta keep waiting . . ." He fumbled with the door, in the darkness and his haste.

8

THE LADIES OF THE METHODIST CHURCH WERE holding a rummage sale in the vacant store building beside the Ford garage. Molly planned on going down early that morning, before the stock was picked over. Rummage sales were the delight of Molly's life. She never lost the thrill and the joy of discovering what incredibly fine things she could buy for a dime or twenty-five cents.

She changed her dress and went into the tiny, breathless, hot bedroom where old Jud Higgins drowsed in the middle of the bed. There was one small window in the room, but it was closed. There was no screen for the window. Molly always kept forgetting to measure it for a new one, and besides, Jud preferred to sleep with the window closed. Today, the sun shone through the dusty scarred window panes, with an intense heat that filled the little room and sapped the vitality of the old man in the bed. Flies and insects flew onto the glass and crawled over the warm smooth surface of it, humming in several different keys. Old Jud lay still on his back, his body so small and frail it scarcely humped up the covers over him. He was drowsing, with his eyes closed and his mouth open, drops of sweat standing on his forehead, and a big bluish green fly crawling down his nose.

Once Molly told him of her plans, the old man thought of countless ways to delay her. He objected to being left alone. Sam was not around the house this morning. He insisted that he was dirty and that there ought to be clean sheets on his bed. He asked for a drink of water, complained that it was not cold enough, and after Molly had labored at the pump behind the house to get cold fresh water for him, he refused to drink it, pointing out to Molly that the well needed cleaning, that the water was no longer fit to drink.

He tried Molly's patience until she was almost in tears, and then just as she was going out the front door, he called after her, insisting that despite the heat he wanted a shirt over his heavy, long-sleeved underwear that he wore in bed. Molly found a faded blue shirt for him, but Jud craftily insisted that he wanted to put on his good shirt. When Molly objected that his good shirt was put away all washed and ironed and that it was a pity to crumple and dirty it, Jud accused her triumphantly of wanting to keep the good shirt fresh to bury him in. Then the tears did come to Molly's eyes and silently she put onto him the old shirt of some thick heavy material, white, but yellow now with age, with a thin green stripe in it. When she asked him sarcastically if he wanted his necktie on too, Jud said that he did, and so she knotted loosely under his collar the antique narrow knitted tie.

Jud apparently could think of nothing else to detain her, so he watched her spitefully as she left the bedroom in silence.

Molly was hurt and angry. It was almost too late by now for her to go to the rummage sale at all, if she were to get home at noon to prepare dinner for her family.

But at the front door she repented a little and called back to the old man kindly, "Good-bye. I'm leavin' now, Mr. Higgins. I ain't gonna be gone but just a few minutes. Good-bye."

He did not answer her. He listened to the sound of her heavy footsteps climbing down the porch steps, slowly and ponderously. The house was very still. There were only the drowsy daytime sounds of the village life. The sound of the flies buzzing on the ceiling and over the bed. A freight train went through on the tracks across the street, gently rocking Jud's bed back and forth. It was as if the long, loud, continuous sound of the train was a corporeal thing that came into the room and engulfed the bed with Jud in it, and picked it up and rocked it all enfolded in itself, and then set it down again and retreated out of the bedroom. After the train was gone, it was quieter than ever; somewhere upstairs, a beam or rafter hidden by the walls squeaked loudly. Jud drowsed, enjoying the sensuous delight of half slumber, neither waking nor sleeping, a rapid transition from the one to the other at random, with no conscious choice of his own involved in the matter.

Because he was dozing he did not hear the soft sound that the kitchen screen door made when Dorothy closed it behind her carefully. He did not hear her soft padding feet across the floor as she came into the bedroom either. She stopped still beside the bed and leaned over him. She watched him intently without moving a muscle. Her thin pale little face was intense with curiosity and fascination, her fine yellow hair hung down on either side. She kept staring at Jud's relaxed face, the mouth open, the eyes closed, the breathing, whistling out among the yellow stumps of teeth, and his bristling white whiskers.

Her presence there, her eyes turned on him unblinking, or possibly just her breath on his face awakened him. The old man opened his eyes suddenly and started in the bed as he saw the child hanging over him.

"You bastard imp a Satan!" he gasped. "What you doing hanging around in here? You ain't supposed to come in here. You get outa here now. If you don't get outa here, I swear by heaven, as sick as I be even, I'll get up outa this bed and give you a good tanning, see if I don't."

Dorothy retreated a little out of the reach of his skinny arms. But she was not frightened and apparently she had no idea of leaving the bedroom. She continued to stare at him curiously and impersonally.

"Go on, get outa here, God-damn yuh!" Jud said, bursting with anger.

Dorothy paid no attention to what he said. She tipped her head a little and studied him unblinkingly from another angle.

"You wait'll your grandmother gits home," Jud raved. "You little bastard, you. She'll tend to you proper, by God. You wait and see."

Dorothy scratched her stomach leisurely, without taking her eyes off Jud. He floundered around in the bed, flinging his arms out, but in his condition of near paralysis, it was almost impossible for him to sit up alone. He was weak with the weakness of illness, and he found himself wet with sweat from his exertion. The heat in the bedroom was so intense that for a second he was faint with it. The shirt collar was stifling him. He grabbed hold of it and jerked it, tearing away the button, loosening the knot of his old necktie.

Dorothy scratched her stomach thoughtfully. "Why don't you die?" she asked him.

Jud shrieked at her in anger and in a sudden gripping fear. "Why, you God-damn little bastard, you . . ."

He stared at her in horror, but gradually the crafty look came back to his face. "Whatcha want me to die for?" he asked her.

"Because," Dorothy answered him elaborately.

"Don't you like me?"

Dorothy stared at him out of her wide blue unblinking eyes, as if she did not understand what he meant.

Jud tried another tack, grinning eagerly and malevolently. "Do they talk about me dying? Is that where you got it? Do they all want me to die?

"You come on and tell me," he wheedled the child. "You been hearing them folks say they wished I was dead?"

"They never said they wished you was dead," Dorothy answered him unexpectedly. "They don't want you to be dead."

"How do you know?"

"Because," Dorothy said profoundly.

Jud relaxed on his pillow and stared back at her intently, out of his wizened spiteful bewhiskered old face. "What you been hearing them talking about me?"

Dorothy did not answer him.

His eyes glittered with anger and exasperation. "By God, you tell me now, or I'm gonna beat hell outa you!" As he spoke he thrashed around in the bed, trying to sit up.

Dorothy watched his feeble grotesque flounderings, and laughed suddenly, her high-pitched, hysterical mirthless laugh.

Jud trembled all over in his rage. He recovered his self-control and lay still in the bed again. Dorothy diddled up and down at the foot of his bed in complete unconcern.

An inspiration came to the old man then. "Hell," he said craftily and triumphantly. "You're just lying, I can tell. You never heard 'em say nothing about me. You're just lying, pretending you know a lot, I kin tell." He grinned at her in triumph.

"I ain't neither lyin'," the little girl answered him, shrill and angry in an instant. "I heard 'em talking about you dying. Just the other night, I heard 'em talking."

"I don't believe it. You're lying. Who'd yuh hear talkin'?"

"Them," she made a vague gesture with her hands. "You know, her and him . . ."

"Your grandma and grandpa? Hell, I don't believe it. Where'd you hear them talking?" Jud knew his advantage over the little girl now, and he played it deftly for all that it was worth.

"Did too hear 'em talking. They thought I was sleepin', but I wasn't. They was talking upstairs to bed. I heard 'em."

"Ah, you're just making it up," Jud insisted. "I can tell you're making it up. What did they say? See, you can't even tell what they said." He cackled with laughter at her.

"You God-damn little bastard!" she shrieked at him. "I did too hear what they was saying. They was talking about you dying, I heard them talking."

"Then why can't you tell me what they said, if'n you heard 'em?"

"I can too tell you what they said," the little girl talked fast, a torrent of words in her artificial high-pitched voice. "They didn't want you to die, neither one of 'em did. She didn't on account a she said you was just like a father to her, and the only grandfather her kids ever had, and she said she'd always feel kinda like it was all her fault because she didn't watch you alla time and keep you from running off and drinkin' whiskey, that's what she said, 'cause I heard every word they was saying, and he didn't want you should die neither 'cause he said so. He didn't want you to die, 'cause who the hell is gonna pay for burying you? And he said it would be a shame for Ernie and Mary to haveta do it, that's what he said. He said he hoped you didn't die because he didn't know where in the world the money would come from to bury you. He said Ernie was ugly right now, and it was bound to make trouble in the fambly and he hoped you didn't die, and she said he hadn't oughta talk like that, but she said it was true, and she wished to goodness that Ernie wouldn't get mad about it, and she said . . ."

Dorothy stopped then, completely out of breath, her face twitching and her eyes popping out of her head.

Jud lay still with the furious anger at all of them racking his frail tired body. They could talk like that about him! All they wanted him alive for, by heaven, was because they was worrying about raising money for burying him. That was all he meant to them, and after he had come to think of them through the years as his own children.

Jud chewed his stumps of teeth together with the sparse beard on his chin quivering.

Dorothy grabbed hold of the iron footrail of his bed, and swung back and forth on it. Her anger was gone now. She looked at him slyly and secretively out of the sides of her eyes. "I guess if you went out on the track and a train run over you, you'd be dead right away."

Back and forth she swung by her puny arms while the old man lay still in the middle of the bed, chewing his rough, sore, diseased gums together. She watched him secretively and meditatively. "I know something that's dead," she said. "It got dead on accounta something squeezed it by the neck. Something squeezed it by the neck and it got dead right away."

She stopped swinging on the footrail, and hung from the top of it by her arms, and peeped in at him between the iron spokes.

Jud looked at her silently with hot, glittering eyes.

"You git outa here and quit your pestering . . ." He said it half-heartedly, abstractedly.

She let go of the footrail and edged away to the door, looking back to him with her incredibly aged wise little face. "I should think you'd hurry up an' die. It's gonna make 'em all awful mad if you die. It's gonna make trouble in the fambly. They'll all be as mad as anything if you die." She said it all in her monotonous singsong voice. She kept watching him while she talked.

"You go on outa here now," Jud said to her abstractedly. "You go on outa the house and go play somewheres, go on, git!"

She looked at him intently, once more, and then she walked out of the bedroom. On a strange unreasoned impulse that she could not have explained to herself, if she had taken the trouble to have tried, she closed the bedroom door behind her. Under the strange spell of this impulse in her, the little girl tiptoed through the house to the front door, and closed that door also. Then she ran back through the house as if the devils were at her heels. She slammed shut the heavy kitchen door, tugging at it, pulling it over the warped boards, a heavy wooden door that was never shut except in the wintertime. She strained at it, tugging and pulling, and at last she closed it too. She went down the steps from the back porch two at a time. She ran across the garden, leaping over the rows of vegetable and weed clumps. She ran into the thick weeds of the vacant lot behind the house. She did not stop running. She floundered in the thick tall weeds. They came above her shoulders, some of them, but she did not stop running. She crossed the vacant lot at last and came out onto the street the other side of it. With sidewalk under her feet, she ran like a thing possessed, the hot sun beating down on her, bathing her with her own perspiration. Even the trees stood silent in the heat, their great leaves hanging crumpled and limp and dusty from the branches. But Dorothy ran on, as if she never would stop running again.

And back in the house in the little hot bedroom, old Jud lay still, staring blankly at the wall. He knew exactly now what it was that he must do. His thoughts swung back and forth, an overtone to his anger and hurt. His thoughts were all mixed with the things that

Dorothy had said to him. Over and over again, he kept repeating to himself, 'cause who the hell is gonna pay for burying you? A shame for Ernie and Mary to haveta do it . . . Didn't know where in the world the money would come from to bury you . . . Ernie is ugly right now, bound to make trouble in the family . . . Hadn't oughta talk like that, but it's true. She said you was just like a father to her, the only grandfather her kids ever had. She said she'd always feel kinda like it was all her fault because she didn't watch you all the time . . . She said she'd always feel kinda like it was all her fault . . . She'd always feel like it was her fault because she didn't . . . She'd always feel, she'd always feel . . .

Molly came home, laden down with groceries and several mysterious bunchy paper sacks that contained her purchases at the rummage sale. She was so elated by these purchases that she did not even mind the sun that was pouring down on her. Her arms ached with her load, sweat ran down under her arms and along her legs and her feet pained her. One of the cotton stockings was bunching up at her heel and a blister was forming there, but Molly did not particularly mind.

She hobbled up the front walk on her sore feet, thinking gratefully of the relatively cool temperature of the interior of the house, a chair to sit in, the right to remove her shoes and stockings, and a drink of cold water. She had an impulse to let dinner go, and then get a hot meal at night when the sun was down.

She noticed then that the front door was closed, and she was positive that she had not closed it. Molly was a relatively unimaginative woman, particularly when her feet hurt and she was hot and tired. She found nothing especially out of the way in this closed door. The function of doors was, after all, to close. She opened it, clumsily and noisily, and got through it some way with all of her packages and dropped them down on the center table in the living room. "Whew!" she said. "It sure is hot in here, and it sure is hot outdoors. What, for Lord's sakes, was this door doing shut—and the kitchen one too? Why, it's just like an oven all over this house. There ain't much air stirring outdoors, and what there is is hot, but it's better to have the doors open and the air a-coming in than . . . ."

She started through to the kitchen to open that door also. "Well, sir, I'd like to know who'd wanta shut up all the doors. It don't make it a bit cooler in here; it just shuts the air off so it feels like an oven. Why, it must be a hundred degrees right in this house with no air stirring like this and . . ."

And then she saw that Jud's bedroom door was closed also. She was not frightened. She thought that it was peculiar, that was all, and she went to it unhesitatingly and opened it, turning the knob in her sweaty fingers and pushing the door open into the room. She was aware first of all that the room was distressingly hot and full of the buzzing sound of flies, and then she saw Jud.

She screamed to the top of her lungs, and shut her eyes. She could not move, and with her eyes closed she could still see him distinctly. He was hanging from the bedpost, secured by the old green necktie, with his face turned to the wall, his body limp and grotesque. He had the appearance of armlessness. The shirt had twisted around on him in his struggle to free his arms, and an empty sleeve dangled away from the middle of his back. The body was perfectly still, and the flies had settled over him.

Molly opened her eyes again, and it was just the same with her eyes closed or open. It did not occur to her to touch him. If he had been struggling yet she would have gone to him, but there was something extremely final, over and done with, about the way his body dangled.

She wanted only to run away, but she could not move for the life of her. The only emotion that she felt was the great overpowering single one of somehow getting out of this room. She was screaming loudly and continually but she was not aware of that. It seemed to her that a century or two of time passed while she stood rooted there inside the bedroom door. And suddenly the stiffening went out of her and left her weak and trembling, and then Molly ran, for all her bulk and her sore feet, Molly ran. The kitchen door was the nearest, and she broke her fingernails, and ran slivers of wood into her hands, getting it open. It was a heavy wooden door, the floor under it was warped, and it stuck to the floor. Somehow or other Molly got it opened, and burst out onto the back porch.

The backyard, and the garden and the vacant lot seemed perfectly strange to her; whatever she had expected to find the other side of the door, in her fear, was not there. She came into the kitchen again and ran back through the house to the front door. She flung open the screen door, still screaming, and burst out onto the front porch and nearly collided with Sam, who was moving toward the front door, the swiftest he had moved in many years, under the impetus of Molly's screams that he had heard way out on the sidewalk. "Molly, what in God's name . . . You sick? What's a matter? You got a pain? Tell me what's a matter."

"It's Mr. Higgins," she wailed. "Come quick, Sam. He's gone and . . . Oh, why don't you go in there quick? Oh, it's awful, it's the terriblest thing I ever . . . Hurry, why can't you hurry?"

Sam tripped over the furniture in his haste to reach the bedroom, and Molly trailed him as far as the kitchen, but she did not offer to enter the bedroom again.

Whatever Sam had been prepared to see inside the bedroom it was not precisely this, but somehow he was not surprised. He had a momentary and almost overwhelming impulse to run away, just as Molly had had, but he managed to control himself. And then his curiosity got the better of him. It seemed to him a marvelously ingenious job. He congratulated Jud on it mentally, and drew nearer to view it at closer hand. It seemed a wonderful thing to him that Jud from the bed could have accomplished this. The closer he came to Jud, the more painfully aware he became suddenly of several things: the terrible pathetic looseness of that dangling body, the swarm of flies hanging to it, and the face, dark and contorted and unrecognizable save for the sparse bristling whiskers. He felt some sensation or other in his stomach and retreated hastily from the room.

He found Molly sitting in the chair by the kitchen table, crying loudly.

"I guess he's dead, all right," Sam said to her weakly. "Well, sir, it sure looks like he did a good job of it all right."

"Well, Lord, don't just—stand there . . ." Molly wailed at him between sobs. "Do something, get somebody quick. Mary's to the hotel, and Ernie's out on the job, and Carl's to the meat market, and Josie's way off up there to Ashbury, and there ain't no telling where Jen is, and Kenny . . ." Here Molly really wailed . . . "And I ain't got no idea even where Kenny is. Oh, I wished Kenny was only here. If Kenny was only here . . ."

Sam stood helplessly by. "Well, sir," he said mildly. "I suppose there's certain things we're bounden to do in a case like this, but I can't just remember what they are. You suppose we oughta get a doctor?"

"What's he need of a doctor?" she wailed. "Poor Mr. Higgins is way past a doctor helping now. Oh, Lord, I never should have left him alone here when I went uptown. I never should have left him here. Oh, Lord, oh, Lord, how was I to know he'd go and do a thing like that the minute our backs was turned?"

"You suppose we oughta call the sheriff of this county?" Sam asked her again. He had a guilty feeling that they were committing some crime or other by permitting Jud's death to go this long a time unreported to some authority or another. As if Jud was now the property of the government, and it was a crime to keep him here in the house, without telling the government about it.

"Why, I don't know what you'd want to go and call the sheriff for," Molly cried. "If I only hadn't went off downtown and left him all alone here. He seemed just like he always is. He seemed just like he always is, and then to think the minute my back was turned . . . Sam Veech, for Lord's sakes, what you standing there for? You ain't no more good to me than nothing. Why don't you do something? Oh, I wish that Kenny was here, if only we knew where to get Kenny . . ."

Sam searched his mind desperately for something that he could do or say. He honestly wanted to do something, anything, but he could think of nothing. Molly had rejected the doctor and the sheriff and it appeared to him that all that was left was the undertaker. Yet somehow he did not want to mention the undertaker to Molly, as if it would be indelicate, as if Jud was not already dead. Besides, he didn't know how long you should decently wait after a thing like this before you called the undertaker. Sam was upset, and bewildered, and so he grabbed at Molly's last words eagerly.

"Well, sir, where is Kenny? Seems like you'd know where we could get a hold of him. Did he come home from town last night? I ain't seen nothing of him around here today."

"I don't suppose he come home last night," Molly said. "I suppose he's up there to Ashbury some place. I wish to Lord he was here.

He'd know what to do for poor Mr. Higgins. Kenny'd know just what to do, if only he was here . . ."

Sam was grasping at straws now. "Maybe he come home late and is still up there in bed asleeping. I'll go right up there and look. It wouldn't do no harm to look, the way he sleeps, nothing ever wakes him up, you could yell the roof off."

Molly smeared her tears around on her face. "Well, what you standing here blabbing for? Go on and see if Kenny's up there, go on, hurry up . . ."

Sam ran up the stairs, his rheumatism forgotten. He was hoping now desperately that Kenny would be there, but he did not think that he was. He had only mentioned it in his anxiety to be doing or saying something helpful. The bedroom door was closed, and he opened it and could not believe his eyes. It did not seem possible to him that that could really be Kenny lying there in the middle of the bed, sleeping peacefully, with his mouth a little open, a flush of color in his face, and his blond hair falling over his face. It was a miracle to Sam. He went weak with relief. He rushed to the bed and started shaking Kenny, eager to rouse him, eager to shift the responsibility of this thing to him.

Kenny swam up out of sleep regretfully. Someone was clawing at his shoulder and babbling words at him. Some of the words that Sam was saying began to filter into his consciousness. He sat up suddenly, his eyes clearing. "You mean the old boy hung himself? For God's sakes, when?"

Without listening to what his father was saying he got out of bed and started downstairs. He went just as he was, in his shorts, and that was all. He heard his mother crying in the kitchen, and his father clattering down the stairs behind him, and from far off the sound of Smith's rooster crowing. He went out to the kitchen, and just as he got there a train came through, and made all speech impossible. Molly kept right on talking although he couldn't understand a word she was saying or even hear the sound of her voice. She got up out of the chair and flung her arm around him, crying hard.

He patted her shoulder absently, loosened her arms, and went into Jud's bedroom. His father trailed in behind him and stood in the doorway.

Once before Kenny had seen a man who had hung himself. When he was just a kid, and the coppers picked him up drunk on the streets of Ashbury and put him in the bull pen. The first thing he saw when he woke up in the morning was this Negro hanging, only he hung himself with his belt.

Kenny walked up to Jud. He thought that he certainly looked as if he was dead, all right. He peered around into Jud's face, and concluded that it must have been a whole lot harder for that Negro that time, if the looks of them was any way of telling. He wondered first of all if Jud was really dead. He wasn't kicking any more, and he certainly looked dead, but you never could be sure. Kenny wondered about his pulse, and then he discovered that Jud to all appearances didn't have any hands or arms, just dangling empty sleeves in the wrong places.

Kenny swore a little. "What the hell . . ." he was saying.

"It sure is an awful thing," Sam said in an awed voice.

"Where in hell's his arms?"

Sam brightened up a little in his admiration of Jud's ingenuity. "Why, ain't you seen where his arms are yet? You know, that's the first thing that struck me right off. Where's his arms? And then I see his arms is right there under that shirt. He worked his arms out of his shirt sleeves, and the shirt kept his arms down. I guess he thought of just about everything."

"So that's where his arms is," Kenny said shortly. "Hell, I thought for a minute the flies had et 'em off." He swung his hand savagely at the swarm of flies crawling around on Jud as he spoke. "I was going to take his pulse, but I better not reach up there under his shirt to get ahold of his wrist."

"Well, don't you suppose we oughta . . ." Sam paused delicately. "Wouldn't it be better to git him down on the bed?"

"Naw, we can't," Kenny scowled ferociously, wrinkling up his forehead. "We gotta leave him hanging there till the sheriff and the coroner get here. You ain't supposed to cut 'em down, unless they're still alive, a course."

"Well, now I had a feeling that was the way it was," Sam said triumphantly. "I was trying to tell your mother I had a feeling the law was something like that."

"Look," said Kenny impatiently. "I'll get some clothes on and go uptown and do the telephoning. Gotta get holda the sheriff and the coroner and some of them guys to come out here. We ain't got no right to touch him or nothing, till after they see him. I'll go uptown and do the phoning." He waved savagely at the flies on Jud again.

But before going to dress, Kenny put his arm around Molly and led her firmly to the stairs. "Come on, Mom, take it easy now. You'll make yourself sick, crying like this. You better go upstairs and lay down awhile. That'll make you feel better. There ain't nothing you can do down here anyway right now."

Crying and protesting, Molly let Kenny help her up the stairs. He took her to her bedroom and got her to lie down on the bed. She clung to him, but he worked her hands loose. "I can't stay, Mom. I gotta get downtown and do some phoning. It won't take but a minute and then I'll be right back. You lay still here an' rest and you'll feel better." He took her shoes off, and then left her. He decided that this was an occasion that warranted notifying Mary at the hotel immediately.

After dressing, Kenny started for the front door and then he thought of something. He returned to the kitchen and looked in the customary place for his mother's purse. He couldn't find it and then he remembered the pile of groceries and packages on the center table in the living room. Sure enough the purse was among them. He took a dollar bill and a little change out of it. The way he was feeling, Kenny thought, by the time he got through making phone calls he'd need a little whiskey to straighten him up, stiffs on empty stomach and gassing over telephones to lousy coppers like up to the sheriff's office.

When Kenny came out of the front door he met Carl just coming up the porch steps, home from the meat market to get his dinner. Carl's unconcern, and his unmelodic whistling struck Kenny as being irresistibly funny under the circumstances.

"Hi, kid," he said. "What you got to feel so good about?"

"Hell, you up already?" Carl answered him scowling. "What's the matter with you, Tarzan? Where's your shirt?"

Kenny was more pleased every second. "Here, you better have a cigarette," he said to his brother.

"What's the matter, they stale or something?" Carl said suspiciously as he took the cigarette.

Kenny grinned as he held the match. "Naw, I just got a feeling you're gonna be needing a cigarette in a minute, that's all."

Carl brushed past him blowing the smoke out of his mouth.

"Go in quiet, why can't you?" Kenny said. "Ma is upstairs laying down."

As Carl went through the screen door, Kenny called back to him, "Got a surprise for yuh out in the kitchen. Go out there and look right outside of Jud's door. I bet you'll be surprised."

Carl was only mildly interested in any form of family surprise. He wondered vaguely if Ernie had bought his mother the kerosene stove that he'd been talking about buying for her for the last two or three summers.

Kenny called to him once more from the street. "Go on out and look at the surprise, but don't touch it, see?" Kenny laughed. Carl stood in the shadows of the doorway and looked out to his brother. He thought that he had never seen Kenny look so beautiful as he did at the moment.

He edged out to the kitchen, but he saw nothing that looked like food or dinner preparations anywhere. He was angry and disappointed. And then he remembered about the surprise that Kenny had spoken of. He turned around expectantly and looked toward the door of Jud's room. He couldn't see anything there, so he walked over toward the door. Out of the corner of his eye, he caught a glimpse of the bed in Jud's room and, for a second, it looked to him as if Jud wasn't in the bed. He walked through the doorway to make sure, idly, hoping that the old man would be asleep, so that he wouldn't be forced to say anything to him. He stood in the doorway, and it was not necessary that he say a word.

And so that was how it happened that Carl fainted, and fell headlong into Jud's room, hitting his head against the edge of the little dresser.

Sam heard the sound of his fall upstairs and it gave him a nasty shock, for he wasn't aware that Carl was in the house.

He tiptoed down the stairs cautiously, and went out to the bedroom prepared for the worst. What he found was the long ungainly length of Carl spread out along the floor, face down, with blood trickling out of the cut on his head.

Sam cursed then, for the first time that day, and went to get water from the pail in the corner of the kitchen.

The cigarette that Kenny had given Carl rolled away out of his fingers, under the bed, and burned out there unnoticed on the floor.

9

T HAT NIGHT THE VEECHES SAT TOGETHER STIFFLY and solemnly in the living room, in unexpected family conclave. They had been gathering one by one all afternoon, and now they were at last alone together. The police and coroner had departed. The house was at last empty of the stream of sympathetic friends and neighbors who had been pouring in all day ever since the news of Jud's death spread through the village. The house was even empty of Jud himself. But Molly had insisted that Jud should not be compelled to wait over night at the undertaking parlors, so his return was expected at any moment.

The Veeches were alone together, and strangely quiet for them. The windows were all open and the night spread over the house, warm and vaporous and illusive. Occasionally soft rain fell soundlessly. The sky was silvery and luminous as bluish-white corrugated clouds curdled from horizon to horizon, the moon cutting through here and there unexpectedly.

Molly occasionally sighed audibly over the squeaking of her rocker. She could not cry another tear now to save her. She was completely wept out, and no wonder. She had wept sincerely and unashamedly with, or for the benefit of, every single caller that had come in all day long.

Sam sighed a little too, and shuffled his feet on the floor. More than anything else in the world he wanted to take off his shoes and stretch his hot cramped feet in the cool air, but he did not dare run the risk of Molly's displeasure. She had the expression on her face that he had long since learned to recognize and dread; a certain tightening of the lips and lengthening of the eyes, which meant that she was on the verge of being difficult. Sam shuffled his feet along the floor and sighed again.

Kenny tilted his chair further back on the two legs, until his head could rest against the wall. He coughed a little, contentedly, and let his eyes droop almost shut. He was looking at Mary. She was sitting beside him, in the low rocking chair from upstairs. Her hands were folded quietly in her lap, her eyes were downcast and there was a flush of color in her cheeks. She rocked gently back and forth, for all the world like a demure child. My God, Kenny thought, it was worth having the old bastard kick the bucket to have Mary home for awhile like this.

There was a sound from upstairs of Dorothy's voice, in a fretful incoherent cry. Both Molly and Mary stopped rocking instantly and listened.

"I guess she was just crying out in her sleep," Molly said. "That poor little thing. I swear, I never see a little kid take a death in the fambly so hard as Dor'thy did. Why, she liked to never stopped crying all afternoon. It'll be a wonder if she ain't sick."

After that the terrible silence fell again. Molly hitched her chair around a little and sighed once more.

Josette, sitting beside Jen on the piano bench, cleared her throat loudly. A night bird flew against the window screen hard, his wings scraping on the wire, and then he was gone.

They all heard the car stop out in front, saw the headlights shining on the wet sidewalk and shiny wet black tree trunks. Molly said, "I guess that's them, bringing Mr. Higgins back now."

It was the undertaker, a soft-footed, morose man with his several assistants. They went about their duties, while the Veeches sat awkwardly by. The coffin was to be placed in Jud's room, the bed having been taken down during the afternoon in readiness for it.

One of the undertaker's assistants was attaching a slightly mussy spray of flowers to the front door. The Veeches listened to the short discreetly soft strokes of his hammer disconsolately, and each one of them was thinking dark thoughts of death and destruction.

With every stroke of the hammer Ernie became more irritated, more aware of the money that all this was going to cost. Not a word about burial expenses had been mentioned yet, but he knew that it was coming, and that he would be expected to pay the bills. The whole thing made him furious. He hated old Jud as he had never hated him before. He was so angry with his mother that he could hardly contain himself. What in God's name did she mean chasing off uptown and leaving the old bastard all alone? Just handing him the chance to string himself up. Hell, she shoulda known. . . . And then Kenny, that lazy, good-for-nothing son of a bitch, sleeping right upstairs all the while, laying up there in bed and letting the old devil pull a stunt like that. Maybe he was asleep and maybe he wasn't, Ernie kept thinking. And for a fleeting moment, he even toyed with the idea that Kenny had strangled Jud himself and hung him to the bedpost just to take out his grudge against his elder brother, knowing very well that Ernie would be called upon to pay the bills.

But down underneath, in the dark sensitive vital areas of his thinking, Ernie was trying his best to unravel the tangle of his personal affairs. Erma had left him two days ago. She had returned to her parents and she was out to make trouble. He conceded that it was partially his fault, but he was glad to be rid of her, glad and relieved. She was a tricky little devil, that's what she was. He would admit that she was justified in leaving. He would admit that he was drunk, that was true enough; and without a doubt he did beat her, he often did when he was drunk; and it was even possible that he had beaten her cruelly and unmercifully, but how was he to know that she was pregnant? He didn't believe that story, anyway. Well, if she was, that was just too bad, the tricky little devil, he could see what she was up to. She figured if she got in the family way he'd marry her, the scheming, tricky little devil. Well, that was all over now, anyway. Maybe she had really been pregnant, and maybe she hadn't. My God, a baby! Who did she think she was, having a baby of his? She knew how he felt about stuff like that. Why, she wasn't fit to have a baby. Anyway, she wasn't fit to have his baby. When would a woman come along who would really love him and stick to him no matter what happened? A nice girl, who would have children for him and really love him. And what did Erma have up her sleeve now? She had a God-awful temper. And that family of hers, they would make trouble . . . He was wondering if he could get Leatha Owens to come and keep house for him. Leatha, who used to be married to one of his boys, only she ran off with some guy and Dick Owens divorced her. And the last couple of years she had been working as hostess in a joint up to Ashbury. Leatha was a swell girl, swell figure, blonde, laughed a lot, and he wouldn't wonder if she wouldn't be glad to come down and keep house for him for awhile, kind of a vacation for her, and he wouldn't mind having her around the house.

The undertaker and his assistants set up the frame on which the coffin was to rest. The sound of it was almost more than Molly could bear. Poor, poor Mr. Higgins, she thought, to have to die like he did. She would never forgive herself if she lived to be a hundred. It was all her fault, going off uptown and leaving him. She'd never get over it, never. Underneath these pensive thoughts, Molly was seething with anger. She kept looking at Ernie sitting across the room, scowling and not saying a word. She could tell what was wrong with him, she thought grimly. It was the funeral expenses that was worrying him. He hadn't as much as mentioned helping out and he knew very well that that was what was on his mother's mind. Oh, she'd like to take him over her knee and give him a good thrashing, Molly thought wildly. And that wasn't all, she'd like to thrash them all while she was at it, this whole family of hers, Sam too. Not a one of them had a single decent feeling among them. She wondered if they'd sit around like this, all unmoved and silent and spiteful when she died. She just wished that she didn't have to ask odds of Ernie at all. She knew very well that Mary could get the money for the burial. Mary had offered already, and for two cents she'd just let Mary do it, too. She guessed she could show Ernie if she wanted to.

Carl lit a cigarette with shaking fingers, dreading more than anything the moment when they would carry the coffin with Jud in it into the house. Carl's head was aching and his nerves were unstrung. There would be no use in his attempting to sleep tonight. If he ever dared to shut his eyes, he knew exactly what he would see. Even if he didn't close his eyes he was going to see Jud hanging to the bedpost. When that happened he was going to scream and scream. He didn't care what they thought about him, he was going to scream.

Carl realized that he was afraid of death. It sickened him to think that a time would come when he too must die. If he had his way, Carl thought, they would never have funerals. As soon as somebody died, the undertaker would rush there quick with the sirens blowing like an ambulance, and take the corpse away. He had thought of suicide himself, Carl remembered, but he knew now that he never could kill himself. No matter what, he would have to live, because he was so terribly afraid of death. Carl looked away out of the door anxiously, to see if they were ready to carry the coffin in yet.

And at that very moment the undertaker and his assistants were preparing to bring the coffin in. Kenny wondered absently if he should offer to help them. Jud wouldn't weigh next to nothing, a little withered up old bastard like him. Hell, ran Kenny's reverie, old Ernie was sure going around with a sour puss on him, thinking about the money he was gonna have to part with. Well, wasn't that just too bad. For once he would spend it on something besides clothes, women and liquor. Old Ernie was tight with his money, and it was sure gonna be fun to see him have to shell out. There was a story going around that this last dame Ernie had had up there living with him had left him, on account of he beat hell outa her when he was drunk or something. Good old Ernie, he sure was hard on women, but the kind of women Ernie wanted he could buy any place for a dime a dozen. That was one thing about Ernie, he never had woman trouble, because the kind of women he wanted he could always get as long as he had money. Kenny felt immeasurably superior to Ernie, because in his time Kenny had had intimate knowledge of women who couldn't have been reached for any amount of money, the kind of women that he imagined that Ernie did not dream existed.

They brought the coffin in, carrying it through the living room out to Jud's bedroom. Molly began to cry again softly.

Poor old Mom, Kenny thought, she was the only one on earth that gave a damn whether Jud Higgins was alive or dead. Kenny wondered suddenly in an imaginative burst that was rare for him, if when he died, sometime in the remote future, there would be anybody on the whole earth to mourn for him. It was a chilly thought that sent Kenny reaching for a cigarette and his eyes straying to that comforting warmth that was Mary. His thoughts clogged and became incoherent with tenderness. Mary must have felt his eyes, for she raised her head ever so slowly, and looked at him a moment. Funny, thought Kenny, that however many times Mary had looked at him he was still always surprised to see her eyes so blue. Mary smiled, and lowered her gaze again to her hands in her lap. Kenny felt a familiar warmth go through him like quicksilver. He still watched her. A very funny thing, there were times when he could tell what was in her mind, like reading words out of a newspaper, times when it was a waste of time for either one of them to talk because they didn't need to put into words the things they had in their heads. But tonight, this moment, he could not reach her. By God, he ruminated, he'd give a million dollars to know what was going on in her head right this minute, a million dollars. It must be something she didn't want him to know. It must be something she couldn't share with him. He wondered where she learned the trick of doing that. He couldn't ever shut her away from him even if he wanted to. Any time Mary looked at him, slow, the way she did, she could see right through him like tissue paper. She knew more about him than he knew himself, he conceded in a burst of generosity. It sobered him suddenly, the thought that although Mary sat there so close beside him that he could reach out his hand and touch her, that really she was a million miles away, totally beyond his reach. It was as if she had gone off some place far away, and left him, without even waiting to say good-bye or to tell him where she was going or when she would return. The sense of the loss of her overwhelmed him. He felt a cold ill feeling in his stomach, and it was as if a chill wind blew upon his body. The world became strange and unreal for him, colorless and uninhabited, not this room any more, or any place that he had ever been. He reached out his hand instinctively and touched the soft warmth of her arm, closing his fingers tight around it, feeling the very blood of her coursing under the tight circle of his fingers. Mary looked at him once more, and he saw a world of good and tender things beyond her eyes. She smiled a half-smile, and made the little weaving motion of her shoulders, ducking her head, in the pantomime of a boxer, touching his chin momentarily with her doubled fist.

Kenny came back to reality and his normal plane of thoughts in an instant. Poor old Mom, crying away over there. Where did all them tears come from? Before they got Jud planted she was likely to lose twenty pounds, crying off the fat right under their eyes. And good old Ernie looking uglier and uglier. Kenny chortled with glee. Old Ernie, old scout, he better come through with the dough too, by heaven, because if he don't, Mary will, and if Mary has to pay the bills for planting the old bastard, I'll beat the hell outa Ernie myself, and don't think I couldn't do it and don't think it wouldn't be a pleasure. Who the hell says it wouldn't be a pleasure? A pleasure, I say, a puh-lezyuh, yassah, uh puhlezyuh!

They carried the coffin through the room, and Jen had to put her hand tight over her mouth to keep from crying out loud suddenly. Because this very night, Franny lay up at Ashbury in the hospital unconscious, and the doctors said that she was never going to wake up again. It wasn't fair, Jen told herself for the thousandth time, it wasn't fair that soon they would carry another coffin so, only one containing all the youth and aliveness of beauty that had been Franny. It wasn't so bad for some nasty mean old son of a bitch like Jud to die, but for Franny it was awful. Jen wanted to cry but she would be damned, she thought, if she would cry here, because if she cried now they would all think she was crying over Jud and she wouldn't have them thinking that. Franny can't die, Jen thought again, over and over, but already down under, in her thinking, she had accepted the fact of Franny's death, and she was already trying to arrange her easy loose-patterned scheme of living to a world with no Franny in it, and the process left her puzzled and unsettled and bewildered. Out of the corner of her eye, Jen saw Kenny reach out and put his hand on Mary's arm, with his face so blank and quiet that she could not tell what he was thinking or why he did it, and Mary in return touched her fist against his face; it was a gesture between them that Jen had seen as long as she could remember. She wondered why they did that, and what meaning it had for them. She wondered why Mary liked Kenny better than any of the rest of her brothers and sisters. Mary, who was the kindest, nicest, swellest person on earth, and a louse like Kenny. Some day she was going to tell Mary just what he did to Franny, and then see if Mary thought he was such a good guy. By God, I'll cook your goose, Kenny Veech, she thought, if it's the last thing I ever do I'll get even with you.

Then at last the undertaker went away. Each of them sighed a little and put away from himself as much as possible his private thoughts. This was the moment they had all been waiting for. Jud home once more, the reality of the death here in the house with them at last.

Ernie yawned prodigiously, covering his wide-open mouth with his hand with the cameo ring on it. "Damn, I gotta get home and get some sleep. I gotta go to work tomorrow."

Molly out of her annoyance with him, did not answer.

"Who's gonna set up here?" Sam asked mildly.

Ernie shrugged his shoulders and darted a glance at Molly, rocking back and forth in her chair determinedly, with her lips folded together, and her eyes narrowed in her face.

Kenny teetered his chair back and forth on two legs, carelessly. "Mary and me'll set up. Hell, it ain't gonna be long now till morning, anyways."

Ernie stood up and pulled at the cuffs of his shirt. "I should think the resta yuh would get to bed. You're gonna be busy around here tomorrow all right, folks comin' in, and cleaning up the house and stuff . . ."

Nobody answered Ernie and he started toward the door uncertainly under the combined battery of the eyes of all of them.

Just as he reached the door Molly spoke to him icily. "Don't you want to see Mr. Higgins?"

"Naw, I don't!" Ernie spoke shortly, angrily, before he thought. He realized as soon as he spoke the words that he had said the wrong thing. He groped for other words to mend and modify them, but it was too late now.

"No, acourse you don't wanta see Mr. Higgins. That ain't no surprise to me." Molly took a deep breath and went on talking loudly and angrily. "Ernie Veech, you oughta be ashamed of yourself. That old man just exactly like a grandfather to you and then you act like this. Why, him dying don't mean no more to you than nothing, no more than nothing. I tell you it's a terrible, terrible thing, him dying the way he did, and it don't mean no more to you than . . ."

"Damn it!" Ernie said dryly and containedly. "Whatcha want me to do, bawl from now till breakfast and lay off work the rest of the week? Is that whatcha think I oughta do?"

"Well, Lord, it wouldn't hurt you to show a little respect, I guess."

Ernie was catching the contagion of anger from his mother, and he broke in on her rudely. "Sure, you betcha it's an awful thing. Yeah, you betcha it is, in a minute I suppose you'll be blaming that on me too. Sure, you will. Hell, yes, it was me I suppose that went chasing off uptown and left the old bastard alone . . ."

"No more feeling in you than nothing," Molly raised her voice over his. "Calling Mr. Higgins nasty names and everything and him laying right in here in the other room dead right this minute. Lord, I guess I know now the way that you'll talk about me when I'm dead and gone . . ."

"For Lord's sakes, Ma!" Ernie pleaded. "I never said . . ."

Molly began to cry loudly. "Oh, you don't need to worry, Ernie Veech. I ain't gonna ask you for a cent to pay for the burying. I ain't gonna ask you for one single red cent. I know better'n to ask you. I know I wouldn't get it. I know the way you feel, so you don't need to worry about me asking you no more. I know . . ."

"I never said I wouldn't pay for burying him," Ernie roared. "I dunno where you get such crazy ideas in your head. I never said I wouldn't pay . . ."

"You did too!" Molly shrieked.

"Well, I didn't. I guess I oughta know what I said and what I didn't. I never said no such God-damn thing!"

"Well, I guess you did. You just as good as come right out and said it." No matter how loudly Molly cried, her voice was always high and distinct over her sobbing. "You come right out and said it was all my fault Mr. Higgins killing himself, that I was the only one to blame for him being dead, and all the expense . . ."

Ernie floundered down in his mother's peculiar and characteristic logic. "I never said . . . All I said was . . . I never claimed I wouldn't pay for burying him," he shouted helplessly.

"Yes, you did too. You claim it's all my fault poor Mr. Higgins hanging himself like he done. I guess I heard what you said to me. I ain't deef, nor I ain't no fool . . ."

"My God," Ernie yelled wildly, "I wish you'd keep still and let me talk once. I never said I wouldn't pay for burying him. I expect to have to. I expected it all along. And I never said it was your fault he hung himself neither."

"Yes, you did!"

"I did not. Hell, how was you to know the old devil would string himself up the minute your back was turned? It ain't none of it your fault. It ain't nobody's fault, unless . . ." Ernie was floundering and grasping at straws and he turned on Kenny viciously, "unless—it was yours, you lazy God-damn bastard laying up there in bed all day long, instead of getting a job or helping out here around home, or . . ."

"Go on and have your fun, sonnyboy," Kenny said to him softly, "but keep me outa this, see?"

Molly sprang into the breach to turn the tide of Ernie's anger away from Kenny. "I always done the best for my fambly I knew how, and now I'm getting to be an old woman this is all the thanks I get. It ain't very often that you're asked to do nothing here, Ernie. It's precious little money you ever hand over here, precious little money. Do you ever give me ten dollars and say to me . . ."

Sam exploded forth into the argument indignantly. "You haven't got no cause to be bawling out Ernie. He's done an awful lot for this family. Maybe he don't keep peddling out money to you all the time, because he knows where all your money goes to. Every cent you can git hold of you're a-handing out to Kenny to buy booze with and to lay around up to Ashbury in them . . ."

"You shut up, Sam Veech," Molly shrieked. "You just be careful the things you say right here in front of your own daughters. This ain't none of your business, anyway. I'd like to know what you think you ever done for this fambly that gives you any right to jibe in when we're a-talking about money, that's what I'd like to know."

"He's right, Ma," Ernie said. "Damn it, if Pa ain't right. That's just the way it is. I'd be handing out money to you all the time, if it wasn't that I knew that that lazy bastard was a-getting it away from you just as fast as I could give it to yuh . . ."

Kenny inserted his voice into the bedlam easily. "Hell, Mom, don'tcha let 'em kid you. You know why Ernie can't give you no money. Poor old Ernie's got his own family expenses. My God, no man ever had more family expenses'n poor old Ernie. He's got a big one coming up right now. Did you hear about it? His itty bitty witty up there left him and it's gonna cost him plenty before he's done with her. And then when he gets done he'll have to spend a whole lot more money buying himself a new mama . . ." Kenny laughed uproariously and turned aside coughing and laughing.

"You shut your God-damn mouth," Ernie said in his normal tone of voice, his face flushing red.

"Why, sure," Molly yelled triumphantly. "You can spend all kinds of money on them women, but when it comes to doing something for your own fambly, why . . ."

"Oh, sure," Ernie roared, "I never do a single God-damn thing for this family, do I . . ."

Josette stood up suddenly with her face pale and determined and yelled at them at the top of her voice. "Oh, you all make me sick. You ought to be ashamed. What do you suppose people are going to say, you all yelling and hollering like this. Jud dead right here in the house and then you fighting and yelling about the money for the funeral to the top of your lungs. What do you suppose people are going to say, they can hear you from one end of this town to another, the noise you're . . ."

Ernie got his breath while Josette was talking and then he launched forth again as if he had never been interrupted. "No, I never do nothing for this family, do I? There's something right there. Who in hell is paying the bills for sending Josie up to business college, I'd like to know. Just tell me that, who's paying the bills for sending Josie to . . ."

Josette laughed then, suddenly and bitterly. "Ernie Veech," she said, "you've bragged for the last time about what a wonderful thing you are doing, sending me up there to school. I've had to stand around here and listen to you brag about what a swell fellow you were, and I've had to keep still and be nice to you when I hate you, and hate the kind of a life you live, but I don't have to any more. Now I can say just what I think of you, because you're not sending me to business college any more. You didn't know that, but you aren't. They canned me out of there today. Flunked, see? You'll have to get something new to brag about. Now I can tell you for once just what I think of you, and . . ."

"Ma!" Ernie howled, aggrieved and bewildered. "You gonna let her talk to me like that after all I done for her, sending her up there to Ashbury to school?"

"Josie Veech," promptly answered Molly, "ain't you ashamed to talk to Ernie like that after all he's done for you? And that ain't all, after all that money he spent, ain't you ashamed to fool around and miss your lessons so's they have to kick you out up there to school? You oughta be ashamed . . ."

"Oh, of course, it's all my fault," Josette said. "It's all my fault!"

Molly looked at her and began to cry again at the top of her lungs. "Well, sir, I tell you, I just can't understand it, that's all. There ain't a one a you that's got a spark of decent feelin' in you, not a one a you. That poor old man that's been a grandfather to you a-laying out there in his casket, and after dying the awful way he did too, and there ain't a one of you that's got a spark of decent feeling in you. Yelling around here like nothing had happened, and Ernie here a-arguing and fighting a-tryin' to git outa paying poor Mr. Higgins' funeral bill . . ." Molly's voice dissolved away into her sobs.

"Oh, hell," Ernie said wearily. "We gotta start that all over again?"

Kenny had started to laugh uproariously, with his head back against the wall, and Mary sat beside him in the rocking chair, wreathed in her cigarette smoke until she looked like an idol in a wall niche.

"Don't have to start nothing over again," Molly said.

"Look, Ma," Ernie said, his voice was hoarse and cracked from strain, and he talked slowly. "I give up, honest I do. I never said I wasn't gonna pay for burying Jud. I always figured on paying the bills when Jud finally kicked off. And I'm gonna pay 'em too. So what you want to start jumping all over me for?"

"You don't have to pay for Mr. Higgins no such a thing," Molly said. "I ain't gonna ask a cent of you, not a cent. You don't need to worry about it no more."

"Okay, now you're mad," Ernie said. "I don't see what call you got to be mad. I said I'd pay for burying Jud, didn't I?"

"Let's not talk about it," Molly said with dignity over her sobs. "I ain't gonna ask a cent off from you."

What control Ernie had retained over his temper snapped now. His face looked flushed and brutal, and his voice was cold. "Oh, I get it," he said. "My money ain't good enough for you, I guess. So that's it. You been listening to stories little Kenny goes around telling behind my back. That's how it is. Now you think I'm one hell of a guy and you won't touch my lousy money. Of course, little Kenny, he's a swell guy, he is," Ernie laughed unpleasantly. "The only trouble is nice little Kenny ain't got any money to give you. So now it looks like you're gonna have to get your money the same place that nice little Kenny boy gets his all the time. By heaven, talk about lousy money! If you think my money is lousy, what in hell you think the money she gets is?"

Kenny was out of his chair and halfway across the room all in one motion. "You better shut your mouth," he said softly to Ernie. "You can talk about me all you wanta, see, but you leave Mary outa this, or I'll push you to sleep."

"Well, now," Ernie said unpleasantly, "ain't you touchy about Mary, though. Somebody oughta have licked the pants offa you for hanging around her years ago. It would have been better for you, and for her too, a hell of a lot better." He laughed dryly and mirthlessly as he spoke and looked away over Kenny's shoulder to Mary in the chair across the room.

That was why he did not see Kenny coming, and why the impact of Kenny's heavy body, hurtling forward like a spring unloosed, sent Ernie sprawling and cursing to the floor. The table in the middle of the room was overturned, the lamp fell with it, the cord pulling out of the socket and leaving the room in shadows, lighted only by the lamp on the piano. Molly clutched for the lamp too late, and heard the crashing sound of the big glass bowl breaking and saw the bright-colored shade with the long bead fringe break into pulp under their rolling struggling bodies. Then Molly fled out of the mêlée to the kitchen where the others had taken refuge.

The semidarkness of the room was filled with the sound of sliding breaking furniture, the impact of heavy bodies, their hard breathing and their muttered incoherent cursings as Ernie and Kenny wrestled on the floor. Carl stood flat against the wall at the end of the piano, too stunned to move. Every nerve and muscle of his body cried out against the brutality of what was going on before his eyes. He pressed the palms of his hands against the wall hard, and for the second time that day he felt a faintness coming over him, a dimming of vision, a sagging of the knees, but this time as much as he might have desired to, he did not lose consciousness completely. He could only stand there with a deathly sickness in his stomach and a blur before his eyes and the unfamiliar frightening sounds of the fight in his ears.

Molly wailed at them incessantly at the top of her lungs. "You cut out that fighting this minute! Kenny, you hear me? Stop it, now! Somebody's gonna git hurt and you're a-smashing all the furniture to pieces. Lord, a-fighting and a-carrying on like this, two great big grown-up men like you, and poor Mr. Higgins a-laying out here in his casket. Kenny, you hear me, stop it now before you git hurt . . ."

But apparently neither one of them had any intention of stopping. They had not fought like this since they were boys at home together. They rolled over and over on the floor, hitting each other hard with doubled fists. And although it was obvious that Ernie was no match for the precise relentless fury of his brother, he was not ready to give in easily.

They stopped momentarily for a second wind, facing each other, Kenny in a semicrouch, his shirt torn to ribbons, the blood on his face testimony to the utility of Ernie's cameo ring, and Ernie squatting on one knee with his elegant suit and shirt ripped off him, and his face already marked and swollen.

Taking advantage of this lull, Mary crossed the room from the corner where she had been standing near the piano. She righted the piano bench and stepped daintily from the bench to the keyboard and, shoving aside some of the glittering Scotty dogs and photographs, sat down beside the lamp on top. She crossed her knees, perfectly unperturbed, but always keeping her grave intent face upon her brothers below.

"Mary," Molly wailed in desperation, "make them stop. Make Kenny stop that fighting. Somebody's gonna git hurt bad. They're smashing every stick a furniture we got—and poor Mr. Higgins right here in the house . . ."

Mary paid no attention to her mother.

Molly stopped for breath, and found Sam clawing at her shoulder. "Say," he kept saying, "what was Ernie saying? What did Kenny git so mad for? What did Ernie mean, what he said to Kenny about he oughta been licked. How come Kenny got so mad?" But Molly could not remember for the life of her just what it was that Ernie had said to Kenny, but something of little importance, she was sure. She shook Sam's hand off her shoulder and began her wailing again, and Sam muttered to himself unheard.

"Kenny!" Mary spoke suddenly, her voice sharp and clear over the noise below her, "look out for his right!"

Kenny broke loose from Ernie, shook him off, just as Ernie swung at his brother's head with his doubled fist, swung hard with every ounce of his strength. Kenny ducked away, under his arm, and Ernie floundered off balance. Kenny caught hold of his arm and they struggled for a moment, and then Kenny pulled it loose from Ernie's right hand and threw it the length of the room hard against the wall, that little cupped piece of metal that Ernie had slid over his knuckles.

"You bitch!" Ernie shrieked at Mary. "You bitch, you!" He started to say something else but he never finished it, because Kenny hit him hard and clean in the mouth. Ernie sagged down to the floor, but Kenny dragged him to his feet once more and hit him again and again.

Molly began to scream then with all of her strength, and Josette without a sound turned away and hid her face in her hands.

When his mother screamed, Carl's vision miraculously cleared, and he saw something before his eyes that he never forgot. Kenny, bare to the waist, blood-smeared, beating that limp swollen insensible mass that was Ernie, beating it with bare hard fists in his fury, hard impact of fists against flesh and bone.

Mary slid down from the piano and ran across the room, in and out among overturned pieces of furniture. She caught hold of Kenny's arms from the back and hung on with all her strength. He tried to shake her off, to be loose of her, and she spoke to him with her mouth muffled against his bare back, as she clung to him. "Kenny, you hear me, stop!"

Kenny stopped then, with his arms hanging at his sides and his head drooping, and Ernie lay at his feet on the floor.

Everyone for one moment was perfectly still; there was not a sound or motion in the room.

At that moment, the little Smith boy—the Smiths were the nearest neighbors the Veeches had—hopped up out of the darkness onto the front porch. He was only partially clothed, and yawning and rubbing his eyes. But when he looked into the room he was instantly alert. He cupped his hands on either side of his face and flattened his nose against the screen. "Judas Jenny!" he said appreciatively. "Kenny sure been knocking hell outa somebody. We heard the noise over to our place. My Pa wants to know if he should come over or call the police or som'p'n. Huh?"

Molly wailed to him from the kitchen. "Tell your Pa to git over here just as quick as he can. Hurry!"

The little Smith boy looked at Mary questioningly. "Should I, Mary?"

She shook her head and smiled at the little boy. "No, not now. But if you want to help us, you run over there to the doctor's house on the other street and tell him to come over here right away. You think that would be worth a dime to you?"

"Sure," the little Smith boy said. He took one last look into the room as if he regretted leaving the scene of the conflict. "Judas Jenny!" he said. "Kenny sure been knocking hell outa somebody!" With one last admiring look at Kenny he disappeared, his bare feet pattering on the sidewalk as he ran upon his errand.

When he was gone, Mary bent down over Ernie, and Molly came into the living room with Sam trailing behind her.

"He hurt bad?" Molly asked tremulously.

"I don't think so," Mary said. "The doctor can tell for sure."

Molly's voice deepened and richened in relief. "Well, I sure hope he ain't. Lord, for a minute there I thought . . . Kenny, what in the world got into you? For Lord's sakes, what in the world possessed you to . . ."

"Ernie oughta have you locked up in jail, that's what he oughta do," Sam said bitterly. "That's the place for you. Ernie oughta have 'em lock you up and keep you there, that's what Ernie oughta do!"

Kenny's face was perfectly blank, his eyes far away, unseeing.

It was then that Carl, whose eyes had had far more than their fill of the limp battered figure on the floor at Kenny's feet, turned around and pillowed his face on his arms on the end of the piano top and began to cry, softly and miserably.

Jen spoke sharply from the doorway. "Kenny wanted to kill Ernie. He likes to kill people and hurt 'em. He almost killed Franny, too. He's a killer. He hadn't oughta run around loose!"

Kenny did not move or give any sign that he had heard. But Mary made an odd little gesture with her hand. Her face was still and quiet, but she doubled her hand up tight as if she felt a sudden sharp pain in her. She doubled her hand up tight and then relaxed the fingers and laid her flat warm palm against Kenny's chest for a second, and then doubled her hand again.

"I wouldn't talk about this any more," she said gently. "Ernie won't want to either, you know."

She repeated that strange gesture, doubling her hand up tight and turning it a little at the wrist.

She spoke again, almost with an effort, but with her voice still soft and even. "Kenny won't be wanting to see the doctor. I'll take him up to my room for awhile. That must be the doctor now."

The headlights of the automobile that had just stopped in front of the house glittered across the lawn. It had begun to rain again. The air was so soft and black that you could almost hear the sound the sharp light made tearing through it.

10

THE DAY BEFORE THE FUNERAL WAS INTERMINABLE and hot and full of unaccustomed activity. Molly insisted that she would not feel right about the funeral unless the house was clean from top to bottom, so Aunt Maggie Hoyer became chairman of a housecleaning committee that included Carl, the twins, and even Dorothy and Sam. It was a full day's work for all of them; Molly had done no housecleaning in the last three years.

Molly sent out to a neighbor's and borrowed a vacuum cleaner to speed the cleaning. While Carl was attempting to clean the living-room rug with it, it suddenly and mysteriously ceased to operate, at the same instant blowing out every fuse in the house and giving Carl a slight electric shock that unnerved him completely.

It was then that Molly discovered that Kenny was missing from the family group. No one had seen him all morning. Apparently he had disappeared from the house at the time that Mary had departed for the hotel. Molly burst into tears. Why, oh, why, she asked of everyone, couldn't Kenny have remained at home this one particular day of all days?

In the midst of the confusion, the Copes stopped in to bring the news that Jen had been expecting. Franny had died in the night, easily and painlessly, without ever recovering consciousness.

Jen and Aunt Maggie collapsed simultaneously. Everyone knew that deaths came in threes to a family, Aunt Maggie explained. Jud first, and now Frances Cope who was almost one of the family, and where would it strike next?

Molly outwept all of them.

By the time that work was resumed, Ernie arrived and put another halt to it. Ernie was in a ferocious bad temper. He made a strange-looking sight and was unhappily aware of it. He was impeccably overdressed as usual, but today no one would be looking at his clothes. His face was discolored and swollen, and covered with a maze of adhesive tape. He was wearing an enormous pair of dark glasses that only served to accentuate the puffy blackened condition of his eyes. One of his hands was completely bandaged.

He had decided that it would be unwise for him to appear at work this morning. His appearance, he felt, would have a demoralizing effect on his men, who, he hoped, were firmly convinced that he was invincible in battle. But he had not felt like staying at home alone either, so he came to his family because he had been sure that they at least would not dare to laugh at him to his face. None of them did, except Dorothy. She laughed long and loudly until he stopped her with a stream of profanity out of his swollen cut lips.

He spent most of that day there, sitting morosely in a corner of the kitchen, well out of the public gaze, smoking chains of cigarettes that did not taste good to him and planning fantastic schemes for revenge on Kenny.

The casket was finally moved into the living room and the few sprays of flowers arranged about it to the best possible advantage. Flowers had become one of Molly's chief worries. There was no one to send Mr. Higgins flowers, and she was not willing that he should be so slighted. At her insistence the family money was divided and two smaller sprays were bought, in preference to one larger one. She had found or borrowed two faded dusty baskets and Aunt Maggie had filled them generously with the blooms of her garden. But Molly found them slightly less than she hoped for; those honest homely flowers looked exactly what they were, and in no way the product of a florist's art. Molly used them nevertheless, shoved back against the wall in the shadows she hoped that they might be mistaken for florist's flowers.

The more immediate neighbors of the Veeches took up a collection among them, as was customary, and contributed a small spray of stiff, wired carnations that Molly detested the moment she laid her eyes on it.

When Molly had reached the lowest depths of her despair and was just at the point of asking Ernie for the money for at least one more spray, a floral offering arrived that made all other flowers extraneous. It bore no card, and it was not necessary that it do so. There was no doubt in Molly's mind where it came from, and she sighed deeply at the sight of it, because she knew that there would be no doubt in anybody else's mind concerning the donor of these flowers either. It was a blanket of pink and white roses, an exquisite, elaborate thing that completely overshadowed all of the other flowers, and called immediate attention to itself, draped over the cheap plain casket in that poor room in that sagging weatherbeaten house. Lew Lentz had ordered it sent on an impulse, partly as a sincere gesture to please Mary, partly because he knew how conspicuous and obvious it would be there, and that gave him pleasure. He also hoped that it might have some subtle psychological effect upon Kenny. It would be too much to hope for, Lew thought, that Kenny might suffocate in its fragrance during the funeral, but it would be there continually before his eyes, as a reminder of several things.

But that was a miscalculation on the part of Lew Lentz, because Kenny didn't get back for the funeral. All the next morning, in the midst of the alterations on her old black silk dress, Molly had looked for him. She could not believe that he would deliberately stay away from Jud's funeral. She had wept and repeated over and over that something must have happened to Kenny, because he would never stay away on purpose. She begged Ernie to go to Ashbury and look for him, but Ernie had declined emphatically to do so. Even after the first mourners had begun to congregate and to examine the flowers, Molly had still looked for Kenny. She listened anxiously for his step all the while the minister was preaching the funeral sermon, it seemed so incredible to her that Kenny would actually stay away from Jud Higgins' funeral.

But he did. And one of the undertaker's damp affable assistants had to take his place among the pallbearers.

When the party left for the cemetery, north of town, in solemn procession behind the hearse, Aunt Maggie remained behind. Aunt Maggie always remained behind at this point in every funeral she ever attended. She was somewhat of an expert at this. Her function was to remove as many traces of the funeral as possible from the house, and prepare a meal for the family to eat on their return. She folded up the undertaker's chairs and stacked them on the porch, and resurrected as much of the living room furniture as she could find that was all in one piece, and returned it to its usual position. Then she withdrew to the kitchen and poked up the fire and got the coffee pot on and went about setting the table.

While she was working in the kitchen, Kenny came home. She did not hear his feet, noiseless in the thin worn soles of his old shoes, and when she looked up and saw him standing there on the back porch it gave her such a start that she dropped a stack of cups and broke one of them.

He was not a very prepossessing sight. His clothes wrinkled and dirty, shirt unbuttoned down his chest, his hair tousled into his eyes, and his face loose and blank with alcohol.

"Sure, Kenny Veech, if you didn't give me an awful scare!" Aunt Maggie said tolerantly. Kenny was a favorite with Aunt Maggie. She diagnosed his condition immediately, and although she disapproved, she made up her mind illogically that she was going to see to it that nobody scolded him or criticized him.

"You come on in here, Kenny, and sample a cup of my coffee and tell me if it's gonna be fit to drink," she said to him briskly.

He came into the kitchen without a word and sat down on the chair just inside the door at the end of the table. To do him justice, Kenny had intended to come home in time for the funeral. But after a day and a night of prolonged drinking, he was in such a mood that he had been very easily persuaded to linger on in Ashbury instead of returning to the village the first thing in the morning as he had planned to do. He was relieved now to find that the funeral was over.

Physically, he was feeling weak and ill. He wondered if he would vomit if he could get out to the wooden toilet the other side of the garden. He decided that he probably wouldn't, and that the walk out there would not be worth it. He buried his head in his arms on the end of the table.

Aunt Maggie had been watching him out of the corner of her eyes, and her heart was touched for him. She hurried to get a cup, hoping that the coffee would make him feel better. The sight of Kenny beaten down and miserable invariably affected all women alike. It aroused a strong protective maternal urge in all of them. They always wanted to protect him and comfort him and help him.

Aunt Maggie set the black steaming cup down in front of him and mixed her hand into his tangled blond hair. "There now," she said with a tremble in her voice, "you come on and drink your coffee, and you'll be feelin' better in a little."

Kenny pulled his head up from his arms and looked at her out of his dull bloodshot eyes. He made the great effort and managed to smile at her.

That brief three-cornered smile was too much for Aunt Maggie. She hugged Kenny tight in her arms. "Kenny boy, if you ain't the limit!" she said to him tenderly.

She hurried about her work again, while he drank the coffee down in great gulps. "The funeral was real nice, Kenny."

"Ma mad at me?" he asked.

"Well, you know how your mother is," Aunt Maggie said hesitantly. "I wouldn't say she was mad exactly, but she was just terrible disappointed. She kept a-looking for you all morning, and worrying and stewing her head off 'cause you didn't show up. She was afraid something mighta happened to you. She kept trying and trying to get Ernie to go up to Ashbury and see if he could find you."

Kenny laughed mirthlessly. With the coffee hot in his stomach, he thought perhaps that he was going to live after all.

"Wouldn't be surprised'n they'd be back any minute now," Aunt Maggie said, peering out of the window. "I got dinner for 'em just about on. It was a kind of nice funeral, lots more people come than I expected, but you know how it is. Lots of folks in this town don't never miss a funeral, don't make no difference if they know 'em or not. And then the way that Jud died and everything, there was bound to be a lot of folks a-coming. Say, the flowers looked real nice, and after all that worrying your Ma done about flowers, too . . ."

"Who in hell would send Jud flowers?"

"Course the neighbors chipped in on a spray, but wait till you hear! There wasn't no card or nothing on this one nor nothing," Aunt Maggie explained elaborately. "It was one of them swell expensive blankets made right out of roses, pink and white roses, a regular blanket of them to drape over the coffin, you know how they do. Say, if that wasn't the swellest thing I ever saw though. It sure did look pretty . . ."

Kenny wrinkled his forehead, but he didn't say anything.

"I sure thought that was nice of him to do," Aunt Maggie offered carefully. But still Kenny did not answer her.

She changed the subject rapidly. "Yes, sir, it was a nice funeral. Your Ma didn't have no music on account of some remark she claims she heard Jud make some time or other about how he didn't like to hear singing at funerals. They had the minister from the Methodist church for the preaching, and he certainly preached a real good sermon, if I ever heard one. 'Twas real short and right to the point. He talked about Jud real nice, and about him committing suicide and everything and judge not lest ye be judged and . . ."

"Yeah, sure, sure, sure . . ." Kenny said impatiently.

"Say, I bet you ain't heard yet. There's gonna be another funeral in this town," Aunt Maggie said importantly. "That Cope girl died up there to the hospital night before last. It sure seems a pity, don't it, when you stop to think about it. A young girl like that having to go the way she did . . ."

Kenny stretched hard, suddenly, and slid down in his chair and began his characteristic search for a cigarette. "Say, Aunt Maggie, you know you're getting better-looking every day? How in hell you do it, anyway? By God, before long you're gonna be the best-lookin' woman in this town. By God, you're gonna have all the old baches in town chasing after you, you mark what I tell you . . ."

"Say, what got into you all of a sudden?" she asked him. "Right this minute you're feeling too good to set still, and a spell back you come a-dragging in here limp as a rag, without a word to say for yourself. What got into you anyway, I'd like to know?"

"Shure now, Maggie, and I'll be afther telling you what got into me. 'Twas your own foine coffee, faith and bejabbers, that's what got into me. Why, shure now, 'tis just loike it driv the currrrrse off me, Maggie, me girrrrl . . ."

Aunt Maggie laughed at him, delighted to see him good-humored again. And strangely enough he could not have told any more than she could what was responsible for this sudden lift to his spirits. All he could tell was that a moment ago he had felt low and depressed, like death in him, and now that feeling was gone and it was life instead that he felt, pushing the chill out of his veins.

He laughed uproariously, and struck a match down his trouser leg. His head felt as if it would split apart when he laughed, so he laughed again at the top of his lungs, with his mouth wide open and the cigarette hanging to his lower lip, wobbling away from the dancing match flame.

In the midst of the laughter in the kitchen, the family arrived.

"Hush your laughing now," Aunt Maggie warned him. "Here they come!"

Kenny rose from his chair instantly, and met them at the living room door. "Greetings, my good people, greetings!" he roared at them. He attempted to bow low to them from the waist, lost his balance when he clutched for the doorjamb and his head found it first with a loud whack. Somehow he managed to keep on his feet, rubbing his head vigorously. "Think nothin' of it, my good people, think nothin' of it. Merely a slight wound, merely nothin' at all. Step right this way, folks, dinner is being served in the dining car. Madame, my arm!"

Molly was a great massive figure in the stiff old-fashioned black dress. Her face was moist and red and she kept wiping it with her limp handkerchief. She was dripping with perspiration in the long-sleeved dress, and already she had ripped the seam under one arm, where it fit too snugly. When her eyes fell upon Kenny, her face turned radiant with relief and joy. "Kenny Veech! Where you been?"

She held her arms out to him dramatically, and when he came to her she kissed him loudly. "You old bum, you," she cried. "Where you been, I want to know? Ain't you ashamed a-trailin' in here after the funeral is all over and everything? Lord, we been worried to death about you. We figured you'd got hurt or died or something up there to Ashbury. What you been doing, anyway?"

She led the way into the kitchen, unfastening the cuffs of her dress at her fat sweaty wrists.

"Well, sir, it sure is hot today!" she said cheerfully, pushing at the dress sleeves, in a burst of relief to be returned once more to the normal plane of living, this plane of easy normal emotional responses.

11

WITH JUD'S FUNERAL OVER, THE FAMILY SETTLED back into their easy comfortable pattern of living. But now Josette was at home every day, and Molly was content to let the greater share of the housework fall to her. Josette worked continually and uncomplainingly. She kept the house cleaner than her mother had ever bothered to do. She worked hard all day long and after the supper dishes were done at night, she went to bed. Several times Pat Thompson came in to see her in the evening, and each time Josette declined to get out of bed and dress again on his account.

Jen's problem of readjustment proved to be a difficult one. Without Frances Cope, her entire scheme of living was out of balance, precarious, unsatisfactory. She sat around the house listlessly day after day, making no effort to help Josette with the housework. She seldom bothered to dress, left her hair wound up on curlers and spent hours mechanically manicuring her fingernails, removing the paint, and substituting a new shade.

Molly advised the family to let her alone. It was just going to take time, Molly said.

The change came, however, even sooner than Molly had anticipated. Five days after Fran's funeral, several boys came to the Veeches to see Jen. When they asked her to go to a dance that night, Jen demurred, and the boys complained that it was bad enough for them to have lost Franny, without losing Jen too. Jen agreed to go then, reluctantly.

She went out that night, and from that night on she did not remain at home a single evening when she could possibly arrange to do otherwise.

On a night several weeks after Fran's funeral, Jen came home close to morning in a queer state of suspension between sobriety and drunkenness. She went about the ritual that marked the end of every evening. She made plans for the succeeding night. She kissed her date good night the required number of times in the automobile, and the required number of times on the front porch.

The moon tinseled the trees and houses and paled the street lights, and the insects went about their business vociferously. Jen's young man with the smooth wet-looking black hair kissed her repeatedly, holding her in an impassioned Hollywood-style embrace.

As Jen crept up the stairs a concert of the sounds of slumber greeted her. She stopped before the first door at the top. She leaned her body against the closed door, and put her lips tight to the crack.

"Mary," she said, "are you there? Are you awake, Mary?"

The low voice beyond the door answered her whispering immediately. "Come in," Mary said. The room was quiet save for the loud insistent concert of snoring that issued from Sam and Molly's bedroom. Jen approached the subject of her visit with a rush.

"Mary, you know what I wanta do?" Her voice was defiant.

"What?" Mary said.

Jen hunted the little scrap of paper out of her purse and gave it to Mary. "That's the ad they had in the paper. I cut it out."

Mary read the printing, her face expressionless.

"I bet you think I'm crazy," Jen said. "But I want to. It would make me feel better, honest."

Mary looked at her with thoughtful eyes, and wadded up the paper in her hand. "Yeah," she said. "Get my purse from on the bureau."

Jen brought the purse, and Mary took several bills out of it and gave them to her. And then she hunted in the purse till she found a card, and she gave that to Jen too. "Go there," she said. "It's a better place than the other. You could go to Ashbury on the bus first thing in the morning."

Jen stood still, incredulous, crumpling the bills tight in her hand, and then the affection and admiration came into her face. "Honest to God, Mary, I can't get over you. You're—good, Mary. I always come to you when I got my chin on the ground. Not on account of this," she said hurriedly, holding out the money. "But because you always understand things, and you—the way you make me feel . . ."

"You better go to bed now," Mary said.

"Yeah. I come bustin' in here and I bet you was just about ready to go to bed yourself. I'll scram."

But at the door she hesitated with her hand on the knob. "Mary," she said.

"Yeah."

Jen hesitated, her forehead wrinkling. "Listen, Mary," she said at last, talking rapidly. "I was awful mad at Kenny about something, see? But you tell him for me some time that I ain't mad at him any more. He don't need to think, though, it was him that made me feel different. It's on account of you, Mary. You tell him I said I wasn't mad any more. He'll know what I meant."

Mary matched her hands together and looked down to her fingertips. "You mean on account of what he said to Fran up there in the hospital?"

Jen turned around from the door with her eyes widening in surprise. "How come you knew about that? Why, I never told a soul!"

When Mary was silent, Jen said incredulously, "You mean—Kenny—told you himself?"

Mary nodded.

Jen said, shaking her head. "I can't make you out; you nor Kenny either, the both a you!"

Jen turned to the door again, but she stopped and slid the knob in her fingers, as if there was something more that she wanted to say. At last she said briefly, "You tell Kenny what I said." She opened the door and glided out, closing it noiselessly behind her.

Mary got up and turned the light off on the bureau and then returned to her chair once more.

Smith's rooster crowed suddenly in the distance, loudly and excitedly, as if he had just awakened out of a sound sleep with the guilty feeling that the day was already here before he had announced it.

The next morning Jen was out of bed early. She bathed and dressed hurriedly and announced to her surprised family at breakfast that she was going in to Ashbury, but she declined to tell them precisely what for. She was feeling very good. She sang before breakfast, until Molly stopped her with the reminder that those who sing before their breakfast invariably weep before they sleep. She refused to help Josette with the breakfast dishes, and while she waited for her bus, she practiced tap-dance steps across the kitchen floor. And then she was gone at last with a burst of song and laughter, swinging her hat in her hand. Josette watched her go, and then went about sweeping the kitchen floor methodically. Jitterbrain, she was thinking, that's all she is, just a jitterbrain. She never is serious about anything; nothing ever matters to her; there isn't a thing to her more than the paint on her face and the curl in her hair.

Jen did not return until the family were done eating supper, and the sun was already down. Ernie had been invited to supper that night. Inasmuch as he had not been able to arrange for a new housekeeper as yet, he was forced to buy his meals at the restaurant, and nothing was more intolerable to Molly than the knowledge that any of her family was forced to subsist on restaurant fare. She insisted that if Ernie would not come home for all of his meals, he at least come occasionally for supper. The first few times he came, she went about preparing a meal of the food that he was most fond of, but after that she was only too glad to leave it to Josette. And so that afternoon it was Josette who stayed in the kitchen near the unbearably hot stove to bake the cherry pie that Molly insisted upon having for supper because it was Ernie's favorite pie next to apple pie and butterscotch pie.

Just as Josette was putting the last pie into the oven, the pale crust pinched around the edges exactly and a precise scroll drawn in the middle, she heard voices on the front porch—her father talking to someone. While she was scraping up the last of the dough, Pat Thompson came out into the kitchen.

"Hello, Josette," he said awkwardly.

She threw her knife down on the table with a clatter and brushed the flour off her hands. She would not look him in the face. "Hello," she said.

He sat down in a chair beside the table uncertainly. "I got out of work early, so I stopped in on my way home. Seems like every time I come over here after supper lately, you been to bed."

Josette nodded. "Yes, I know. I've been working hard. I get so tired, I go to bed right after supper."

Pat frowned, wrinkling his forehead. Whatever it was that he had come to say to Josette, he could not find the right words for it.

"I heard you wasn't going to school any more," Pat blurted out at last.

"No, I'm not," she said. "I suppose they're telling all kinds of stories about me all over town. Well, they can talk all they want to, I don't care."

"I haven't heard any stories about you," Pat said. "The only thing they're saying is that you flunked out up there. That's all I heard anybody saying, anyway."

Josette wiped her hands on the towel over and over again.

"That is the reason you aren't going up there to school any more, isn't it, Josette?"

"Of course it is. What did you think? Did you think I just got tired of it and quit? I couldn't keep my lessons up, that's all."

"Well, you know how I felt about you going up there to school all along. I kept trying to get you to quit. I'm glad you're not going any more."

Josette felt the anger come to her, and the helplessness, because there wasn't anything that she could think of to say that would hurt him enough, or that would make him feel differently about her.

"Pat," she said, in a strained tight voice, "would you mind if we didn't talk any more now? I haven't felt very good today. I think I ought to go lay down awhile before I get supper."

Pat got up immediately and pulled a chair around close to the screen door. "Here, why don't you sit down here? It's cool right by the door. It would rest you just as much to sit down as anything else. Anyway, you can't go off and lay down with them pies still in the oven."

Josette sat down in the chair and looked out of the door to the dried-up garden, the green plants sprawling wilted on the ground, and the soil around them baked dry and powdery by the sun.

"You see," Pat said, "you are tired out."

Josette made a little choking sound in her throat.

"What did you say, Jo?" Pat asked considerately.

"I said 'Go to hell!' " Josette said loudly and distinctly.

Pat was completely astonished. He stared at her without saying a word.

"Well, what are you waiting for?" Josette said angrily. "Get out of here!"

Pat went then, without a word, and Josette opened the oven door again nervously and stared in with unseeing eyes. She held the hot handle with one holder, and kept the other one pressed over her mouth, as if she could not trust it, as if she had no idea now what might be coming out of it next.

While the family were still sitting around the table finishing up Josette's cherry pies, they heard the bus stop at the corner to let Jen off. The powerful noisy motor roared again as the bus went on, and they heard her feet on the porch. She burst in the front door out to the kitchen and confronted her family. "Hi, everybody! How do you like it?" As she spoke she pulled the white felt hat off her head. For once even Molly was temporarily speechless. Jen had had her hair bleached. It lay now over her head in waves and curls, a light-yellow color, but just a little darker than Dorothy's. After the first shock of seeing it so, the effect was admittedly not so bad as it might have been. Jen's skin was just light enough, her eyes just dark enough and her features just pretty enough so that this drastic lightening of her hair gave her an added attractiveness, in spite of an added artificiality.

"Well, for Lord's sakes," Molly said. "If you ain't gone and had your hair bleached like a regular hussy. If you ain't a sight to see! What in the world ever put such an idea in your head, I'd like to know."

"It looks just awful," Josette said grimly. "You can tell the minute you look at it that it's been bleached. What made you go and have your hair bleached? You won't be able to curl it or nothing from now on. It'll be brittle. Bleaching makes hair brittle. It will break off every time you comb it, even. You've simply ruined your hair now."

"What I want to know, young lady, is where in the world you got the money to go up there and have your hair all fixed up fancy like this?" Molly said angrily.

Jen ruffled her hair triumphantly. "Mary give me the money to do it with."

Molly was completely bewildered. "Well, sir, I don't know whatever got into Mary to let you chase off and do something like this. Why, Mary never would let 'em fool around with her hair if it was the last thing she ever did on earth."

"Neither would I," Jen said, "if my hair had been as pretty natural as Mary's is. Look at the way my hair used to be, a nasty dark, dirty, old brown color." As she spoke she looked straight at Josette, whose neat, carefully combed hair was the identical shade that Jen's had been.

"Well, it's too late to do nothing about it now, but you've gone and ruined your hair for good, that's what you've done."

"Aw, pooey!" Jen said as she walked out of the kitchen.

"You better set down here and eat some supper," Molly called after her.

"Nope. I had a lunch up to the beauty shop before I left, and I ain't got time, anyway. I got a date with Jimmy. Boy, is Jimmy gonna be surprised when he sees me tonight."

"He sure is," her mother said. "If he had any sense in his head he wouldn't want to be seen with no such looking thing as you are either."

"Oh, pooey," Jen said again, her voice contented and happy. "Jimmy likes blonde hair, he said he did. He's gonna be crazy about my hair when he sees me."

Josette followed Jen upstairs a few minutes later, and found her standing in front of the mirror still admiring her hair. "My God, does this look gorgeous in the electric light! Just look at it shine! My God, just look!"

Josette went around her to the bureau without answering and picked up a bottle of hand lotion. She poured the cream into her red roughening hands, puckered up by the perpetual dishwater.

"My hands are getting to be a mess," she said. "I just hate to put them into dishwater again tonight. I don't suppose you got time to help do 'em?"

"Gee, I haven't," Jen said with real concern, although she did not take her eyes away from the reflection of her shining hair for a second. "I'm late right now. Why don't you stack the dishes up and let 'em go for once? Let Ma do 'em if she wants 'em done."

"I might as well do them and get them over with," Josette said.

"It's a shame," Jen said. "Why don't you leave 'em and go out some place tonight? You been cooped up in this house for days. I betcha Pat would be tickled to death to take you some place if he knew you wanted to go."

Josette stood silent, rubbing her hands together, working the lotion into her rough, chapped skin. "Jen," she said reflectively.

"Uh-huh."

"This—Clim Hawkins . . . You said he wanted to have a date with me?"

"Holy cow!" Jen threw her comb down on the dresser top with a clatter. "You don't mean to tell me!"

"I just asked you, that's all," Josette said indignantly, a flush of color coming into her face.

"What's got into you, anyway?" Jen asked her. "I bet you and Pat had a fight. Aw, Jo, go on and make it up with Pat. What you want to keep having fights with Pat for, and treating him nasty and stuff?"

"You tell Clim Hawkins that it's all right," Josette said determinedly. "You make a date with him for me for whenever he wants to!"

"Well, okay . . ." Jen was puzzled. She kept staring at Josette, fingering her hair automatically all the while. She opened her mouth to speak again, but Josette walked out of the room quickly.

Anyway, Josette thought, I'll show Pat Thompson that he doesn't own me. In all the books she read, girls did things like this. They dated one man to make another, the one they really cared about, jealous. That was it. She must make Pat jealous; it was the only thing she could think of that might bring Pat to her on her terms instead of his. And if Pat did not come on her terms she knew that she would not let him come at all. She knew herself that well, and though she would not admit it to herself, she was more anxious than anything else in the world to smooth a path for her pride, by which she might go into a marriage with Pat.

12

WHEN JOSETTE GOT OUT OF THE CAR THAT NIGHT, after her date with Clim Hawkins, she was surprised and somehow faintly disappointed. Whatever misgivings she had felt before she went with him, she might have saved herself. He had not in the slightest lived up to his lurid reputation. He had called for her promptly at eight and escorted her to the car deferentially. They went to a movie in Ashbury, and he had sat beside her sedately, not even attempting to hold her hand. Afterward, he bought her a sandwich and a glass of ginger ale. And now, at not quite eleven-thirty, he had stopped the car before her door.

Just as she got out of the car, Josette saw the flicker of a lighted cigarette in the shadows on the porch. "Don't bother to get out with me," she said to Clim, hastily. She did not want to have to say good night to him on the porch in the hearing of any member of her family.

"Okay," he said instantly, "if you say so."

Josette closed the car door and smiled at him determinedly. "Well, I had a very nice time. I—I really enjoyed it a lot."

He smiled back at her, moving his crooked eyebrows into little peaks on his forehead. His hair was brown, like his eyes, and there was a deep cleft in his chin. There was no doubt about it, thought Josette, he was almost the best-looking man she had ever seen.

"You mean that?" he said. "You're not just saying you had a good time to be polite?"

"No, I mean it," Josette said honestly.

"Did you have a good enough time so you'd like to do it again?"

"Well . . ." Josette answered. She had not thought about that. She searched her mind for some reaction to the idea. Either way, it made no difference to her. Anyway, it was better to go out than to sit around the house night after night. She had to admit that she had enjoyed herself this evening, or that she would have, if she had not been continually worrying about what he would do next.

He was waiting for her to answer him, watching her face patiently.

Josette felt a little surge of tenderness toward him. He had behaved so perfectly to her. He was so undeniably attractive.

She smiled again. "I'd like to do this again very much," she said.

"That's good," he said. "I was hoping you would say that. How about Wednesday night? Is it a date?"

"Why, I guess so. I mean—yes. Yes, it's a date, Wednesday night."

"That's good," he said again softly. "That's what I was hoping you would say. It means a lot to me. Maybe you don't know that, but it does. I been hopin' for this to happen for a long time now."

Under his eyes, Josette felt oddly confused. "Good night," she said uncertainly.

He leaned out of the door, closer to her. "Wednesday night."

"Yes. Good-bye."

"It's a million years to wait," he said.

She turned away, uncertain, and as she walked to the porch she heard the car drive away. Pat Thompson, she thought, never said anything to me as nice as that. Of course, it isn't what you say that counts really, but just the same . . .

Josette came up the steps, and looked curiously into the shadows at the dark slouching form behind the cigarette in the porch swing.

"Hi yuh," Kenny said lazily, over the gentle sawing of the porch swing.

"Hello," Josette said distantly.

"Well, I'm damned!" he said. "I thought you was Jen when you come up on the porch then."

"Well, I'm not," Josette said. "It should be easy to tell us apart now, I should think. I'm the one that hasn't got blonde hair."

Kenny laughed softly, ending it in his delicate little cough. Now that his ribs were completely healed the cough was only a habit. "Oh, I guess I shoulda been able to tell, anyway. That wasn't the way Jen says good night to her dates . . ."

He sang the words softly and ironically:

"A fine romance, with no kisses
A fine romance, like hell this is . . ."

Josette turned her back on him and started toward the door.

"No kidding," Kenny said. "I thought you was Jen, as sure as hell. I thought you was Jen, and I thought that was that Hawkins squirt's car you got out of . . ." He laughed again.

Josette turned back to him defiantly. "Well, it was Clim Hawkins' car I got out of!"

"No!" He slouched down in the swing, and doubled up one leg, resting his heel on the edge of the seat. "Hell, you're sure playin' ball in a different league tonight. You had a fight with Thompson?"

Illogically, it made Josette angrier to be thus reminded of Pat by Kenny than by any other member of her family.

"No, I didn't have a fight with Pat Thompson. That's what you all keep yelling at me: Did I have a fight with Pat Thompson? Well, I'm getting sick of hearing it. You'd think the way you talk I was engaged to Pat Thompson, or something. You'd think he was the only man around here that would take me out."

"Okay," Kenny said. "Relax, will yuh? You wanta wake up everybody in the house? I don't know what in hell cause you got to fly off'n the handle like that. Ain't you going to marry Pat Thompson?"

"No, I'm not!"

"Well, well, how rumors do get around."

"Is there anything else you want to know?" Josette said to him sarcastically.

Kenny sent his cigarette butt spinning through the darkness out into the thick grass in front of the porch. "Well," he said, pondering elaborately on it, "lemme see. Seems like there was one or two other things I was gonna ask you the first chance I got. Like, for instance, what do you think of the Brooklyn Dodgers, and who do you like in the fourth at Belmont tomorrow—and what you doing out mugging around with a puke like Hawkins?" he snapped at her suddenly.

He caught Josette off her guard, as he had intended to do. She stammered, trying to answer him. "Well, I don't see what business it is of . . . At least, he's just as good as some of the people that you . . . What's the matter with Clim Hawkins, anyway?"

"What's the matter with Clim Hawkins?" he repeated. "My God, too numerous to mention, sister, too numerous to mention. For one thing he ain't been sober one day in the last three years."

"You're just saying that," Josette said coldly. "He was certainly sober tonight or I wouldn't have been out with him. You just like to say that about everybody because . . ."

She stopped before she finished, and Kenny said, "Because why?"

"Because you drink all the time yourself," she said.

"Sure, sure," he said impatiently. "Old 'ten years in a bar room' Veech, that's me, but we ain't talking about me, see? Listen, no kiddin', why don't you leave Clim and that bunch of mugs to Jen and her little girl friends?"

"Well, if Clim Hawkins is so terrible, I'm surprised that you think he's good enough for Jen, even."

Kenny began to get angry. "Look, toots, I ain't saying nothin' about nobody bein' too good for nobody. Get that idea outa your head for once. You ain't a damn bit better'n anybody else on this earth, get that. I wasn't trying to say you was better'n Jen. I'm just saying that Jen is smarter'n you are. If Jen wants to play around with Hawkins, that's fine; he'd make a nice little playmate for her, but not for you. Baby, they play rough in that league. They don't play drop the handkerchief, they're way outa your class."

"Well, I don't know what you're talking about, but I suppose you do," Josette said. "All I know is that I had a date with Clim Hawkins tonight and he behaved like a perfect gentleman. That's all I know about him, and that's all I want to know. There's a lot of people in this town who don't amount to very much themselves and they like to make out that nobody else amounts to anything either just to make themselves feel better. Clim Hawkins treated me perfectly all right, and I had a good time and I'm going to have another date with him."

"Okay," Kenny said. "Okay, don't mind me. Old big brother Veech spewin' a speech. Go right ahead, do just as you damn please. Start playing around with Hawkins, the little horse's ass, when you could marry an up-and-coming guy like Thompson and quit living off'n Pa and Ma in their old age. Sure, go right ahead, what I always say is . . ."

But Josette closed the screen door behind her and put an end to what he was saying. Never was Kenny more annoying than when he struck this mood compounded of anger and humor, boredom and flippant cynicism—all combined with a gift for fluent speech.

She ran upstairs noisily. Jen was sprawled across the bed, flat on her back, clad in faded and frayed blue silk pajamas that belonged to Josette. The little wet heap of pink elastic and wool that was Jen's bathing suit was lying on the floor beside the bed just as she had stepped out of it. As Josette walked around it, her sister said, "Hang it up for me, huh?"

Josette threw her purse on the dresser, picked up the bathing suit, shook it out disapprovingly and hung it over the foot of the bed. "You been swimming tonight?" she asked morosely.

"Uh-huh. Boy, do I feel good!" Jen humped her stomach up into the air like a contented baby and dropped back flat again on the bed. "Wimpy and a bunch of guys come tearing in here tonight and wanted to go swimming, so we went over to Perkins' Lake . . . What did you and Climie do?"

"We went to the movies. Afterward we went to a drugstore and had something to eat and then we came on home."

Josette brushed her hair vigorously and methodically in front of the mirror. Jen watched her from the bed with a little smile puckering her mouth. "You did, huh? Poor old Climie!"

Josette dropped the hairbrush on the dresser. "Well, I guess he didn't have too bad a time with me tonight. He made another date with me for Wednesday."

"Gosh, love sure is wonderful," Jen said raptly. "Tonight must have been the longest, quietest, driest evening Clim's had since he wore long pants, and not only does he eat it up, but he sticks his neck way out and asks you to do it again. Wow!"

"Well, it all goes to prove," Josette said with her mouth full of hairpins, as she pinned her curls up in place for the night. "It's like I've always said. When boys are out with tough girls they act tough too, but when they're out with a girl that they know is a nice decent girl, they respect her and act just as good as anybody."

"Yes, sir, Gentleman Clim, the nice girl's delight!" Jen said. She stared at the ceiling dreamily. "So Climie's in love again. Now lemme see . . . I bet I could remember, yes, sir, I bet I could tell you what he said to you tonight."

She sat up straight on the bed suddenly. She clasped her hands together, pressed them against her breast and then stuck them out in front of her dramatically. She closed her eyes and spoke in a burlesque of restrained passion. "That's good," she said. "That's fine, that's what I was hoping you would say!" And then she attempted to raise one eyebrow in imitation of Clim Hawkins' crooked, winged eyebrows. She tried, but both of her eyebrows lifted together, so she held one down with one hand, and lifted the other one, shoving up the skin into wrinkles across her forehead.

Josette pressed her lips together tightly.

Jen flopped over to the foot of the bed and stretched her arms out to Josette over the footboard. She spoke again in the ridiculous exaggerated voice, husky, restrained and tremulous. "Wednesday night. It's a million years to wait."

"Oh, shut up!"

Jen laughed delightedly, and fell back on the bed again. She lit a cigarette while Josette fussed around the dresser. "Okay, I'll shut up. Just don't let Climie make a sucker outa you."

The sounds of their voices died away, and down below Kenny squeaked the porch swing monotonously. He was completely relaxed, perfectly comfortable. He had brought out cushions from the rocking chair and davenport in the living room and padded the slats of the wooden swing under him. The night was warm and quiet. The moon hid behind a thin cloud, so that the night was neither too bright nor too dark. It was Sunday, an off night, and there was no place in the world that he would have cared particularly to go. Kenny was at peace, a state more deep and healing and precious than sleep ever was. He submerged himself consciously into the sound of the swing creaking, the chorus of insect voices. He submerged himself onto those sounds so completely that automobiles passed on the highway and he did not hear them, so completely that trains came by and shook the house and he never even felt it. He was in a semiconscious state, a condition bordering on self-administered hypnosis. Kenny had lost himself this night in the squeaking noise that a chain made rubbing over a metal hook and in the sound of insect voices; and lost therein, he found freedom and release. After a while Carl came up the steps, and stumbled over his feet.

"God-damn it," said Kenny crossly, "why don'tcha look where you're going for once, anyway! Gimme a cigarette!"

Carl was just going in the screen door when the sound of Kenny's voice stopped him. He came back scowling in the darkness. He rattled the paper package in his fingers exploringly. "I ain't got but one left," he said plaintively.

"Gimme it."

Kenny took the package out of his hands before he could answer, and extracted the one crushed cigarette. He lit the cigarette with a great flare of the match and a great cloud of smoke. After he had a puff on it, he gravely offered it to Carl, who stood shuffling his feet over the porch boards.

Carl sat down in the swing beside him and puffed the cigarette, then handed it back to his brother.

"Where in hell you been hanging out to pretty near morning?"

"Nowhere," Carl said sullenly.

Kenny handed the cigarette to Carl. "You're a nice friendly kind of a guy, ain't you?"

Carl inhaled the smoke without answering Kenny.

"Got a girl, huh?" Kenny said, mockingly.

"No, I ain't!"

"Aw hell, don't gimme none of that B.S."

"No such a thing," Carl muttered.

Kenny took the cigarette out of his fingers. "Well, well," he said coolly. "You sure didn't let the grass grow under your feet. Here you are mooning around about Franny Cope, and she dies, and already you forgot she ever lived, and are staying out half the night with some other girl. Boy, I'd sure like to get a gander at the girl that's giving you hot pants nowadays." Kenny laughed unpleasantly.

Carl flared up under Kenny's calculated goading.

"Shut your mouth up, why don'tcha. I ain't hanging around after no girl!"

"You don't mean to tell me? Then where was you tonight?" Kenny said rapidly.

"I was just walking around by myself!"

Kenny's voice dropped and became as soft and guileless as a kitten's. "Oh, so you was just walking around by yourself half the night, huh?"

Carl did not answer him. Kenny was keeping the swing in gentle motion, and Carl braced his feet against that motion stubbornly.

Kenny did not believe that he had told him the truth, and Carl knew it, and suddenly he was frightened, for no reason.

"Come on, give. You been mugging around with some girl?" Kenny said mildly. "You been hanging around with the boys, shooting a little crap maybe, drinking beer, looking at picture postcards, what?"

Carl was panicky, and he did not say a word.

"You deaf? I said what?" Kenny's voice was soft and deadly. Carl felt weak and defenseless under the barrage of such an attack from his brother. It was humiliating to him. It destroyed his self-respect and self-confidence. It always left him feeling stripped and naked, and somehow reviled. He wanted to burst into tears now, but instead he tried to control his voice and tried to give Kenny a true and coherent answer.

"I was just walking. It's a nice night. I took a walk."

"That's fine," Kenny said. His voice was deadly and broken by his gentle cough. "That sure is fine. Well, you can save that stuff for suckers. What you been up to?"

Kenny reached out his hand so quickly in the darkness that Carl never saw it come. Kenny reached out his hand and closed it over Carl's leg, up above his knee, close to the groin. Carl jumped so that the whole porch swing rattled, his hard body whacked against the flimsy wooden slats. He jumped to his feet, trembling all over.

"My God," Kenny said in amazement. "Damnation, whatsa matter with you?"

Carl was trembling all over and his breath came in gasps between his teeth.

"Why, you little puke, you . . ." Kenny said.

He never finished his sentence because Carl never waited to hear it. His panic got the best of him and he bolted and ran, his feet clattering on the porch steps. He ran up the street and cut across the vacant lot and disappeared under the trees as if Kenny had been right at his heels.

Kenny rocked the porch swing back and forth. The little puke, he thought, the God-damn little puke. He was suddenly gnawed with discontent and dissatisfaction, with himself, with his life, with everyone he knew. He hated the village suddenly and overpoweringly. The sound of the squeaking chain and the insect voices were mocking him now. He hated the very quiet and placidity around him. His nerves and muscles strained and stretched and ached for motion and action, to be doing. He wanted a cigarette, and there was no place then in the village except Lew Lentz's hotel. He thought of that and swore angrily under his breath. He also wanted a drink, and there was no place in the state where he could buy one legally on Sunday night, and no place where he would consider buying one illegally this side of Ashbury.

A train went through, tearing the quiet night like a flaming comet. Kenny got out of the swing and walked down the steps out to the highway. He turned toward Ashbury and began to walk. He walked slowly but steadily, with a certain rhythm, a swagger in his walk, a catch, almost like a limp in one leg. When he was just about opposite the air beacon north of town, he saw headlights from a car slanting up over the hill. He walked into the bright headlights without blinking, facing this one lone automobile scudding down the pavement with its tires singing against the concrete.

Ernie Veech was at the wheel of that car, his eyes on the shining pavement ahead of him. When he broke over the crest of that hill he saw the figure of the man walking at the side of the road, saw the headlights pick him out and illuminate him. At first he was an unreal figure, the baggy brown pants and coat, a sweat shirt, and a shock of blond curly hair. Ernie recognized him and was delighted. Yes, sir, he thought, there goes poor old Kenny bumming his way up to Ashbury and here goes me sailing along in this year's Lincoln Zephyr. Because Ernie was feeling very good that night he leaned on the horn hard as the car roared past Kenny.

The latter paid no attention. He did not even recognize Ernie. Kenny kept walking and the car went on down the road behind him. Ernie was driving fast that night because he was feeling good. He had had a long and successful interview with the fascinating, yellow-haired Owens woman, and she had agreed to move in with him, bag and baggage, the following night. Ernie was excited and young again. She's a swell girl, he kept thinking, a very swell girl. And, damn it, if that little bitch Erma or any of her God-damn crazy family starts making trouble for me I'll marry Leatha Owens, that's what I'll do. And then Erma and all the rest of them can go jump in the lake for all their trouble.

Kenny kept on walking and a big combination trailer truck came lumbering up behind him. He waved it down and the driver stopped and opened the door for him gladly in spite of the "no riders" sticker on the windshield.

"Hi yuh, bud. Going as far as Ashbury?" the driver said, glad to hear even his own voice again over the drone of the motor in that lonely little world, the truck cab in the darkness.

"Yeah," Kenny said as he clambered up beside him.

Book Three

1

KENNY IDLED THE MOTOR WHILE HE WAITED IN front of the gas station on a corner in downtown Ashbury, and felt no premonition of disaster. It was a warm night, sultry, close, and as black and thick as velvet. Kenny made the motor of the long shiny automobile purr. He liked cars; he liked to drive them. And now he liked to sit here at the wheel of this one and idle the motor, keep it muted under the radiator, soft husky-throated purring, and feel the little vibration of the floor boards under his feet. There wasn't much traffic on the street because it was late. A few people loitered on the sidewalks, warm, dispirited-looking people who, having exhausted all possibilities for prolonging the evening, were now forced to give up and go home to their stifling little rooms and flats and try to sleep.

The bright streetlights hung motionless and made black clear-cut shadows of buildings and signs across the sidewalk. The restless neon light ran back and forth within the tubes in which it was bottled, up and down the street as far as Kenny could see, in front of every build-ing. And the buildings themselves stretched up to the dark sky and were lost in it just above the neon signs. For all you could tell that building right over there with the light in just one window way up there in the blackness might keep right on stretching up and up into the sky, taller and taller, more windows and more windows all cov-ered and lost in the darkness, until, for all you could tell it was twice as high as the Empire State Building, for all you could tell.

Kenny idled the motor and wondered how long it was going to take the boys, not that he minded waiting for them. Kenny felt fine and good all over, just sitting here at the wheel of a good car late at night, with the city spread around him on every side, the city that never failed to delight him.

This night he had gone over to Gitlo's. Gitlo and some of the boys were having a poker game, and they dealt him in the next time around and he sat over there four, five hours maybe, playing poker. That is, playing poker most of the time, except for once or twice when he went out for some liquor or something, for Gitlo. Kenny didn't care much about poker. He liked to play once in a while, but he didn't care for it twenty-four hours of the day the way some guys did. Gitlo, for instance. They said that Gitlo really kept the game going in his apartment twenty-four hours a day, so that no matter when he felt like playing a little poker he could find a good lively game all started that would cut him in. Kenny laughed, thinking about that. This guy Gitlo was the damnedest, funniest little guy. He had an idea he was Jesus Christ Almighty Himself. And he didn't even know what the big-time rackets were all about. Gitlo was just a little shot that had got to thinking that he could get away with any-thing, and whatever he said people had better run and do it right away, or else. It was too bad about Gitlo, Kenny was thinking. He had seen little guys like Gitlo before, seen 'em coming, and seen 'em going. Little guys that get to thinking that they're Jesus Christ Almighty Himself and get to acting like regular little rattlesnakes without the rattle, until everybody, the boys that work for 'em, the guys they do business with, everybody gets sick to death of them, and gangs up on them and starts them on the way out.

Poor little Gitlo, an awful nice little guy for all that, that is, if he liked you. It was easy enough to see why Gitlo liked him, Kenny was thinking. It was because he was somebody out of the rackets. He didn't want nothing from Gitlo, and Gitlo couldn't hand him out orders. Pretty soon Gitlo would start to get sick of him, and when that time came Kenny knew from experience what to do, run, and run fast, and keep out of sight of Gitlo long enough for him to for-get that he'd ever lived.

He liked Gitlo, too, and he liked the prestige of being Gitlo's favorite at a time when everybody in town knew Gitlo and talked about him and was afraid of him. Then Gitlo's apartment was some-place to go, where there was always a good gang of boys around, and liquor. Seemed like Gitlo was never happy unless Kenny had a snoot-ful, Kenny thought regretfully, and look at himself right this moment, driving a good car that belonged to Gitlo, too.

That was another reason Gitlo liked him. Kenny had never so

much as chiseled a nickel change from Gitlo and Gitlo knew it and appreciated it. Gitlo trusted him, like tonight, for instance:

He peeled off some bills and give 'em to Robotelli and Sam and said to 'em to go down to that gas station on Michigan and Lermont and pay the guy the money he owed him. Then he kind of winked at Kenny, and said you better drive the boys down there. He made some joke about making sure they didn't ride around the block and put the money in their own God-damn pockets and come back and tell him they paid the bill. Gitlo said it real funny, like it was all a big joke, but you could see that it wasn't no joke with him, and that he really wanted Kenny to drive 'em down there and kind of keep an eye on them.

Kenny liked to have Gitlo send him on errands like that in the presence of the boys. It made him feel good. And he liked to drive a car; even when he had been drinking a whole lot heavier than he had any business to, he still liked to drive a car.

And that was why Kenny sat in Gitlo's car outside the gas station on Michigan and Lermont, idling the motor and wondering why in hell Robotelli and Sam didn't hurry up and pay that bill and get to hell outa there. He couldn't see through the windows of the gas station because they were full of gadgets and inner tubes and automobile truck like that. Kenny thought of honking the horn, and he reached his hand out toward it, but he never honked that horn.

Because just then he heard the noise, heard it plain, out of the open door of the gas station, a shot, or rather two shots, close together. Kenny really never had a chance. It was just as natural for him to run toward trouble as it is for a lot of people to run away from it. Without thinking, before he knew it, he had the car door open and was out of it and running across the cement toward the oil station, in between the gas pumps. While he was there between the gas pumps, right in front of the steps, the gun came sliding out of the door toward him, low, as if someone had tossed it along the floor. Kenny reached down and scooped the gun up automatically, before it went off or something, and because it occurred to him that it might be a handy thing to have once he got in the station. He got to the door, but no farther. The gas station was bright with light from an unshaded electric bulb, and the little radio with the automatic tuning buttons in the corner was filling the room with loud music. The oil-station attendant in black-striped overalls was lying on the floor with his mouth open and blood on his face, and a lot more of it running into a big puddle on the floor. The cash register was open. Kenny saw all of that in a fraction of a second, the first look he took through the open door, but he saw something else that was a great deal more important. He saw Sam and Robotelli just climbing out of the window into the alley that ran back from Michigan parallel to Lermont Street. He started to yell at them, but he knew suddenly that all the yelling in the world was never going to stop Sam and Robotelli.

In that moment, for the first time, he felt danger to himself. He was in a spot, and he knew it. Sam and Robotelli were running up the alley. He could hear the sound of their running feet, and that sound suggested just one thing to him, as his scalp began to prickle under his hair and his skin began to gooseflesh.

He wanted to run too, and he wheeled away from the door of the gas station. What he saw when he turned around drove the last effect of the liquor out of him and left him deathly cold and sober and tense for action. There were six or seven people gathered on the sidewalk across the street, milling around and hollering and pointing and there was a cop tooting his whistle and coming across the street toward the oil station on a run. There was also a car drawn up in front of the gas pumps that hadn't been there when Kenny went into the gas station. The car was empty.

Kenny threw down the gun as if it had burned his hand and ran for Gitlo's car. Kenny boy, his mind kept saying idiotically, just try and talk yourself outa this one! He heard shouts, but he paid no attention to them. A half-dozen steps from the car he felt the sharp numbing blow against his right shoulder that spun him halfway around, at the exact moment that he heard the shot from the pistol. He realized that the policeman was shooting at him, and that he had been struck in the shoulder. He stumbled and nearly fell, as he tried to get his bearings again to reach the car. He knew that he was close to the car. Hell, he had been just three or four steps away when that lousy bastard cop winged him, but now he was bewildered and stood still momentarily, swaying on his feet. He had lost his sense of direction. He was weak and sick and dizzy. He could see nothing, nothing but whizzing stars and comets, and all the neon in the world let loose chasing up and down the streets, red and blue and green and yellow and white, and his ears full of their shouting voices, and the sound of the policeman's whistle. It was as if a great net was falling over him while he stood helpless, stifling, breathless, blind, without even the sense to tell where the car was, or the policeman or the oil station or anything.

That agonizing second of helplessness caught and held him like a vise. Kenny stood stock-still under the lights, swaying a little, clutching at his shoulder, only a step or two from Gitlo's automobile that waited docilely by the curb with its motor humming.

The policeman could have taken him where he stood, but he was excited, and in his nervousness he shot at Kenny again. The bullet did not strike him, but Kenny felt the air stir as the bullet cleaved it, and he heard and smelled the report, and saw the flare of light from the gun.

He was angered. He hated that policeman more than he had ever hated anything before. He made the greatest effort of which he was capable. Gotta find that car before that God-damn bastard shoots me down . . . His vision cleared, and he whirled around to the car. He opened the door with his good left hand, the right arm flopping useless at his side. He got into the car, all right, but he had trouble with the shift, reaching for it with his left hand.

He got the car under motion, heading it up Lermont Street, but before he could pick up speed the police cruising car arrived on the scene and started chasing him.

If the whole thing hadn't been deathly serious, it would have been ludicrous. It was all like a gangster movie, Kenny thought. You read about things like this in the paper, but they didn't happen to you, not to you, Kenny Veech. Kenny drove the car automatically, twisting and turning up one quiet side street and down the other, in the dark hot summer night, trying to keep away from the railroad tracks that at any time could make a blind alley out of a through street, with the police car right behind him. He kept thinking, That lousy Sam and Robotelli, God, what Gitlo won't do to them guys, they sure crossed Gitlo up. What he won't do to them guys once he gets his hands on them.

His ears were full of the sound of the motor roaring and the screaming of the brakes as he cut around corners, and the music of the car radio, and the siren on the police car and the rush of the wind. The lurching of the car and the motion of it made him sick, he was sick all over and tired from head to foot, and he wanted to wake up from this dream and go back to sleep again. The police car kept just behind him. He could see the headlights of it dancing in the rear-vision mirror at the top of the windshield. Sometimes, just after he got around a corner, while he was struggling to straighten the sliding car with one hand on the steering wheel, he would look up to that mirror and it would be dark, but before he could get to the next corner those two dancing spots of light from the headlights would appear again.

Kenny was tired and sick all over, and sick of all of this. He wanted to stop playing, and stop the car, and tell them how all this happened and say, well, so long boys, and go on home and go to bed.

His right arm was so numb it was beginning to ache. Without even meaning to, he slackened speed a little, before he realized it, and the police car gained on him, and the policemen started shooting at the tires and the back of the car. He heard the spat-spat of the bullets, and the ripping sound when the rear-window glass broke out.

Kenny wasn't afraid. He simply hated the cops ferociously and wanted to keep alive more than anything.

He gave the car all it had, and stopped thinking and concentrated on trying to keep a careening, twisting, turning automobile right side up when you have only one hand and arm to do it with.

The car radio was on. A girl with a deep, lush, insistent voice was singing at Kenny:

> *"I've got you, under my skin*
> *I've got you, deep in the heart of me . . ."*

Yeah, boy, that sure is gonna be your theme song, all right, because before you get done with this it looks like you're gonna have a whole skinfull a bullets deep in the heart of you . . .

His mind was alert and ringing insistent warnings to him. These damn police cars had radios. There'd be half a dozen of them after him in a couple of minutes now. He'd got to be careful and watch for them before he turned up side streets. They'd try to sneak up on him and trap him. God, what chance did one guy have against a million cops and a couple of million police cars and a billion bullets bouncing off the back end of his car?

He saw the alley then, a nice wide alley, stretching away between two brick buildings, a nice alley with the other end of it open on the next street; he could even see the streetlight hanging at the foot of it. He slammed the brakes as hard as he dared turning in to it. He almost side-swiped the brick wall. For a minute he thought he was going to lose a wheel instead of just crumple the fender.

The police behind him for once were caught off their guard, he exulted. They were going too fast to stop or to turn, but there was nothing in the world to prevent them spraying Gitlo's car with bullets. Kenny listened to the rain of bullets and the breaking glass objectively, and out of the corner of his eye he saw the two clean little holes bored through the windshield suddenly, to the right of him, leaving the wrinkles around them in the shatterproof glass.

He was halfway through the alley by then, bumping over the rough bricks. Then in a split second he saw the other alley running parallel to the street, and the great truck rolling out of it onto him. He even saw the truck driver's agonized face, the mouth, wide open, yelling at him. He pressed his foot to the floor boards and the car leapt out of the way. He looked back for a second and there was the truck blocking off the alley, come to a dead standstill, with a shriek of brakes. It was a trailer truck. One trailer blocked the alley like a barricade, and, best of all, even as he looked he saw headlights behind it. Them damn sucker cops had turned their car around and shoved her nose into the alley before they ever saw the truck.

Kenny must have shouted out loud then, but the sound of his voice was lost. He did not fool himself, though. All the cops had to do was wheel that car outa there and beat it around the block either way they wanted to, and it was only a minute before they'd pick him up again, and anyway, by now they probably had every cruiser in the city waiting for him, with his license number all down on paper. He wondered if they had shot his taillight off. That would help. The headlights were still going, and over these streets he did not dare try to drive without them.

Gitlo's car came bounding out of that alley onto a street that was an inclined plane, going downhill to the left, going uphill to the right, up over a bridge built over the railroad. Kenny knew the street. It wasn't far from the depot. He knew the street and felt that this would be a swell chance to get across the railroad tracks without being stopped by some God-damn freight train. He started pulling on the wheel, trying to turn the car uphill over the bridge. The car skidded and slid; the tires shrieked on the cement; Kenny kept pulling and pulling desperately on the steering wheel with his one good hand, knowing all the while that he wasn't going to make it, and he was never going to be able to pull that steering wheel around far enough with one hand.

"*Close your eyes,*" the girl sang out of the radio.
"*Rest your head on my shoulder and sleep,*
Close your eyes,
For this is divine. . . ."

Kenny was right about it; he couldn't make it. He spun and spun the steering wheel, wet and weak with sweat, but he didn't make it. The car slid into the cement bridge abutment. The crash was not half so hard as he anticipated. The radiator simply crumpled up gently and the car came to rest. The lights were gone, and the radio music. The windshield didn't break, and the steering wheel, although it projected Kenny, knocked all the breath out of him when the crash came.

The motor stopped. It was dead-still there by the bridge, and dark. Somewhere near a train whistled and the rails under the bridge began to sing and hum. There were dark buildings on all sides, and dark empty streets running in all directions. Kenny was slumped over the top of the steering wheel, wandering in a fog, splintered through by rosy-pink lightning running jagged here and there; he was wandering in a fog so dense that there was no air to breathe and he was choking in it. And in his ears all the while was the rushing sound of great winds blowing, piling the fog up over him.

But some instinct in him was too strong to let him rest there, to allow him to settle down gratefully into the fog where all things were like all other things and nothing mattered because you did not know.

His whole body and being pleaded for this chance to lose itself in this merciful fog that piled over him layer after layer, but some one part of him would not have it so. The door on his side of the car was hanging open already, and Kenny undraped himself from the steering wheel, forced his body out of balance and fell out of the door onto the street. The jolt when he hit the ground sent the pink lightning jangling and running through him in all directions. It also brought the breath back into his body, released the vise that gripped his lungs and cleared his head. His numb right arm jolted dully. The only real feeling he had was the scrape his leg received on the brake as he left the car. His leg smarted and stung and he felt the warm blood where the skin was scratched away.

Kenny scrambled to his feet. The roaring in his ears he realized was a train underneath him. The streets were still dark, but at every second he expected the police car to come tearing around a corner. He caught hold of his numb swinging arm and held it close to his body and ran. The impulse to get across the railroad tracks by the bridge was still dominant. He ran up the hill onto the bridge. It was not fear that he felt, it was just a horrible vulnerability—to be out of the car, here on the ground with only his two unsteady legs to carry him away, and only his one good hand to fight back at guns, and nothing but his clothes to keep bullets away from his body. He felt a complete and terrible helplessness. And there was still in him that great desire and resolve to live in spite of all that they could do to him.

2

THE BRIDGE OVER THE TRACKS WAS A FLIMSY AFFAIR of wood and metal. With the train rushing by under it, the whole structure vibrated and shook under Kenny's feet.

Before he even got halfway across it, he saw the thing that he had been dreading: headlights, searchlights, shining out of a side street; in a second's time, the police car would come out of that side street, turn up the hill toward the bridge and envelop him in the illumination of its lights. Instantly he dropped to the wooden sidewalk on the outer railing of the bridge. He pressed his body flat to the boards. The whole bridge was vibrating so, with the train underneath it, that for a moment he had the sensation that comes in dreams sometimes of a fall from a great height. With that feeling in him, he clutched at one of the metal braces on the railing with his good hand and hung on to it tight. The feeling of that cold metal in his hand cleared his head still more. Automatically, he started to examine the structure of the brace. It extended down the edge of the bridge, and ended in a loop of solid iron below the lower side of the bridge.

While he was still exploring its possibilities, he was already sliding onto it. He wrapped his legs and his good arm around it tight, and his feet, groping for the end of it in the darkness, found the loop of metal that gave him a substantial footrest. While he was still feeling for the most comfortable and secure foothold, he heard the sirens and motor as the police car went over the bridge. He also heard the squeal of their brakes when their headlights picked up Gitlo's car. He even heard their voices, but all sounds after that were drowned out in the sound of the train underneath him.

His shoulder was throbbing, and he was beginning to feel a weak, sick dizziness. He reminded himself grimly that if he fainted he would fall down under the wheels of the train beneath him. His good arm was beginning to cramp and prickle, he was hanging to the bracing so tightly with it. He conquered his fear of falling, and forced himself to relax.

But it would just be a matter of minutes anyway, he was thinking, before some smart copper would start sticking his flashlight down into the metal bracework underneath the bridge. Besides, the cops would hang around up there half the night, and he wasn't going to fool himself about it, he wouldn't be able to keep hanging down here forever.

Then, in a hideous flash, Kenny realized that it would be impossible for him to climb back onto the bridge, even if he had the opportunity. Physically impossible, for he had only one arm left with which to pull himself up.

For the first time, Kenny lost all hope, but it did not occur to him to call the police to his rescue.

He hadn't wanted to die tonight, Kenny thought weakly, clinging tight to his metal bracing with the warm tears pushing at his eyelids. He hadn't planned on dying at all.

The train droned under him sadly in accompaniment to his thoughts of death.

But all the hope had not gone out of him yet, no matter what he thought. He was busy with his half-formulated plans already. He would have to risk the drop from here onto the railroad tracks. If he didn't split his head open on a rail, he would probably break his back and both legs, he thought grimly, but there was no alternative. He couldn't go up, and he couldn't stay here, so he had to go down, it was simple and obvious.

He wanted to act immediately, but the train still droned along a few feet beneath him. He swore at the train. God-damn freight train, was it gonna take all night? Must be an end to it some place. Was it gonna take all night? What in hell did it think he was? He couldn't hang up here like no God-damn monkey forever.

He listened to the train anxiously, speeding it on its way with every ounce of mental energy he had, all the while that every bit of physical energy was being drained from him to maintain his precarious position.

But the freight slackened speed. It was coming into the yards. It slackened speed until it was barely moving, crawling along underneath him. He knew then that he was not going to be able to outwait this train. He was going to drop in a minute, whether things were ready for him below or not.

Until now he had avoided looking down at the cars rushing by underneath him, for fear that the sight would make him dizzy. Now he bent down, straining his eyes to accommodate them to the darkness. In a few seconds he was able to discern the shadowy shapes of the cars as they slid along not ten feet underneath him.

It was all over in a minute. He loosened his feet from the loop of metal, hung there free for one terrible moment by his aching arm, and then dropped. He lay flat on the top of the car and drew his breath in great sobbing gulps. His bad arm was beginning to throb with pain. He went off into the fog again where the rosy lightning played. He did not feel the jolting vibrating boards of the top of the freight car under him, or hear the sound of the wheels grinding over the bright steel below.

The freight slid into the yards. There were signals flashing off and on, red and green and amber lights, and bells ringing, and train whistles. The switches were set, the freight went onto the siding, and in a minute or two it stopped.

The train stopped with a jerk that was transmitted from car to car all down the line. The bell on the engine began to ring slowly, tolling a dirge, punctuated by the violent hiss of escaping steam. It continued to dominate all the myriad sounds of the freight yards: men's voices, and whistles and bells and signals and trains in and out, and light engines coming and going.

When the car under him stopped, Kenny was altogether bewildered. He could not tell where he was, or why, or what had happened. He was weak and aching in every muscle, and his right arm was red-hot with pain from the fingertips deep into his chest. His shirt front and coat were wet and sticky, and when he touched the wounded arm with his left hand, his fingers came away from it wet with the warm slime of blood. For one moment a great wave of despair came over him, so that he wanted to scream aloud with it. And then he began to remember things.

Immediately Kenny started crawling down to the end of the freight car. His whole body was numb and stiff, so that he had to drag it along. His right arm sizzled and burned until he half expected to see sparks showering out of it into the darkness. Somehow, he got to the end of the freight car and groped around in the dark till he found the little iron ladder onto the coupling between the two cars and from the coupling onto the ground. His trembling legs buckled under him and he almost fell. There was a string of empties on the next siding, and Kenny leaned up against one of them, lost in the deep shadows.

It seemed as if the top was blowing off his head. On the other side of the freight he saw in a kind of haze the flashlights and heard the voices of the trainmen as they made their little excursion up the line of cars.

Kenny knew by then that somehow he had to get on that freight before it pulled out. He wasn't going to be walking any place, not tonight. Either he left town with this freight, or he just crumpled up in a few minutes here on the cinders.

It took such a concentrated effort for him to keep himself on his feet that he had no energy left for thinking or planning. If he could only get to Gitlo, he thought confusedly, Gitlo would fix it for him. Or would he? With the doubt he became panicky. In his ears once more he heard the gentle spat-spat noise the bullets had made against the back end of Gitlo's car. By God, he'd tell the world that this town wasn't big enough for him and the police department both, he kept crying to himself. He was going to get out of this town . . . I don't know where I'm going, but I'm on my way . . . California, here I come . . . Go west, young man, go west or east or south or north . . . What the hell difference? Just get going to hell outa here . . .

Just then the cars gave a little jerk one after another all down the line. It startled Kenny so that he jumped and prickled all over. The trainmen came back along the cars, but Kenny scarcely noticed, he was so afraid that the train was going to pull out without him. It was dark along here except for a few colored signal lights, and quiet. The engine whistled sharp a couple of times, and way down to the other end of it some place, where the caboose was, he saw lanterns flashing. He was prickling all over with excitement. No fooling, the freight was all set to pull outa here.

He looked along the length of the train, the dark shapes of the cars just discernible in the thick darkness of the night. He was standing right in front of the one that he had ridden into the yards.

He came close and groped for the door. The engine up at the other end was doing a lot of puffing and twitching. He was nervous, expecting the train to start moving any minute. He found the door, all right, and it was open just enough for him to slide his hand in. The car was an empty, all right.

He grabbed hold of the door and tried to push it back, but he was weaker than he thought and he couldn't move it. He swore at himself, and the sweat poured off him. The engine up ahead was making a chugging noise. Now take it easy, relax, get a-hold of yourself. You gonna keep fooling around like this all nervous, and you ain't gonna get nowhere. Now take it slow and easy, and don't be in such a God-damn sweat, or you're gonna get left, Kenny boy.

He pushed again on the door, but he couldn't get it rolling. Just then another spasmodic twitching passed along the cars. Their wheels started to turn, ever so slowly, and the freight began moving, just perceptibly.

Kenny was in an agony. He walked along beside the car, over the uneven tie ends, with his hand still in the crack of that car door, up above his head, pushing as hard as he could.

It seemed overwhelmingly senseless and bitter to him that he should be allowed to come this far, only to be defeated because he didn't have enough strength left in his arm to push back a door on a freight car.

The freight was rolling along now easily, faster and faster, and Kenny kept hanging onto the car, running and stumbling to keep up.

And then all of a sudden the door opened, rolled away from his hand all by itself. Over the grinding of the wheels and the roaring in his own ears, and the whistling of his own breathing, Kenny heard a man's voice, a low husky amused voice, speaking to him out of the doorway of the freight car.

"Goin' my way, bo, or can't you make your mind up?"

Kenny tried to speak words back to the voice up above him, but he couldn't say a word. His strength was gone. All he could do was keep his hand tight on the doorsill and keep running and stumbling along beside the car.

The voice up above him spoke again, but this time the amusement was all gone out of it. "Scram, you! Go home and sleep it off and quit playing around the railroad tracks. There's a whole flock a lights up ahead."

The sole of the man's shoe ground down mercilessly on Kenny's fingers on the door ledge, but Kenny hung on tight.

"God-damn son of a bitch!" the man in the car said, and he started to pull the door shut.

With the first of the lights he got a good look at Kenny, and changed his mind. The desperate bloody fingers still clinging to the doorsill, and the limp arm swinging, the blood-soaked front of him, and most of all, his face tipped up, his head rolling on his shoulders as he stumbled along, and his eyes under his tangled hair, glazed and unseeing, as if he was dead on his feet and didn't know it yet.

The man in the car dropped down on his knees in an instant and braced his body against the edge of the car door for support and leverage. He reached his hands down to Kenny on the ground.

"Come on, come on," he said rapidly, "jump for it. You expect me to do the whole damn job?"

With the last strength he had, Kenny swung himself up on his one good arm, and, as his body dropped back, he felt the hands under his armpits. His body hung precariously for a minute, half in the car and half out of it.

The man in the car pulled with all the strength he had. He wasn't a very big man, and Kenny's body was big and solid and a dead-weight. He pulled and hauled, and got Kenny up into the car. He rolled him over quickly and slammed the door shut just as the car was coming up under the bright lights at the edge of the freight yards.

The last thing that Kenny knew was the good solid feeling of the wooden floor of the car under him, shaking and vibrating as it was over the roaring wheels. He realized that he was safe in the freight car, that the door was shut, that the car was under motion, rolling away from Ashbury. What else there was didn't matter. The fog got him then. Only it wasn't any ordinary gray fog this time. It was a thick hot black fog, as thick and black and hot as the night itself that was pressing down on top of the jiggling freight cars rushing along blindly one after the other in a mad stampede over the thin silver rails.

The man stood by the door a moment. Then he turned around, flexing his arms, and spoke to Kenny on the floor conversationally, with his voice amused again.

"Well," he said, "here you are. I thought we was never going to make it. My arms feel like they're pulled out of the sockets. I bet you weigh a ton, a solid ton of bones and muscles . . ."

He was apparently not at all surprised that Kenny did not answer him.

He edged over to Kenny in this special, stifling, darker-than-darkness inside the car, and knelt down beside him. He reached out a hand cautiously, and touched him on the chest, and took his fingers away sticky with blood. He rubbed his fingers up hard in the palm of his hand until the blood was rubbed away. He felt around in his pocket for a match and struck it along the floor boards. He held the little flaring torch of it up in his fingers and studied Kenny. Kenny was lying on his back with his legs straddled apart. His right arm was at his side and the other one was flung up over his head. His shirt and coat were soaked with blood, and his whole right arm was bathed in it. The blood was beginning to dry. There was blood smeared over his face, and up into his hair. His face was white, under the dirt and blood, and his eyes were closed. He was breathing short and hard out of his open mouth. His head kept knocking against the vibrating floor, up and down, knocking on the floor gently.

The match burned out in his fingers, and in the darkness the man felt around for some of the wads of paper left in the empty car, and made a pillow for Kenny's head.

He lit another match, and with quick sure fingers, pulled the shirt and coat away from Kenny's shoulder. There wasn't much he could see, with all the blood on it, and in just that short space it took the match to burn. He felt the shoulder, and nodded his head as if satisfied with his own diagnosis. There wasn't much bleeding from it now, only a trickle. A clean enough hole, but he couldn't tell whether there were bones smashed or not.

He lit another match. He jerked a cigarette package out of his pocket and worked a cigarette out of it quickly, to get a light before the match burned out. He got the light, and threw the match away just as the flame started licking at his fingers, burning his fingernails yellow on the edges.

The flare from the match when he lit his cigarette illumined his face. He was a short man, but broad across the shoulders. His face was dark and smooth, a bland, controlled face. He was young; not as old as Kenny. His eyes were dark-brown, with a hardness in them, but a humor also. His mouth didn't match the rest of his face. His mouth was alive and restless, full, loose, sensuous lips. His hair matched his complexion and eyes, black and curly, blue-black, and slicked back in waves on his head, except for a couple of little straggling locks that hung in two curls on his forehead.

He sat on the floor beside Kenny with a wad of papers under him, puffing on his cigarette appreciatively.

The inside of the car was a solid chunk of thick black heat, and the very air seemed charged with the vibrations and the deafening noise of the wheels below.

After awhile the dark-haired man wiped the sweat off his face and snuffed out the stub of his cigarette. Beside him on the floor Kenny stirred a little, and muttered and groaned under his breath.

The man leaned over close to him once and listened.

Kenny grunted and hunched his body on the floor. "Mary," he said, and then his body relaxed again and there was only the sound of his hard short breathing.

"Mary, huh!" the dark man said.

He stretched out on his back on the rocking floor of the car, pillowing his head on his arms.

He must have slept for awhile, and after a long time he pulled another cigarette out of the package and in the flare of the match he looked at Kenny.

"Mary, huh!" he said again.

He laughed suddenly, full and loud rich laughter in the freight car, echoing and re-echoing against the walls.

Then he smoked, contentedly lulled by the sharp monotonous noise that filled that little chunk of the night that was the freight car and made it a world apart.

The engine shrieked its whistle at a white-painted whistle post, and the freight car went lurching and jiggling up over a rough crossing.

The dark-haired man yawned hard and deep. "No foolin'," he said. "I'll bet Mary is a swell kid. I bet I'd like meeting up with Mary some day."

3

THAT DARK NIGHT DRAGGED ITSELF OUT TO A PALE sultry sluggish dawn at last.

Mary Veech was awakened from a troubled sleep in a room in

Lew Lentz's hotel by a soft insistent tattoo on her door, and found a little evil vaporous light coming through the window. She got out of bed, left the negligee across the footrail, and searched for another robe out of the closet, a warm thick wine-colored chenille robe, not because it was cold—the air was still close and hot—but because of this cold and cheerless quality of the dawn.

Lew Lentz had spent most of the night in Ashbury, and at his request she had remained at the hotel. Now, as was his custom, he had returned with the dawn and was waiting for her to come down and share a breakfast with him before he went to bed. She found the robe and slipped it on, and combed out her silky hair before the mirror without looking into it. She was still half asleep. She felt tired and beaten and bruised, as if she had had no sleep for weeks.

She went downstairs to Lew's office. At the other end of the room from his desk a small table had already been laid for two, snowy white tablecloth, and better table service than ever appeared in the hotel dining room.

Lew met her at the door and put his arms around her. "Sleepy baby!" he said to her tenderly.

She was shivering with cold, and her eyes were almost shut. She clung to him tightly, nestled against him. She opened her eyes, but they would not stay open, so she gave it up and burrowed her head under his chin, yawning.

Lew led her to the chair across the table from his own and seated her in it solicitously. He kissed her on the mouth, bending down to her, and at the same moment he dropped the inky fresh morning paper over her plate. Then he went around the table to his own chair.

"Wake up," he said cheerfully. "Wake up and read the papers . . ."

Mary opened her eyes wide and looked at Lew Lentz curiously.

He nodded his head to her, smiling all over his face. "Good morning, Merry Sunshine!"

She kept on looking at him. For Lew Lentz, good humor at dawn was so rare as to be miraculous. There was no doubting her ears and eyes; he was in the very best humor this morning. He was smiling, his coat was off, his shirt sleeves rolled up, vest unbuttoned, and, what was particularly unusual, he had loosened his necktie under his collar, shoving it around till it hung rakishly out of place. Never, as long as she had known Lew Lentz, had she known him to allow his necktie to become disarranged. He was a meticulous man. He did not like to see careless attire, and he did not feel comfortable when carelessly attired himself. Mary stared at him curiously, trying to imagine what it could be that had made him feel so exorbitantly good this early in the morning.

She found a clue suddenly, in the words that he had just spoken to her, and she picked up the sticky new morning paper from her plate.

The streamer head across the top of the paper was something about the Ashbury City Council selling the site of the old city building to a department-store company, and she could see no connection there because Lew did not have any interests in that transaction that she knew of. The next most prominent headline was about a gas station robbery, or rather an attempted robbery, and Mary read down through the subheads into the story idly:

An attempted robbery of the gas station at Michigan and Lermont in downtown Ashbury, a daring lone bandit (possibility admitted that there may have been two of them). One set of fingerprints on gun, station attendant fighting for his life in Receiving Hospital. Witnesses' description of bandit, as seen coming out of station with gun in his hand, account of police chase, wrecked car found and now being traced (probably a stolen car anyway), bandit unaccountably missing, details of police search around railroad bridge, small probability that bandit would be able to leave city, police dragnet spread for him, all citizens of Ashbury and outlying communities urged to co-operate with the police in the apprehension of this dastardly robber who had shot down a man in cold blood. Identification of blond bandit made easy by striking size and appearance of the man and the bullet wound in his right shoulder, and possibility of other bodily injuries received from bullets or from the automobile crash . . .

Mary read the whole story through, and when she finished she read it all through again, carefully, slowly, with Lew's eyes upon her. And then she laid the newspaper down and looked up to Lew Lentz dumbly.

Lew cut his bacon painstakingly, and waited until the waiter was out of the room before he spoke to her. He did not keep the triumph out of his voice. "Well, it certainly is too bad. I've been afraid of it, though. He's been playing around in bad company for years."

When Mary did not answer him he covered up her hand on the table with his. "God, Mary, I wish there was something I could do for him. Soon as I see the papers I called up Gitlo right away. He's been hanging around with Gitlo's boys a lot lately and I put two and two together. Gitlo says it was his car he had, all right. Asked him to borrow it, and hell, how was Gitlo to know? Gitlo feels just as bad as I do, but there ain't a thing he can do either. He's in a spot himself, being his car. He's got it fixed to say he took the car from out in front without his permission, and he's got good alibis for all of his boys, just in case."

Mary withdrew her hand from Lew's and took the cigarette case out of her pocket. Lew hurried to strike a match and he kept talking. "Mary, you see how it is, sweetheart. What can I do? You read it in the paper yourself. Six or seven witnesses and a policeman see him come running outa that oil station with the gun right in his hand. If the gas station attendant dies, you know what that means. Some of those lousy politicians up there are gonna make an awful hullabaloo about this. They're going to pick him up, just as sure as shooting."

Mary's hands were shaking so that the ashes from the cigarette spilled over the white tablecloth.

Lew Lentz made a sad little clucking noise in his mouth. "It's too bad, all right, but there isn't nothing anybody can do for him now."

Mary got up from her chair abruptly and went over to the desk and picked up the telephone and then changed her mind and laid it down again. She walked to the window and looked out into the alley.

Lew Lentz hitched his chair around so that he could look at her. "There isn't nobody you can call up; there isn't nothing you can do. Honest, if there hada been anything anybody could have done, you know I'd have done it for you."

Mary stuck her hands out in front of her and spoke with the cigarette wobbling in her mouth. "You can can that stuff, Lew!"

She came back to the table quickly, sat down in her chair again, and leaned toward him across the table. "Just tell me this much; do you know where he is now?"

"No," Lew said. "How in hell would I know where he is?"

"On the level?"

"Yeah, on the level. I got connections around Ashbury that would let me know right away if they knew where he was, but I haven't heard nothing from none of them yet."

"Does Gitlo know, do you think?"

Lew shook his head. "Uh-uh," he said. "Gitlo don't know and he don't want to know."

She got up again and went toward the telephone.

"I wouldn't make any phone calls if I were you, no kidding," Lew Lentz said. "They haven't got him identified yet, and a few phone calls from you would hurry it up a lot. Besides, where could he go up there that I wouldn't hear about it?"

Mary stopped still by the telephone and thought over what he said and came back to the table. Her face was perfectly calm and controlled. She lit another cigarette from the stub of her first one and her hands had stopped shaking. She picked up the newspaper again and read a paragraph or two in the middle of the story, the part about the automobile crash and the disappearance of the bandit.

She dropped the paper down on the table again. "Lew, where do you think he is?"

Lew shrugged his shoulder. "I dunno. It's a funny thing. Myself, I don't see how he got away from there after the automobile smashed." He picked up the paper and read that part of the story over again.

And then he laid it down and blew lazy, precise little smoke rings toward the ceiling.

"Lew, you think the police chief is playing for the publicity? You think they have got him already but they don't want it in until the afternoon editions?"

Lew shook his head. "No, the police haven't got him yet. I'll know as soon as the police pick him up."

She sat down at the table again, and poured herself another cup of the strong black coffee out of the electric percolator.

"Mary," he said to her, "would it make you feel any better to know what I think, off the record?"

"Go ahead," she said.

He spoke with the confidence of a man who is proud of his own shrewd wits and seeks to win the admiration of others. "I was just thinking right now, reading the story again, about that bridge. If I was a policeman, I'd do a hell of a lot of thinking about that bridge. It don't say in the paper, but it would be a funny thing if it just happened there was a train going along under that bridge right the time the automobile piled up there. That bridge isn't so far from the freight yards, you know. The freight train would be slowing up coming into the yards, and a guy, if he was quick and smart and in a big enough of a hurry, could let himself down offa that bridge onto the top of a freight car real easy. The whole thing would be so dead easy. Ride the car into the yards, and then beat it down and get inside of an empty and be rolling outa town while the police were still running around in circles up by the bridge . . ."

Mary listened to him gravely, and gave his idea due consideration. She shook her head a little. "If he had been all right, not shot or anything, maybe he could have done it, but with a bullet in his shoulder, I don't see how. I don't believe anybody could do it, anyway. I never heard of anybody doing that. What made you think of it?"

"I know it can be done," Lew said. "He's big and strong and he could do it easy and not think nothing about it. Even if he was hurt . . . When you're trying to get away from somebody, you can do a lot of things you wouldn't be able to do any other time. I know he could do it all right. What made me think of it, when I was just a kid back in my home town, bunch of kids used to hang around the railroad tracks. There was a bridge a lot like that over the tracks quarter mile or so from the depot. We used to hang around on the bridge and wait for freights to come in slow, and then drop down from the bridge onto the tops of the cars. Nothing to it, just gotta judge the speed right and know when to jump."

Mary listened to him attentively. When he was through, she said, "You used to hop off from bridges onto freight cars when you was a kid, or did you just used to watch the other kids do it?"

Lew closed his hand over Mary's fondly. "Hell, you know I didn't. I was always too God-damn scared to try it."

He laughed, and Mary answered him with her lovely smile.

He kept hold of her hand, and they leaned back in their chairs and looked at each other across the table.

"And you was so scared that you did this to Kenny."

"Sure, I was scared," Lew Lentz said readily. "I was scared of losing you. Besides, I couldn't stand having him hang around you."

"You don't happen to have a yen to tell your bright ideas about bridges to the coppers, do you?" she asked him after awhile.

"Hell, no," Lew said. "Look, let's get this straight, beautiful. I don't give a damn whether the coppers pick him up or not. In fact, I hope they don't. All I want to be sure of is that he won't dare to poke his nose in around this part of the country again for years and years and years."

"And suppose he bleeds to death, jouncing around in a freight car without anybody to look after him," Mary said softly, with none of the smile left on her face any more.

"Then I send roses," Lew Lentz said promptly.

4

JUST ABOUT THE TIME MARY WAS TALKING ABOUT it, or a little earlier maybe, the freight train pulled into a siding at a little depot just outside of Detroit to wait for a fast passenger. The dark-haired man awoke as soon as the freight began to slow down. He got up from the floor, stretched himself, went over to the door and slid it open a little. There wasn't much to see; it was still more dark than light, nothing anywhere but the bedraggled backs of stores and buildings, and the backyard of a house with soot-covered washing hanging on a line.

He craned his neck around until he saw a sign with the name of the town on it, and then he slid the door almost closed, and went over and knelt beside Kenny. Kenny was still sleeping or unconscious, it was hard to tell which, but his breathing was slower and more regular, he thought. He knelt there beside him and studied him carefully. He sat back on his heels and rested his hands on his knees and waited. He yawned once, wide, for a long time.

The passenger train went through then, a burst of noise and vibration, and then it was gone. The engine on the freight started chugging and steaming again, and, in a couple minutes, it slid off the siding onto the track, and started to pick up speed.

As soon as the noise and monotonous vibration of the wheels began again, the little dark fellow began working on Kenny. He kept patting him on the face and talking to him in a low insistent voice. "Come on, pal, wake up, can't yuh? We gotta get off this train in a minute or two, what you think? You think I'm gonna carry you offa here piggy back? Come on now, snap out of it. Come on, you hear me talking to you. I'm not just talking, I mean it. Wake up, you hear me, wake up?"

He kept at it, and Kenny began to stir and mumble. The muscles in his face twitched, and he rubbed at his nose with his good left hand.

"Attaboy, pal, wake up. You can hear me talking now. Wake up. We gotta get off this train in a few minutes; you hear me, wake up!"

He kept patting Kenny's face, only not so gently as at first, and all of a sudden he slapped him hard across the cheek a couple times.

Kenny's eyes fluttered half open, and he swung at him weakly with his left hand. "Cut it out," he mumbled hoarsely. "Who in hell you think you can . . ."

"Ah, good!" he said delightedly. "Come on now, pal, we gotta get offa this train."

Kenny's eyes stayed open, but he kept blinking them, and the little guy leaned down over him and waited a minute while he got his bearings.

"What the hell!" Kenny said at last wonderingly. He started to sit up, and changed his mind about it. "My arm . . ." And then he began to remember a good many things, and his face turned hunted and desperate. He focused his eyes on the dark-haired man with difficulty and struggled up onto his elbow. "Who are you? Where in hell did you get mixed up in all this?"

"I should be asking you," he answered cheerfully. "It was my private car you come flopping down on top of last night without the benefit of parachute, remember? You come flopping down on the top of my private car right outa the sky, like pennies from heaven . . ."

Kenny struggled to sit up straighter. "Look, I'm in a hell of a spot. Where are we? How long I been sleeping? Say, I gotta get offa this freight . . ."

"Good!" the little guy crowed delightedly. "Now you're talking, pal. That's the old stuff." He went to the door of the car, shoved it open a crack, looked out and closed it and came back to Kenny.

"We're gonna be getting off in just a few minutes now. The last stop they gonna make before they roll way into Detroit. You gonna jump when they slow down, like a nice guy, or do I have to roll you out?"

"Look, you don't get it," Kenny mumbled impatiently. He kept rubbing his face up against his shoulder. "How long I been out? Where are we now?"

"Just call me Butch or Eddie or Joe," the other said impudently, with his eyes sparkling. He fumbled with his cigarette package and stuck a twisted bent cigarette into Kenny's mouth, and held a match to it.

"That's better, huh, pal?"

Kenny puffed on his cigarette, and eased himself down on his back again. He took the cigarette out of his mouth and held it between his fingers and rubbed at his face with the palm of his hand. "Feel rotten," he admitted with something like a grin. "Must have a fever."

"Sure, you have," the little guy said sympathetically, and he felt Kenny's face with his hand. "Yeah, you got a fever, all right."

He got up and went to the door again and looked out. The car was slackening speed, and he slid the door open, and stood a moment silhouetted against the gray light, a short stocky figure in a baggy, dirty, black suit. He whistled a little softly, out of key and no particular tune, "Another morning," he said. "*E pluribus unum!* I always say '*e pluribus unum*' in the morning," he explained to Kenny. "I don't know what it means, but it sounds nice; it's kind of appropriate to say in the morning."

He peered ahead into the dim light. "Kind of foggy around here this morning. Ain't that a break for us, though? Now look, pal, you let me jump first, and then maybe I can keep you from splitting your head on a tie."

He watched while Kenny crawled over to the doorway and swung his feet out over the sill.

"How you doing?" he said anxiously. "Dizzy, huh?"

"Old rockin' chair's got me," Kenny said, with another one of his lopsided attempts at a smile.

The car was barely moving. They had come abreast of a string of empties on a side track, with a wide strip of cinders in between. The little guy crouched on his heels in the doorway, constantly peering ahead of them into the foggy morning air.

"Get ready," he said suddenly. "Here's where we get off."

He jumped down easily as he spoke. He whirled around the minute he hit the ground, rocking on his feet like a boxer. Kenny came down after him clumsily, out of balance once his feet were on the ground. He did not fall, but he draped over the top of his smaller companion for a minute or two. They stood still and the rest of the freight rolled past them down the track, and then everything was very quiet to their ears, grown accustomed to the clatter of the train wheels. There was nobody in sight any place. The backsides of buildings again, shadowy in the dim light, and down the track an unpainted wooden depot building, with a wide, bleak, empty platform of brick in front of it.

"Well, here we are, pal, and from now on it's gonna be easy."

Kenny's legs were beginning to quiver. His eyes were glassy and his lips were dry and cracked a little from fever. His bad shoulder was lumpy with swelling, and the dried blood all over him didn't help his appearance any.

"You better set down here," the little guy said. All the time he was talking his dark eyes were darting this way and that, taking in everything there was to see in all directions. "There won't be nobody coming along here for a minute. I want to beat it out to the street and take a gander; maybe I can find a drinking fountain, or something. I sure would like to wash you up a little, pal, before I take you out walking with me."

Kenny sat down gladly on the cinders. "Look, you don't get it . . . Where we gonna . . . What am I gonna . . ."

"Leave it to your cousin Slapsy," he said as he walked off. Kenny watched him as he went. A slouching, stocky figure, with his head lifted up to the clean gray morning sky, sniffing the foggy fresh morning air as if he had nothing more in the world than that on his mind. He walked with his hands deep in his pockets, down across the brick platform, until he was around the corner of the depot.

Kenny felt bad all over. Funny little guy. Bet he just walks off and never comes back, and who in hell would blame him? But it was only a halfhearted thought, because Kenny really didn't believe that the little guy with the dark hair was going to just walk off and leave him setting there on the cinders in front of a string of empty freight cars at the back door of nowhere. His head was light and throbbing until it felt as if the blood pounding there would break through the tissue-thin walls of his enormous bobbing skull.

"*E pluribus unum!*" Kenny whispered to himself, and he laughed out loud hysterically.

He didn't keep any track of the time, so it seemed just like a couple of seconds to him or a couple of hours when he came back. He came up so quietly, with just a gentle slap-slapping of his old thin soles against the brick, that Kenny never heard him or knew that he was back until he touched his shoulder.

"How you doin'?" he said to Kenny. "Miss me?" And he grinned his peculiar impudent grin. He carried a soiled white handkerchief soaked with cold water, and he went directly to work, mopping over Kenny's face and hands.

"We gotta get movin'," he said cheerfully, while he rubbed the cloth over Kenny's face not any too gently. "Seems like people in this damn town get up early in the morning. The shift is gonna change over to the shops in a minute and if we don't get a move on first thing we know there we'll be right out in front leadin' the Easter parade, and me without a new hat too, wahoo!"

He flopped the rag over, and laid it across Kenny's forehead for a minute.

"Well, you don't look so pretty," he said critically, "but let's get moving."

He gave Kenny a hand up, and when he was on his feet he slipped his arm around Kenny's waist to give him support.

"You just keep walking," he said cheerfully. "Let me do the worrying."

They moved off down the depot platform, an odd-looking pair, with the top of the little guy's dark head just coming above Kenny's shoulders. They slipped around the corner of the depot and out to the foggy street, where the street lights still shone in the dim light. He guided Kenny across the street, and into an alley that cut back away from it.

"We wanta make for the residential section," he said. "A hell of a lot easier traveling."

Kenny heard his voice from a vast distance and the words meant nothing to him. He felt removed and alone and utterly strange. There was the strangeness that came from the pain and fever. There was the strangeness to find himself here, deprived even of his physical strength that he had always taken for granted, dependent upon a stranger, a bullet in his shoulder and the knowledge that policemen all over the state were on the lookout for him by now. The time was lost to him again so that he could not tell whether there had been hours of this, or only minutes.

By striking back from the main highway, they had come out in a residential section of the suburb, empty streets in front of trim new suburban homes, smart, comfortable, modern, and identical. They slipped along the misty streets past the dark, closed houses like a couple of shadows. The little guy was breathing quickly from the exertion of bearing up part of Kenny's weight. He kept them moving, with his eyes darting out this way and that continually.

They walked for quite awhile, and then the little guy saw the back end of the place at last, a neat white, wooden building facing out on the main street that dissected the suburb, and he became more cautious.

There was a store building facing the side street, and he cut across behind it. There was no one in sight, so he started for the back door, dragging Kenny after him. He moved fast, put every ounce of strength he had into it, and when he finally slid his clumsy burden in the back door, he had the satisfaction that nobody had gotten any kind of a close look at them crossing the vacant parking space between the store building and the back door.

Inside he could hear voices and music from records on the nickel machine. This was the time of day when they cleaned up the beer gardens and got them manicured for the afternoon trade. He kept hoping that Mungo would be around. He would have to bluff it out at best, but it would be better if Mungo was there himself. He slid Kenny back against the wall, and kept him like that, resting partly against the wall and partly over his shoulders, while he got his breath again and thought things over.

He was still thinking things over when a waiter in a dirty white coat, carrying a pail of water and a mop, came along and stuck his head out in the entry.

The waiter came out and set the pail down, instantly hostile. "What you doing in here?" he said. "Go on, scram!"

While he was talking, he looked Kenny up and down curiously. All of a sudden, he noticed the blood-soaked shirt and coat. His face tightened up and from then on he didn't look at anything else.

"Mungo here?" the little guy said, shifting his shoulders a little under the weight of Kenny's body.

The waiter looked at him again. "Yeah, and you better get goin' outa here, I'm telling you."

"I want you to go take a message to him," he said steadily. "Tell Mungo his cousin George just dropped in from out yonder to drink a glass of beer with him. Go on, tell him!"

The waiter stood uncertain.

"Go on and tell him, and tell him I want my beer out in the back room; I never been much on drinking up in front where the plate-glass windows was."

The waiter started to go, and he called after him, "Tell Mungo I got a friend with me." The waiter looked back at them hostilely, and disappeared.

The little guy waited, whistled his odd snatch of off-key tune, and waited.

In a couple of minutes the waiter came back and he had a tall thin man in shirt sleeves with him. He had dark hair, thin on top, and a cigar in his mouth, and when he spoke without bothering to take the cigar out, his voice was curiously high and monotonous.

"Hello, kid!" he said. If he was surprised, he didn't look it.

"How are you, Mungo?"

"I'm fine." He looked over what he could see of Kenny appraisingly. "Don't look like your friend will be wanting a drink," he said.

"Just take a look close at the front of that guy," the waiter said unpleasantly.

Mungo did. When he spoke it was back over his shoulder to the waiter. "Go mop a floor, will you!"

The waiter picked up his pail and went.

"Shot, huh?" Mungo said to him after the waiter was gone.

"You got a cigarette?"

"You don't think I'm gonna . . ." Mungo's high voice ended on a querulous note.

"Yeah," the little guy said flatly.

Mungo puffed on his cigar, biting at the end of it in his mouth. "Who is he?"

"A friend of mine!"

"How long you been in town?"

"Just got in this morning." He smiled impudently, with his dark eyes snapping. "I imported him."

Mungo took the cigar out of his mouth and knocked off the ashes and put it back in his mouth again. He looked at Kenny with unblinking eyes for a long time.

"I got friends in this town," Mungo said at last. "Maybe this guy has got the wrong kind of friends. How can I tell?".

"You're doing a favor for me, not for him. If there is any trouble, it's gonna be me that's on the receiving end of it, not you. That is, unless," he added delicately.

"Yeah," Mungo said. "I'll call a couple of the boys to carry him upstairs," Mungo said at last in his high voice that never varied in tone or expression no matter what he was saying.

He stuck his head back in the door and yelled, and made a motion with his arm.

"I'll have to have a doctor," the little guy said.

A couple of waiters in white coats came out, and Mungo motioned to Kenny. "Take him upstairs," he said, and then he answered him. "Don't you suppose I can see he's gotta have a doctor?"

Mungo stood back beside him as the men lugged Kenny through the doorway. "Reminds me of Prohibition," Mungo said, in his high-pitched flat voice.

The little guy laughed delightedly, his mouth relaxing for the first time.

5

IN THE SECURE DARK LITTLE WORLD OF THE AUTO-mobile, Josette and Clim sat together, their arms tight around each other and their bodies pressed close.

Clim spoke after awhile, with his lips muffled in her hair. "Jo, I can't stand it. I can't let you go back there. I can't stand seeing you feel bad like this . . ."

Josette spoke softly, with her eyes closed, with her voice gentle and enriched with feeling. "Clim, you don't know what I have to go through living there. It's awful. It just seems like I can't do it any more. I wish this moment right now could go on forever and ever . . ."

"Oh, God!" he said.

"I don't know what I'd do if it wasn't for you, Clim," Josette said. "I don't know how I'd live, how I'd get along . . ."

"Oh, God," he said again. "You know the kind of a heel you make me feel like?"

"I don't care what you feel like," she said. "You aren't any kind of a heel . . ."

"Yes, I am. If I wasn't, I could see to it we never had to be separated again. I'd take you to Indiana tonight and we'd get married, right tonight. But look at me—I'm no good, I ain't got a job, I got debts, my old man is all set to kick me outa the house . . ."

"Oh, Clim, don't. What do things like that matter . . ."

Clim sat up straight in the seat suddenly and shook her by the shoulders. "Darling, say that again, say what you just said again . . ."

"What I just said . . ." Josette stared at him in bewilderment. "What I just said, Clim? Why, I said that—that—nothing else was important—except us being together the way we are now . . ."

He caught hold of her and kissed her hard on the mouth, and then he started the motor and sent the automobile hurtling down the road.

Josette caught hold of his arm. "Clim, what got into you? Where are we going?"

"Darling, don't you know?"

Josette's heart began to pound against her ribs. He wouldn't do that, he wouldn't dare to, and besides, it didn't matter what he wanted to do, she wouldn't do that, she wouldn't get married like this, she wouldn't get married, she didn't want to marry Clim Hawkins. When he had his arms around her and was making love to her it was very easy to kid herself into thinking that she was half in love with him, because it was romantic. But when she was out of his arms and away from him it was altogether different. Her thoughts began to tangle in her panic.

She pulled at his arm. "Clim, stop. We can't do anything like this. It wouldn't be . . . It wouldn't be . . ."

"Sure, it would," he said. "Honey, it's the only way to get married. You're of age and I sure as hell am; what's to stop us? Do it quick this way, no messing around. No five days to wait, no stuff printed in the papers, no doctor exam . . ." He looked at her suddenly, sharp. "Jo, is that what's on your mind? Look, I swear to God, I'm perfectly all right. The doctor was checking me over not more 'n three weeks ago, and he said I was perfectly all right."

A sort of nausea swept over her. "Don't, Clim," she said. "Don't say any more. That wasn't what I was thinking about . . ." She was trying so hard to make an order out of her thinking, to put all the feelings she had into words to speak to him, to stop him.

He put his arm around her and pulled her over across his chest. "Indiana, here we come," he sang. "Indiana, here we come . . ."

He drove the car fast, guiding it with one hand. They came to the place where the road intersected the pavement, and he swung the car up onto the smooth cement and stepped down harder on the accelerator.

Josette felt a kind of weakness catch hold of her and relaxed her body against his. After indecision for so long, wanting to do something, but not knowing exactly what or how, after existing so long under the compulsion to make some kind of plan for her life, after all of that, it was so good to have any kind of a decision, any plan at all thrust upon her. So good to have Clim always with her and always loving her, always a comfort to her when things went wrong. Maybe he isn't the best man on earth, she thought recklessly, but what the hell? Maybe he isn't any better than I am. What does it matter? Her thoughts were all scattered and chaotic. And what a good joke this is going to be on Pat Thompson. Maybe I won't get far, but anyway, I'll get away from my family and that house. I couldn't live another day in that house. I'll show them. They all think they can run my business and tell me what to do, but they can't. They expect me to stay home and work day after day till I get so sick of it that I can't stand it any more, and then go and marry Pat, like a good girl. Well, they're crazy. I'll show them. I'll do what I want to do. I'll marry whomever I please. I'll live my own life any damn way I see fit to live it. This may not be what I wanted, Josette was thinking, but at least it's something. I can't wait forever. I've got to do something with my life. I can't wait forever; I've got to do something; at least this is something. She felt a pang of remorse. It isn't as if Clim was just something, anything, a way out of all this mess I'm in. Clim is swell; he loves me; I love him—anyway, I'm terribly fond of him. Anyway, he's the nicest person I know. Besides, I've got the right to marry anybody I please, whenever I feel like it. They can say anything they like, it's my right to.

The car shot up over a hill and when it dropped down over the other side, there was a kind of sinking feeling in Josette's stomach. "Don't drive so fast, Clim," she murmured.

"Okay," he said. "Okay, anything you say. Anything the bride says, goes." But he did not slow down.

He slipped his arm further around her until he was cupping her breast in his hand. She felt his fingers, pressing and stroking her breast. She reached up and moved his hand away.

"Please don't, Clim."

"Okay," he said again, squeezing her tighter up against him. "There ain't any short cuts with you, are there, honey? How about stopping the car side of the road down in Ohio or some other God-damn place just for the hell of it, so we can always say we done it before we was married?" He squeezed her tight against him again and laughed loudly, his sudden loud laughter that always irritated her.

Josette felt a revulsion in her, her head was whirling. She started off on another whole cycle of thinking that she knew would lead her no place at all. She only felt tired and weak, too weak and too tired to protest or to talk to him or to think any more. Something she had heard Jen say popped into her mind—Jen saying, "What the hell, the first marriage never counts anyway . . ."

Clim Hawkins swung the car from one side of the road to the other adeptly, just to show that he was feeling good.

"Indiana bound, da da da da da da," he sang. "Indiana bound, da da da da da da . . ."

6

HOURS LATER, WHEN THE VEECH HOUSEHOLD WAS dark and wrapped in slumber, an automobile stopped outside and the faint sound of voices came from it for an hour or more.

Eventually, another car drew up in front of the Veech house. The boy named Jimmy, with the patent-leather hair, stopped his car at a discreet distance back of the other one, and switched off his lights instantly. Jen lingered in the car a moment yawning. They were both fatigued. The excitement of the evening was over for them, the tri-umph, and the liquor afterwards; even the excitement of each other. They admired the tall ugly silver cup which they had won as the most proficient dancers out of a floor full of a couple hundred others. They made plans for going to a dance the next night to practice and perfect some new steps they had originated.

Then Jen slid away from him and opened the car door. "What you better do is go home and go to bed for a change," she said affectionately.

They smiled at each other, and Jen leaned over and kissed him briefly and slid out of the car. She stood by the door, hugging the cup up against her in both arms, the bright yellow curls standing up all over her head. "Scram, you!"

He slammed the door shut, and started the motor. Jen watched him wheel around onto the pavement. He tooted the horn softly at her, and she turned around and started toward the house. She walked with the cup hugged up tight against her, humming to herself, her feet scuffling along over the sidewalk in dance patterns.

Just before she got to the porch steps, someone called to her softly. "Hey, Jen, come here a minute, will you?" It was Clim Hawkins' voice, calling from the car parked in front of the house, calling to Jen, softly and urgently.

Jen turned around, and zigzagged down the walk toward the car. She felt gay and detached, and not in any way curious about anybody or anything.

The window was rolled down, and Jen leaned through into the car. "Hi yuh," she said brightly.

By the little muted light of the dashboard, she saw Josette sitting with her shoulders slumped, her face in her hands, her elbows on her knees. And Josette was crying, softly and miserably.

"Whassa matter?" Jen asked without concern. She lifted the big silver cup up and rested it on the door ledge. "Look what we got!"

Clim ignored the cup. His face was earnest and worried. "Jo, honey," he said, "if you'd only cut out that God-damn sniveling for a minute maybe I could . . . Jen, she been crying here like this for a half-hour; see if you can't talk to her or somethin'."

"Oh, damn, Clim!" Jen said complainingly. "I'm tired! I want to go to bed, my feet are just killing me. If you two kids can't get along without . . . What you 'spect me to do anyway?"

"Well, you could talk to her, couldn't you?" he said distractedly. "God, she been crying like this for a half-hour maybe, without stopping!"

"Oh, sure, talk to her!" Jen reached into the car, and shook Josette's shoulder roughly. "Hey, come on, quit blubbering and spill it. Come on, tell it to auntie. Spill it, I'm a reg'lar little Dorothy Dix, you know me. What has nasty bad mans been doing, huh?"

"Jen, for heaven's sakes," Clim said, as Josette shook Jen's hand loose from her shoulder without answering her.

"Okay, okay," Jen said wearily. "Look, Josie, what's the matter? Come on and tell me?"

But still Josette did not answer. She only kept up her miserable, monotonous crying in the darkness of the car.

"Clim, why don't you go on home and let me take her in to bed?" Jen said. "She's all pooped out. You can see yourself. You can't talk to her when she's like this. Go on home, and come back tomorrow."

Clim Hawkins' face set in his determination. "I ain't going a step nowhere," he said shortly.

"Okay, you don't have to take my head off," Jen said. "I just thought you'd wanta do it, that's all. Hell, I don't care what you do, this is your business, and it ain't none of mine. You can sit out here all night if you wanta, I don't care."

Jen turned away from the car, but Clim called after her. "Jen, for God's sakes, I'm gonna go nuts. Talk to her, or something. I don't know what to do with her when she's like this. Don't you run out on me . . ."

Jen hesitated, and then she came back to the car once more, and again she leaned in through the window. "Josie, now listen to me. I'm not gonna hang around here all night, while you carry on. Spill it, come on, tell me what happened."

Josette spoke at last, out of the midst of her crying, incoherent, spaced words. "I don't know—what made—me do it. Oh, I wish—I hadn't done it—if I—only—hadn't—done it . . ."

Jen's face instantly turned stormy with anger. She rested the silver cup on one hip, put her foot up on the running board, and doubled her arm against the door ledge, and cupped her chin in her hand. "So this is what you get me out here to hear," she said to Clim, softly and sweetly. "Well, isn't this just too bad. I sure do feel just terrible for both of you." She looked at Clim, and began to sing, softly and tantalizingly:

> "Oh, I got a girl and she lives on a hill
> She won't do it but her sister will—
> How'm I doin', hey, hey . . ."

"Shut up!" he said. "We got married tonight down in Indiana. We just got back from there."

"Married!" Jen said. "Holy God! Married!"

She clutched at the cup with both hands to keep it from falling. She sat down suddenly on the running board of the car.

They were all quiet then, except for Josette, who kept gulping as she tried to stop crying. Jen rested her forehead on the edge of the silver cup, and listened to the insects and frogs and the stir of the wind in the leaves.

She stood up suddenly, leaving the silver cup on the running board, and stretched out a hand into the dark interior of the car. "Gimme a cigarette," she said briefly.

Clim shook a cigarette out of the package from his pocket, and held a match out to her, the little flame crinkling in the darkness, and then he lighted his own.

"Shut up your crying! Bawling ain't gonna help none," Jen said to her sister impersonally. She drew deep on the cigarette, and her forehead wrinkled with thought. "Clim, you damn fool you," she said at last.

"I didn't figure on coming back here tonight," he said. "I figured we'd get a room in some hotel some place, but Jo wanted to come back. She claimed everybody'd throw a fit around here if she didn't come home tonight."

Jen was silent for awhile. A train went through, and when the clatter of it died down, she said. "Look, Clim. She's all nerved up, she don't know what she's doing or saying. Why don't you go on home? I'll take her upstairs and put her to bed, and then you can come over in the morning and thrash this thing out."

"The hell I will," Clim Hawkins said. "I'm married to her, ain't I? The place for me is where she is. If she wants to come home with me, okay. But we're gonna be together, that's all I gotta say. God, this has sure been some wedding night—so far . . ."

"Take it easy," Jen said. "In case you're feeling so good, you heard what she said, didn't you? She don't want to be married to you. She's sorry she ever got married to you. You know where that puts you, don't you? Go on, get out of here, and go home and leave her alone tonight."

"The hell I will," Clim Hawkins said again. "I ain't that dumb. She's married to me and I ain't goin' no place without her. There's one awful easy grounds in this state for getting marriages annulled, and I ain't taking no chances on pulling outa here right now, and then having you talk her up into going and having it annulled tomorrow."

Jen was completely baffled. She shivered a little as a breeze struck her body, and she kept pressing one knee into the top of the silver cup on the running board. "Ah, Clim, please go on home," she said helplessly.

"Not without Josie, I ain't," he said stubbornly.

Jen reached into the car and grabbed hold of Josette's shoulder and shook her hard. "Jo, for God's sakes, snap outa it. You just can't go all to pieces like this. If you're gonna change your mind about marrying Clim this is the time to do it right now. If you don't want him, tell him to get to hell outa here, and it don't make no difference if you been married by every God-damn justice of the peace in the state of Indiana, Ohio and Kentucky. Jo, snap outa it!"

"I don't know what made me do it," Josette said in an uneven whisper. "I don't know what made me do it."

"For God's sakes," Jen said urgently. "If you don't want to be married to him now, tell him to get to hell outa here, and then forget all this. Damn it, make your mind up, you want him or don't you?"

"I wish you'd all go away and leave me alone," Josette moaned. "I wish you'd all just leave me alone. I just don't know what to do. I don't know what made me do it."

"Jo, you make me so mad," Jen said. "You ain't got no more guts than nothing, and sometimes I don't guess you got a brain in your head."

"You heard what she said," Clim said. "She don't want you picking on her no more. I'm going to take her down to my house right now."

"Oh, no, you aren't," Jen said. "Jo, listen, quit setting there mumbling. You wanta go down to Clim's house tonight, or don't you?"

Josette pulled her face out of her hands suddenly. Her face was waxy white and swollen around the eyes. "Oh no," she said. "I won't go down there. I don't want to."

"There, you see!" Jen said triumphantly.

"I don't see nothin'," Clim said. "All I see is you're just trying to get her more worked up than she is. You're just a-trying to bust us up before we ever get started."

"You betcha," Jen said. "That's just what I'm tryin' to do, and you know why, just as well as I do. Josie don't want to be married to you no more than nothing."

"The hell you say! She went down there to Indiana with me tonight, didn't she?"

"So what!" Jen said curtly. "Even the best of people go off their nuts once in a while. Come on, Josie, get outa this car and go on in the house. I got some talking I wanna do to your boy friend."

Whether Josette reached out her hand for the door, or not, Jen could not see in the darkness, but it didn't make any difference, because Clim got hold of the handle first.

"She's married to me; she ain't going nowhere. Josie honey, my God, you gonna let that little bitch stand there and bust us up like this? You gonna let her get away with it?"

Josette dropped her head down into her hands again.

"Clim Hawkins, you open that door and let her get outa this car. Her nerves are all shot to hell. She didn't know what she was doin'."

"Go on, scram!" Clim said. "I'm taking her home with me, see? We're married, ain't we? There ain't a law in the land says I can't."

Jen felt weak and panicky and she tried to think of what she was to do. If only Mary was here, she kept thinking. If Mary was here she would know what to do. She could straighten out a mess like this and there wouldn't be any argument about it. She was panicky, and she didn't know what to do. She had a feeling that whatever she did or didn't do this moment, this very moment, was going to change the whole life of her sister. Jen had never felt such a responsibility in all her life, and she went dizzy with it, and hung onto the top of the car door, with her throat and mouth dry.

"Go on, scram!" Clim Hawkins said again in a thick angry voice. He switched the key over and put his foot on the starter.

"You're not going nowhere with Josie," Jen said, the words tumbling out of her mouth. She hung onto the door hard, and shut her eyes, more angry than she could ever remember being. She began to scream.

"Shut your mouth, you God-damn little . . ."

Jen hung onto the door tight and danced up and down on the ground and shrieked to the top of her lungs. A part of her that was cool and detached from all of this looked on approvingly and said to her, atta girl, atta way to do it, keep it up now, atta way to show that stinkin' bastard where to get off . . .

Clim Hawkins swung out at her blindly in the darkness and connected with her face, high up, over her right eye. It sent Jen reeling, but she kept on screaming over the rasping of the starter louder than ever.

At the same time that she got her hands fastened to the top of the door again and heard Clim Hawkins' curses over the sound of Josette's sobbing, she heard the ventilator clatter out of Molly Veech's window.

"Say! What's a-goin' on down there?" Molly whooped into the darkness, her head of straggling gray hair, her shoulders and a wide expanse of white nightgown sticking out of the window. "A-screaming and a-yellin' down there, an' pretty near morning! What's a-goin' on down there?"

"There, you see!" Jen screamed at Clim Hawkins triumphantly. "Kenny Veech'll knock your head right off'n you for this, you lousy son-of-a-bitching, dirty double-crossing pismire, you . . ."

"You hush up that kind of talking down there right this minute, Jen Veech, you hear me!" her mother yelled. "A-talking dirty, and swearin' and yellin' to the top of your voice. You come right into the house this minute, and you out there with that car, you drive away in it right now, you hear me, a-yelling and hollering and talking dirty around here when it's pretty near morning."

"I ain't coming a step into no house unless Josie comes with me," Jen yelled back up to her mother. Sam and Dorothy were trying to peep out of the window around the bulk of Molly, so that she looked for all the world like a many-headed idol carved in ivory, with the vast white nightgown in the moonlight.

"Josie, you out there?" Molly called. "You come on in the house, you and Jen both, right now. Lord, a-carrying on and yelling and hollering out in the front of the house when it's pretty near morning. I have a notion to whip the both of you as big as you are, no more sense'n to . . . Well, come on in the house, you hear me telling you, and I ain't gonna have no more monkey business. Clim Hawkins, if that's you down there in that automobile you just get away from here, and I don't never wanta see you crawlin' around here again, a-foolin' and yellin' and swearin' and . . ."

"C'mon, c'mon, c'mon," Jen said to Josette rapidly. "You heard what Ma said. C'mon in the house."

Jen picked up the cup from the running board and jerked the car door open, and Josette crawled out of the automobile like a sleep-walker. For one moment Clim Hawkins was daunted and helpless.

"You get outa here now, Clim Hawkins," Molly bawled at him. "I ain't gonna have you hangin' around here a-tall. No more sense'n to start hollering and yellin' and carryin' on. Lord, I wish to goodness Kenny was here, I guess he would shut you up in a hurry. Go on now, go away from here!"

Clim Hawkins sprang out of the car in one leap, his face dark and angry. "Mrs. Veech, you don't understand the way it is. You gotta let me tell you . . ."

"You ain't a-goin' to tell me nothing," Molly yelled. "Go on now, you git, you heard me. I ain't gonna have you down there a-yellin' an' swearin' at me. You're drunk, that's what's the matter with you, and I ain't gonna have nobody hanging around here that's so drunk they can't tell how to act nor if they're . . ."

"Mrs. Veech!" Clim roared. "Lemme tell you. Josie and me are married. We got married down to Indiana tonight. Josie and me are married."

Molly stopped yelling, and the night suddenly was still and quiet. The girls stood together in front of the porch steps, and Clim stood defiantly with his legs wide apart on the sidewalk in front of the house, and they all looked up to Molly in the window. Molly was quiet, and for just a moment, in the moonlight, it looked as if she grew smaller, settled together somehow. But in a second she was erect and powerful again. Her voice was loud and authoritative. "You come in the house now, all of you. Ain't none of you got no better sense than to yell and holler about fambly business to the top of your lungs out in front of the house? Lord, I'd like to know what you think the neighbors think. Come on in the house now."

She disappeared from the window and none of them ever stopped to think of the miraculous speed with which she came down those stairs.

Carl, on the couch in the living room, swam out of sleep into a tangle of yelling voices out in front of the house. The first thought that he had was that the police had come for Kenny. He sat up bewildered on the couch in the darkness, and in no more than a few seconds he heard feet on the front porch at the exact moment that his mother opened the door and came bounding out of the stairway, with her nightgown billowing and her bare feet slapping against the floor.

Molly caught up an old piece of blanket that served for a pad on the back of a wooden rocking chair, and draped it modestly around her shoulders that were already more than adequately covered by the sleeves of the thick white nightgown. She switched on a light, and turned around to the twins and Clim Hawkins where they stood inside the door. None of them noticed Carl at all. Carl was bewildered. He could not imagine what had happened. They all looked strange to him, like people out of a dream, Josette with her strained dead-white face, and Clim Hawkins with his legs braced apart and his brown hair on end and his face flushed and red. But the oddest of them all was Jen. She was clutching the tall silver cup. Her absurdly yellow curls were in disorder around her pale face where the rouge and lipstick stood out. There was a little spot of blood from a light cut on her right eyebrow, and her right eye was swelling shut rapidly, the dark color settling around it.

Jen had not escaped her mother's eye, either. "Well, if you ain't one pretty-looking sight," Molly said. "I never see the beat. You look like a regular little toughie."

Sam came out of the stairway uncertainly, holding his pants up with one hand, and twitching at his twisted suspenders with the other, and Dorothy crept down behind him like a little ghost in faded pink pajamas.

"Now, what's this you're blabbing about you and Josie being married?" Molly said to Clim Hawkins directly.

"We are married, Mrs. Veech," he said. "Ain't we, Jo? Show your Ma the certificate we got."

Josette was holding it in her hand, a piece of stiff white paper, with a wrinkle along one side of it. Josette held it out, and Molly took it and glanced at it and threw it down onto the table.

"Well, you gone and done it all right, ain't you, young lady?" she said to Josette with her blue eyes snapping. "So now I wanta know what all this hullabaloo is about?"

Clim started to speak, but Jen broke in on him. "I can tell you what the matter is, all right!"

"Lord, by the looks a you I guess you can," Molly said calmly. Sam stood by the table behind her with the certificate in his hand and his face drained and expressionless.

"Josie hadn't got no business being married to him. She don't even want to be married to him. She was all tired out tonight, and nerved up, and he just talked her into running off down there and getting married. But now she doesn't want to be married to him, and I'm not gonna stand around and . . ."

Molly looked at Josette hard. "Well, what you standing there like a reg'lar idjit for? It looks to me like this is your say . . ."

"What about Pat?" Sam said in a shocked voice. "She was going to marry Pat. He was a-planning and . . ."

Clim Hawkins took hold of Josette's arm and shook her a little. "Josie, you gonna let Jen bust us up like this? Why don't you just tell 'em the way you feel about me and stuff and . . ."

Carl watched Josette's face from the couch, and he thought that she had a look on her face like he must have had years ago after he had his tonsils out, and was trying to come back into the world out of the strange hopeless mazes of the ether world.

Sam began to talk from behind Molly desperately. "Josie, you just go on upstairs there, and this young feller can just go on home. There's such a thing as an annulment law in this state, and it ain't gonna be nothing at all to it. You don't want to get married to a no-good drunk that can't keep a job nowhere. You just go on upstairs and forget about it, and we'll get you annulled just like nothing. You got all your life ahead a-you, and young Thompson for one is gonna be mighty tickled to . . ." Sam's voice was excited, oddly urgent and tender.

"Sure," Jen broke in. "Josie, you musta been crazy running down there and marrying Clim. Why, Pat is worth more'n a couple of dozen a him . . ."

"Some day you're gonna pull just about one stunt too often on Pat Thompson," Molly said sarcastically. "How you suppose Pat is gonna feel when he hears about you tearing down to Indiana an' marrying up with a worthless drunken no-good like this Hawkins. There's them that always claimed you was smarter'n anybody else in this fambly, but they can just see you ain't got the brains to pound sand in a rathole. A-tearing off somewhere and marrying some good-for-nothing, and not knowing what or who you want no more than nothing, and a-standing here right now with your eyes a-hanging out on your face, like a bump on a log, if you ain't a sight, and not a word to say, or . . . For Lord's sakes, if it don't beat all, running off like that, giving your fambly no warning at all, and coming back here in the middle of the night and sniveling around . . ."

Under the lashing of her mother's angry words, the color began to come back into Josette's face.

"Jo," Jen said to her softly. "Oh, Josie, don't do it!"

Josette took hold of Clim Hawkins' hand and held it hard and whirled around toward Jen. "Jen Veech, you keep your mouth shut and leave me alone," she said. "You're just jealous, that's everything in the world that's the matter with you. You're jealous, because you're in love with Clim yourself, and you don't want to see him married to me."

Josette turned around to face her father and mother, hanging tight to Clim's hand. "You're always rubbing it in to me. Well, maybe I'm not so smart, but I'm smart enough to know what I want to do and do it, and there isn't any of you that can stop me. I hate Pat Thompson, and I wouldn't be married to him if he was the last man on earth, so there." Her voice was rising, hysterically . . . "And if you think I'm just going to stay around this house all of my life and do all of the work and just . . . I'm going to do as I please, and I don't care what any of you say or think. I'm married to Clim and—and—and that's all there is to it, so!" Josette's hands were trembling, and she held them tight together to stop their trembling, and then she began to tremble all over. Clim put his arm around her protectingly, and Carl felt a sickness all through him at no more than the lost frightened look that Josette was struggling to keep off her face. He felt hate for her, and more hate because he pitied her. Fool, damn fool, he kept saying to himself, what does she want to run off and get herself into a mess like this for. What made her do it? Why couldn't she have waited? She must be crazy. I hate her, but she must be feeling terrible to have such a look on her face.

Jen was the first one of them to move after Josette spoke. She shrugged her shoulders elaborately, with her face expressionless and the anger only showing in her eyes. "Okay," she said. "Do as you please. You can go to hell, for all of me, Jo. Go ahead." She went to the table and set the shiny silver cup down and stood back from it admiringly. "Well, what you standing around for?" she said over her shoulder. "Why don't you go on to bed? That's what you been trying to do for the last couple hours."

Molly settled the problem practically. "Well, there ain't no sense a-staying up all night that I can see. Jen, you go on upstairs and sleep in Mary's room. It don't look like she's gonna get home tonight, anyway."

Josette turned to Clim, her face pleading. "Clim, can't we—you said . . ."

"I guess we better stay right here, Josie," Clim said easily. "As long as it's all right with your folks, I guess we better. We gotta be careful spending money, you know that."

Jen walked to the stair door, with all of her curls bobbing. "Sweet dreams!" she said spitefully over her shoulder, as she began to climb the stairs.

Dorothy was hanging over the edge of the table examining the silver cup curiously, and at Jen's words she began to laugh immoderately in her high mirthless way.

Her grandmother turned to her, properly shocked. "Why, Dor'thy, you just hush right up now!"

Sam made his last appeal to Molly. "Don't you think she oughta think this over a little? Ain't no sense of her rushing headlong into somethin' . . ."

"She already rushed," Molly answered grimly. "If she had any thinking to do she oughta done it a long time before this. Now she's gone and flew right in the face a Providence, and done as she pleased and jilted a nice boy like Pat and told her own fambly right to their faces that it ain't none of their business what she does, so just let her be. She's made her bed, now let her lay in it," Molly finished dramatically.

Josette moved suddenly, as if she could not endure another word that her mother spoke. Carl caught a glimpse of Josette's face as she walked to the stair door with Clim at her heels, and he was sickened and horrified by the hurt and bewilderment and terrifying lack of courage that he saw there. It was awful, Josette's face, he thought, like a—like a prisoner being led to execution. The trite old phrase popped into his mind, and that brought him back to Kenny and to this much more terrible thing that had happened to him. It was all too much for Carl, these two things that had happened mixing in his head. He got up and stumbled out of the room and out of the back door into the darkness, and no one saw him go but Dorothy who stared after him with blank incurious eyes.

Jen heard their footsteps in the hall and she came out of Mary's room and followed them to the door. Josette switched on the light and stood still in the middle of the floor. Jen, in the doorway, carefully avoided looking at Clim. She spoke to her sister impersonally. "Here," she said. "It's brand-new. I guess Mary must have got it the last time she was in Detroit." She threw it down on the bed, and it spread out there, an exquisite peach satin night-gown, low cut and covered with lace. Jen closed the door behind her and went back to Mary's room.

Downstairs, to break the silence that had built itself around the patient squeaking of Molly's rocking chair, Sam spoke hesitantly to her. "I wished you hadn't a-been so hasty about . . ."

"For Lord's sakes," Molly said angrily. "I wasn't the one that was being hasty. Josie was the one that was being hasty, chasing off down there to Indiana and marrying the one fellow that ever asked her besides Pat Thompson, and then coming back here sniveling one minute and talking up sassy the next. Just let her be now, and see how she likes it. I guess she'll find she bit off more 'n she can chew before she's done with it. She's always been so smart and uppity she's just gotta learn the same as everybody else."

Sam opened his mouth to say something more when Molly finished talking, but she spoke again impatiently. "For Lord's sakes, go on up there to bed again and take this young one with you. She's gonna catch a cold as sure as anything running around on this drafty floor in her bare feet."

Something in her voice told Sam that he had received a dismissal. He went to the stairs without another word, and Dorothy trailed after him looking back over her shoulder.

7

MOLLY RELAXED IN HER CHAIR. SHE TURNED HER face toward the open door, out to where the light shone into the blackness. She wished that Kenny would come. Her need for him suddenly was a great thing that encompassed her consciousness. Her concern over Kenny drove away all her disappointment in Josette. She forgot that Josette had in any way disturbed the pattern of family living. She said a kind of prayer to nobody in particular for Kenny. Make him be all right, make him come home soon, take care of him—make him come.

Molly hoisted herself out of her chair suddenly and went out to the kitchen and switched on the light. She filled the coffee pot with water out of the pail, and measured the black grains of coffee into the percolator. It was a small electric percolator, a gift from Mary several years ago, for this very purpose: coffee in the night when the kitchen range was black and cold.

She waited for her coffee patiently. She thought about Kenny, called up the image of him and pondered over it, feature by feature, lovingly. She remembered other nights when they had shared coffee at unorthodox hours before the dawn. She tried to devise a scheme whereby she would not listen for his feet on the porch, and then he must surely come. While the water gurgled in the coffee pot, she recklessly tried to bargain with some unknown power. Do anything else you want to me, but only send Kenny back. Take any one of the rest, if it must be someone, but let it not be Kenny, let Kenny live and stay out of trouble always. Let me die if it has to be that way to make a bargain, take anything else that I have in this world, but I must have Kenny back.

She heard feet on the porch, and her heart jumped. But these steps were even lighter and quicker than Kenny's and she knew that Mary was home at last. Molly's face brightened with her pleasure and the brooding look went out of her eyes, as she hurried to get another cup out of the cupboard.

"Hi yuh, Mom," Mary said. Her face looked tired and pinched, and the severe dark suit that she wore accented her slimness. She sat down to the cup of steaming black coffee gratefully.

"Lord, if it don't seem good to have you come home," Molly said cozily, spooning her coffee to cool it. "I give up you comin' home tonight, it got so late."

Mary did not answer her. Her head drooped over the steam from her cup. Molly looked at her. "Mary," she said, "you know where Kenny is?"

Mary parried the question with one of her own. "What's the silverware on the table?" she asked her mother.

Molly glanced into the living room where the light from the kitchen illuminated the shiny silver cup a little, but it was to the white slip of paper beside it that she looked. "Oh, I dunno," she said absently. "Some kind of jigger Jen come lugging home from some place."

"Cup," Mary said briefly. "Dance contest prize."

Molly was not interested. "Well, sir, she's gone and done it," she said to Mary dramatically.

Mary looked up from her cup, the thick lashes rising, and the quick blue eyes imprisoned in the great shadow of her face. "Who's done what?"

"Josie got married down in Indiana some place tonight. Don't that beat all?"

Mary remained quite unperturbed. "How did she talk Pat into running away like that?" she asked.

Molly savored her surprising news for a moment, built up her crisis expertly, took a great gulp of hot coffee, and looked fixedly at

Mary. "She didn't have to talk Pat into nothing. It wasn't Pat she got married to."

However surprised Mary might have been, her face was no indication, and Molly was somewhat disappointed.

"Hawkins, huh?" Mary said.

Her mother nodded. "Lord, don't that beat the cars though? I swear I just don't know what got into Josie to make her do a thing like that. I don't mind telling you, you coulda knocked me over with a feather, I was that surprised and disappointed when she come a-walking in here. You know how I always counted on Josie to do something special, her being kind of different than the common run. What possessed her to run off with that no-good bum when Pat Thompson was hanging around here just waiting for her to say the word, I don't know."

Mary shrugged her shoulders. "Where are they now?"

"Who? Josie and that Hawkins? Why, Lord, upstairs there to bed in Josie's bed. Jen's a-sleeping in your bed, but you can have her come down here on the couch."

"I'll sleep in my chair," Mary said absently. "I do half the time, anyway."

"Say, you think Jen is in love with that Hawkins fellow?" Molly asked confidentially.

"Why?"

"Well, she sure acted funny about them getting married, at first. She got into a regular screaming fight with that fellow about it right out in front of the house here, and he let her have it, a good one right in the eye, the prettiest shiner you ever did see. She got to yelling at him and calling him every name she could lay her tongue to, faster'n a horse could run, and she claimed . . ."

"What did Josette say?"

"At first, she didn't say nothing. She bawled, and then she stood around like a bump on a log without saying a single word, and finally she got kind of peeved and come right out and accused Jen a-being jealous of her getting married to Clim. Then she told the whole fambly it wasn't nobody's business what she done nor who she married nor nothing about it."

"What did Jen say, besides swearing at him?"

"Oh, Lord," Molly said, wearily, filling up her coffee cup again. "A whole lot of junk about Josie not knowing what she was doing and being all nerved up or something when she got married to him down there, and wanting to quit now she'd got home with him. You want your coffee warmed, Mary?"

Mary shoved out her cup, and Molly spooned a flake of cigarette ash out of it carefully, and filled the cup up to the top. "Just between you an' me, Mary," she said softly, "I wouldn't be more'n half surprised if Jen was right. Josie had a kind of a sick look all over her face. I don't figure she 'tended getting married tonight at all, and, once she had, she'd a-give most anything if she hadn't by the time she got back home here."

Mary touched the hot cup tentatively with one finger.

"Well, sir, it's too bad if that's the way it is," Molly said comfortably, "but Josie will just have to learn the way the rest of us do."

"Clim Hawkins drinks all the while," Mary said impersonally. "When he lost his last job up to Ashbury, they blacklisted him in every shop in the city. He can't stick to no one thing, not a job, nor a woman. His father has been figuring on kicking him outa the house down there and, after this, he will."

Molly sighed deeply and spooned her coffee. "Oh, well," she said philosophically, "I figure she'll get her belly fulla Hawkins before long, and the next time she won't go a-flying off with the first man that comes along. I ain't one to be mean, but Josie sure had it coming to her, the way she's been acting around here."

"It won't take Josette long to get her belly full in more ways than one," Mary said mildly, and Molly was silenced. "And I'll lay you any odds you want that she never quits him neither."

"I don't see how you figure," Molly said, perturbed.

"Josie has pride," Mary said. "People with pride are funny. They never make any mistakes."

Molly was silent. "I wish . . ." she said at last, and let her voice trail away. "Mary," she said soberly. "Sometimes I just don't know. I done the very best for you kids I knew how, but sometimes I just don't know. There's a whole lot more to raisin' up a family of kids than just feedin' 'em and clothin' 'em. And I always had to do the whole job alone. You know how your father is, no more help 'n as if he wasn't here at all. All I know is I done the best I could, the very best I could, with what I had to do with. Sometimes I think that . . ."

Mary reached out and put her hand over her mother's big rough red one. "You're okay, Mom," she said.

"Mary," Molly said with her voice shaking and falling apart, "I just can't stand this no more. Where's Kenny? You know what's happened to him! You got to tell me, I can't stand this not knowing no more!"

Mary took her hand away from her mother's. "Yeah," she said.

Molly waited, leaning forward over her fat arms, watching Mary's face.

Mary's face was cool and detached and her eyes far away. When she spoke at last, she said, "Mom, Kenny has got into about the worst jam he ever has."

Molly's face began to crumple up. "Oh, I knew it! I had a feelin' all along. Where is he? Did he get hurt? What did he do? Mary, where is Kenny at?"

"You gotta take it easy, Mom," Mary said. "It isn't gonna help him none, nor you none, or nobody if you let yourself go all to pieces."

"Mary, tell me!" Molly said, her face quivering.

"First off," Mary said, "Kenny didn't do it. He was framed. But he can't prove that, so it's just as bad as if he did do it. But you want to remember that Kenny didn't do it."

"Do what? Do what? Mary? Oh, why don't you tell me?"

"There was an oil station robbery up to Ashbury," Mary said rapidly. "There was a man shot. But Kenny didn't do it. The only trouble was he was along with the guy that did. The guy must have shot the fellow in the oil station and then got away some place without nobody seeing him. The only one they saw was Kenny, so they thought that Kenny did it . . ."

Molly seemed to fold together and grow smaller, small and still. Her voice was breathless. "Mary, you sure—that—that Kenny didn't do it?"

Mary answered her positively. "I'm sure. I know. You don't have to worry, Mom. That kind of stuff is way out of Kenny's line."

"Where is Kenny? They got him in jail? Where is he?"

Mary shook her head, and for one second she drew her brows together as if it was a hard thing for her to sit here across the table from her mother, and tell her these things about Kenny.

"He got away from the police. They don't know where he is, but they are still looking for him. They'll come down here tomorrow and ask you questions. You want to be careful. You want to say that you don't know where Kenny is, but that you aren't worried because lots of times he goes away from home to work, and stays with friends of his and looks for jobs. You have to be careful. We don't want the police to get any more suspicious than they are. I wish that I hadn't had to tell you nothing about it at all, but everybody in town is talking about it, and I was afraid you'd hear it anyway, tomorrow morning."

Molly sat by the table as if she had been stunned. She raised a numb and heavy hand and smoothed some hair away from her face behind her ears. Her shoulders were caved in, as if all the strength and energy had gone out of her. She said something that Mary could not hear, half under her breath. And then suddenly a look of horror came over her face.

"Mary," she said urgently, with her blue eyes wide and tortured. "Mary! It wasn't Kenny that your father was reading to me about in the paper. The one that the policeman shot in the shoulder, and then they chased him all over town and found his car all smashed to pieces up against a bridge. That wasn't Kenny, was it?"

Mary did not have to answer her because Molly spoke out of the certainty of her knowledge.

Molly spoke again in a dry whistling whisper, as if her voice had gone out of her too, along with her strength and will. "Where is Kenny? You know where he is? He must be hurt something awful. Where is he?"

"I don't know," Mary said. "He isn't in any of the hospitals around here. The police can't find any trace of him any place. Maybe he wasn't hurt so bad. You know how lucky Kenny is. They can't find him, so that must mean that he is well enough to get away from them and hide."

"You ain't heard from him? You don't know where he is? Where could he a-run off to? Why didn't he come right here to home? How could he a-got away from them police, when it claimed right there in the paper . . ."

"He couldn't come home," Mary explained patiently. "That would have been the first place the police would look for him, once they found out who he was. There is one way he could have got away. Lew says that that must have been what he did . . ."

Molly straightened herself slowly in her chair. "Lew," she said. "Can't Lew find Kenny and help him? Lew has got a lot of money and everything . . . Why can't Lew . . . ?"

Mary shook her head.

"I don't see why he wouldn't if you was to ask him special . . ."

"Lew is out," Mary said shortly.

Without any warning at all the snap came back to Molly's eyes and the life and energy to her body. "Well, for Lord's sakes, if that ain't the best thing I ever heard. Lew Lentz a-setting down there in his hotel, with all the money he's got, and being in with all the big folks and things like that, and him practically one a this fambly, and then him not willing to turn over a finger to do a thing for Kenny! If that don't beat anything I ever heard tell of! Well, sir, Mary Veech, if you want to just set around here and let them put Kenny in jail for something he never done no more than nothing, you can, but I ain't a-going to. You go on over to Smith's and call me up Ernie right now this minute, and we'll just see whether they gonna put Kenny in jail or not for something he didn't do no more than nothing . . ."

Mary smiled suddenly, and some of the strain went out of her face.

"Take it easy, Mom," she said. "You think Ernie's gonna break his neck to help you get Kenny outa a jam?"

Molly was silenced, defeated temporarily, but indomitable. She shifted her tactics somewhat, and went on talking.

"Lord, if this ain't the awfulest thing I ever heard of. Them dirty, double-crossin' toughies up there to Ashbury getting Kenny into a jam like this. The trouble with alla them is they're just jealous of Kenny, them toughies up to Ashbury, and Ernie, yes, and Lew Lentz too, the whole of them. All of them always been jealous of Kenny because he's more of a man than any of them ever will be. I tell you and I ain't just braggin' on account of him being my son, Kenny

Veech is a man if there ever was one, every inch a man. You suppose he's just gonna set around here and let them police put him in jail for something he never did? Well, I'll tell the world he ain't. The police needn't think they gonna catch up with Kenny right away. He's too smart for 'em. I guess Kenny'll show 'em . . ."

"You better go to bed. You can't do nothing till morning, anyway. If they come down here, the less you know about it, the better it's gonna be for Kenny," Mary said. She opened the flat silver cigarette case.

"You just shut that thing right up," Molly said. "Lord, you ain't done a thing but set here and smoke them things right down one after another ever since you been home. I been a-telling you, you ain't got no business smoking them things like that, you and Kenny both . . ."

"Yeah," Mary said, rolling the cigarette slowly in her fingers. "Me and Kenny, both . . ."

8

MARY TOOK THE PHONE CALL THAT MORNING from the corner of Lew Lentz's desk. Lew stopped his work and listened to her talking, his fingers closed around one of the tall heels of her pumps as she sat in front of him on the edge of the big desk. It was Julia who ran the dress shop in Ashbury where Mary bought clothes sometimes. She was talking about a new dress that had just come in, a very peculiar dress, but one that she knew that Mary would want. She thought that Mary ought to come in for a fitting that morning, or, in fact, as soon as she could get to Ashbury. Mary agreed with her. Julia talked a little incoherently, and she was oddly breathless. Julia's talents did not run to intrigue, Mary thought. On several occasions in the past, Kenny had sent messages to Mary through Julia. It was not strange that Kenny should be trying to reach her through Julia now. Mary was not at all surprised. As soon as she had heard Julia's voice on the telephone she had known perfectly well why Julia had called her. But it seemed incredible to her that Kenny could be in Ashbury, and in any position so that he would be free to get to Julia. Her mind became clear and alert and wary, as she listened to Julia talk, and all of her intuitions rang alarm warnings of suspicion. And yet it was so natural a thing that Kenny would make an effort to reach her, and so natural a thing that he would attempt to make that effort through Julia.

Mary dropped the phone back on the hook carelessly, when she was through with it, and leaned back against the top of the desk. "I have to go uptown," she said to Lew.

"Today is going to be a scorcher all right," he said irrelevantly. "I thought we was all done with hot weather for this year." He was right. The air was hot and breathless, and outside the sunlight was dancing and shimmering in the narrow streets, creeping in through the slats of the Venetian blinds and grilling the floor in hot bright strips.

"Wait till this afternoon," Lew said, "and I'll take the day off and go in with you."

Mary shook her head indifferently. "I have to go this morning. I have to have a dress fitted."

"Julia wouldn't care, she'd just as soon do it this afternoon. Go on, call her up and tell her you're coming in this afternoon."

"Okay." Mary picked up the phone, and then suddenly she dropped it back in the cradle. "I just remembered. This is Julia's afternoon off today."

"That's a woman in business for you," Lew said. "Afternoon off and all that stuff. Just lock up her shop any time she feels like it and walk off. It's a wonder she makes enough money to keep the sheriff from locking it up for her."

"I guess I better go this morning."

"Okay, you run along. I got some business I oughta attend to this afternoon, anyway. You keep where it's cool and I'll come up tonight and we'll have dinner somewhere."

"Okay," Mary said. "I'll have lunch with Julia and go to a show or something. Where shall I meet you?"

"How about at Marcossi's in the bar at six?"

Mary nodded and stood down from the desk leisurely.

"I tell you," Lew said, "after dinner we'll do the rounds. We haven't done that in a long time. We need to catch up on our night life. Remember how we used to do that, start out some night and hit every place in town? Hell, last summer during the hot weather it got so we was celebrating something just about every damn night."

"Maybe I can think up something this afternoon for us to celebrate," Mary said, with her sudden smile.

"There's at least one thing you could think up, that I ain't got to mention, that I'd buy every drop of champagne they got in Ashbury to celebrate, and you know what I mean."

Mary turned her face away, and Lew Lentz looked at her hard. And then he flicked off an imaginary speck of dirt from his shirt cuff, and reached in his pocket for his wallet.

He gave her the bills and she took them silently. "Buy a new dress, and a hat and jiggers. We're celebrating tonight." He sighed profoundly as he put his wallet away. "My God, but there certainly is an awful overhead to keeping a little doll like you around, baby. Sometimes I ask myself why I do it, when I see them bills roll in . . ."

"Smile when you say them words, pardner," Mary said.

He kissed her affectionately, and she walked toward the door.

"You gonna want the car this afternoon?" he asked.

She shook her head, and held out the money he had given her. "I got taxi fare."

"Okay. I'll have one of the boys take you up, and bring the car back." He stood up and switched on another electric fan, a new small powerful one, on the other end of the desk top. "Hey," he shouted after her, "tell Dutch I said he better buy me a couple more fans and get to hell back here with 'em, when he takes you into town. You keep outa this sun today, honey—and be a good girl; you sure better."

The little dark-haired guy whom Mungo called kid waited out in the lobby of the building where Julia had her dress shop in Ashbury. While he waited, he amused himself by trying to imagine what this girl named Mary would look like. All he knew about her was what Kelly had told him. He had dubbed Kenny "Kelly" because of something the doctor had said when he took the slug out of his shoulder, something about how Kenny reminded him of a big Irishman named Kelly who had been a patient of his once, the finest body of a man he had ever seen.

From all that Kelly had said about her, the kid had this girl Mary all added up to be a tall, long-legged, dark-haired girl with a lot of energy and very serious-minded. According to Kelly, she was plenty smart and independent. But also according to Kelly, she was some kind of an angel, and he could get tender to the melting point just thinking about her. The Kid whittled his picture of her down into a medium-sized blonde, very luscious and at the same time an angel-face and a halo.

He didn't think so much of Julia. She was all right, and straight on the level, he figured, about sending the tip along to Mary and then forgetting all about it. But it was women like Julia who messed up things. They couldn't help it; they were nervous and jittery. He wondered if Mary could possibly be anything like that. Maybe Kelly was just prejudiced about her, maybe she wasn't any different than the fluttery dress-shop dame. He swore a little at the thought.

Kelly had done a lot of talking. He told the kid about the whole thing, and how it was a frame, and the kid believed him. At first Kelly wanted him to beat it up here to Ashbury and get in touch with the guy Gitlo, because Kelly figured it was the two boys that gave Gitlo the doublecross that night. But the kid thought better of it, and pretty soon Kelly did too. This Gitlo is the guy that put the frame on you it looks to me, he had said, and Kelly said I think you got something there. And then his face had turned blank and hard and he hadn't said a word for a long time. The kid said, this Gitlo must have had one hell of a grudge against you. And Kelly said no, but he had a friend that didn't like me. Kelly hadn't said anything more than that, but there had been little things that the kid had pieced together. He was willing to bet that the real guy behind this whole frame was this boy friend of Mary's. Hell, was any woman worth all this trouble on both sides? Not for his money, anyway, the kid thought.

He watched the people pour across the lobby to the elevators, and the cars flash by out in the streets in the sizzling sun. This Mary girl was sure taking her time coming up here. He didn't like anything about it. He kept watching the blonde elevator girl, a very nice piece in her black uniform. Between hauls she came out of the elevator over to the newsstand and looked at pictures in the movie magazines. She looked at him sometimes too, and all the while she kept singing softly. Pretty soon the bells would start ringing and jangling, all the people who were up and wanted down. But the elevator girl never hurried or stopped singing. She closed the movie magazine leisurely, pulled her uniform dress down smooth over her hips, looked at him, and then walked over to the elevator slow and hippy as if she had all the time there was.

After a few minutes of that, he got tired of the elevator girl, her face was always the same and she always sang the same song, as if she was feeble-minded or something. It was hot and he would have liked to go out and have a drink. He was tired of standing around waiting for a dame who took her own time about coming up to see him when the only real reason he was out here at all was as a kind of favor to her. This Mary sounded like just about the most selfish dame he had ever heard of, anyway. And if she wasn't, then why hadn't she cut Kelly loose years ago when he was younger and it would have been easier. She was Kelly's sister and she was older than he was, and at some time or another the fault was all hers. If she packed the dynamite that Kelly claimed she did, she never had to look around for men, so why didn't she cut Kelly loose, instead of waiting until a jam like this one came along.

Just then a thin girl with red hair came in carrying a suit box and went across the lobby to the elevator. He looked at her, up and down and up, and she looked back at him with her face expressionless. Then she turned away and lit a cigarette, and when the door opened, the kid admired the casual way that she carried the cigarette into the elevator in defiance of the sign that hung in the lobby between the elevator doors. He watched her go regretfully.

The doors from the street swung, and several people came in. One among them was a tall blonde girl, striding along in a messy pink suit of some kind, with the skirt about three inches too long. A very messy-looking dame; for a moment he was scared, but she went across to take the elevator too.

And then he saw her, when Mary walked in the door. And as soon as he saw her he knew that this was the one. This girl couldn't be anybody else but Mary, and the Mary that Kelly had talked about could not be anybody else in the world but this girl. She walked toward him slowly with a kind of indolent flowing rhythm. She had on a white suit with a very short skirt and short sleeves. The skirt was full and there was blue braid around it, and it arched around her knees when she walked. There was more blue braid on the front of her jacket and blue on her hat, and her purse and shoes were blue. She looked perfectly cool and immaculate, and the kid thought, a million miles away from a poor bloody bum in a box car with a slug of lead in his shoulder.

She turned away from him to go down the corridor to Julia's shop, and he smelled her perfume as she passed. And then she stopped still and turned around and came back to him slowly. She raised her eyes to him from the hat brim, and he felt the shock of the blueness of her eyes in the midst of the great weary brown shadows.

"You might be waiting for me," she said simply.

"I might," he said.

He rocked back on his feet suddenly with the fluid grace of a boxer, ducked his head, and caricatured a feint, and then stepped in and cocked the other fist at her. And she answered him with the slight, rapid, half-developed motions of the pattern, touching his chin momentarily with her small doubled fist under the soft white glove.

"I'll see Julia a minute and then we'll get out of here," she said. She walked off down the corridor and disappeared. The kid stepped on the cigarette butt that still lay burning on the stone floor, where he had dropped it when he first saw her come in. Damn, he kept thinking, whatever produced a woman like that? What bred her? What made her the way she is? Why doesn't she happen more often, or is she one of the kind that one's enough of? He couldn't get the way she looked and talked and walked out of his mind. He felt very sorry then for his big fellow. I never thought she'd be like this. Speaking of understatement, why didn't Kelly tip me off, warn me what I was gonna be up against?

Mary came back down the corridor, and he fell into step with her. When he came out the door behind her, onto the hot street, she turned to him and smiled briefly. "This is a good time to go get a drink, don't you think?"

"It sounds good to me."

She looked up and down the street a moment and then she said, "There's a place around the corner."

The kid grinned. "Today is the first I ever been in this town. It still looks all alike to me."

"You're from the East, aren't you?" Mary said.

He nodded. "How could you tell my Brooklyn accent?"

"East, but not quite so far East as New York," Mary said.

"That's right."

They came up to the corner and Mary said, "This way." They didn't talk any more after that. He kept watching her, and all of a sudden she turned around and found his eyes on her. They looked at each other hard, and unashamedly, and then they both looked away.

"This is the place." Mary stopped by a basement entrance with iron railing around it. She went down first, and the motion of her descent stirred the air and puffed out her skirt wide and higher above her knees, like a figure skater's.

The interior was dimly lighted and crowded and smoky, full of people, although it wasn't noon yet, a great hubbub of voices and music.

"The booth in the corner," the kid said to the waiter. "Right?"

"Right," Mary said.

They ordered drinks first to dispose of the waiter, and while they waited for him to come back, the kid held a match to her cigarette. I could understand I guess, he thought, how any woman who had been knocked around a lot could have eyes that look the way hers do, but where does that sweet baby mouth fit in? My bet is that she is the kind of a woman that could keep a man running around her in circles for about ten years, and at the end of that time he still wouldn't know very much about her.

Mary put a bill from her purse on the corner of the table for the waiter. He came back at last with their drinks—an old-fashioned for Mary and plain whiskey for the kid. Then they waited for him to come back with the change.

The waiter turned away from the table in the booth, and Mary said, "How is he?"

"He's coming fine," the kid said. "Fever all gone. It was a nice clean hole in his shoulder. No bones broken. He's up on his feet already. I don't think you could stop him with an axe."

"Where is he?"

"Detroit, the edge of it."

"You live in Detroit now?"

"No," he said. "It happened like this. You know all about this end of the story. I happened to be riding in the box car he happened to land on when he jumped from that bridge onto the top of the freight as she came into the yards. After it stopped in the yards he got down and tried to get into the car. He was weak—loss of blood and shook up from the whole thing—and he couldn't make it. He was game. He hung on to the bottom of the car even after she got moving. I happened to be in the car, so I hauled him in. He passed out right then. When we rolled into the edge of Detroit in the morning, I got him off, and walked him over to a friend of mine's. He has been having good care, and a good doctor. He's as safe there as if he wasn't there, and once he leaves, he hasn't been there."

Mary looked at him curiously. "You must have connections in Detroit."

He shook his head. "Me? No. My brother it just happens has got plenty of big connections all over out this way. Sometimes it happens I use them." He looked away from her then, doubled his fist up and pressed it into the palm of his other hand and tried to stretch his short blunt fingers up over it.

He looked up at Mary suddenly. "You know how this frame on him works?"

She nodded. "Yeah. Does he?"

"He didn't at first, but now he does." He kept thinking, how can she be so cool about it, as if this was happening to somebody else and some other guy. "First off, he wanted me to get over here and get this guy Gitlo busy at trying to fix up something for him. But then he got to thinking it over a little."

She nodded.

"Any chance a-getting him out from under?" he asked. He leaned over to reach for the ash tray, and stayed that way, so he could look up into the cool angles and shadows of her face.

She shook her head slowly, and turned her glass in her fingers.

"That's the way I had it figured. I bought some papers. They didn't leave any loose ends any place. I guess he takes the rap, that's all."

"How soon can he get out of Detroit?" Mary asked.

The kid began to get uneasy. Sooner or later he'd have to tell her what she didn't want to hear, and she knew it too. He said, "Couple days. Any time now, if he takes it kind of easy. The sooner he'd get out of the state the better it would be for him."

"Maybe," she said. She raised her eyes to him suddenly. "But there isn't any future in it," she said simply.

"Yeah, I know what you mean. I've seen guys on the road. Always on the move, always waiting for it to catch up with them. It's a hell of a life, all right."

"Maybe a good lawyer," Mary said. "A few years isn't so long, and he'd have it all done with."

They were silent together, and then they smiled suddenly together.

"I guess that's out, all right," the kid said. "He wouldn't get along so good in a jail. He wasn't built for that. The only thing to do, I guess, is turn him loose and let him go."

For a minute he thought he could see some pain and hurt in her eyes, but she dropped the lids down over them, and thinking back, he couldn't quite be sure what he had seen there. A girl like this, you never could be sure.

They were silent again, and he kept his eyes down on his glass on the table top. He knew what she wanted to ask, what she knew already before she even had to ask. He moved the glass, set it here and there, precisely, as if he were building an elaborate pattern with it.

"How is he?" Mary said again.

He knew what she meant, when she asked it this time, and he thought a little before he answered. "Well, he's still in a kinda daze, you know how he would be. It all happened so quick. And what he went through there for a few minutes was no picnic. He took a beating. I don't see how he gets over it so quick. And then it's all awful—awful—new to him. Having to depend on other people to look out for him, getting caught off base the way he is, being on the run now.

Then, too, I guess he always figured he was a wise guy, and now he isn't so sure. That's hard on him." The kid folded his fingers up over his fist again, and spoke carefully without looking at her. "Of course, he hates like hell to think of leaving his—family and everything. Oh, I don't know, I guess you know the way he feels better than I do. There isn't any use me trying to tell you about how he feels."

Mary leaned back in the seat and followed a spiral of smoke away from the table with her eyes. "Any hard feelings?" she said, her voice even and flat.

"I guess you know without having to ask that one either," the kid said, looking at her quick out of the corners of his eyes.

"Yeah," she said. "I don't have to ask that one." And then her face closed up.

God, this is sure one screwy setup, he kept thinking. I never come across one just like it. With a setup like this, somebody is bound to get hurt bad, maybe two or three people. A woman like this is bound to make trouble wherever she happens. How can she be cool like this, a million miles away? You could sleep with her, you could beat her up, you could maul her around, and you wouldn't get a bit nearer than I am right now, sitting across the table from her. What makes her be like this?

"What does he expect me to do?" Mary said abruptly. "Does he think I can fix things up here? What does he want?"

Hell, the kid thought before he spoke, here we go!

"Nothing. He knows you can't do anything. He said you couldn't. He doesn't blame you for none of it. He says he was dumb, that was all. He doesn't expect you to do anything. He just wanted me to come over here and tell you where he was and get some dough if you could manage it. He—" he took a deep breath. "He said to tell you that—he'd be seeing you any day now, that he had to make a call out your way."

This time the kid saw it for sure, something moved and was alive in her eyes for a second.

"I was afraid of that," she said simply.

She picked up her purse from the table and opened it and took a wad of bills out of the coin purse and began to fold them automatically in her hand.

The kid watched her slender, unsteady fingers, and said at last, "He's plenty sore. He's not the kind to take something like this laying down."

"Tell him I said not to come," she said, without conviction in her voice. "Tell him to use his head . . ."

"I'll tell him," the kid said, "but I wouldn't guarantee anything."

She handed him the little packet of bills along the table top, and he slid them away into his pocket.

She closed her purse, and shook her head at the waiter who came up to the booth. "Unless you want another?"

"No," he said. "I don't even like the liquor in this town. Thanks, just the same."

After the waiter was gone, he put out his cigarette in the tray. "Well, I guess this takes care of everything. He'll get the dough tonight, all right. I'm glad you think I got an honest face. I—I—take kind of an interest in the big guy, he . . ." The kid couldn't think of anything to say. This was pretty bad for her, he could tell, not from how she acted on the outside, but he could feel it.

"Tell him," she said suddenly, "tell him I said . . ." She stopped and her lips quivered a little, but the rest of her face was still and detached. She stopped without saying what the kid was to tell him. Should I just get up and get to hell out of here and leave her, or what, he was thinking.

He looked at her, and then he looked away quickly, to his hands locked together in front of him, and then he looked back to her again in a minute.

She had gotten control of herself. Her mouth was still, her face wasn't strained, it was only very tired. She spoke softly, in her low husky voice, without hardly moving her lips. "Tell him that I'm going to marry Lew."

The kid wasn't surprised, as if he had known all along that that was what she would say. He couldn't get any reaction to it. It didn't seem to have any less meaning, or any more, than any of the rest of this mess.

She stood up suddenly in the booth, at the end of the table. "Good-bye," she said. "Thanks for—everything. I guess we both talk the same kind of language . . ." But she didn't walk away yet.

The kid stood up too, and he didn't know what to say or do. He felt sick. He couldn't think of anything to say to her that would make it any easier. I know what she's got in her mind, he kept thinking. She's really come to the end of something now, and she knows it. What did she ever do to get a kick in the face like this, or what did he do, or her boy friend or any of them? The sweat stood out on the kid's forehead and on his upper lip, because he knew what this was meaning to her, the moment that she walked out of here, it was like the big guy himself was sitting here at the table and she was saying good-bye to him for God knows how long, and maybe never to see him again. The only thing he could think of to do for her was to somehow cut this short. He did it without thinking about it. He went through that funny set of motions that the big guy had showed him. Rode a punch that wasn't there, ducked his head, and feinted with his left, and stepped in and touched her soft and quick on the chin with his right doubled. And she repeated the pattern after him, quick, in caricature of half-formed gestures. Touched her fist to his chin with her eyes soft and shining, and then she smiled at him, her sudden lovely, childish smile, and before he knew it she was gone.

"My God, my God!" he said. "Hey! Waiter!" and he sat down again to the table, and shoved his glass out to the edge. For once, maybe, I got it right, there at the end . . .

9

LATE THAT NIGHT, THE LITTLE DARK-HAIRED FELLOW they called the kid climbed the stairs of Mungo's white, painted air-conditioned beer garden, and went in the second door to the left off the hall. But he found the room dark and empty. He turned around and went down the stairs again. He moved swiftly and noiselessly. He had been drinking too much maybe, but he didn't feel it, and he didn't show it at all.

He went out into the bright lights and the smoky, noisy interior of the beer garden and sure enough there at one of the tables in the back sat Kenny. Kenny was sharing the table with a thin consumptive-looking Negro with an incessant, deep, hacking cough. The Negro was drunk, and talking to Kenny. Kenny sat lounged back in his chair with his head resting against the wall. He was wearing light summer trousers, and a very clean, fine white shirt. Just as the kid came up behind him, he was giving his sore arm a rest, trying to roll a cigarette in one hand.

"Oh, hell!" the kid said. He threw a package of cigarettes down on the table in front of Kenny, and pulled a chair out and turned it around and sat down on it with his knees straddling the back.

For a minute Kenny's face looked excited and eager at the sight of him. "Naw," he said casually. "I'm getting the hang of this, no kiddin'. I could use my other hand okay, if I wanted to. Knew a guy once that could roll 'em with one hand so you couldn't even tell the difference. It's a nice trick, all right." He kept rolling the tobacco in the paper with his fingers as he talked, rolling it together firm and tight and even, his face blank and serious with concentration. He got the tobacco all packed together and then he rolled it out to one edge of the paper, and pulled the paper tight across it. "Now if the damn paper don't tear . . ."

"Pal, you going stir-crazy . . ."

Kenny pulled the paper tight, the look of infinite concentration on his face, and then swiftly and expertly he rolled it up, and licked the other edge of the paper down.

"There you are," he said triumphantly, tapping the end of the cigarette against his thumbnail. "You couldn't tell this one from a regular. Now all I gotta do is figure out some way to put cork tips on 'em . . ."

The Negro began to talk a little louder, and still incoherently. Kenny leaned over a minute and listened to him and then he said impatiently, "Naw, sit still. Stick around awhile."

"Miss me today?" the kid said.

Kenny grinned wide across his face. "I had company. The Doc came the last time this morning. Then I set around and talked to Mungo most the afternoon."

"What was eating Mungo?"

"The damnedest thing . . ." Kenny stretched his whole great body back in the chair leisurely and comfortably. "We got to talking and come to find out Mungo used to be with a gang that used to float liquor outa my home town when I was just a kid—prohibition. Hell, we got to talking most of the afternoon. I wasn't nothing but a kid, but I got to know all them guys, used to hang around with them when they brought the stuff in. I was the only one outside the mob that knew right where the cache was. Ain't that the nuts? I never did know what become of the boys . . ."

"Old home week," the kid said. "It's a small world, huh, pal?"

Kenny's face turned serious, shadowed momentarily. "I dunno. Sometimes I figure it is a hell of a lot too big, and then I get to thinking it ain't half big enough. I dunno."

The kid took the roll of bills out of his pocket silently and slid them under Kenny's hand on the table.

Kenny closed his hand on them and smoothed them in his fingers. His face turned tense and blank. He coughed a little, his habitual, delicate little cough, and kept smoothing the bills with his fingers.

The kid signaled a waiter with his hand, and in a minute the waiter came and set the bottle of beer and the empty glass down in front of him.

The Negro kept on talking to himself, something about winter coming, and the cold rains.

After awhile Kenny said without looking at him, "You saw her, huh?"

"Yeah."

Kenny hunched his big shoulders and then straightened them out again, the muscles rippling under the white shirt. "How was she?"

The kid looked at his own short blunt fingers closed tight around the glass. "If looks got anything to do with it, she was feeling swell. You shoulda warned me, pal."

Kenny laughed a little, mirthlessly, ending his laughter with his gentle cough. "What was she wearing?"

The kid studied his fingers carefully. "Some kind of white dress with blue on the front of it. It had short sleeves and a real short full skirt. All the stuff to go with it. She looked—swell. . . ."

"Yeah," Kenny said with his voice warm and tender, so low the kid hardly heard him over the noise and music.

"Yeah," the kid said, looking at Kenny.

Kenny looked back at him, and his face turned suddenly hard and sullen. "You tell her what I said?"

The kid nodded. "Sure."

Kenny was silent then, and looked away. The Negro had stopped talking, too. He was leaning over the corner of the table staring with glazed eyes like one hypnotized at the old battered red upright piano shoved back in the corner.

The kid emptied his beer at a gulp, and filled the glass again.

"She said I was to tell you . . ." He stopped and cleared his throat a little. "She said to tell you she was gonna marry Lew."

He didn't look at Kenny. The light was just right, so he could see the tip of Kenny's cigarette reflected on his glass, and he saw it turn bright red as Kenny drew on it hard.

Over at a table in the front of the room two guys were talking loud. They stood up suddenly and one chair fell over. A couple of waiters got there at the same time. They all milled around a little and then one of the guys left, jamming his hat down on his head as he went out the door. The other guy stood and talked to the waiters a minute, waving his arms, and then he sat down at the table and picked up his glass again. The waiters faded away.

The Negro got up from the table unsteadily and weaved over to the piano. He dragged a chair away from a table and sat down in front of it. He lifted the dusty cover and sat still, staring solemnly and fixedly at the keys.

Finally the kid said, "You don't need to think it's just you, pal. This woman stuff ends up with a kick in the teeth for just about everybody."

Kenny said, "He's been wanting to marry her for a long time. I'm glad . . ." He didn't finish that sentence.

The kid waved down a waiter again for more beer.

Kenny spoke suddenly with his voice rough and unsteady. "I'm all washed up. I'm gonna beat it outa here tomorrow."

"Back there?" the kid asked carefully.

Kenny's face looked almost surprised. "Hell, no! I mean I'm all washed up. I'm gonna get to hell outa this part of the country."

The Negro got up suddenly, lurching on his feet, and removed a flimsy piece of board from the front of the piano over the keyboard. He laid it down on the floor carefully and then he went back to his chair and sat down. He had a long spasm of coughing, and after that he just sat still staring into the depths of the strings and panels in the dusty interior of that worn-out piano.

Kenny slumped down in his chair. He put his hand over his eyes as if the light hurt them.

The kid finished his beer and set his glass down and got up from his chair all in one fluid motion. "I gotta go see Mungo," he said to Kenny. "I'll tell a waiter you could use some liquor maybe."

Kenny did not answer him or look up. He dropped his hand onto Kenny's shoulder momentarily and then he turned away. He walked slowly, with the swagger in his walk, and his head up and his black hair shining even in the blue mist of smoke that dimmed the light in the room. He went out of the door to the back.

After a few minutes the waiter came with the liquor. Kenny sat up on his chair and poured himself a series of stiff whiskies. He drank them rapidly one after another, without paying any attention to anything or anybody.

The Negro was still sitting in front of the old red piano. His back was hunched over, his face close to the keys. His bony hands were stretched out wide, and sometimes he touched the keys softly without striking them. He kept whispering to the keys lovingly, caressing them with his long fingers and speaking to them affectionately.

Sometime a little later, the waiter stopped at the table again. This time he handed Kenny a folded sheet of white paper. Kenny unfolded it with clumsy, uncertain fingers. There were words typewritten on the paper. He had to look at it a long time before his eyes would focus right and make words out of the letters, and before his mind would make any sense out of the words.

"I'm keeping a date with a freight train tonight. I talked to Mungo. After closing time he's going to drive into Chicago on business. He knows a nice road over the state line that nobody else

*knows about. Chicago is a nice town to leave. Go ahead and get
drunk. So long, pal. Some time when you hear a train whistle at
night you can pray for me if you want to.*

"*P.S. It's a small world. I might be seeing you.*"

Kenny finished the liquor in his glass, and poured the next one
straight and kept on looking at the piece of paper in his hand.

A big heavy guy came out of the men's room and stood still just
outside the door. He began to laugh uproariously. Everybody in that
part of the room twisted their heads around over their shoulders to
look, everybody except Kenny.

The big guy kept laughing and he was pointing his finger toward
the old red piano in the corner. "Come on dere," he shouted, "give
us some a dat boogie woogie." He laughed again uproariously.

The Negro had passed out at the piano. His head rested against
the ledge over the keyboard, his knees slumped underneath, and one
of his arms lay limp over the old dirty black and white keys.

Kenny finished his drink at a gulp and poured another one
straight. He licked at his lips a little and his eyes were blank and
unseeing. In his big sweaty hand he still held tight to the crumpled
piece of paper.

10

THE VEECHES SAT DOWN TO A LATE SUPPER WITH
the last rays of the sun slanting through the dirty streaked window over the table. Molly set the coffee pot down, and lowered her
bulk onto her chair wearily. "Sam Veech, you get on out here to the
table now," she yelled. "Lord's sakes, go to a lot of trouble around
here to get vittles on the table and then folks won't come to the table
and eat."

Josette and Carl were already in their places. Molly pushed the
potato dish and the bread plate around in front of her impatiently.

Sam appeared in the door from the living room with the newspaper still in his hands.

"You just put that paper down now, and come on here to the table," Molly scolded.

Sam dropped the paper obediently, and went to the mirror over the sink and slicked his hair down neatly before he sat down.

While Molly poured the strong hot coffee, Jen came in, yawning, and the bright blonde hair done up on curlers on the top of her head. "Hi," she said brightly to nobody in particular. "Thanks for calling me to supper. Looks like nobody around here cares whether I eat or not."

"Well, sir," Sam said indignantly, "all you do around here is eat. It's getting so you won't turn over a hand to help your mother and Josie do nothing around here. All you want to do is sleep all day and go chasing off to dance all night, with that skinny, half-baked feller from up to Ashbury. It's getting so . . ."

"Oh, can it!" Jen said as she slipped into her place. "Somebody always gotta be the goat around here. Now Kenny's gone, looks like I'm it."

"Well, sir," Molly said judiciously, "it seems to me, young woman, that it wouldn't hurt you a bit to take a hold and do your share of the work around here, long as you expect to live here with your fambly and have us feed and clothe you . . ."

Carl paused from his rapid eating long enough to insinuate himself into the conversation. "Boy, that is sure some boy friend you got! Boy, that guy ain't even what I call half-baked, he's . . ."

"Where's Climie?" Jen said sweetly as she passed the platter of cold meat to Josette.

Josette frowned a little. "He went to Ashbury this afternoon to see about a job."

"Honest, I don't see why you kids don't just go on W.P.A. and be done with it," Jen said.

"Clim has a very good chance of getting a job any day now," Josette said with dignity. "A friend of his father's is a foreman up there in one of the shops, and he told Clim himself that it would be just a matter of time before he got him in up there."

"Yeah, sure, just a matter of time, and what I mean, time," Jen said flippantly.

Josette folded her lips together tightly, and Carl burst out into loud laughter.

"Well, it seems to me," Molly said innocently, with her eyes snapping, "that Clim has took to doin' a lot of jobhunting nights up there to Ashbury lately. Why, he ain't been home here till way late at night all this week. Lord, if he was a husband of mine, I believe I'd . . ."

Sam began to tremble with anger. "When Kenny was to home a-tearing off to Ashbury every single night and never getting back till morning, that was different, wasn't it? That was all right. Kenny was a-hunting himself a job, and that was all right . . ."

"Lord, that's a different thing altogether," Molly said. "Kenny wasn't no married man with a wife to support and everything. It just seems to me that if I was Josie I'd begin to wonder, that's all, the way he goes ramming around up there night after night and . . ."

"I guess I can run my own business," Josette said. "I guess if I'm not worrying about Clim, the rest of you don't need to start worrying about him. And you don't need to think that Clim likes you one bit better than you like him either. He'll be just as glad to get a job and get out of here as I will, or as you'll be to have us go, so there."

"My, you don't need to get so mad and uppity about it," Molly said. "We're your fambly, and I guess if we want to be interested in your business that's all right. And you don't have to tell us that Clim Hawkins don't like us. Lord, we know that, all right. He's acted just as snotty as he can around here. We're good enough for him to live off from, and hand him out his three square meals a day and that's all."

Jen licked marmalade out of a spoon blissfully. "Guess who I saw last night? Pat Thompson. You won't believe this, but honest to God, he got promoted again up there to the shops. Ain't that the limit? Gee, I never saw a boy like him . . ."

Molly's eyes kept snapping with suppressed humor. "Pat is an awful fine boy," she said. "There is one boy who's gonna get ahead, you just mark my words. There ain't gonna be no stopping him. Why, it wouldn't surprise me none if some day . . ."

Sam tried awkwardly to stem this tide of attack away from Josette. "Ernie coming over here tonight? I thought Ernie said he was coming over tonight?"

"Why, I don't know . . ." Molly said. "I can't remember him saying . . ."

"Ernie won't be here tonight," Jen said. "He'll be taking Leatha down to the street dance downtown."

Molly put her fork down on her plate in amazement. "Lord, is tonight the street dance?"

"Sure," Jen said. "This is Wednesday night. This is the last band concert this summer."

"For Lord's sakes," Molly said. "I'd like to know where this summer has gone to. It just don't seem possible, does it, that this summer has just about gone already? Why, I can't make it seem right that's all, where the time goes to. Why, it don't seem no time at all that the summer was just a-starting, and I was getting the garden in, and setting the plants outdoors, the first warm weather, and now . . ."

"The days are getting shorter, you can tell," Sam said pessimistically. "And it's getting kind of chilly nights and mornings. I can feel it in my back and legs, let me tell you. It ain't gonna be long before them fall rains set in, and that's the worst time of the whole year for my rheumatism . . ."

"Whatcha mean, it still seems like summer," Carl said impatiently to his mother. "Ain't I started back to school already? Whatcha think, I go to school in the summertime?"

"I hate to see the cold weather come," Molly said broodingly. "Seems like I hate to see it come worse every year. House all shut up—and fixin' fires and everything . . ."

Dorothy came in the back door silently and slid into her place at the table.

"Well, sir, looks like you got here just in time," her grandmother said fondly. "Lord, in a few minutes more these fellers woulda had everything all et up. What you been doin' so late, sweetie?"

"Playin'," Dorothy said cautiously.

"Her Ma don't want her out running the streets like this till almost dark," Sam said accusingly.

"Oughta send her to bed without any supper," Carl said.

Dorothy looked at him obliquely. "Carl stole my money," she said.

Carl exploded with anger, pushing his plate away from him on the table. "My God, Ma, you gonna let her go around saying things like that all the time? She's the worst liar I ever saw in my life. I like to know what you think she's going to grow up into, lying around here all the time. My God, lie, lie, lie, that's all she does. She never told the truth in her life if she could help it. I can't stand it the way she goes around here lying all the time. Now her mother's got married, why in hell can't she take her away from here?"

"You shut your mouth, Carl Veech and hush up that swearin'," Molly said. "That hotel down there would be a fine place to bring up a kid, wouldn't it?" Molly smiled at Dorothy fondly, and made her voice warm and affectionate as she spoke to the little girl. "You're Grandma's girl, ain't you, Dor'thy? Lord's sakes, I'd like to know what they think Grandma'd do around here without her girl, that's what I'd like to know. Your Ma said I could keep you just as long as you was a good girl, that's why Grandma wants you to be careful about telling stories when you know they ain't so. You gonna be careful, ain't you, honey-bunch?"

"My God! My God!" Carl marveled in his despair.

"Honestly, I think it's just terrible myself, the way she lies all the time," Josette said. "There is something wrong with a child when they lie all the time like she does, it isn't natural. Somebody ought to do something . . ."

"Somebody oughta lick the pants off her," Jen said.

Dorothy looked up slyly from one to another of them, delighted by the attention and concern she was commanding.

"No," Josette said seriously. "It never does any good to whip a child. You have to reason with them and—and . . ."

Jen laughed delightedly. "Will you listen to Josie! She must have been reading the books on bringing up kids. You know what it sounds like to me. Boy, I been waiting for the great news. Soon I am to be an auntie . . ."

"Oh, shut up," Josette said.

Jen shoved her chair back from the table, finished her coffee at a gulp and pattered across the floor in dance steps. She contorted her body in weird rhythms and sang in an exaggerated, hot husky voice:

"Just Climie and you,
With nothing to do.

But have a baby or two—
Sure must—be—Heaven . . ."

They all laughed at her together, Molly and Carl and Dorothy and even Sam. Amid their laughter, Josette got up from the table and left the room, and they heard her quick angry steps on the stairs. And then Jen joined in their laughter too, uproariously.

Molly stopped laughing at last and wiped her eyes. "It ain't no laughin' matter," she said absently, "but I guess it ain't no matter if we laugh." She took the fork up from her plate and impaled on it a great mushy chunk of pickled cucumber from the dish in front of her, and put it into her mouth. "Them always used to be Kenny's favorite kind of pickles," she said wistfully as she poured herself another cup of lukewarm coffee.

Molly drank her coffee silently, her eyes turned toward the west window. Carl had already disappeared from the kitchen, and Sam had retreated back to the porch with his paper. Only Dorothy remained with her at the table eating the cold greasy food.

"Getting kind of dark," Molly said at last. "Oughta turned the light on before we started eating. Bet you can't see to find your mouth."

Dorothy laughed mirthlessly and immoderately.

"Looks like them girls, neither one of 'em, intend to do any dishes around here," Molly said. "Well, I sure as the world ain't going to do no dishes tonight. They can just set here on the table for all a me. Save 'em for seed."

Molly hoisted her heavy body up out of the chair.

"You go right on eating now, Dorothy, just take your time. Grandma's going out on the porch a minute and get kinda cooled off before I change my dress to go uptown . . ."

She went out through the house to the front porch, where Sam swung back and forth in the squeaky porch swing in the dusk with the newspaper in his hands.

"Move over," Molly said.

Sam slid along in the swing obediently, and Molly sat down in one end of it, sagging it down with her weight.

A stream of automobiles was already pouring past the house,

bound for downtown and the annual festivities. The street lights had just come on, and made golden misty spots here and there in the dusk, and over the other side of town the sabre blade of light from the air beacon swung back and forth through the air.

"Looks like there is gonna be a crowd downtown tonight, all right," Sam said mildly.

"Lord, yes. The way they're coming in here already," Molly said. "Can't make it seem possible that the summer's over. I don't know where the time goes."

"Sure goes flying right along," Sam said. "Especially when you begin to get along in years the way me and you are . . ."

Molly was in a soft mood of gentle nostalgic melancholy that was not altogether unpleasant to her. "This summer sure seen a lot of changes in this fambly," she said plaintively. "Mr. Higgins gone, and Kenny—and the girls getting married . . .

"Say," Molly said suddenly, making her voice confidential, "you suppose that Hawkins is stepping out on Josie already? Lord, it looks funny to me, all right, the way he keeps chasing up there to Ashbury or some place night after night. That feller has got an awful shifty deceitful look. You figure that's what he's up to, and him and Josie just married the way they are?"

"Well, sir, I don't know nothing about it," Sam said. "I'd a-give most anything though if she hadn't never married him. Him just a-coming in here and living here like he intended to do it all the rest of his life. You wouldn'ta caught Pat Thompson pulling no trick like that. Once he got married, he'd be out earning money to support his family the way he should . . ."

"You know," Molly said meditatively, "I just believe I'll talk to Ernie about it, and see if he's heard any stories about Hawkins around town. I'll just bet you a dollar that Hawkins is up to something, and him and Josie just married like they are, too. The next chance I get I'm gonna talk to Ernie about it, and see if he's heard anything . . ."

Sam squeaked the swing back and forth.

"You hear about that Hammet girl?" Molly asked. "They claim she's got to git married. She goes up there to high school, you know. Come to find out the teachers got to suspecting something, and one of them took her over to the doctor's herself, and sure enough that was what was wrong with her. I ain't a bit surprised, though. She always been a little toughie. And you mark my words, that younger sister of hers will be getting into trouble too some of these days. That little Ruthie's just like her, a regular little toughie, chasing after the boys ever since she was big enough to run around. It sure beats everything. You'da thought their folks woulda straightened them girls up, wouldn't you? Lord, I guess if they don't care what becomes a their own kids, it ain't anybody else's lookout."

"That little Ruthie is kind of a nice-looking little girl," Sam said in mild defense. "I don't figure she's any worse acting than a whole lot of others . . ."

"Looks ain't everything," Molly said. "You mark my words now, she'll be getting into trouble pretty soon. Say, I bet they're going to have an awful time about that oldest one, though. She's been foolin' around with so many different fellers that it wouldn't surprise me none if she didn't know herself. You remember that Winkle girl last year and all that muss? Why, they had to go to court and take blood tests and everything before they finally got her married to the Gillis boy."

The swing squeaked in the darkness for a little while. "Say," Sam said suddenly, "they was telling uptown today they was some drugstore gonna come in here in that vacant building the other side of the meat market where Herb Sweet's grocery store used to be before he had to go outa business."

"For Lord's sakes, I don't believe it! Like to know who'd be fool enough to come in here with another drugstore. One drugstore's enough in a town this size, an' the one we got don't hardly do any business at all, everybody chasing up there to Ashbury to buy stuff at them cut rates."

Dorothy came out onto the porch, banging the screen behind her noisily. "You got the paper out here?" she said, peering at them in the gloom.

"You git enough to eat, Dor'thy?" her grandmother said fondly.

"Here's the paper, but mind you don't tear it now, or get it all pulled apart and lost . . ."

Sam watched Dorothy vanish with the paper regretfully. "Hadn't got around to get it all read before dark."

Molly yawned deeply. "I like to look over the births and deaths and marriage licenses, but it ain't more'n one day a week around here I ever get a chance to look at a paper."

"It sure looks pretty bad," Sam said gloomily. "Now they finally got that war started over there in Europe it won't be long before they'll have us mixed up in it, you just wait and see."

"All you want to talk about is war," Molly said impatiently. "What good you think it's gonna do to talk about it or even think about it? There ain't nothing we can do about it. Them big fellers in the government will get us into it when they get ready and that's all there is to it. I don't like to talk about it at all."

A train came through then and drowned out whatever reply Sam might have been disposed to make to her. It was a passenger train, a short dotted row of bright lights, the violent sound, the whistle blowing, and then it was gone.

And as it went through, Molly was looking away up the street, the sidewalk losing itself under the big trees. A man was walking along toward town slowly, and when she first saw the dark silhouette of him, her heart lifted up, as it used to when she first glimpsed Kenny coming home like that. She was suddenly overcome with an unbearable longing for Kenny.

Once the train was gone, she hoisted herself up out of the swing. "Kind of chilly out here," she said uncertainly. "Guess I'll go on in and git my dress changed and go uptown there for awhile. I kind of like to see the people."

"Gitting along toward fall, all right," Sam said, his voice mixing with the sound of the screen door slamming behind her.

The twins were in Mary's old room that Jen had now fallen heir to, when they heard their mother's heavy tread upon the stairs.

Jen was sprawled across the bed, scantily clad, her curls in disorder around her face, just as she had taken them from the curlers. Josette sat straight and prim in Mary's big chair in front of the window.

"Don't tell me Ma's going downtown to the dance!" Jen said.

"They'll probably have a table of bingo going, for the older folks," Josette said.

Jen stretched her body and shivered. "You wanta shut that window, Josie? It's kinda chilly in here . . ."

Josette got up and lowered the window obediently. "If you'd put on some clothes instead of lopping around all naked you wouldn't be cold."

Jen blew smoke rings ceilingwards. "Oh sure, sure, sure!"

"Are you going to the dance downtown?"

"Hell, no!" Jen said. "You think Jimmy and I go around wasting ourselves with the hicks? We're in the bigtime now. My God, you can wear out your feet, say nothing about your shoes scraping around down there on that cement with corn meal on it, or whatever it is. 'Sides, they ain't gonna have no orchestra that amounts to nothing, and just about every other dance a square dance . . ."

"I don't see what you want to keep chasing around to dance contests for. I don't see what you think it's getting you," Josette said.

Jen studied the ashy tip of her cigarette curiously. "I dunno. It makes something to do around here. Keeps you busy, that's all."

"Are you in love with Jimmy?" Josette asked directly.

Jen squirmed around onto her stomach and ran her hand through the tight yellow curls. "No. I wish I was. Jimmy ain't in love with me either. It's getting so that now wherever we are, once we get through dancing we mix up with other people, set at different tables and everything. It's just business with us, that's all. We happen to dance perfect together, so we just go around and dance together. Oh, we neck a little and stuff like that, but neither one of us gives a damn." She sighed profoundly.

Josette fanned the smoke from Jen's cigarette away from her with her hand.

"You goin' downtown?" Jen asked her.

Josette shook her head. "No. Not unless . . ." She stopped without finishing.

"You mean not unless Climie darling comes home and wants to go down, huh?"

Josette did not answer her.

"Honest kid, you're a sucker. Take it from me. I knew Climie about three years longer than you did. I mean, knew him well. I know he's cute, sure, something you'd like to take home and put on the piano maybe, but nothing if you was in your right mind you'd ever want to marry up with."

Josette smoothed the bright cretonne cover over the arm of the big chair. "I don't want to talk about it," she said coldly.

"Say, Josie," Jen said after a minute.

"Yes?"

"Promise you won't get mad?"

"Mad at what?"

"At what I'm gonna talk to you about. It ain't none of my business, remember. I just promised him I'd tell you."

"For heaven's sakes, what are you talking about?" Josette asked.

"Well, I saw Pat last night, and we talked for a while and—now wait, and listen—please, Josie."

"All right," Josette said, her face tight and strained. "But it doesn't make any difference to me what he had to say to you. I should think you'd know more than to sit around and talk with him about me . . ."

"Well, you don't have to be so—so—personal about it, do you?" Jen said. "Any girl would be crazy to know what he had to say, just for the hell of it, if she was you."

"All right, go ahead!"

"Well, we talked a little, and naturally we couldn't help talking about you, and I didn't say a thing, honest, I didn't. I just said that you seemed to like Clim a lot, and that you kids seemed to get along swell, and stuff like that, honest, Josie. You know I wouldn't say nothing behind your back you wouldn't want me to, don't you?"

"All right, what did he say?" Josette asked tonelessly.

"Well, he seemed to be awful crazy to hear about you, how you was and stuff like that. He didn't seem all broke up or nothing; 'course I could tell he felt real bad and all that, but he wasn't all shot to hell the way some kids would have been. He got to talking about you being married to Clim, and he said he couldn't get it out of his head that you didn't know what you was doing when you done it, that you was just all nervous and unstrung and run off down there with Clim without thinking it over or anything."

"I suppose you sided right in with him."

"Josie, I didn't say a thing either way, honest. Well, Pat kept talking like that, and then he asked me to tell you this. This is just what he wanted me to tell you, honest. He said he had quite a little money in the bank, and he didn't feel like it was too late yet for you and him to get together, and he'll be glad to pay the bills if you'll go ahead and get a divorce from Clim."

Josette's face tightened with anger and she sat stiff and straight in Mary's chair.

Jen looked at her anxiously. "Josie, take it from me, you got something there. For God's sakes, go ahead and let him do it. Please."

Josette got up out of the chair. "I don't want to talk about it," she said stonily.

Something in her voice silenced Jen. "Okay," she said, with her face sullen and pouting. "Okay. So what the hell, it don't make no difference to me one way or another. Many happy returns of the day!"

"You're getting so you talk more like Kenny every day you live," Josette said disapprovingly.

"So maybe I do, so what?"

"Well, it just doesn't sound very ladylike, that's all."

"I never claimed I was a lady." Jen crawled off from the bed, and stretched her arms high above her head. "If I couldn't be the kind of a lady Mary is, I wouldn't be any kind, and I couldn't be like Mary if I tried a hundred years, so—skip it!"

"A fine lady Mary is, getting married to Lew Lentz after she lived with him for years, and it getting in the papers and everything. I think it was a disgrace . . ."

Jen laughed merrily. "You think it was a disgrace for Mary to get married to Lew instead of just going on living with him?"

"You know what I mean," Josette said. "And a fine lady Mary is, just walking out of here and leaving Dorothy as if she—she—didn't belong to anybody."

"Well, she couldn't take Dorothy down to the hotel very well, you know that yourself, just like Ma said, and—oh—I don't know." Jen went over to the bureau and rumpled up her curls in front of the glass. "Honest, I can't get used to living here in Mary's room yet, it seems so funny . . ."

Josette pulled the window shade down to the sill thoughtfully.

"You know, it was funny, Mary marrying Lew Lentz all of a sudden, the way she did. I just wonder. I wonder if Kenny's getting into trouble and going away had anything to do with it."

Jen studied a fancied blotch on the soft skin of her forehead minutely. "I don't know. Why should it?"

"I don't know," Josette said. "But I just wonder, that's all."

Jen straightened up and considered the idea momentarily. "You know," she said slowly, "I think maybe you got something there!"

"What do you mean?"

"Oh, nothing. It just kind of fits in with a feeling I always had about Mary and Ken . . ."

"What do you mean a feeling you always had about . . ."

Jen flung herself across the room suddenly to the clothes closet and sent clothes flying out of it onto the bed helter-skelter. "Well, I gotta get dressed up all beautiful. Who knows, tonight I might meet a great big beautiful man with a job and an automobile and he might take just one good look at me and say, 'Baby, I'm nuts about you,' and I might take just one good look at him and say . . ."

"You don't really believe that, do you?" Josette asked curiously.

"I sure do!" Jen said. "At this stage of the game, I better."

She dumped a dark sheer dress on a wire hanger onto the bed and danced about the room, viewing herself appreciatively in the mirror.

"Someday he'll come along," she sang,
"The man I love—
And he'll be big and strong
The man I love . . ."

11

CARL STALKED AROUND AMONG THE PEOPLE DOWN-town, profoundly bored. He did not want to be here, but there was no other place for him to go.

The entire block of Main Street was roped off. At one end of it, under bright electric bulbs, a bingo game had been established, the incessant monotonous noise of the callers, the display of gaudy blankets and cheap table lamps and hams. At the other end, the local orchestra had taken its place on a wooden platform and dancers were already choking that part of the cement covered with cornmeal to facilitate the dancing. Onlookers formed a vast ring around the dancers, three deep, and small children ran and slid in the cornmeal at the corners of the impromptu dance floor, and were threatened constantly by officials, dancers and parents.

Carl himself did not dance and took no interest in it. Giggling high-school girls who looked first at Carl and then wistfully at the dancers and then back to Carl again, quick and sideways, might have saved themselves the trouble. He looked carelessly at the dancers moving fast and jerkily to the uneven music. Down at the far end in the shadows he saw Ernie, impeccably dressed as usual, his panama hat shoved back on his head, dancing with the very blonde, thick-bodied Leatha Owens, holding her tightly in his arms, dancing determinedly and ungracefully. Carl turned away in disgust. Dancing always seemed to him to be a peculiarly revolting public exhibition of something that he firmly believed should be performed in private. The bingo game did not lure him. He knew very well that his mother would be found there, and quite likely Dorothy hanging around as well. His father he had seen already, leaning against the wall in front of the poolroom, talking earnestly about politics and the war in Europe.

The music stopped suddenly, and then began again with a change in tempo. The orchestra was playing a waltz and the dancing space was jammed full with the hurried addition of older people, calling to each other delightedly, older people, and country people, gray-headed men with rolled shirt sleeves, gray-haired women in low-heeled shoes and limp, sweaty, unfashionable dresses.

Carl decided that he could stand no more of it. He turned his back on the energetic and rather proficient waltzers. He came up to the beer garden and someone clapped him on the shoulder heartily. "Hi, kid!" It was the little guy, Smitty, whom Carl particularly detested.

"Hi," Carl said distantly, looking away from Smitty immediately into the crowd, hoping that he was giving the appearance of someone entirely preoccupied with searching out some one person out of all this mob.

Smitty was entirely pleased with the world, due partially perhaps to the festive occasion, but largely due to the beer that he had been drinking. "Been down looking 'em over yet?" he asked Carl cheerfully. "I'm goin' down there and pick me a nice little young tender one all for myself.

"Look," Smitty said mysteriously, lowering his voice. It was a key case that Smitty held in his hand, with dangling automobile keys hanging out of it, shining in the dim light. "I got the keys to Joe's car," Smitty said. "He's got it parked out back in the nice dark quiet alley. Now all I gotta do is go down there and pick myself a nice little young tender one!" He nudged Carl in the ribs and wrinkled up his little monkey face with laughter.

Carl wanted only to get away from this person, and he started to edge off into the crowd again. Smitty slapped him on the shoulder once again. He sighed deeply. "It ain't the same old town without Kenny helling around here, is it?" Smitty said wistfully.

Carl started to cross the street toward the façade of the hotel and then he changed his mind. He felt panicky and hemmed in by the crowd and he thought to take refuge at last in a booth in the back of the drugstore. He retraced his steps down the street again, and he came face to face with someone who gave him a shock. He stood stock-still in the surging, pushing mass of people that choked the sidewalk and stared at her, open-mouthed. It was Rita Sibley, supported by two crutches, a smiling grotesque ghost of herself. He had not even realized that she had been released from the hospital. She hobbled now among the crowd like a veritable ghost, with a ripple of whispering on all sides of her. She kept a smile on the scarred inhumanly masklike face, and carried her head high. Occasionally she stopped to talk to someone, and Carl was horrified that even her voice was different, scarred also, artificial, toneless and inhuman. She looked him full in the face, and for a second Carl was afraid that she meant to come near him, speak to him, perhaps. He did not wait to see. He fled, elbowing through the crowd, to his refuge in the last booth in the back of the drugstore. He ordered a lemon Coke and waited, with his shoulders hunched over, his heart pounding and his whole body shaking.

A kind of fancy took hold of him. Kenny was gone now, without a trace, without a word, as if he never had existed; and now this horrible inhuman thing that was Rita Sibley walked the streets instead, a ghoulish symbol of what Kenny's life had been here. Carl admired his own versatility of mind that had produced such an imaginative idea, but at the same time it terrified him.

When the waiter brought his Coke at last he threw away the straws and drank it straight down, chewing on the chipped ice impatiently. The sound of the voices and music surged up like waves against the walls of Carl's booth. Carl felt indescribably lonely and miserable. Must he always be alone like this, and unhappy? he thought. Must all his life be exactly like this night, with the sounds of happy, noisy people all around him, and he alone some place apart from them, unhappy and afraid and lonely? If it was, then he wished that he was dead. What was the use of living like this? How could he live, anyway, when he couldn't endure this town another hour or day, and could conceive of no way in the world for him to make a living in any other place.

He envied all the people outside profoundly and childishly, only he, Carl Veech, of all the world, alone, unloved and unhappy. With one of his rare flashes of insight that struck out beyond where his thinking left off, he granted suddenly that all these people might be lonely and dissatisfied deep in themselves too, but he envied them nonetheless because they possessed an ability for the positive action of living; if only he too might be caught up in some violent rhythm of life apart from any mere desire for happiness or change in status, to live hard, drink hard, love hard, and hate hard, to expend himself and his energies and his talents and explode himself wide open and die here to the same tempo of life as his fellow townsmen.

And then that flash of feeling was gone as quickly as it came, and Carl was left only with a great dissatisfaction and feeling of a kind of inadequacy and failure in himself.

He got up suddenly and rushed out of the drugstore. Better to get away from the lights and sounds and people, and walk alone some place in the darkness than stay here and walk his loneliness up and down the streets among happy people. He paused at the edge of the dancing space momentarily, for one last look at the dancers. The music was at a temporary standstill. The musicians were moving about the bandstand under the hot, blazing lights, drinking Coca-Cola out of bottles and wiping their moist hands and faces with soiled white handkerchiefs.

A little man with a red face and grizzled hair was suddenly hoisted up out of the crowd onto the bandstand. He yelled out in an amazing, hoarse, loud voice, "All right, folks! Take your places for a square dance!"

The crowd instantly began to seethe with activity. The dancing space was cleared, but only momentarily. Sets were made up here and there in a few seconds, some unaided, people shouting and waving one to another; some with the aid of the little man on the bandstand with his amazing lung capacity, sending his shout out over the crowd. "Another couple right over here. Fill her up, there, that's fine. Get yourself a girl, sonny, and fill up that set there in the corner. Come right over here, folks, room for another set right in here in front of the bandstand!"

Sets formed miraculously until the space was filled to capacity, and the rest had to be turned away. Sets of white-haired people, sets of excited high-school students, a set made up of the village banker, hardware merchant, grocer, and creamery manager, and their respective wives, all manner and kinds of people grouped together in the close little community of the square. Excitement was high, even among the onlookers. A wave of laughter started when a heavy, elderly gentleman deserted his place in one of the sets long enough to run to the sidelines and deposit his felt hat and lighted cigar with an amazed and embarrassed girl with long, dark curls. Carl saw the flush of soft color spread up over her white neck and face and was somehow inordinately pleased and soothed.

The crisis pitch was reached when the music actually began. The little man began his strident rhythmic chant, and the sets dissolved magically into separate active patterns of individuals in motion, punctuated by screams of laughter and excitement.

"Oh, the center two ladies cross over
And by your partners stand
The end two ladies cross over
And wait for my command
Honor at the corners, honor your partners all
Swing the corner lady
And promenade the hall.

"Oh, if I had a girl and she wouldn't dance
I tell you what I would do—
Buy me a boat and send her afloat
And paddle my own canoe.
Oh, the end two ladies cross over
And by your partners stand . . ."

The train came then, rushing carelessly through the night with the great strident clatter of noise, a stampede of grotesque silhouettes of freight cars following the engine blindly one after another, the monstrous powerful engine that shrieked and belched fire at every whistle post like a creature tormented. And that sound smothered all sounds, the voices and the laughter, and the music, and the dancers went on moving in their active, grotesque patterns like the silent meaningless figures in a dream.

ABOUT THE AUTHOR

Maritta Wolff was born on December 25, 1918, in Grass Lake, Michigan, where she grew up on her grandparents' farm and attended a one-room country school. At the age of twenty-two, after graduating the University of Michigan as a Phi Beta Kappa with a bachelor's degree in English composition, her Hopwood Award–winning novel *Whistle Stop* was published by Random House in 1941, going through five printings and earning glowing reviews for her raw, vital characters. A special Armed Forces edition of *Whistle Stop* brought a flood of letters from servicemen and began her lifelong practice of writing to her fans.

Wolff moved to Los Angeles in the late 1940s. A year after her first husband, author Hubert Skidmore, died in a house fire, she married Leonard Stegman. They had one son, Hugh. Between 1941 and 1962 Wolff wrote and published five more novels. After a disagreement with her publisher, her seventh novel was not published and languished in a refrigerator until after her death on July 1, 2002.